magic and bustles with realistic people and spine-chilling amounts of skullduggery." —DAVE DUNCAN

"A splendid read, filled with magic, mystery, adventure, and taut suspense. Lynn Flewelling, bravo! Nicely done."
—DENNIS L. McKIERNAN

"An engrossing and entertaining debut . . . full of magic, intrigues, and fascinating characters. Witty and charming, it's the kind of book you settle down with when you want a long, satisfying read." —MICHAEL A. STACKPOLE

"Exceptionally well-done and entertaining." —LOCUS

"Lynn Flewelling has written a terrific first novel, a thrilling introduction to this series . . . Highly recommended."
—STARLOG

Stalking Darkness

"Flewelling is . . . bringing vigor back to the traditional fantasy form. In this highly engaging adventure novel, the most powerful magic is conjured out of friendship and loyalty. The author has a gift for creating characters you genuinely care about." —TERRY WINDLING,
The Year's Best Fantasy and Horror,
Eleventh Annual Collection

"Events move forward in this second adventure . . . it's up to four companions to stop Mardus's schemes. Things get very violent and there's also a strong emotional undercurrent . . . an amusing twist on the old 'damsel in distress' scenario." —LOCUS

"While fans . . . will find enough wizardry, necromancy, swords, daggers, and devilishly clever traps here to satisfy the most avid, this book also provides entry to a complete and richly realized world that will please more mainstream readers." —BANGOR DAILY NEWS

Traitor's Moon

"What most fantasy aspires to, *Traitor's Moon* achieves, with fierce craft, wit and heart. It is a fantasy feast—richly imagined, gracefully wrought and thrilling to behold. An intoxicating brew of strange and homely, horror and whimsy, lust and blood, intrigue and honor, great battles and greater loves. It is a journey through a world so strange and real you can taste it, with companions so mysterious and memorable you won't forget it. Lynn Flewelling is a fine teller of tales who delivers all she promises, cuts no corners and leaves us dazzled, moved and hungry for more. *Traitor's Moon* is a wonderful book."

—PATRICK O'LEARY

Bantam Books
by Lynn Flewelling

LUCK IN THE SHADOWS
STALKING DARKNESS
TRAITOR'S MOON
THE BONE DOLL'S TWIN

The Bone Doll's Twin

Book One of the Tamir Triad

Lynn Flewelling

BANTAM BOOKS

New York   Toronto
London Sydney Auckland

THE BONE DOLL'S TWIN

A Bantam Spectra Book / October 2001

SPECTRA and the portrayal of a boxed "s" are trademarks of Bantam
Books, a division of Random House, Inc.

All rights reserved.
Copyright © 2001 by Lynn Flewelling
Cover art copyright © 2001 by John Jude Palencar
Maps by James Sinclair
No part of this book may be reproduced or transmitted in any form or
by any means, electronic or mechanical, including photocopying,
recording, or by any information storage and retrieval system, without
permission in writing from the publisher.
For information address: Bantam Books.

If you purchased this book without a cover you should be aware that
this book is stolen property. It was reported as "unsold and
destroyed" to the publisher and neither the author nor the publisher
has received any payment for this "stripped book."

ISBN 0-553-57723-9

Published simultaneously in the United States and Canada

Bantam Books are published by Bantam Books, a division of Random
House, Inc. Its trademark, consisting of the words "Bantam Books" and
the portrayal of a rooster, is Registered in U.S. Patent and Trademark
Office and in other countries. Marca Registrada. Bantam Books, 1540
Broadway, New York, New York 10036.

PRINTED IN THE UNITED STATES OF AMERICA

OPM   10   9   8   7   6   5

For l.e. and the knapp kids
up the magic staircase a long time ago

Acknowledgments

Thanks as always to my husband, Doug, and our boys for their love, support, and feedback. Matt pronounced this one "Disturbing, but in a good way." Quite apt, I think.

Thanks also to my parents, because. To Pat York and Anne Bishop for their feedback on the early chapters. To Anne Groell and Lucienne Diver, for their help and patience. To Nancy Jeffers, for her boundless enthusiasm for this project. To all the good folks at the Internet Fantasy Writer's Association, for their always swift and valuable replies to last-minute research questions. To the late Alan M., for being a good friend to writers, too briefly known.

To Mike K. wherever he is, for being.

The Skalan Year

I. WINTER SOLSTICE—Mourning Night and Festival of Sakor; observance of the longest night and celebration of the lengthening of days to come.

1. Sarisin: Calving
2. Dostin: Hedges and ditches seen to. Peas and beans sown for cattle food.
3. Klesin: Sowing of oats, wheat, barley (for malting), rye. Beginning of fishing season. Open water sailing resumes.

II. VERNAL EQUINOX—Festival of the Flowers in Mycena. Preparation for planting, celebration of fertility.

4. Lithion: Butter and cheese making (sheep's milk pref.) Hemp and flax sown.
5. Nythin: Fallow ground ploughed.
6. Gorathin: Corn weeded. Sheep washed and sheared.

III. SUMMER SOLSTICE

7. Shemin: Beginning of the month—hay mowing. End and into Lenthin—grain harvest in full swing.
8. Lenthin: Grain harvest.
9. Rhythin: Harvest brought in. Fields plowed and planted with winter wheat or rye.

IV. HARVEST HOME—finish of harvest, time of thankfulness.

10. Erasin: Pigs turned out into the woods to forage for acorns and beechnuts.
11. Kemmin: More plowing for spring. Oxen and other meat animals slaughtered and cured. End of the fishing season. Storms make open water sailing dangerous.
12. Cinrin: Indoor work, including threshing.

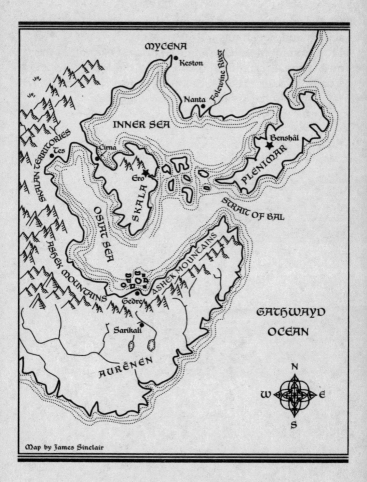

MYCENA

Keston

Nanta

Folcwine River

INNER SEA

Cirna

Tes

Benshâl

PLENIMAR

Ero

SKALA

STRAIT OF BAL

OSIAT SEA

ASHEK MOUNTAINS

SKALAN TERRITORIES

ASHEK MOUNTAINS

Gedre

GATHWAYD

OCEAN

Sarikali

AURËNEN

N

W   E

S

Map by James Sinclair

SKALA

Map by James Sinclair

Part One

An old man looks back at me from my mirror now. Even among the other wizards here in Rhíminee, I'm a relic of forgotten times.

My new apprentice, little Nysander, cannot imagine what it was like to be a free wizard of the Second Orëska. At Nysander's birth this beautiful city had already stood for two centuries above her deep harbor. Yet to me it shall always and forever be "the new capital."

In the days of my youth, a whore's cast-off like Nysander would have gone unschooled. If he were lucky he might have ended up as a village weather-caller or soothsayer. More likely, he would have unwittingly killed someone and been stoned as a witch. Only the Lightbearer knows how many god-touched children were lost before the advent of the Third Orëska.

Before this city was built, before this great house of learning was gifted to us by its founder, we wizards of the Second Orëska made our own way and lived by our own laws.

Now, in return for service to the Crown we have this House, with its libraries, archives, and its common history. I am the only one still living who knows how dear a price was paid for that.

Two centuries. Three or four lifetimes for most people; a mere season for those of us touched by the Lightbearer's gift. "We wizards stand apart, Arkoniel," my own teacher, Iya, told me when I was scarcely older than Nysander is now. "We are stones in a river's course, watching the rush of life whirl past."

Standing by Nysander's door tonight, watching the lad sleep, I imagined Iya's ghost beside me, and for a moment it seemed as if it was my younger self I gazed at; a plain, shy nobleman's son who'd shown a talent for animal charming. While guesting at my father's estate, Iya recognized the magic in me and revealed it to my family. I wept the day I left home with her.

How easy it would be to call those tears foreshadowing—that device the playwrights are so enamored of these days. But I have never quite believed in fate, despite all the prophecies and oracles that shaped my life. There's always a choice in there somewhere. I've seen too often how people make their own future through the balance of each day's little kindnesses and cruelties.

I chose to go with Iya.

Later, I chose to believe in the visions the Oracle granted to her and to me.

By my own choice, I helped rekindle the power of this good strong country, and so may rightly claim to have helped the fair white towers of Rhíminee rise against this blue western sky.

But on those few nights when I sleep deeply, what do I dream of?

An infant's cry, cut short.

You might think after so many years that it would be easier to accept; that one necessary act of cruelty could alter the course of history like an earthquake shifts a river's course. But that deed, that cry, lies at the heart of all the good that came after, like a grain of sand at the heart of a pearl's glowing nacre.

I alone carry the memory of that infant's brief wail, all those years ago.

I alone know of the filth at the heart of this pearl.

Chapter 1

Iya pulled off her straw wayfarer's hat and fanned herself with it as her horse labored up the rocky trail toward Afra. The sun stood at noon, blazing against the cloudless blue. It was only the first week of Gorathin, far too early for it to be this hot. It seemed the drought was going to last another season.

Snow still glistened on the peaks overhead, however. Now and then a plume of wind-blown white gusted out against the stark blue of the sky, creating the tantalizing illusion of coolness, while down here in the narrow pass no breeze stirred. Anywhere else Iya might have conjured up a bit of wind, but no magic was allowed within a day's ride of Afra.

Ahead of her, Arkoniel swayed in his saddle like a shabby, long-legged stork. The young wizard's linen tunic was sweated through down the back and stained drab with a week's worth of road dust. He never complained; his only concession to the heat was the sacrifice of the patchy black beard he'd cultivating since he turned one and twenty last Erasin.

Poor boy, Iya thought fondly; the newly shaven skin was already badly sunburnt.

Their destination, the Oracle at Afra, lay at the very heart of Skala's mountainous spine and was a grueling ride any time of year. Iya had made the long pilgrimage twice before, but never in summer.

The walls of the pass pressed close to the trail here, and centuries of seekers had left their names and supplications to Illior Lightbearer scratched into the dark stone.

Some had simply scratched the god's thin crescent moon; these lined the trail like countless tilting smiles. Arkoniel had left one of his own earlier that morning to commemorate his first visit.

Iya's horse stumbled and the reason for their journey bumped hard against her thigh. Inside the worn leather bag slung from her saddle horn, smothered in elaborate wrappings and magic, was a lopsided bowl crudely fashioned of burnt clay. There was nothing remarkable about it, except for the fierce aura of malevolence it gave off when not hidden away. More than once over the years she'd imagined throwing it over a cliff or into a river; in reality, she could no more have done that than cut off her own arm. She was the Guardian; the contents of that bag had been her charge for over a century.

Unless the Oracle can tell me otherwise. Fixing her thin, greying hair into a knot on top of her head, she fanned again at her sweaty neck.

Arkoniel turned in the saddle and regarded her with concern. His unruly black curls dripped sweat beneath the wilted brim of his hat. "You're red in the face. We should stop and rest again."

"No, we're nearly there."

"Then have some more water, at least. And put your hat back on!"

"You make me feel old. I'm only two hundred and thirty, you know."

"Two hundred and thirty-two," he corrected with a wry grin. It was an old game between them.

She pulled a sour face. "Just wait until you're in your third age, my boy. It gets harder to keep track."

The truth was, hard riding did tire her more than it had back in her early hundreds, although she wasn't about to admit it. She took a long pull from her waterskin and flexed her shoulders. "You've been quiet today. Do you have a query yet?"

"I think so. I hope the Oracle finds it worthy."

Such earnestness made Iya smile. This journey was merely another lesson as far as Arkoniel knew. She'd told him nothing of her true quest.

The leather bag bumped against her thigh like a nagging child. *Forgive me, Agazhar,* she thought, knowing her long-dead teacher, the first Guardian, would not have approved.

The last stretch of trail was the most treacherous. The rock face to their right gave way to a chasm and in places they rode with their left knees brushing the cliff face.

Arkoniel disappeared around a sharp bend, then called back, "I can see Illior's Keyhole, just as you described!"

Rounding the outcropping, Iya saw the painted archway glowing like a garish apparition where it straddled the trail. Stylized dragons glowed in red, blue, and gold around the narrow opening, which was just wide enough for a single horseman to pass through. Afra lay less than a mile beyond.

Sweat stung Iya's eyes, making her blink. It had been snowing the first time Agazhar brought her here.

Iya had come later than most to the wizardly arts. She'd grown up on a tenant farm on the border of Skala's mainland territory. The closest market town lay across the Keela River in Mycena, and it was here that Iya's family traded. Like many bordermen, her father had taken a Mycenian wife and made his offerings to Dalna the Maker, rather than Illior or Sakor.

So it was, when she first showed signs of magic, that she was sent across the river to study with an old Dalnan priest who'd tried to make a drysian healer of her. She earned praise for her herb craft, but as soon as the ignorant old fellow discovered that she could make fire with a thought, he bound a witch charm to her wrist and sent her home in disgrace.

With this taint on her, she'd found little welcome in her village and no prospect of a husband.

She was a spinster of twenty-four when Agazhar happened across her in the market square. He told her later that it was the witch charm that had caught his eye as she stood haggling with a trader over the price of her goats.

She'd taken no notice of him, thinking he was just another old soldier finding his way home from the wars. Agazhar had been as ragged and hollow-cheeked as any of them, and the left sleeve of his tunic hung empty.

Iya was forced to take a second look when he walked up to her, clasped her hand, and broke into a sweet smile of recognition. After a brief conversation, she sold off her goats and followed the old wizard down the south road without a backward glance. All anyone would have found of her, had they bothered to search, was the witch charm lying in the weeds by the market gate.

Agazhar hadn't scoffed at her fire making. Instead, he explained that it was the first sign that she was one of the god-touched of Illior. Then he taught her to harness the unknown power she possessed into the potent magic of the Orëska wizards.

Agazhar was a free wizard, beholden to no one. Eschewing the comforts of a single patron, he wandered as he liked, finding welcome in noble houses and humble ones alike. Together he and Iya traveled the Three Lands and beyond, sailing west to Aurënen, where even the common folk were as long-lived as wizards and possessed magic. Here she learned that the Aurënfaie were the First Orëska; it was their blood, mingled with that of Iya's race, that had given magic to the chosen ones of Skala and Plenimar.

This gift came with a price. Human wizards could neither bear nor sire children, but Iya considered herself well repaid, both in magic and, later, with students as gifted and companionable as Arkoniel.

Agazhar had also taught her more about the Great War than any of her father's ballads or legends, for he'd been among the wizards who'd fought for Skala under Queen Ghërilain's banner.

"There's never been another such war as that, and pray Sakor there never shall be again," he'd say, staring into the campfire at night as if he saw his fallen comrades there. "For one shining span of time wizards stood shoulder to shoulder with warriors, battling the black necromancers of Plenimar."

The tales Agazhar told of those days gave Iya nightmares. A necromancer's demon—a *dyrmagnos,* he called it—had torn off his left arm.

But gruesome as these tales were, Iya still clung to them, for only there had Agazhar given her any glimpse of where the strange bowl had come from.

Agazhar had carried it then; never in all the years she'd known him had he ever let it out of his possession. "Spoils of war," he'd said with a dark laugh, the first time he'd opened the bag to show it to her.

But beyond that, he would tell her nothing except that the bowl could not be destroyed and that its existence could not be revealed to anyone but the next Guardian. Instead, he'd schooled her rigorously in the complex web of spells that protected it, making her weave and unweave them until she could do it in the blink of an eye.

"You'll be the Guardian after me," he reminded her when she grew impatient with the secrecy. "Then you'll understand. Be certain you choose your successor wisely."

"But how will I know who to choose?"

He'd smiled and taken her hand as he had when they'd first met in the marketplace. "Trust in the Lightbearer. You'll know."

And she had.

At first she couldn't help pressing to know more about it—where he'd found it, who had made it and why, but Agazhar had remained obdurate. "Not until the time comes for you to take on the full care of it. Then I will tell you all there is to know."

Sadly, that day had taken them both unaware. Agazhar

had dropped dead in the streets of Ero one fine spring day soon after her first century. One moment he was holding forth on the beauty of a new transformation spell he'd just created; the next, he slipped to the ground with a hand pressed to his chest and a look of mild surprise in his fixed, dead eyes.

Scarcely into her second age, Iya suddenly found herself Guardian without knowing what she guarded or why. She kept the oath she'd sworn to him and waited for Illior to reveal her successor. She'd waited two lifetimes, as promising students came and went, and said nothing to them of the bag and its secrets.

But as Agazhar had promised, she'd recognized Arkoniel the moment she first spied him playing in his father's orchard fifteen years earlier. He could already keep a pippin spinning in midair and could put out a candle flame with a thought.

Young as he was, she'd taught him what little she knew of the bowl as soon as he was bound over to her. Later, when he was strong enough, she taught him how to weave the protections. Even so, she kept the burden of it on her own shoulders as Agazhar had instructed.

Over the years Iya had come to regard the bowl as little more than a sacred nuisance, but that had all changed a month ago when the wretched thing had taken over her dreams. The ghastly interwoven nightmares, more vivid than any she'd ever known, had finally driven her here, for she saw the bowl in all of them, carried high above a battlefield by a monstrous black figure for which she knew no name.

Iya? Iya, are you well?" asked Arkoniel.

Iya shook off the reverie that had claimed her and gave him a reassuring smile. "Ah, we're here at last, I see."

Pinched in a deep cleft of rock, Afra was scarcely large enough to be called a village and existed solely to serve the

Oracle and the pilgrims who journeyed here. A wayfarer's inn and the chambers of the priests were carved like bank swallow nests into the cliff faces on either side of the small paved square. Their doorways and deep-set windows were framed with carved fretwork and pillars of ancient design. The square was deserted now, but a few people waved to them from the shadowy windows.

At the center of the square stood a red jasper stele as tall as Arkoniel. A spring bubbled up at its base and flowed away into a stone basin and on to a trough beyond.

"By the Light!" Dismounting, Arkoniel turned his horse loose at the trough and went to examine the stele. Running his palm over the inscription carved in four languages, he read the words that had changed the course of Skalan history three centuries earlier. "'So long as a daughter of Thelátimos' line defends and rules, Skala shall never be subjugated.'" He shook his head in wonder. "This is the original, isn't it?"

Iya nodded sadly. "Queen Ghërilain placed this here herself as a thank offering right after the war. The Oracle's Queen, they called her then."

In the darkest days of the war, when it seemed that Plenimar would devour the lands of Skala and Mycena, the Skalan king, Thelátimos, had left the battlefields and journeyed here to consult the Oracle. When he returned to battle, he brought with him his daughter, Ghërilain, then a maiden of sixteen. Obeying the Oracle's words, he anointed her before his exhausted army and passed his crown and sword to her.

According to Agazhar, the generals had not thought much of the king's decision. Yet from the start the girl proved god-touched as a warrior and led the allies to victory in a year's time, killing the Plenimaran Overlord single-handedly at the Battle of Isil. She'd been a fine queen in peace, as well, and ruled for over fifty years. Agazhar had been among her mourners.

"These markers used to stand all over Skala, didn't they?" asked Arkoniel.

"Yes, at every major crossroads in the land. You were just a babe when King Erius tore them all down." Iya dismounted and touched the stone reverently. It was hot under her palm, and still as smooth as the day it had left the stonecutter's shop. "Even Erius didn't dare touch this one."

"Why not?"

"When he sent word for it to be removed, the priests refused. To force the issue meant invading Afra itself, the most sacred ground in Skala. So Erius graciously relented and contented himself with having all the others dumped into the sea. There was also a golden tablet bearing the inscription in the throne room at the Old Palace. I wonder what happened to that?"

But the younger wizard had more immediate concerns. Shading his eyes, he studied the cliff face. "Where's the Oracle's shrine?"

"Further up the valley. Drink deeply here. We must walk the rest of the way."

Leaving their mounts at the inn, they followed a well-worn path deeper into the cleft. The way became steeper and more difficult as they went. There were no trees to shade them, no moisture to lay the white dust that hung on the hot midday air. Soon the way dwindled to a faint track winding up between boulders and over rock faces worn smooth and treacherous by centuries of pilgrim's feet.

They met two other groups of seekers coming in the opposite direction. Several young soldiers were laughing and talking bravely, all but one young man who hung back from his fellows with the fear of death clear in his eyes. The second group clustered around an elderly merchant woman who wept silently as the younger members of her party helped her along.

Arkoniel eyed them nervously. Iya waited until the

merchant's party had disappeared around a bend, then sat down on a rock to rest. The way here was hardly wide enough for two people to pass and held the heat like an oven. She took a sip from the skin Arkoniel had filled at the spring. The water was still cold enough to make her eyes ache.

"Is it much further?" he asked.

"Just a little way." Promising herself a cool bath at the inn, Iya stood and continued on.

"You knew the king's mother, didn't you?" Arkoniel said, scrambling along behind her. "Was she as bad as they say?"

The stele must have gotten him thinking. "Not at first. Agnalain the Just, they called her. But she had a dark streak in her that worsened with age. Some say it came from her father's blood. Others said it was because of the trouble she had with childbearing. Her first consort gave her two sons. Then she seemed to go barren for years and gradually developed a taste for young consorts and public executions. Erius' own father went to the block for treason. After that no one was safe. By the Four, I can still remember the stink of the crow cages lining the roads around Ero! We all hoped she'd improve when she finally had a daughter, but she didn't. It only made her worse."

It had been easy enough in those black days for Agnalain's eldest son, Prince Erius—already a seasoned warrior and the people's darling—to argue that the Oracle's words had been twisted, that the prophecy had referred only to King Thelátimos' actual daughter, not to a matrilineal line of succession. Surely brave Prince Erius was better suited to the throne than the only direct female heir; his half-sister Ariani was just past her seventh birthday.

Never mind the fact that Skala had enjoyed unparalleled prosperity under her queens, or that the only other man to take the throne, Ghërilain's own son, Pelis, had brought on both plague and drought during his brief reign. Only when his sister had replaced him on the throne had Illior protected the land again as the Oracle had promised.

Until now.

When Agnalain died so suddenly, it was whispered that Prince Erius and his brother, Aron, had had a hand in it. But the rumor had been whispered with relief rather than condemnation; everyone knew Erius had ruled in all but name during the last terrible years of his mother's decline. The renewed rumblings from Plenimar were growing too loud for the nobles to risk civil war on behalf of a child queen. The crown passed to Erius without challenge. Plenimar attacked the southern ports that same year and he drove the invaders back into the sea and burned their black ships. This seemed to lay the prophecy to rest.

All the same, there had been more blights and drought in the past nineteen years than even the oldest wizards could recall. The current drought was in its third year in some parts of the country, and had wiped out whole villages already decimated by wildfires and waves of plague brought in from the northern trade routes. Arkoniel's parents had died in one such epidemic a few years earlier. A quarter of Ero's population had succumbed in a few months' time, including Prince Aron, as well as Erius' consort, both daughters, and two of his three sons, leaving only the second-youngest boy, Korin, alive. Since then, the words of the Oracle were being whispered again in certain quarters.

Iya had her own reasons now for regretting Erius' coup. His sister, Ariani, had grown up to marry Iya's patron, the powerful Duke Rhius of Atyion. The couple was expecting their first child in the fall.

Both wizards were sweating and winded by the time they reached the tight cul-de-sac where the shrine lay.

"It's not quite what I expected," Arkoniel muttered, eyeing what appeared to be a broad stone well.

Iya chuckled. "Don't judge too quickly."

Two sturdy priests in dusty red robes and silver masks sat in the shade of a wooden lean-to beside the well. Iya joined them and sat down heavily on a stone seat. "I need time to compose my thoughts," she told Arkoniel. "You go first."

The priests carried a coil of heavy rope to the well, motioning for Arkoniel to join them. He gave Iya a nervous grin as they fixed a loop of it around his hips. Still silent, they guided him into the stone enclosure to the entrance to the oracle chamber. From the surface, this was nothing but a hole in the ground about four feet in diameter.

It was always daunting, this act of faith and surrender, and more so the first time. But as always, Arkoniel did not hesitate. Sitting with his feet over the edge, he gripped the rope and nodded for the priests to let him down. He slid out of sight and they paid out the line until it went slack.

Iya remained in the lean-to, trying to calm her racing heart. She'd done her best for days not to think too directly on what she was about to do. Now that she was here, she suddenly regretted her decision. Closing her eyes, she tried to examine this fear, but could find no basis for it. Yes, she was disobeying her master's injunction, but that wasn't it. Here on the very doorstep of the Oracle, she had a premonition of something dark looming just ahead. She prayed silently for the strength to face whatever Illior revealed to her today, for she could not turn aside.

Arkoniel's twitch on the rope came sooner than she'd expected. The priests hauled him up and he hurried over and collapsed on the ground beside her, looking rather perplexed.

"Iya, it was the strangest thing—!" he began, but she held up a warning hand.

"There'll be time enough later," she told him, knowing she must go now or not at all.

She took her place in the harness, breath tight in her chest as she hung her feet over the edge of the hole.

Grasping the rope with one hand and the leather bag with the other, she nodded to the priests and began her descent.

She felt the familiar nervous flutter in her belly as she swung down into the cool darkness. She'd never been able to guess the actual dimensions of this underground chamber; the silence and faint movement of air against her face suggested a vast cavern. Where the sunlight struck the stone floor below, it showed the gently undulating smoothness of stone worn by some ancient underground river.

After a few moments her feet touched solid ground and she stepped free of the rope and out of the circle of sunlight. As her eyes adjusted to the darkness, she could make out a faint glow nearby and walked toward it. The light had appeared from a different direction each time she'd come here. When she reached the Oracle at last, however, everything was just as she remembered.

A crystal orb on a silver tripod gave off a wide circle of light. The Oracle sat next to it on a low ivory stool carved in the shape of a crouching dragon.

This one is so young! Iya thought, inexplicably saddened. The last two Oracles had been old women with skin bleached white by years of darkness. This girl was no more than fourteen, but her skin was already pale. Dressed in a simple linen shift that left her arms and feet bare, she sat with her palms on her knees. Her face was round and plain, her eyes vacant. Like wizards, the sibyls of Afra did not escape Illior's touch unscathed.

Iya knelt at her feet. A masked priest stepped into the circle of light with a large silver salver held out before him. The silence of the chamber swallowed Iya's sigh as she unwrapped the bowl and placed it on the salver.

The priest presented it to the Oracle, placing it on her knees. Her face remained vacant, betraying nothing.

Doesn't she feel the evil of the thing? Iya wondered. The unveiled power of it made Iya's head hurt.

The girl stirred at last and looked down at the bowl. Silvery light bright as moonshine on snow swelled in a nimbus around her head and shoulders. Iya felt a thrill of awe. Illior had entered the girl.

"I see demons feasting on the dead. I see the God Whose Name Is Not Spoken," the Oracle said softly.

Iya's heart turned to stone in her breast, her worst fears confirmed. This was Seriamaius, the dark god of necromancy worshipped by the Plenimarans who'd come so close to destroying Skala in the Great War. "I've dreamt this. War and disasters far worse than any Skala has ever known."

"You see too far, Wizard." The Oracle lifted the bowl in both hands and by some trick of the light her eyes became sunken black holes in her face. The priest was nowhere to be seen now, although Iya had not heard him go.

The Oracle turned the bowl slowly in her hands. "Black makes white. Foul makes pure. Evil creates greatness. Out of Plenimar comes present salvation and future peril. This is a seed that must be watered with blood. But you see too far."

The Oracle tilted the bowl forward and bright blood splashed out, too much for such a small vessel. It formed a round pool on the stone floor at the Oracle's feet. Looking into it, Iya caught the reflection of a woman's face framed by the visor of a bloody war helm. Iya could make out two intense blue eyes, a firm mouth above a pointed chin. The face was harsh one moment, sorrowful the next, and so familiar that it made her heart ache, though she couldn't say then of whom those eyes reminded her. Flames reflected off the helm and somewhere in the distance Iya heard the clash of battle.

The apparition slowly faded and was replaced by that of a shining white palace standing on a high cliff. It had a glittering dome, and at each of its four corners stood a slender tower.

"Behold the Third Orëska," the Oracle whispered. "Here may you lay your burden down."

Iya leaned forward with a gasp of awe. The palace had hundreds of windows and at every window stood a wizard, looking directly at her. In the highest window of the closest tower she saw Arkoniel, robed in blue and holding the bowl in his hands. A little child with thick blond curls stood at his side.

She could see Arkoniel quite clearly now, even though she was so far away. He was an old man, with a face deeply lined and weary beyond words. Even so, her heart swelled with joy at the sight of him.

"Ask," the Oracle whispered.

"What is the bowl?" she called to Arkoniel.

"It's not for us, but he will know," Arkoniel told her, passing the bowl to the little boy. The child looked at Iya with an old man's eyes and smiled.

"All is woven together, Guardian," the Oracle said as this vision faded into something darker. "This is the legacy you and your kind are offered. One with the true queen. One with Skala. You shall be tested with fire."

Iya saw the symbol of her craft—the thin crescent of Illior's moon—against a circle of fire and the number 222 glowing just beneath it in figures of white flame so bright they hurt her eyes.

Then Ero lay spread before her under a bloated moon, in flames from harbor to citadel. An army under the flag of Plenimar surrounded it, too numerous to count. Iya could feel the heat of the flames on her face as Erius led his army out against them. But his soldiers fell dead behind him and the flesh fell from his charger's bones in shreds. The Plenimarans surrounded the king like wolves and he was lost from sight. The vision shifted dizzyingly again and Iya saw the Skalan crown, bent and tarnished now, lying in a barren field.

"So long as a daughter of Thelátimos' line defends

and rules, Skala shall never be subjugated," the Oracle whispered.

"Ariani?" Iya asked, but knew even as she spoke that it had not been the princess' face she'd seen framed in that helm.

The Oracle began to sway and keen. Raising the bowl, she poured its endless flow over her head like a libation, masking herself in blood. Falling to her knees, she grasped Iya's hand and a whirlwind took them, striking Iya blind.

Screaming winds surrounded her, then entered the top of her head and plunged down through the core of her like a shipwright's augur. Images flashed by like windborne leaves: the strange number on its shield, and the helmeted woman in many forms and guises—old, young, in rags, crowned, hanging naked from a gibbet, riding garlanded through broad, unfamiliar streets. Iya saw her clearly now, her face, her blue eyes, black hair, and long limbs like Ariani's. But it was not the princess.

The Oracle's voice cut through the maelstrom. "This is your queen, Wizard, this true daughter of Thelátimos. She will turn her face to the west."

Suddenly Iya felt a bundle placed in her arms and looked down at the dead infant the Oracle had given her.

"Others see, but only through smoke and darkness," said the Oracle. "By the will of Illior the bowl came into your hands; it is the long burden of your line, Guardian, and the bitterest of all. But in this generation comes the child who is the foundation of what is to come. She is your legacy. Two children, one queen marked with the blood of passage."

The dead infant looked up at Iya with black staring eyes and searing pain tore through her chest. She knew whose child this was.

Then the vision was gone and Iya found herself kneeling in front of the Oracle with the unopened bag in her arms. There was no dead infant, no blood on the floor. The Oracle sat on her stool, shift and hair unstained.

"Two children, one queen," the Oracle whispered, looking at Iya with the shining white eyes of Illior.

Iya trembled before that gaze, trying to cling to all she'd seen and heard. "The others who dream of this child, Honored One—do they mean her well or ill? Will they help me raise her up?"

But the god was gone and the girl child slumped on the stool had no answers.

Sunlight blinded Iya as she emerged from the cavern. The heat took her breath away and her legs would not support her. Arkoniel caught her as she collapsed against the stone enclosure. "Iya, what happened? What's wrong?"

"Just—just give me a moment," she croaked, clutching the bag to her chest.

A seed watered with blood.

Arkoniel lifted her easily and carried her into the shade. He put the waterskin to her lips and Iya drank, leaning heavily against him. It was some time before she felt strong enough to start back for the inn. Arkoniel kept one arm about her waist and she suffered his help without complaint. They were within sight of the stele when she fainted.

When she opened her eyes again, she was lying on a soft bed in a cool, dim room at the inn. Sunlight streamed in through a crack in the dusty shutter and struck shadows across the carved wall beside the bed. Arkoniel sat beside her, clearly worried.

"What happened with the Oracle?" he asked.

Illior spoke and my question was answered, she thought bitterly. *How I wish I'd listened to Agazhar.*

She took his hand. "Later, when I'm feeling stronger. Tell me your vision. Was your query answered?"

Her answer obviously frustrated him, but he knew

better than to press her. "I'm not sure," he said. "I asked what sort of wizard I'd become, what my path would be. She showed me a vision in the air, but all I could make out was an image of me holding a young boy in my arms."

"Did he have blond hair?" she asked, thinking of the child in the beautiful white tower.

"No, it was black. To be honest, I was disappointed, coming all this way just for that. I must have done something wrong in the asking."

"Sometimes you must wait for the meaning to be revealed." Iya turned away from that earnest young face, wishing that the Lightbearer had granted her such a respite. The sun still blazed down on the square outside her window, but Iya saw only the road back to Ero before her, and darkness at its end.

Chapter 2

A red harvest moon cast the sleeping capital into a towering mosaic of light and shadow that nineteenth night of Erasin. Crooked Ero, the capital was called. Built on a rambling hill overlooking the islands of the Inner Sea, the streets spread like poorly woven lace down from the walls of the Palatine Circle to the quays and shipyards and rambling slums below. Poor and wealthy alike lived cheek by jowl, and every house in sight of the harbor had at least one window facing east toward Plenimar like a watchful eye.

The priests claim Death comes in the west door, Arkoniel thought miserably as he rode through the west gate behind Iya and the witch. Tonight would be the culmination of the nightmare that had started nearly five months earlier at Afra.

The two women rode in silence, their faces hidden by their deep hoods. Heartsick at the task that lay before them, Arkoniel willed Iya to speak, change her mind, turn aside, but she said nothing and he could not see her eyes to read them. For over half his life she'd been teacher, mentor, and second mother to him. Since Afra, she'd become a house full of closed doors.

Lhel had gone quiet, too. Her kind had been unwelcome here for generations. She wrinkled her nose now as the stink of the city engulfed them. "You great village? Ha! Too many."

"Not so loud!" Arkoniel looked around nervously. Wandering wizards were not as welcome here as they had been, either. It would go hard on them all to be found with a hill witch.

"Smells like *tok*," Lhel muttered.

Iya pushed back her hood and surprised Arkoniel with a thin smile. "She says it smells like shit here, and so it does."

Lhel's one to talk, Arkoniel thought. He'd kept upwind of the hill woman since they'd met.

After their strange visit to Afra they'd gone first to Ero and guested with the duke and his lovely, fragile princess. By day they gamed and rode. Each night Iya spoke in secret with the duke.

From there, he and Iya spent the rest of that hot, sullen summer searching the remote mountain valleys of the northern province for a witch to aid them, for no Orëska wizard possessed the magic for the task that Illior had set them. By the time they found one, the aspen leaves were already edged with gold.

Driven from the fertile lowlands by the first incursions of Skalan settlers, the small, dark-skinned hill people kept to their high valleys and did not welcome travelers. When Iya and Arkoniel approached a village, they might hear dogs barking the alarm, or mothers calling their children; by the time they reached the edge of a settlement, only a few armed men would be in sight. These men made no threats, but offered no hospitality.

Lhel's welcome had surprised them when they'd happened across her lonely hut. Not only had she welcomed them properly, setting out water, cider, and cheese, but she claimed to have been expecting them.

Iya spoke the witch's language, and Lhel had picked up a few words of Skalan somewhere. From what Arkoniel could make out between them, the witch was not surprised by their request. She claimed her moon goddess had showed them to her in a dream.

Arkoniel felt very awkward around the woman. Her magic radiated from her like the musky heat of her body, but it was more than that. Lhel was a woman in her prime. Her black hair hung in a tangled, curling mass to her waist and her loose woolen dress couldn't mask the curves of hip and breast as she sauntered around her little hut, bringing him food and the makings for a pallet. He didn't need an interpreter to know that she asked Iya if she might sleep with him that night or that she was both offended and amused when Iya explained the concept of wizards' celibacy to her. The Orëska wizards reserved all their vitality for their magic.

Arkoniel feared that the witch might change her mind then, but the following morning they woke to find her waiting for them outside the door, a traveling bundle slung ready behind the saddle of her shaggy pony.

The long journey back to Ero had been an awkward time for the young man. Lhel delighted in teasing him, making certain that he saw when she lifted her skirts to wash, and losing no opportunity to bump against him as she moved about their camp each night, plucking the year's last herbs with her knobby, stained fingers. Vows or no, Arkoniel couldn't help but notice and something in him stirred uneasily.

When their work in Ero was finished this night, he would never see her again and for that he would be most thankful.

*A*s they rode across an open square, Lhel pointed up at the full red moon and clucked her tongue. "Baby caller moon, all fat and bloody. We hurry. No *shaimari*."

She brought two fingers toward her nostrils in a graceful flourish, mimicking the intake of breath. Arkoniel shuddered.

Iya pressed one hand over her eyes and Arkoniel felt a moment's hope. Perhaps she would relent after all. But she was merely sending a sighting spell up to the Palatine ahead of them.

After a moment she shook her head. "No. We have time."

A cold salt breeze tugged at their cloaks as they reached the seaward side of the citadel and approached the Palatine gate. Arkoniel inhaled deeply, trying to ease the growing tightness in his chest. A party of revelers passed them, and by the light of the linkboys' lanterns Arkoniel stole another look at Iya. The wizard's pale, square face betrayed nothing.

It is the will of Illior, Arkoniel repeated silently. There could be no turning aside.

Since the death of the king's only female heir, women and girls of close royal blood had died at an alarming rate. Few dared speak of it aloud in the city, but in too many cases it was not plague or hunger that carried them down to Bilairy's gate.

The king's cousin took ill after a banquet in town and did not awaken the next morning. Another somehow managed to fall from her tower window. His two pretty young nieces, daughters of his own brother, were drowned sailing on a sunny day. Babies born to more distant relations, all girls, were found dead in their cradles. Their nurses whispered of night spirits. As potential female claimants to the throne dropped away one by one, the people of Ero turned nervous eyes toward the king's half sister and the unborn child she carried.

Her husband, Duke Rhius, was fifteen years older than his pretty young wife and owned vast holdings of castles and lands, the greatest of which lay at Atyion, half a day's ride north of the city. Some said that the marriage had been a love match between the duke's lands and the Royal Treasury, but Iya thought otherwise.

The couple lived at the grand castle at Atyion when

Rhius was not serving at court. When Ariani became pregnant, however, they had taken up residence at Ero, in her house beside the Old Palace.

Iya guessed that the choice was the king's rather than hers, and Ariani had confirmed her suspicions during their visit that summer.

"May Illior and Dalna grant us a son," Ariani had whispered as she and Iya sat together in the garden court of her house, hands pressed to her swelling belly.

As a child Ariani had adored her handsome older brother, who'd been more like a father to her. Now she understood all too well that she lived at his whim; in these uncertain times, any girl claiming Ghërilain's blood posed a threat to the new male succession, should the Illioran faction fight to reestablish the sacred authority of Afra.

With every new bout of plague or famine, the whispers of doubt grew stronger.

In a darkened side street outside the Palatine gate Iya cloaked herself and Lhel in invisibility, and Arkoniel approached the guards as if alone.

There were still a great many people abroad at this hour, but the sergeant-at-arms took special note of the silver amulet Arkoniel wore and called him aside.

"What's your business here so late, Wizard?"

"I'm expected. I've come to visit my patron, Duke Rhius."

"Your name?"

"Arkoniel of Rhemair."

A scribe noted this down on a wax tablet and Arkoniel strolled on into the labyrinth of houses and gardens that ringed this side of the Palatine. To the right loomed the great bulk of the New Palace, which Queen Agnalain had begun and her son was finishing. To the left lay the rambling bulk of the Old Palace.

Iya's magic was so strong that even he couldn't tell if

she and the witch were still with him, but he didn't dare turn or whisper to them.

Ariani's fine house stood surrounded by its own walls and courtyards; Arkoniel entered by the front gate and barred it behind him as soon as he felt Iya's touch on his arm. He looked around nervously, half expecting to find the King's Guard lurking behind the bare trees and statuary in the shadowed garden, or the familiar faces of the duke's personal guard. But there was no one here, not even a watchman or porter. The garden was silent, the air heavy with the scent of some last hardy bloom of autumn.

Iya and the witch reappeared beside him and together they headed across the courtyard toward the arched entrance. They hadn't gone three steps when a horned owl swooped down and pounced on a young rat not ten feet from where they stood. Flapping for balance, it dispatched the squeaking rodent, then looked up at them with eyes like gold sester coins. Such birds were not uncommon in the city, but Arkoniel felt a thrill of awe; owls were the messengers of Illior.

"A favorable omen," Iya murmured as it flapped away, leaving the dead rat behind.

The duke's steward, Mynir, answered her knock. A thin, solemn, stoop-shouldered old fellow, he'd always reminded Arkoniel of a cricket. He was one of the few who would help carry his master's burden in the years to come.

"Thank the Maker!" the old man whispered, grasping Iya's hand. "The duke is half out of his mind—" He broke off at the sight of Lhel.

Arkoniel could guess the man's thoughts: witch, unclean, handler of the dead, a necromancer who called up demons and ghosts.

Iya touched his shoulder. "It's all right, Mynir, your master knows. Where is he?"

"Upstairs, Mistress. I'll fetch him."

Iya held him a moment longer. "And Captain Tharin?"

Tharin, the nobleman in charge of Rhius' guard, was seldom far from the duke's side. Illior had not spoken for him, but Iya and Rhius had not discussed how he was to be kept away from this night's business.

"The duke sent him and the men to Atyion for the rents." Mynir led them into the darkened audience hall. "The women have all been sent to sleep at the Palace, so as not to disturb the princess in her labor. It's just your Nari and myself tonight, Mistress. I'll fetch the duke." He hurried up the sweeping staircase.

A fire burned in the great fireplace across the chamber, but no lamps were lit. Arkoniel turned slowly, trying to make out the familiar shapes of furniture and hangings. This house had always been alive with music and gaiety. Tonight it seemed like a tomb.

"Is that you, Iya?" a deep voice called. Rhius strode down the stairs to meet them. He was nearly forty now, a handsome, broadly built warrior, with arms and hands knotted from a life spent clutching a sword or the reins. Tonight, however, his skin was sallow beneath his black beard and his short tunic was sweated through as if he'd been running or fighting. Warrior that he was, he stank of fear.

He stared at Lhel, then seemed to sag. "You found one."

Iya handed her cloak to the steward. "Of course, my lord."

A ragged scream rang out overhead. Rhius clutched a fist to his heart. "There was no need for the herbs to start the birthing pangs. Her waters broke at midmorning. She's been like this since sunset. She keeps begging for her own women—"

Lhel muttered something to Iya, who interpreted the question for the duke.

"She asks if your lady has any issue of blood?"

"No. Your woman keeps claiming all is well, but—"

Upstairs, Ariani cried out again and Arkoniel's stomach lurched. The poor woman had no idea who was in her house this night. Iya had given the couple her solemn pledge to protect any daughter born to the royal house; she had not revealed to the child's mother the means the Lightbearer had given her to do so. Only Rhius knew. Ambition had guaranteed his consent.

"Come, it's time." Iya started for the stairs, but Rhius caught her by the arm.

"Are you certain this is the only way? Couldn't you just take one of them away?"

Iya regarded him coldly. She stood two steps above him and in this light she looked for an instant like a stone effigy. "The Lightbearer wants a queen. You want your child to rule. This is the price. The favor of Illior is with us in this."

Rhius released her and sighed heavily. "Come then, and let's be done with it." Rhius followed the two women up and Arkoniel followed him, close enough to hear the duke murmur, "There will be other babes."

Princess Ariani's bedchamber was stifling. The others went to the bed, but Arkoniel halted just inside the doorway, overwhelmed by the heavy odor of the birthing chamber.

He'd never seen this part of the house before. Under different circumstances he'd have thought it a pretty room. The walls and carved bed were covered with bright hangings embroidered with fanciful underwater scenes, and the marble mantel was carved with dolphins. A familiar workbasket lay on a chair by the shuttered window; a cloth head and arm protruded from beneath the half-open lid—one of the princess' lady dolls, half finished. Ariani was famous for her clever handiwork and all the great ladies of Ero and some of the lords had one.

Tonight the sight of this one knotted Arkoniel's guts.

Through the half-open bed hangings he could see the bulging curve of Ariani's belly and one clenched hand gleaming with costly rings. A plump, sweet-faced serving woman stood over Ariani, murmuring to her as she bathed the laboring woman's face. This was Nari, a widowed kinswoman of Iya's, chosen to be the child's wetnurse. Iya had intended for Nari to bring her own babe to be the companion of Ariani's, but the gods had other plans. A few weeks earlier Nari's child had succumbed to pneumonia. Even in her grief, Nari had faithfully squeezed the milk from her breasts to keep it flowing. The front of her loose gown was stained with it.

Lhel set to work, issuing quiet orders while she laid out the things she needed at the end of the bed: bunches of herbs, a thin silver knife, needles of bone, and a skein of silk thread, impossibly fine.

Ariani lurched up with another wail and Arkoniel caught a glimpse of her face, glassy-eyed and drugged now, behind a tangle of lustrous black hair.

The princess was not much older than he was, and though he seldom allowed himself to think on it, he had harbored a secret admiration for her ever since her marriage to Rhius had brought Arkoniel into her sphere. Ariani was the most beautiful woman he'd ever seen and she'd always treated him graciously. Hot shame washed over him; this was how her kindness was repaid.

Too soon Iya turned and motioned for him to join her by the bed. "Come, Arkoniel, we need you now."

He and Nari held Ariani's feet as the witch felt between her thighs. Ariani moaned and tried weakly to pull away. Blushing furiously, Arkoniel kept his face turned away until Lhel had finished her examination, then hastily retreated.

Lhel washed her hands in a basin, then bent to pat Ariani's cheek. "Is good, *keesa*."

"There are—there are two, aren't there, Midwife?" Ariani gasped faintly.

Arkoniel shot Iya a concerned look, but she only shrugged. "A woman needs no midwife to tell her how many babes she has in her belly."

Nari brewed a dish of tea from some of the witch's herbs and helped Ariani to sip it. After a few moments, the woman's breathing slowed and she grew quiet. Climbing onto the bed, Lhel massaged Ariani's belly, all the while murmuring to her in a soothing, singsong voice.

"The first child must be turned into position to enter the world so that the other may follow," Iya translated for Rhius, who stood now in agonized silence by the head of the bed.

Lhel moved so that she was kneeling between Ariani's knees, still rubbing her belly. After a few moments the witch let out a soft cry of triumph. Watching from the corner of his eye, Arkoniel saw her lift a wet little head into view with one hand. With the other, she held the child's nostrils and mouth shut until the rest of it was birthed.

"Girl keesa," she announced, taking her hand from the child's face.

Arkoniel let out a gasp of relief as the girl child sucked in her first lungful of air. This was the *shaimari,* the "soul's breath" that the witch was so concerned with.

Lhel cut the birth cord with her silver knife and held the child up for all to see. The baby was well formed under the birth muck and had a thick head of wet black hair.

"Thank the Lightbringer!" Rhius exclaimed, leaning down to kiss his sleeping wife's brow. "A first-born girl, just as the Oracle promised!"

"And look," said Nari, leaning forward to touch a tiny wine-colored birthmark on the child's left forearm. "She has a favor mark, too, just like a rosebud."

Iya gave Arkoniel a tight, triumphant smile. "Here's our future queen, my boy."

Tears of joy blurred Arkoniel's vision and tightened his throat, but the moment was tainted by the knowledge that their work was not yet finished.

While Nari bathed the girl child, Lhel began coaxing forth the twin. Ariani's head lolled limply against the pillow. Rhius retreated to the fireplace, mouth set in a grim line.

Tears of a different sort stung Arkoniel's eyes. *Forgive us, my sweet lady,* he prayed, unable to look away.

Despite Lhel's efforts, the second child came wrong way around, a footling breach. Muttering steadily in her own tongue, Lhel worked the other leg free and the little body slid out.

"Boy keesa," Lhel said softly, hand poised to cover the child's face as it emerged, to prevent that all-important first breath so that the soul might not be fixed in the flesh.

Suddenly, however, there was a loud clatter of horsemen in the street outside, and a shout of, "Open in the name of the king!"

Lhel was as startled as the rest of them. In that instant of distraction the child's head slipped free of his mother's body and he sucked a breath, strong and clear.

"By the Light!" Iya hissed, whirling on the witch. Lhel shook her head and bent over the squirming babe. Arkoniel backed quickly away, unable to watch what must follow. He shut his eyes so tightly he saw flashes of light behind the lids, but he could not escape the sound of the child's loud, healthy cry, or the way it suddenly choked off. The silence in its wake left him dizzy and sick.

What followed seemed to take a very long time, although in truth they had only minutes. Lhel took the living child from Nari and placed her on the bed next to her dead twin. Chanting over them, she drew patterns in the air and the living child went still. When Lhel took up her knife and needle, Arkoniel had to turn away again. Behind him, he could hear Rhius weeping softly.

Then Iya was at his side, pushing him out into the cold corridor. "Go downstairs and hold off the king. Keep him as long as you can! I'll send Nari down when it's safe."

"Hold him off? How?"

The door swung shut in his face and he heard the key turn.

"Very well, then." Arkoniel dried his face on his sleeve

and ran his hands back through his hair. At the top of the staircase he paused and turned his face up to the unseen moon, sending a silent prayer to Illior. *Aid my faltering tongue, Lightbearer, or cloud the king's eyes. Or both, if it's not asking too much.*

He wished now that Captain Tharin was here. The tall, quiet knight had a manner that put everyone at their ease. With a lifetime of hunting, fighting, and court intrigue behind him, he was far better suited than a green young wizard to entertain a man like Erius.

Mynir had lit the bronze lamps that hung between the painted stone pillars in the hall and stoked the fire with cedar logs and sweet resins to make a fragrant blaze. Erius stood beside the hearth, a tall and daunting figure in the firelight. Arkoniel bowed deeply to him. Like Rhius, the king had been shaped by a lifetime of war, but his face was still handsome and filled with a youthful good humor that even a childhood spent in his mother's court had not extinguished. Only in recent years, as the royal tomb filled with the bodies of his female kin, had some come to regard that kindly visage as a mask for a darker heart, one that had perhaps learned his mother's lessons after all.

As Arkoniel had suspected, the king had not come alone. His court wizard, Lord Niryn, was there, close to the king as the man's own shadow. He was a plain fellow somewhere in his second age, but whatever gifts he possessed had lifted him high and quickly. For years Erius had had no more use for wizards than his mother, but since the death of the king's wife and children, Niryn's star had risen steadily at court. Lately he'd taken to wearing his thick red beard forked and had affected costly white robes embroidered with silver.

He acknowledged Arkoniel with a slight nod, and the younger wizard bowed respectfully.

Erius had brought along a priest of Sakor, as well,

together with a dozen of his own guard in their pick spurs and gold badges. Arkoniel's stomach did an uneasy roll as he caught the glint of mail beneath their red tunics and saw the long knives they carried at their belts. It seemed an odd sort of company to bring into a royal house on such an occasion.

He forced a respectful smile, wondering bitterly who had alerted Erius. One of the household women, perhaps? Clearly Erius had been prepared for this visit, despite the hour. The king's greying beard and curly black hair were neatly combed. His velvet robes looked as fresh as if he'd been on his way to the audience hall. The Sword of Ghërilain, symbol of Skalan rule, hung at his hip.

"My king," Arkoniel bowed again. "Your honored sister is still in the midst of her pains. Duke Rhius sends his respects and asks me to sit with you until he is able to attend you himself."

Erius raised an eyebrow in surprise. "Arkoniel? What are you doing here? Last I knew, neither you nor that mistress of yours practices midwifery."

"No, my king. I was guesting here tonight and have been making myself useful." Arkoniel was suddenly aware of the other wizard's steady gaze. Niryn's bright brown eyes protruded a bit, giving him a perpetually surprised air that the younger wizard found unsettling. He carefully veiled his mind, praying he was strong enough to keep Niryn from his thoughts without the other man suspecting.

"Your honored sister's labor is a difficult one, I fear, but she will be delivered soon," he continued, then wished he hadn't. The king had attended the births of all his own children. If Erius decided to go upstairs, there was nothing he could do, short of magic, to prevent it. And with Niryn here, even that risky avenue was closed to him.

Perhaps Illior had heeded his prayer after all, for Erius shrugged agreeably and sat down at a gaming table by the hearth. "How's your skill with the stones?" he asked, waving Arkoniel to the other chair. "These birthings generally take longer than you'd expect, especially the first. We may as well pass the time pleasantly."

Hoping his relief was not too obvious, Arkoniel sent Mynir off for wine and sweets, then settled down to losing as best he could.

Niryn sat beside them, pretending to observe the play, but Arkoniel still felt the pressure of his regard. Sweat prickled under his arms and down his back. What did the man want? Did he know something?

He nearly dropped the gaming stones when Niryn suddenly asked, "Do you dream, young man?"

"No, my lord," Arkoniel replied. "Or if I do, I don't recall them when I wake up."

This was true enough; he seldom dreamed in the normal sense, and foreknowing dreams had so far proven to be outside his ken. He waited for Niryn to pursue the question, but he only sat back and stroked the tips of his forked beard, looking bored.

Arkoniel was in the midst of his third game of Geese and Squares when Nari came downstairs.

"Duke Rhius sends his regards, Your Majesty," she said, curtsying low. "He asks if you would like your new nephew brought down to view?"

"Nonsense!" Erius exclaimed, setting the stones aside. "Tell your master his brother is happy to come to him."

Again, Arkoniel had an uneasy sense that the king meant more than he said.

That sense grew stronger when Niryn and the priest accompanied them upstairs. Nari caught Arkoniel's eye as they followed and gave him a quick nod; Iya and Lhel must already be safely away. Entering Ariani's room, Arkoniel could sense no trace of magic, Orëska or otherwise.

Duke Rhius stood on the far side of the bed, holding his wife's hand. The princess was still blessedly asleep, no doubt well drugged. With her black hair combed back smoothly and a hectic spot of color high on each cheek, she looked like one of her own dolls.

Rhius lifted the swaddled child from the bed and brought it to the king. He'd recovered enough to act his part with dignity.

"Your nephew, my liege," he said, placing the infant in Erius' arms. "With your leave, he shall be named Tobin Erius Akandor, in honor of your father's line."

"A son, Rhius!" Erius undid the swaddling with a gentle, practiced hand.

Arkoniel held his breath and blanked his mind as Niryn and the priest extended their hands over the sleeping child. Neither appeared to notice anything amiss; Lhel's magic had covered all trace of the abomination she'd wrought on the little body. And who would think to look for hill witch magic in the chamber of the king's own sister?

"A fine boy, Rhius, to bear such a name," Erius said. The birthmark caught his eye. "And look at the favor mark he bears. On his left arm, too. Niryn, you know how to read such things. What does this one mean?"

"Wisdom, Your Majesty," the wizard told him. "A most favorable trait in your son's future companion."

"Indeed it is," the king said. "Yes, you have my leave, brother, and my blessing. And I've brought a priest to make an offering for our little warrior."

"You have my thanks, brother," said Rhius.

The priest went to the hearth and began his droning prayers, casting resins and little wax offerings into the flames.

"By the Flame, he'll make a great playfellow for my Korin in a few years' time," the king went on. "Just think of the two of them, hunting and learning the sword together when your Tobin comes to join the Companions. Just like you and I were, eh? But there was a twin, too, I believe?"

Yes, thought Arkoniel, the king's spies had been thorough, after all.

Nari bent down and lifted another tiny bundle from behind the bed. Keeping her back to the princess, she brought it around to the king. "A poor little girl child, my king. Never drew breath."

Erius and the others examined the dead child just as closely, moving its flaccid limbs about, verifying the gender, and feeling its chest and neck for signs of life. Watching from the corner of his eye, Arkoniel saw the king cast a quick, questioning look at his wizard.

They know something. They're seeking something, Arkoniel thought dizzily. Niryn's question about dreams suddenly took on a dire resonance. Had the man had a vision of his own, a vision of this child? If so, then Lhel's magic did its work again, for the older wizard replied with a quick shake of his head. Whatever they were looking for, they hadn't found it here. Arkoniel glanced away before any expression of relief could betray him.

The king handed the body back to Nari and clasped Rhius by the shoulders. "It's a hard thing, losing a child. Sakor knows I still grieve for my lost ones and their dear mother. It's cold comfort for you, I know, but it's best this way, before you'd both gotten attached."

"As you say," Rhius replied softly.

Giving Rhius a last brotherly thump on the shoulder, Erius went to the bed and kissed his sister gently on the forehead.

The sight made the blood pound in Arkoniel's head as he thought of the swordsmen in the hall below. This usurper, this killer of girls and women, might love his little sister enough to spare her life, but as the Lightbearer had shown, that forbearance did not extend to her children. He kept his gaze fixed on the floor as the king and his councilors swept out, imagining how differently this little drama would have played out if Erius had found a living girl child here.

As soon as the door closed behind them, Arkoniel's knees turned to water and he sank into a chair.

But the ordeal was not yet over. Ariani opened her eyes and saw the dead child Nari held. Pulling herself up against the bolsters, she held out her arms for it. "Thank the Light! I knew I heard a second cry, but I had the most awful dream—"

The nurse exchanged a look with Rhius and Ariani's smile faltered. "What is it? Give me my child."

"It was stillborn, my love," Rhius said. "Let it be. Look, here's our fine son."

"No, I heard it cry!" Ariani insisted.

Rhius brought little Tobin to her, but she ignored him, staring instead at the child the nurse held. "Give him to me, woman! I command it!"

There was no dissuading her. Ignoring the soft cry of the living child, she took the dead one in her arms and her face went whiter still.

Arkoniel knew in that instant that Lhel's magic could not deceive the child's mother the way that it had the others. Twisting his mind to see through her eyes, he caught a glimpse of the strips of skin Lhel had cut from each child's breast and sewn with spider-fine stitches into the wound left on its twin, just over the heart. With this exchange of flesh, the transformation had been sealed. The girl child would retain the semblance of male form for as long as Iya deemed necessary, just as her dead brother had taken her form to deceive the king.

"What have you done?" Ariani gasped, staring up at Rhius.

"Later, my love, when you're rested— Give that one back to Nari and take your son. See how strong he is? And he has your blue eyes—"

"Son? That is no son!" Ariani cut him off with a venomous glare. No amount of reasoning prevailed. When Rhius tried to take the dead child from her, she lurched from the bed and fled to the far corner of the room, clutching the tiny corpse against her stained nightdress.

"This is too much!" Arkoniel whispered. Going to the frantic woman, he knelt before her.

She looked up at him in surprise. "Arkoniel? Look, I have a son. Isn't he pretty?"

Arkoniel tried to smile. "Yes, Your Highness, he's—he's perfect." He touched her brow gently, clouding her mind and sending her once more into a deep sleep. "Forgive me."

He reached for the little body, then froze in fear.

The dead child's eyes were open. Blue as a kitten's one moment, the irises went black as Arkoniel watched and fixed accusingly on him. An unmistakable chill radiated from the little body, slowly spreading to envelop the wizard.

This was the cost of that first breath. The spirit of the murdered child had been drawn into its body just long enough to take hold and become a ghost, or worse.

"By the Four, what's happening?" Rhius rasped, leaning over him.

"There's nothing to fear," Arkoniel said quickly, though in truth this tiny unnatural creature struck fear to the core of his heart.

Nari knelt beside him and whispered, "The witch said to take it away quickly. She said you must put it in the ground under a large tree. There's a great chestnut in the rear courtyard by the summer kitchen. The roots will hold the demon down. Hurry! The longer it stays here, the stronger it will grow!"

It took every bit of courage Arkoniel possessed to touch the dead child. Taking it from Ariani's arms, he covered its face with a corner of the wrappings and hurried out. Nari was right; the waves of icy coldness pouring from the lifeless body grew stronger by the moment. They made his joints ache as he bore it downstairs and out through the back passage of the house.

The moon watched like an accusing eye as Arkoniel placed his cursed burden at the foot of the chestnut tree and mouthed, *forgive me* once more. But he expected no forgiveness for this night's work and wept as he wove his spell. His tears fell on the little bundle as he bent to watch it sink down into the earth's cold embrace between the gnarled roots.

The faint wail of an infant came to him on the cold night air and he shuddered, not knowing if it came from the living child or the dead one.

Chapter 3

*F*or all their power, these Orëska wizards are very stu- *pid. And arrogant,* Lhel thought as Iya urged her down a back stair and away from the cursed house.

The witch spat thrice to the left, hoping to cut the bad luck that had bound them together all these weeks. A real storm crow, this wizard. Why hadn't she seen it sooner?

Lhel had scarely had time to finish the last stitch on the living child before the elder wizard was urging her away. "I'm not finished! The spirit—"

"The king is downstairs!" Iya hissed, as if this should mean something to her. "If he finds you here, we'll all be spirits. I will force you if I must."

What choice did she have? So Lhel had followed, thinking, *Be it on your head, then.*

But the further they got from that house, the more it weighed on her heart. To treat the dead so brutally was a dangerous affront to the Mother, and to Lhel's craft. This wizard woman had no honor, to abandon a child's spirit like that. Arkoniel might have been made to listen, but Lhel had long since realized that he had no voice in the matter. Their god had spoken to Iya and Iya would listen to no other.

Lhel spat again, just for good measure.

Lhel had dreamed the coming of the two wizards for a full month before they'd appeared in her village: a man boy and an old woman who carried a strange burden in a bag. Every divination she'd done as she awaited their arrival indicated that it was the Mother's will. Lhel must give them whatever aid they asked. When Iya and Arkoniel did finally arrive, they claimed that a vision from their own moon god had brought them to her. Lhel had taken this as an auspicious sign.

Still, she had been surprised at the nature of their request. Orëska must be a pale, milk-fed sort of magic, indeed, for two people possessed of such powerful souls not to have the craft to make a simple skin binding. Had she understood then the true depth of their ignorance, she might have tried to share more of her knowledge with them before the time came to use it.

But she hadn't understood until it was too late, until the moment her hand had faltered, letting the boy child draw his first breath. Iya would not wait for the necessary cleansing sacrifice. There was no time for anything but to complete the binding and flee, leaving the angry new spirit lost and alone.

Lhel balked again as the city gate came into sight ahead of them. "You cannot leave such a spirit earthbound!" she said again, struggling to free her wrist from Iya's grasp. "It grows to a demon before you know it, and then what will you do, you who couldn't bind it in the first place?"

"I will deal with it."

"You are a fool."

Iya turned, bringing their faces close together. "I am saving your life, woman, and that of the child and her family! If the king's wizard caught so much as a whiff of you we'd all be executed, starting with that baby. She's all that matters now, not you or me or anyone else in this whole wretched land. It's the will of Illior."

Once again, Lhel felt the massive power coursing through the wizard. Different Iya might be and possessed of unfamiliar magic, but there was no question that she was god-touched, and more than a match for Lhel. So she'd let herself be led away, leaving the child and its skin-bound twin behind in the stinking city. She hoped Arkoniel had found a strong tree to hold the spirit down.

They bought horses and traveled together for two days. Lhel said little, but prayed silently to the Mother for guidance. When they reached the edge of the highlands, she allowed Iya to give her into the care of a band of caravaneers heading west into the mountains. As they parted, Iya had even tried to make peace with her.

"You did well, my friend," she said, her hazel eyes sad as she took Lhel's hands. "Stay safe in your mountains and all will be well. We must never meet again."

Lhel chose to ignore the thinly veiled threat. Fishing in a pouch at her belt, she drew out a little silver amulet made in the shape of a full moon flanked on either side by slender crescents. "For when the child takes woman form again."

Iya held it on her palm. "The Shield of the Mother."

"Keep it hidden. It's only for women. As a boy, she must wear this." She gave Iya a short hazel twig capped on both ends with burnished copper bands.

Iya shook her head. "It's too dangerous. I'm not the only wizard to have studied your ways."

"Then you keep them for her!" Lhel urged. "This child will need much magic to survive."

Iya closed her hand around the amulets, wood and silver together. "I will, I promise you. Farewell."

Lhel stayed with the caravan for three days, and each day the black, cold weight of the dead child's spirit lay heavier on her heart. Each night its cry grew louder in her dreams. She prayed to the shining Mother to show her why she had sent her here to create such a thing and what she must do to make the world right again.

The Mother answered, and on the third night Lhel danced the dreamsleep dance for her guides, seducing away just enough of their thoughts to remove any memory of her and the supplies she took with her.

Guided by a waning white sliver of moon, she threw her traveling sack over her horse's neck and turned back for the stinking city.

Chapter 4

In the uneasy days following the birth, only Nari and the duke attended Ariani. Rhius sent word to Tharin, sending the captain on to the estate at Cirna to keep him away a while longer.

A silence fell over the household; black banners flew on the roof peaks, proclaiming mourning for the supposed stillbirth. On the household altar, Rhius set a fresh basin of water and burned the herbs sacred to Astellus, who smoothed the water road to birth and death and protected new mothers from childbed fever.

Sitting at Ariani's bedside each day, however, Nari knew it was not fever that ailed the woman, but a deep sickness of heart. Nari was old enough to remember Queen Agnalain's last days and prayed that her daughter was not afflicted with the same curse of madness.

Day after day, night after night, Ariani tossed against her pillows, waking to cry out, "The child, Nari! Don't you hear him? He's so cold."

"The child is well, Your Highness," Nari told her each time. "See, Tobin is in the cradle here beside you. Look how plump he is."

But Ariani would not look at the living child. "No, I hear him," she would insist, staring around wildly. "Why have you shut him outside? Fetch him in at once!"

"There's no child outside, Your Highness. You were only dreaming again."

Nari spoke the truth, for she'd heard nothing, but some of the other servants claimed to have heard an infant's cry in the darkness outside. Soon a rumor spread through the house that the second child had been stillborn with its eyes open; everyone knew that demons came into the world through such births. Several serving maids had been sent back to Atyion already with orders to keep their gossip to themselves. Only Nari and Mynir knew the truth behind the second child's death.

Loyalty to the duke guaranteed Mynir's silence. Nari owed allegiance to Iya. The wizard had been a benefactress to her family for three generations and there were times during those first few chaotic days when only that bond kept the nurse from running back to her own village. Iya had said nothing of demons when Nari agreed to serve.

In the end, however, she stayed for the child's sake. Her milk flowed freely as soon as she put the dark-haired little mite to her breast, and with it all the tenderness she'd thought she'd lost when her husband and son had died. Maker knew neither the princess nor her husband had any to spare for the poor child.

They must all call Tobin "he" and "him" now. And thanks to the outlandish magic the witch had worked with her knives and needles, Tobin was to all appearances a fine healthy boy child. He slept well, nursed vigorously, and seemed happy with whatever attention was paid him, which was little enough by his own folk.

"They'll come 'round, little pet my love," Nari would croon to him as he dozed contentedly in her arms. "How could they not and you so sweet?"

As Tobin thrived, however, his mother sank ever faster into a darkness of spirit. The bout of fever passed, but Ariani kept to her bed. She still would not touch her living child, and she would not even look at her husband, or her brother either, when he came to call.

Duke Rhius was near despair. He sat with her for hours, enduring her silence, and brought in the most skilled drysians from the temple of Dalna. But the healers found no illness of the body to cure.

On the twelfth day after the birth, however, the princess began to show signs of rallying. That afternoon, Nari found her curled in an armchair next to the fire, sewing a doll. The floor around her was littered with scraps of muslin, clumps of stuffing wool, snippets of embroidery silks and thread.

The new doll was finished by nightfall—a boy with no mouth. Another just like it followed the next day, and another. She did not bother to dress the things, but cast each aside as soon as the last stitch was tied off and immediately began on another. By week's end half a dozen of the things were lined up on the mantelpiece.

"They're very pretty, my love, but why not finish the faces?" Duke Rhius asked, sitting faithfully by her bedside each night.

"So they won't cry," Ariani hissed, needle flying as she stitched an arm to a wool-packed body. "The crying is sending me mad!"

Nari looked away so as not to embarrass the duke by seeing his tears. It was the first time since the birth that Ariani had spoken to him.

This seemed to encourage the duke. He sent for Captain Tharin that very night and began to talk of the child's presentation feast.

Ariani told no one of the dreams that plagued her. Who could she tell? Her own trusted nurse, Lachi, had been sent away weeks ago, replaced by this stranger who would not leave her side. Nari was some relation of Iya's, Rhius had told her, and that only made Ariani hate her all the more. Her husband, her brother, the wizards, this woman—they'd all betrayed her. When she thought of that terrible night, all she remembered was a circle of faces looking down on her without pity. She despised them.

Exhaustion and grief had weighed down on her like a stack of wool quilts at first, and her mind had drifted in a grey fog. Daylight and darkness seemed to play sport with her; she never knew what to expect when she opened her eyes, or whether she dreamed or woke.

At first she thought that the horrid midwife Iya had brought had returned. But soon she realized it must be a dream or waking vision that brought the dark little woman to her bedside each night. She always appeared surrounded by a circle of shifting light, mouthing silent words at Ariani and gesturing with stained fingers for her to eat and drink. It went on for days, this silent pantomime, until Ariani grew used to her. At last she began to make out something of what the woman whispered and the words pulled fire and ice through her veins.

It was then that Ariani began to sew again, and forced herself to eat the bread and thin soups Nari brought. The task the witch had set for her would take strength.

𝒞he child's presentation took place a fortnight after the birth. Ariani refused to come downstairs and Nari thought this just as well. The princess' strength was returning, but she was still too strange for company. She would not dress and seldom spoke. Her shining black hair was dull and tangled for want of care and her blue eyes stared strangely, as if she was seeing something the rest could not. She slept, she ate, and she sewed doll after mouthless doll. Duke Rhius saw to it that word of a difficult lying-in was spread around the Palatine, as well as rumors of his wife's deep and continuing grief over the loss of the dead girl child.

Her absence did not mar the celebration too badly. All the principal nobles of Ero crowded into the great hall that night until the whole room seemed to shimmer with jewels and silks under the flickering lamps. Standing with the servants by the wine table, Nari saw some whispering behind their hands and overheard a few speaking of Agnalain's madness, wondering how the daughter could have gone the way of the mother so quickly and with no warning at all.

It was unseasonably warm that night, and the soft patter of autumn rain swept in through the open windows. The men of the duke's personal guard stood at attention flanking the stairs, resplendent in new green and blue. Sir Tharin stood to the left of the stairs in his fine tunic and jewels, looking as pleased as if the child were his own. Nari had taken to the lanky, fair-haired man the day she met him, and liked him all the better for the way his face lit up the first time he saw Tobin in his father's arms.

The king stood in the place of honor at the right of the staircase, holding his own son on one broad shoulder. Prince Korin was a bright, plump child of three, with his father's dark curls and bright brown eyes. He bounced excitedly, craning his neck for a look at his new cousin as Rhius appeared at the top of the stairs. The duke was resplendent in his embroidered robe and circlet. Tobin's dark head was just visible above the edge of his silken wrappings.

"Greetings and welcome, my king and my friends!" Duke Rhius called out. Descending to where the king stood, he went down on one knee and held the child up. "My king, I present to you my son and heir, Prince Tobin Erius Akandor."

Setting Korin down beside him, Erius took Tobin in his arms and showed him to the priests and assembled nobles. "Your son and heir is acknowledged before Ero, my brother. May his name be spoken with honor among the Royal Kin of Skala."

And that was that, though the speechifying and drinking of toasts would go on half the night. Nari shifted restlessly. It was past time to feed the child and her breasts ached. She smiled as she heard a familiar hiccuping whimper. Once Tobin started squalling for his supper they'd soon let him go, and she could retreat to her quiet chamber at the top of the house.

Just then one of the serving maids let out a startled squeak and pointed to the wine table. "By the Four, it just toppled over!"

The silver mazer for Rhius' toast lay on its side, its contents splashed across the dark polished wood beside the honey cake.

"I was looking right at it," the maid went on, voice beginning to rise dangerously. "Not a soul was near it!"

"I can see that!" Nari whispered, silencing her with a pinch and a glare. Whisking off her apron, she blotted up the spilled wine. It stained the linen red as blood.

Mynir snatched the cloth away and balled it tightly under his arm, hiding the stain. "By the Light, don't let any of the others see!" he whispered. "That was a white wine!"

Looking down at her hands, Nari saw that they were stained red, too, where the wine had wet them, though the droplets still clinging inside the rim of the cup were a pale golden color.

There was just time to send the trembling girl away to fetch a fresh mazer before the nobles came to make their toasts. Tobin was growing fussy. Nari held him while the duke raised the cup and sprinkled a few drops of wine over the child, then a few more over the honey cake in the traditional offering to the Four. "To Sakor, to make my child a great and just warrior with fire in his heart. To Illior, for wisdom and true dreaming. To Dalna, for many children and long life. To Astellus, for safe journeys and a swift death."

Nari exchanged a quick look of relief with the steward as the droplets sank away, leaving the cake's sticky surface unstained.

As soon as the brief ceremony was finished Nari carried Tobin upstairs. The babe squirmed and grunted, nuzzling at her bodice.

"You're a pet, you are," Nari murmured absently, still shaken by what she'd witnessed. She thought of the spell sticks Iya had left with her, wondering if she should use one to summon the wizard back. But Iya had been very clear; she was only to use those in the direst circumstances. Nari sighed and hugged Tobin closer, wondering where such portents would lead.

Passing Ariani's door in the upper corridor, Nari caught sight of a small patch of red on the wall, just above the rushes that covered the floor. She bent for a closer look, then pressed a hand over her mouth.

It was the bloody print of an infant's hand, splayed like a starfish. The blood was still bright and wet.

"Maker keep us, it's in the house!"

Cheers and applause burst out below. She could hear the king proclaiming a blessing for Tobin's health. With trembling fingers, Nari wiped at the mark with the edge of her skirt until the handprint smeared to a pinkish smudge. She pushed the rushes up to cover it, then slipped into Ariani's chamber, fearful of what she might find.

The princess sat by the fire, sewing away as madly as ever. For the first time since the birth, she had changed her nightdress for a loose gown and put on her rings again. The hem was wet and streaked with mud. Ariani's hair hung in damp strands around her face. The window was shut tight as always, but Nari could smell the night air on her, and the hint of something else besides. Nari wrinkled her nose, trying to place the raw, unpleasant odor.

"You've been outside, Your Highness?"

Ariani smiled down at her needlework. "Just for a bit, Nurse. Aren't you pleased?"

"Yes, my lady, but you should have waited and I'd have gone with you. You're not strong enough to be out on your own. What would the duke say?"

Ariani sewed on, still smiling over her work.

"Did you see anything . . . unusual out there, Your Highness?" Nari hazarded at last.

Ariani pulled a tuft of wool from a bag beside her and tucked it into the muslin arm she'd sewn. "Nothing at all. Off with you now, and fetch me something to eat. I'm famished!"

Nari mistrusted this sudden brightness. As she left, she could hear Ariani humming softly to herself, and recognized the tune as a lullaby.

She was halfway to the kitchens when she placed the smell at last and let out a snort of relief. Tomorrow she must tell the servants to bring in one of the hounds to root out the dead mouse spoiling somewhere along the upper corridor.

Chapter 5

Arkoniel left Ero not knowing when he would see Ariani or her child again. He met up with Iya at an inn in Sylara and together they set off to begin the next long stage of their mission.

Despite Arkoniel's strong misgivings, Iya decided that it would be safest for everyone if they kept their distance from the child. When Arkoniel told her of his strange conversation with Niryn, it only strengthened her resolve. Nari and the duke could get word to them by sending messages to several inns that Iya frequented in her travels. For emergencies, she'd left Nari with a few small tokens; painted rods that released a simple seeking spell when broken. No matter how far away Iya might be, she would feel the magic and return as quickly as she could.

"But what if we're too far away to reach them in time?" Arkoniel fretted, unhappy with the situation. "And how can we leave them like that? It all went wrong in the end, Iya. You didn't see the demon in the dead child's eyes. What if the tree can't hold it down?"

But she remained adamant. "They are safest with us away."

And so they began their long wandering quest, seeking out anyone who had a spark of magic in them, sounding out loyalties, listening to fears, and—with a select few—cautiously sharing a glimpse of Iya's vision: a new confederation of Orëska wizards. She was patient, and careful in her choices, winnowing out the mad and the greedy and those too loyal to the king. Even with those she deemed trustworthy she did not reveal her true purpose, but left them a small token—a pebble picked up on the road— and the promise that she would call on them again.

Over the next few years Niryn's words would come back to haunt them, for it seemed that they were not the only ones spreading the idea of unity. They learned from others they met on the road that the king's wizard was gathering a following of his own at court. Arkoniel often wondered what answer these wizards had given to Niryn's oblique question, and what their dreams had been.

The drought that had heralded Tobin's birth broke, only to be followed by another the following summer. The further south they went, the more often they saw empty granaries and sickly livestock. Disease walked the land in hunger's wake, striking down the weak like a wolf culling a flock. The worst was a fever brought in by traders. The first sign was bloody sweat, often followed by black swellings in the armpits and groin. Few who showed both symptoms survived. The Red and Black Death, as it came to be called, struck whole villages overnight, leaving too few living to burn the dead.

A plague of a different sort struck the eastern coast: Plenimaran raiders. Towns were looted and burned, the old women killed, the younger ones and the children carried off as slaves in the raiders' black ships. The men who survived the battle often met a crueler fate.

Iya and Arkoniel entered one such village just after an attack and found half a dozen young men nailed by the hands to the side of a byre; all had been disemboweled. One boy was still alive, begging for water with one breath and death with the next. Iya gently gave him both.

Iya continued Arkoniel's education as they traveled, and was pleased to see how his powers continued to flourish. He was the finest student she'd ever had, and the most curious; for Arkoniel there were always new vistas ahead, new spells to master. Iya practiced what she jokingly referred to as "portable magics," those spells which relied more on wand and word than weighty components and instruments. Arkoniel had a natural talent for these, and was already beginning to create spells of his own, an unusual accomplishment for so one so young. Driven by his concern for Rhius and Ariani, he experimented endlessly with seeking spells, trying to expand their limited powers, but with no success.

Iya explained repeatedly that even Orëska magic had its limits, but he would not be put off.

In the houses of the richer, more sedentary wizards, particularly those with noble patrons, she saw him linger longingly in well-equipped workrooms, examining the strange instruments and alchemists' vessels he found there. Sometimes they guested long enough for him to learn something from these wizards, and Iya was delighted to see him so willingly adding to what she could teach him.

Content as always to wander, Iya could almost at times forget the responsibility that hung over them.

Almost.

Living on the road, they heard a great deal of news but were little touched by most of it. When the first rumors of the King's Harriers reached them, Iya dismissed them as wild tales. This became harder to do, however, when they met with a priest of Illior who claimed to have seen them with his own eyes.

"The king has sanctioned them," he told Iya, nervously fingering the amulet on his breast, so similar to the ones they wore. "The Harriers are a special guard, soldiers and wizards both, charged with hunting down traitors to the throne. They've burned a wizard at Ero, and there are Illioran priests in the prison."

"Wizards and priests?" Arkoniel scoffed. "No Skalan wizard has ever been executed, not since the necromantic purges of the Great War! And wizards hunting down their own kind?"

But Iya was shaken. "Remember who we are dealing with," she warned when they were safely alone in their rented chamber. "Mad Agnalain's son has already killed his own kin to preserve his line. Perhaps there's more of his mother in him than we feared."

"It's Niryn leading them," Arkoniel said, thinking again of the way the wizard had watched him the night of Tobin's birth. Had he been seeking out followers even then? And what had he found in his Harriers that he hadn't seen in Arkoniel?

Part Two

From the private journal of Queen
Tamír II, recently discovered in
the Palace Archives

[Archivist's note: passage undated]
My father moved us to that lonely keep in the
mountains not long after my birth. He put it about
that my mother's health required it, but I'm sure
by then all Ero knew she'd gone mad, just as her
mother had. When I think of her at all now, I remember a pale wraith of a woman with nervous
hands and a stranger's eyes the same color as my
own.

My father's ancestors built the keep in the days
when hill folk still came through the passes to raid
the lowlands. It had thick stone walls and narrow
windows covered by splintery red-and-white
painted shutters—I remember amusing myself by
picking off the scaling flakes outside my bedchamber window as I stood there, watching for my father's return.

A tall, square watchtower jutted from the back
of the keep, next to the river. I used to believe the
demon lurked there, and watched me from the
windows whenever Nari or the men took me outside to play in the courtyards or the meadow below the barracks house. I was kept inside most of
the time, though. I knew every dusty, shadowed

room of the lower floors by the time I could walk. That crumbling old pile was all the world I knew, my first seven years—my nurse and a handful of servants my only companions when Father and his men were gone, which was all too often.

And the demon, of course. Only years later did I have any inkling that all households were not like my own—that it was unusual for invisible hands to pinch and push, or for furniture to move about the room by itself. One of my earliest memories is of sitting on Nari's lap as she taught me to bend my little fingers into a warding sign—

Chapter 6

Tobin knelt on the floor in his toy room, idly pushing a little ship around the painted harbor of the toy city. It was the carrack with the crooked mast, the one the demon had broken.

Tobin wasn't really playing, though. He was waiting and watching the closed door of his father's room across the corridor. Nari had closed the door when they went in to talk, making it impossible to eavesdrop from here.

Tobin's breath came out in a puff of white vapor as he sighed and bent to straighten the ship's little sail. It was cold this morning; he could smell frost on the early morning breeze through the open window. He opened his mouth and blew several short breaths, making brief clouds over the citadel.

The toy city, a gift from his father on his last name day, was his most treasured possession. It stood almost as tall as Tobin and took up half of this disused bedchamber next to his own. And it wasn't just a toy, either. It was a miniature version of Ero itself, which his father had made for him.

"Since you're too young to go to Ero, I've brought Ero to you!" he'd said when he gave it to him. "You may one day live here, even defend it, so you must know the place."

Since then, they'd spent many happy hours together, learning the streets and wards. Houses made from wooden blocks clustered thickly up the steep sides of the citadel, and there were open spaces painted green for the public gardens and pasturage. The great market square had a temple to the Four surrounded by traders' booths made of twigs and bright scraps of cloth. Baked clay livestock of all sorts populated the little enclosures. The blue-painted harbor that jutted from one side of the city's base outside the many-gated wall was filled with pretty little ships that could be pushed about with a pole.

The top of the hill was flat and ringed with another wall called the Palatine Circle, though it wasn't exactly round. Inside lay a great clutter of houses, palaces, and temples, all with different names and stories. There were more gardens here, as well as a fish pool made from a silver mirror and an exercise field for the Royal Companions. This last interested Tobin very much; the Companions were boys who lived at the Old Palace with his cousin, Prince Korin, and trained to be warriors. His father and Tharin had been Companions to King Erius when they were young, too. As soon as Tobin had learned this, he wanted to go at once but was told, as usual, that he must wait until he was older.

The biggest building on the Palatine was the Old Palace. This had a roof that came off, and several rooms inside. There was a throne room with a tiny wooden throne, of course, and a tiny tablet of real gold beside it, set in a little wooden frame.

Tobin lifted this out and squinted at the fine words engraved on it. He couldn't read them, but he knew them by heart: "So long as a daughter of Thelátimos' line defends and rules, Skala shall never be subjugated." Tobin knew the legend of King Thelátimos and the Oracle by heart, too. It was one of his father's favorite stories.

The city was populated by scores of little wooden stick people. He loved these the best of anything in the city, and smuggled whole families of them back to his bed to hold and talk to under the covers at night while he waited for Nari to come up to bed. Tobin put the golden tablet back, then lined up half a dozen stick people on the practice ground, imagining himself among the Companions. Opening the flat, velvet-lined box his father had brought home from another journey, he took out the special people and lined them up on the palace roof to watch the Companions at their exercises. These people—The Ones Who Came Before—were much fancier than the stick ones; all but one was made of silver. They had painted faces and clothes and each carried the same tiny sword at their side, the Sword of Queen Ghërilain. His father had taught him their names and stories, too. The silver man was King Thelátimos and next to him in the box was his daughter, Ghërilain the Founder—made queen of Skala because of Oracle's golden words. After Ghërilain came Queen Tamír, who was poisoned by her brother who'd wanted to be king, then an Agnalain and another Ghërilain, then six more whose names and order he still mixed up, and then Grandmama Agnalain the Second. The first and last queens were his favorites. The first Ghërilain had the finest crown; Grandmama Agnalain had the nicest painting on her cloak.

The last figure in the box was a man carved of wood. He had a black beard like Tobin's father, a crown, and two names: Your Uncle Erius and The Present King.

Tobin turned the king over in his hands. The demon liked to break this one. The little wooden man would be standing on the Palace roof or lying in his place in the box when suddenly his head would fly off or he'd split right down the middle. After many mendings, Your Uncle was all misshapen.

Tobin sighed again and put them all carefully back in the box. Not even the city could hold his attention today. He turned and stared at the door, willing it to open. Nari had gone in there ages ago! At last, unable to stand the suspense any longer, he crept across the corridor to listen.

The rushes covering the floor were old and crunched beneath his slippers no matter how carefully he tiptoed. He looked quickly up and down the short passage. To his left lay the stairs to the great hall. He could hear Captain Tharin and old Mynir laughing about something there. To his right, the door beside his father's was tightly shut and he hoped this one stayed that way; his mama was having another one of her bad spells.

Satisfied that he was alone for the moment, he pressed his ear to the carved oak panel and listened.

"What harm can there be, my lord?" That was Nari. Tobin wiggled with delight. He'd nagged for weeks to get her to do battle on his behalf.

His father rumbled something, then he heard Nari again, gently cajoling the way she did sometimes. "I know what she said, my lord, but with all respect, he's growing up strange kept apart like this. I can't think she wants that!"

Who's strange? Tobin wondered. And who was this mysterious "she" who might object to him going to town with Father? It was his name day, after all. He was seven today; surely old enough at last to make the journey. And it wasn't so far to Alestun; when he picnicked on the roof with Nari, they could look east over the valley and see the cluster of roofs beyond the forest's edge. On a cold day he could even make out smoke rising from the hearth fires there. It seemed a small thing to ask for a present, just to go, and it was all he wanted.

The voices went on, too soft now to make out.

Please! he mouthed, making a luck sign to the Four.

The brush of cold fingers against Tobin's cheek made him jump. Turning, he was dismayed to find his mother standing right there behind him. She was almost like a ghost herself, a ghost Tobin could see. She was thin and pale, with nervous hands that fluttered about like dying birds when she wasn't sewing the pretty rag dolls, or clutching the ugly old one she was never without. It was tucked under her arm just now and seemed to be staring at him, even though it had no face.

He was as surprised to find her here as he was to see her free. When Tobin's father was home, she always kept to herself and avoided him. Tobin liked it better when she did.

It was second nature for him now to steal a quick look into his mama's eyes; Tobin had learned young to gauge the moods of those around him, especially his mother's. Usually she simply looked at him like a stranger, cold and distant. When the demon threw things or pinched him, she would just hug her ugly old doll and look away. She almost never hugged Tobin, though on the very bad days, she spoke to him as if he were still a baby, or as if he were a girl. On those days Father would shut her up in her chamber and Nari would make the special teas for her to drink.

But her eyes were clear now, he saw. She was almost smiling as she held out a hand to him. "Come, little love."

She'd never spoken to him like that before. Tobin glanced nervously at his father's door, but she bent and captured his hand in hers. Her grip was just a little too tight as she drew him to the locked door at the end of the corridor, the one that led upstairs.

"I'm not allowed up there," Tobin told her, his voice hardly more than a squeak. Nari said the floors were unsound up there, and that there were rats and spiders big as his fist.

"You may come up with me," she said, producing a large key from her skirts and opening the forbidden door.

Stairs led up to a corridor that looked very much like the one below, with doors on either side, but this one was dusty and dank-smelling, and the small, high-set windows were tightly shuttered.

Tobin glanced through an open door as they passed and saw a sagging bed with tattered hangings, but no rats. At the end of the corridor his mother opened a smaller door and led him up a very steep, narrow stairway lit by a few arrow slits in the walls. There was hardly enough light to make out the worn steps, but Tobin knew where they were.

They were in the watchtower.

He pressed one hand to the wall for balance, but pulled it away again when his fingers found patches of something rough that scaled away at his touch. He was scared now, and wanted to run back down to the bright, safe part of the house, but his mother still held his hand.

As they climbed higher, something suddenly flittered in the shadows overhead—the demon, no doubt, or some worse terror. Tobin tried to pull free, but she held him fast and smiled at him over her shoulder as she led him up to a narrow door at the top.

"Those are just my birds. They have their nests here and I have mine, but they can fly in and out whenever they wish."

She opened the narrow door and sunlight flooded out. It made him blink as he stumbled over the threshold.

He'd always thought the tower was empty, abandoned, except perhaps for the demon, but here was a pretty little sitting room furnished more nicely than any of the rooms downstairs. He gazed around in amazement, never imagining his mother had such a delightful secret place.

Faded tapestries covered the windows on three sides, but the west wall was bare and the heavy shutters open. Tobin could see sunlight shining on the snow-covered peaks in the distance, and hear the rush of the river below.

"Come, Tobin," she urged, going to a table by the window. "Sit with me a while on your name day."

A little spark of hope flared up in Tobin's heart and he edged further into the room. She'd never remembered his birthday before.

The room was very cozy and comfortable. A long table stood against the far wall, piled with doll-making goods. On another table, finished dolls—dark-haired and mouthless as always, but dressed in tunics of velvet and silk fancier than any Tobin owned—sat propped in a double rank against the wall.

Perhaps she brought me here to give me one for my name day, he thought. Even without mouths, they were very pretty. He turned hopefully to his mother. For an instant he could almost see how she'd smile, telling him to pick whichever one he liked best, a special present just from her. But his mama just stood by the window, plucking restlessly at the front of her skirt with the fingers of her free hand as she stared down at the bare table in front of her. "I should have cakes, shouldn't I? Honey cakes and wine."

"We always have them in the hall," Tobin reminded her, casting another longing glance at the dolls. "You were there last year, remember? Until the demon knocked the cake on the floor and—"

He faltered to a stop as other memories of that day came back. His mother had burst into tears when the demon came, then started screaming. His father and Nari had carried her away and Tobin had eaten his broken bits of cake in the kitchen with Cook and Tharin.

"The demon?" A tear rolled down his mother's pale cheek and she hugged the doll tighter. "How can they call him that?"

Tobin looked to the open doorway, gauging an escape. If she started screaming now, he could run away down the stairs, back to people who loved him and could be counted on to do what he expected. He wondered if Nari would be angry with him for going upstairs.

But his mother didn't scream. She just sank into a chair and wept, clutching the ugly doll to her heart.

He started to edge his way toward the door, but his mama looked so terribly sad that instead of running away, he went to her and rested his head on her shoulder, the way he did with Nari when she was sad and homesick.

Ariani put an arm around him and pulled him close,

stroking his unruly black hair. As usual, she hugged too hard, stroked too roughly, but he stayed, grateful for even this much affection. For once, the demon let him be.

"My poor little babies," she whispered, rocking Tobin. "What are we to do?" Reaching into her bodice, she took out a tiny pouch. "Hold out your hand."

Tobin obeyed and she shook out two small objects: a silver moon charm, and a little piece of wood capped on both ends with the red metal he'd seen on the backs of shields.

She picked up one, then the other, and pressed them to Tobin's forehead as if she expected something to happen. When nothing did, she tucked them away again with a sigh.

Still holding Tobin close, she rose and drew him to the window. Lifting him up with surprising strength, she stood him on the wide stone sill. Tobin looked down between the toes of his slippers and saw the river rushing in white curls around the rocks below. Frightened again, he gripped the window casing with one hand, his mother's thin shoulder with the other.

"Lhel!" she shouted at the mountains. "What are we to do? Why don't you come? You promised you'd come!"

She gripped the back of Tobin's tunic, pushing him slightly forward, threatening his balance.

"Mama, I want to get down!" Tobin whispered, clutching her harder.

He turned his head and looked into eyes that were cold and hard again. For an instant she looked as if she didn't know who he was or what they were doing here at this window so high above the ground. Then she yanked him back and they both tumbled to the floor. Tobin bumped his elbow and let out a yelp of pain.

"Poor baby! Mama's sorry," his mother sobbed, but it was the doll she rocked in her arms as she crouched there on the floor, not him.

"Mama?" Tobin crept to her side, but she ignored him.

Heartbroken and confused, he ran from the room, wanting nothing more than to escape the sound of her sobs. He was almost to the bottom of the tower when something pushed him hard in the back and he fell the last few steps, banging his shins and scuffing his palms.

The demon was with him, a dark shape flitting just at the edge of his vision. Tobin couldn't recall just when he'd begun to see it, but he knew he hadn't always been able to. It darted close and yanked at a stray lock of his hair.

Tobin struck out wildly. "I hate you! *I hate you I hate you I hate you!*"

Hate you! echoed back from the shadows overhead.

Tobin limped back downstairs to the toy room, but even here the daylight seemed tarnished. The savor of his earlier excitement had been leeched away, and his shins and hands hurt. All he wanted was to burrow under his bedcovers with the current family of friendly little wooden people waiting there. As he turned to go, his father came in.

"There you are!" Rhius exclaimed, hoisting Tobin up in his strong arms and giving him a kiss. His beard tickled and suddenly the day seemed a little brighter. "I've looked high and low for you. Where have you been? And how did you manage to get so dusty?"

Shame welled up in Tobin's chest as he thought of the disastrous visit. "I was just playing," he said, staring down at the heavy silver broach on his father's shoulder.

Rhius slipped a rough, callused finger under Tobin's chin and examined a smudge on his cheek. Tobin knew his father was thinking of the demon; this at least they both understood without the need for words.

"Well now, never mind that," he said, carrying Tobin next door to his room, where they found Nari laying out a new set of clothes on the bed. "Nari tells me you're old enough to ride down to Alestun with me and look for a name day present. What do you think of that?"

"I can go?" Tobin cried, all dark thoughts swept away for the moment.

"Not looking like that, you can't!" his nurse exclaimed, sloshing water into the basin on his washstand. "How did you manage to get so dirty this early in the day?"

His father winked at him and went to the door. "I'll meet you in the front court when you're presentable."

Tobin forgot all about his scraped shins and sore elbow as he dutifully scrubbed his face and hands, then stood as still as he could while Nari combed the tangles she called rats' nests from his hair.

Dressed at last in a fine new tunic of soft green wool and fresh leggings, he hurried down to the courtyard. His father was waiting, as promised, and all the rest of the household with him.

"Blessings of the day, little prince!" everyone cried, laughing and hugging him.

Tobin was so excited that at first he didn't even notice Tharin standing off to one side, holding the bridle of a bay gelding Tobin had never seen before.

The horse was a few spans shorter than his father's black palfrey and fitted out with a child-sized saddle. His rough winter coat and mane had been curried until they shone.

"Blessings, my son," Rhius said, lifting Tobin up into the saddle. "A lad old enough to ride to town needs his own horse to go on. He's yours to care for, and to name."

Grinning, Tobin twitched the reins and guided the bay into a walk around the courtyard. "I'll call him Chestnut. That's the color he is, just like a chestnut shell."

"Then you could also call him Gosi," his father told him with a twinkle in his eye.

"Why is that?"

"Because this isn't just any horse. He's come all the way from Aurënen, just as my black did. There are no

finer mounts than that. All the nobles of Skala ride Aurënfaie horses now."

Aurënfaie. A flicker of memory stirred. Aurënfaie
traders had come to their gate one stormy night—wonderful, strange-looking folk with long red scarves wrapped
around their heads and tattoos on their cheeks. Nari had
sent him upstairs too early that night, but he'd hidden at
the top of the stairs and watched as they did colorful magics and played music on strange instruments. The demon
had scared them away, and Tobin had seen his mother
laughing with her doll in the shadows of the disused minstrel's gallery. It was the first time he'd ever realized he
might hate her.

Tobin pushed the dark thoughts away; that had been
a long time ago, nearly two years. Aurënen meant magic
and strange folk who bred horses fit for Skalan nobles.
Nothing more.

He leaned down to stroke the gelding's neck. "Thank
you, Father! I'll call him Gosi. Can I go to Aurënen someday?"

"Everyone should go to Aurënen. It's a beautiful place."

"Here, take these to make a name day offering at the
temple." Nari passed him up several little packets tied up
in clean cloth. Tobin proudly stowed them away in his
new saddle pouch.

"I've a gift for you, too, Tobin." Tharin pulled a long,
cloth-wrapped parcel from his belt and handed it up to
him.

Inside Tobin found a carved wooden sword nearly as
long as his arm. The blade was thick and blunt, but the
hilt was nicely carved and fitted with real bronze quillons.
"It's handsome! Thank you!"

Tharin gave him a wink. "We'll see if you thank me after we start using it. I'm to be your swordmaster. I think
we'll wear out a good many of those before we're done,
but there's the first."

This was as good a gift as the horse, even if the blade

wasn't real. He tried to brandish his new weapon, but it was heavier than he'd thought.

His father chuckled. "Don't you worry, my boy. Tharin will soon put you through your paces. You'd best leave your weapon with Mynir for now, though. We don't want you getting into any duels your first time abroad."

Tobin surrendered it grudgingly to the steward, but soon forgot all about it as he rode out the gate and across the bridge behind his father and Tharin. For the first time in his life, he didn't have to stop at the far end and wave good-bye to them. As they continued down through the meadow, he felt like a warrior already, heading off to see the wide world.

Just before they entered the trees, however, he felt a sudden crawly chill between his shoulder blades, as if an ant had fallen down his tunic. Turning, he glanced back at the keep and thought he saw the shutters at the watchtower's south window move. He turned away quickly.

Leaves like round gold coins paved the forest road. Others like hands of red or orange wavered over head, together with oak leaves shiny and brown as polished leather.

Tobin amused himself by practicing with rein and knees, getting Gosi to trot at his command.

"Tobin rides like a soldier already, Rhius," Tharin remarked, and Tobin's heart swelled with pride.

"Do you ride your horse at the Plenimarans in battle, Father?" he asked.

"When we fight on land, but I have a great black war horse called Sakor's Fire for that, with iron shoes that the smiths sharpen before every battle."

"Why have I never seen that horse?" Tobin demanded.

"He stays at Atyion. That sort of mount is only suited for battle. He's strong and fast and has no fear of blood or fire, but it's rather like riding a crate on square wheels. Old Majyer here and your Gosi are proper riding mounts."

"Why can't I ever go to Atyion?" Tobin asked, and not for the first time.

The answer often varied. Today his father just smiled and said, "You will, someday."

Tobin sighed. Perhaps now that he was old enough to ride his own horse, "someday" would come soon?

The ride to town was much shorter than Tobin had imagined. The sun had moved less than two hours across the sky when they passed the first cottages beside the road.

The trees grew thinner here, mostly oak and aspen, and Tobin could see herds of pigs snuffling in the mast beneath their branches. A mile or so further and the forest gave way to open meadow, where flocks of sheep and goats grazed under the watchful eye of shepherds not much older than Tobin. They waved to him and he returned the gesture shyly.

They soon met more people on the road, driving carts pulled by goats or oxen, or carrying loads in long baskets on their backs. A trio of young girls in short, dirty shifts stared at Tobin as he rode past and talked to each other behind their hands as they followed him with their eyes.

"Get home to your mothers," Tharin growled in a voice Tobin had never heard him use before. The girls jumped like startled rabbits and fled across the ditch, but Tobin could hear laughter in their wake.

A river flowed down out of the hills to the town and the road bent to follow its bank to Alestun. Fields laid out in broad strips surrounded the town. Some were tilled for spring; others were yellow and brown with autumn stubble.

His father pointed to a group of people at work in a barley field, gathering the last sheaves of the harvest. "We've been lucky here. In some parts of the country the plague has killed off so many folk the fields have gone to ruin for want of laborers. And those who don't die of the illness starve."

Tobin knew what plague was. He'd heard the men talking about it in the barracks yard when they thought he couldn't hear. It made your skin bleed and black lumps grow under your arms. He was glad it hadn't come here.

By the time they neared the wooden palisade of the town, Tobin was round-eyed with excitement. There were more people than ever here and he waved to them all, delighted to see so many folk at once. Many waved back and saluted his father respectfully, but a few stared at him as the girls by the road had.

Just outside the walls a mill stood on the riverbank. There was a large oak tree beside it, full of children, girls and boys alike, swinging out over the water on long ropes tied to its branches.

"Are they being hanged?" Tobin gasped as they rode past. He'd heard of such punishments but hadn't pictured it quite like this. The children seemed to be enjoying themselves.

His father laughed. "No, they're playing at swings."

"Could I do that?"

The two men exchanged an odd look that Tobin couldn't quite decipher.

"Would you like to?" asked Tharin.

Tobin looked back at the laughing children clambering like squirrels among the branches. "Maybe."

At the gate a pikeman stepped forward and bowed to his father, touching a hand to his heart. "Good day to you, Duke Rhius."

"Good day to you, Lika."

"Say, this fine young fellow wouldn't be your son, would he?"

"Indeed he is, come to visit at last."

Tobin sat up a little straighter in his saddle.

"Welcome, young prince," Lika said, bowing to Tobin.

"Come to see the pleasures of the town? It's market day, and there's lots to look at."

"It's my name day," Tobin told him shyly.

"Blessings on you, then, by the Four!"

Alestun was only a small market town, but to Tobin it seemed a vast city. Low, thatch-roofed cottages lined the muddy streets, and there were children and animals everywhere. Pigs chased dogs, dogs chased cats and chickens, and small children chased each other and everything else. Tobin couldn't help staring, for he'd never seen so many children in one place. Those who noticed him stopped to stare back or point, and he began to feel rather uncomfortable again. A little girl with a wooden doll tucked under her arm gazed at him and he scowled back at her until she looked away.

The square was too crowded for riding, so they left their mounts with an ostler and continued on foot. Tobin held tightly to his father's hand for fear he'd be lost forever in the throng if they got separated.

"Stand up tall, Tobin," his father murmured. "It's not every day a prince comes to Alestun market."

They went first to the shrine of the Four, which stood at the center of the square. The shrine at the keep was just a stone niche in the hall, carved and painted with the symbols of the four gods of Skala. This one looked more like Cook's summer kitchen. Four posts supported the thatch roof and each was painted a different color: white for Illior, red for Sakor, blue for Astellus, and yellow for Dalna. A small offering brazier burned at the foot of each. Inside, an elderly priestess sat on a stool surrounded by pots and baskets. She accepted Tobin's offerings, sprinkling the portions of salt, bread, herbs, and incense onto the braziers with the proper prayers.

"Would you like to make a special prayer, my prince?" she asked when she'd finished.

Tobin looked to his father, who smiled and gave the priestess a silver sester.

"To which of the Four do you petition?" she asked, laying a hand on Tobin's head.

"Sakor, so that I can be a great warrior, like my father."

"Bravely said! Well then, we must make the warrior's offering to please the god."

The priestess cut a bit of Tobin's hair with a steel blade and kneaded it into a lump of wax, along with salt, a few drops of water, and some powders that turned the wax bright red.

"There now," she said, placing the softened wax in his hand. "Shape it into a horse."

Tobin liked the smooth feel of the wax under his fingers as he pinched and molded it. He thought of Gosi as he fashioned the animal's shape, then used his fingernail to make lines for the mane and tail.

"Huh!" the priestess said, turning it over in her hands when he'd finished. "That's fine work for a little fellow like you. I've seen grown men not do so well. Sakor will be pleased." She made a few designs on the wax with her fingernail, then gave it back to him. "Make your prayer, and give it to the god."

Tobin bent over the brazier at the foot of the Sakor post and inhaled the pungent smoke. "Make me a great warrior, a defender of Skala," he whispered, then cast the little figure onto the coals. Acrid green flames flared up as it melted away.

Leaving the shrine, they plunged again into the market-day crowd. Tobin still held his father's hand, but curiosity was quickly replacing fear.

Tobin recognized a few faces here, people who came to sell their goods to Cook in the kitchen courtyard. Balus the knife grinder saw him and touched his brow to Tobin.

Farmers hawked their fruits and vegetables from the backs of carts. There were piles of turnips, onions, rabes, and marrows, and baskets of apples that made Tobin's mouth water. One sour-smelling cart was stacked with waxed wheels of cheese and buckets of milk and butter. The next was full of hams. A tinker was selling new pots and mending old ones, creating a continuous clatter in his corner by the town well. Merchants carried their wares in baskets hanging from shoulder yokes, crying, "Almond milk!" "Good marrow bones!" "Candles and flints!" "Coral beads for luck!" "Needles and thread!"

This must be what Ero is like! Tobin thought in wonder.

"What would you like for your present?" his father asked, raising his voice to be heard over the din.

"I don't know," Tobin replied. All he'd wanted, really, was to come here, and now he had, and gotten a horse and sword into the bargain.

"Come on, then, we'll have a look around."

Tharin went off on business of his own and his father found people who needed to talk to him. Tobin stood patiently by as several of his father's tenants brought him news and complaints. Tobin was half-listening to a sheep farmer rattle on about blocked teats when he spied a knot of children gathered at a nearby table. Bolder now, he left his father and sidled over to see what the attraction was.

A toy maker had spread her wares there. There were the tops and whirligigs, cup and ball sets, sacks of red clay marbles, and a few crudely painted linen gaming boards. But what caught Tobin's eye was the dolls.

Nari and Cook said that his mother made the prettiest dolls in Skala and he saw nothing here to contradict them. Some were carved from flat pieces of wood, like the one he'd seen the little girl carrying. Others were made of stuffed cloth, like his mother's, but they were not so well shaped and had no fine clothes. All the same, their embroidered faces had mouths—smiling mouths—that gave them a friendly, comfortable look. Tobin picked one up and squeezed it. The coarse stuffing crunched nicely under his fingers. He smiled, imagining tucking this funny little fellow under his covers with the wooden family. Perhaps Nari could make some clothes for it—

Glancing up, he saw that the other children and the merchant were all staring at him. One of the older boys sniggered.

And then his father was beside him again, angrily snatching the doll from his hands. His face was pale, his eyes hard and angry. Tobin shrank back against the table; he'd never seen his father look like that before. It was the sort of look his mother gave him on her worst days.

Then it was gone, replaced by a stiff smile that was even worse. "What a silly thing that is!" his father exclaimed, tossing the doll back onto the pile. "Here's what we want!" He snatched something up from the table and thrust it into Tobin's hands—a sack of marbles. "Captain Tharin will pay you, Mistress. Come on, Tobin, there's more to see."

He led Tobin away, gripping him too hard by the arm. Tobin heard a burst of mean laughter behind them from the children and some man muttering, "Told you he was an idiot child."

Tobin kept his head down to hide the tears of shame burning his eyes. This was worse, far worse, than the scene with his mother that morning. He couldn't imagine what had made his father so angry or the townspeople so mean, but he knew with a child's sudden, clear conviction that it was his fault.

They went straight back to the ostler for the horses. No more town for him. As Tobin went to mount, he found he was still holding the marbles. He didn't want them, but didn't dare anger his father further by throwing them away, so he jammed them into the neck of his tunic. They slid down to where his belt cinched in, heavy and uncomfortable against his side.

"Come on, let's go home," his father said, and rode away without waiting for Tharin.

Silence hung heavily between them on the homeward journey. Tobin felt as though a hand was clutching his throat, making it ache. He'd learned long ago how to cry silently. They were halfway home before his father looked back and saw.

"Ah, Tobin!" He reined in and waited for Tobin to ride up beside him. He didn't look angry anymore, just weary and sad as he gestured vaguely back toward the town and said, "Dolls . . . They're silly, filthy things. Boys don't play with them, especially not boys who want to grow up to be brave warriors. Do you understand?"

The doll! A fresh wave of shame washed over Tobin. So that was why his father had been so angry. His heart sank further as another realization came clear. It was why his mother hadn't given him one that morning, too. It was shameful of him to want them.

He was too shocked at himself to wonder why no one, not even Nari, had thought to tell him.

His father patted his shoulder. "Let's go home and have your cake. Tomorrow Tharin will start your training."

But by the time they reached home he was feeling too sick in his stomach to eat any honey cake or wine. Nari felt his forehead, pronounced him played out, and put him to bed.

He waited until she was gone, then reached under his pillow for the four little stick people hidden there. What had been a happy secret now made his cheeks burn. These were dolls, too. Gathering them up, he crept next door and put them down in one of the toy city's market squares. This was where they belonged. His father had made them and put them here, so it must be all right to play with them here.

Returning to his room, Tobin hid the unwanted sack of marbles at the very back of his wardrobe. Then he crawled between the cold sheets and said another prayer to Sakor that he would be a better boy and make his father proud.

Even after he cried again, it was hard to sleep. His bed felt very empty now. At last he fetched the wooden sword Tharin had given him and cuddled up with that.

Chapter 7

Tobin didn't forget the bad memories of that name day, but—like the unwanted sack of marbles gathering dust at the back of his wardrobe—he simply chose not to touch them. The other gifts he'd received kept him happily occupied over the next year.

He learned swordplay and archery in the barracks yard with Tharin, and rode Gosi every day. He no longer cast a longing eye at the Alestun road. The few traders they met on the mountain track bowed respectfully; no one pointed at him here, or whispered behind their hands.

Remembering the pleasure he'd felt making the wax horse at the shrine, he begged bits of candle end from Cook's melting pot, and soon the windowsill in his bedchamber was populated by tiny yellow animals and birds. Nari and his father praised these, but it was Tharin who brought him lumps of clean new wax so that he could make bigger animals. Delighted, Tobin used the first bit to make him a horse.

On his eighth name day they went to town again and he was careful to behave himself as a young warrior should. He made fine wax horses at the shrine, and no one snickered later when he chose a fine hunting knife as his gift.

Not long after this, his father decided it was time for Tobin to learn his letters.

Tobin enjoyed these lessons at first, but mostly because

he loved sitting in his father's chamber. It smelled of leather and there were maps and interesting daggers hanging on the walls.

"No Skalan noble should be at the mercy of scribes," his father explained, setting out parchments and a pot of ink on a small table by the window. He trimmed a goose quill and held it up for Tobin to see. "This is a weapon, my son, and some know how to wield it as skillfully as a sword or dagger."

Tobin couldn't imagine what he meant but was anxious as always to please him. In this, however, he had little luck. Try as he might, he simply could not understand the connection between the crooked black marks his father drew on the page and the sounds he claimed they made. Worse yet, his fingers, so adept at molding wax or clay from the riverbank, could not control the scratchy, skittering quill. It blotted. It wandered. It caught on the parchment and spat ink in all directions. His lines were wiggly as grass snakes, his loops came out too large, and whole letters ended up backwards or upside down. His father was patient but Tobin was not. Day after day he struggled, blotching and scratching along until the sheer frustration of it all made him cry.

"Perhaps we'd best leave this for later," his father conceded at last.

That night Tobin dreamt of burning all the quills in the house, just in case his father changed his mind.

Fortunately, Tobin had no such difficulty learning the sword. Tharin had kept his promise; whenever he was at the keep, they met to practice in the barracks yard or the hall. Using wooden swords and bucklers, Tharin taught Tobin the rudiments of sweeps and blocks, how to attack and how to defend himself. Tobin worked fiercely at these lessons and kept his pledge to the gods and his father in his heart; he would be a great warrior.

It was not a difficult one to keep, for he loved arms practice. When he was little he'd often come with Nari to watch the men spar among themselves. Now they gathered to watch him, leaning out the barracks windows or sitting on crates and log stools in front of the long building. They offered advice, joked with him, and stepped out to show him their own special tricks and dodges. Soon Tobin had as many teachers as he wanted. Tharin sometimes paired him against left-handed Manies or Aladar, to demonstrate how different it was to fight a man who held his weapon on the same side as your own. He couldn't properly fight any of them, small as he was, but they went through the motions in mock fights and showed him what they could. Koni, the fletcher, who was the smallest and youngest of the guard, was closest to him in size. He took a special interest in Tobin, too, for they both liked to make things. Tobin made him wax animals and in return Koni taught him how to fletch arrow shafts and carve twig whistles.

When Tobin had finished his practice for the day, the others would shoot with him, or tell stories of the battles they'd fought against the Plenimarans. Tobin's father was the great hero of these tales, always in the forefront, always the bravest on the field. Tharin figured large as well, and was always at his father's side.

"Have you always been with Father?" he asked Tharin one winter day as they rested between drills. It had snowed the night before. Tharin's beard was white around his mouth where his breath had frozen.

He nodded. "All my life. My father was one of your grandfather's liegemen. I was his third son, born at Atyion the same year as your father. We were raised together, almost like brothers."

"So you're almost my uncle?" Tobin said, pleased with the notion.

Tharin tousled Tobin's hair. "As good as, my prince.

When I was old enough, I was made his squire and later he made me a knight and granted me my lands at Hawkhaven. We've never been separated in battle."

Tobin pondered all this a moment, then asked, "Why don't I have a squire?"

"Oh, you're young for that yet. I'm sure you will when you're a bit older."

"But not one I've grown up with," Tobin pointed out glumly. "No boy has been born here. There aren't any other children at all. Why can't we go live at Atyion, like you and Father did? Why do the children in the village point and stare at me?"

Tobin half expected Tharin to put him off, talk of other things the way his father and Nari always did. Instead, he just shook his head and sighed. "Because of the demon, I suppose, and because your mama is so unhappy. Your father feels it's best this way, but I don't know . . ."

He looked so sad as he said it that Tobin almost blurted out what had happened that day in the tower. He'd never told anyone about that.

Before he could, however, Nari came to fetch him. He promised himself he would tell Tharin the following day during their ride, but Koni and old Lethis came too, and he didn't feel right speaking in front of anyone else. Another day or two passed and he forgot about it, but his trust in Tharin remained.

As Cinrin wore on there was little snow, hardly enough to dust the meadow, but the weather turned bitter cold. Tharin kept the men busy hauling firewood from the forest and everyone slept in the hall, where the hearth fire burned night and day. Tobin wore two tunics and his cloak indoors. During the day Cook kept a fire pot burning in the toy room so that he could amuse himself there, but even so he could still see his breath on the air.

The river froze hard enough to walk on and some of

the younger soldiers and servants went skating, but Nari would only let Tobin watch from the bank.

He was playing alone upstairs one bright morning when he caught the sound of a horse galloping up the frozen road. Soon a lone rider in a streaming red cape came riding up the meadow and across the bridge. Leaning out over the sill, Tobin saw his father come out to greet the man and welcome him inside. He recognized the red and gold badge all too well; this was a messenger from the king and that usually meant only one thing.

The man did not stay long however, and was soon off again down the road. As soon as Tobin heard him clatter across the bridge he hurried downstairs.

His father sat on a bench by the hearth, studying a long scroll weighted down with the king's seals and ribbons. Tobin sat down beside him and peered at the document, wishing that he could read it. Not that he needed to, to know what the message was. "You have to leave again, don't you, Father?"

"Yes, and very soon, I'm afraid. Plenimar is taking advantage of the dry winter to raid up the Mycenian coast. The Mycenians have appealed to Erius for aid."

"You can't sail this time of year! The sea's too stormy, isn't it?"

"Yes, we must ride," his father replied absently. He already had that faraway look in his eyes, and Tobin knew he was thinking of supplies and horses and men. That would be all he and Tharin would talk about around the hearth at night until they left.

"Why is Plenimar always making war?" Tobin asked, angry with these strangers who kept causing trouble and taking his father away. The Sakor festival was only a few weeks away and his father was sure to leave before then.

Rhius looked up at him. "You remember the map I showed you, how the Three Lands lie around the Inner Sea?"

"Yes."

"Well, they were all one land once, ruled by priest kings called hierophants. They had their capital at Ben-shâl, in Plenimar. A long while ago the last hierophant divided the lands up into three countries, but the Pleni-marans never liked that and have always wanted to re-claim all the territory for their own."

"When can I go to war with you?" Tobin asked. "Tharin says I'm doing very well at my lessons!"

"So I hear." His father hugged him, smiling in the way that meant no. "I'll tell you what. As soon as you're big enough to wear my second hauberk, you may come with me. Come, let's see if it fits."

The heavy coat of chain hung on a rack in his father's bedchamber. It was far too big, of course, and puddled around Tobin's feet, anchoring him helplessly in place. The coif hung over his eyes. Laughing, his father placed the steel cap on Tobin's head. It felt like he was wearing one of Cook's soup kettles; the end of the long nasal guard hung below his chin. All the same, his heart beat faster as he imagined the tall, strong man he'd someday be, filling all this out properly.

"Well, I can see it won't be much longer before you'll be needing this," his father chuckled. And with that he dragged the rack across the corridor to Tobin's bedchamber and spent the rest of the afternoon showing him how to keep the mail oiled and ready.

Tobin still clung to the hope that his father and the others could stay until the Sakor festival, but his father's liegemen, Lord Nyanis and Lord Solari, arrived a few days later with their men. For a few days the meadow was full of soldiers and their tents, but within the week everyone was gone to Atyion, leaving Tobin and the servants to celebrate without them.

Tobin moped about for a few days, but Nari cajoled him out of his dark mood and sent him off to help deck the house. Garlands of fir boughs were hung over every doorway, and wooden shields painted gold and black were hung on the pillars of the hall. Tobin filled the offering shelf of the household shrine with an entire herd of wax horses for Sakor. The following morning, however, he found them scattered across the rush-covered floor, replaced by an equal number of dirty, twisted tree roots.

This was one of the demon's favorite tricks, and one Tobin particularly hated, since it upset his father so. The duke would always go pale at the sight of them. Then he had to burn sweet herbs and say prayers to cleanse the shrine. If Tobin found the roots first, he threw them away and cleaned the shelf with his sleeve so his father wouldn't know and be sad.

Scowling to himself, Tobin pitched the whole mess into the hearth fire and went to make new horses.

On Mourning Night, Cook extinguished all but one firepot to symbolize Old Sakor's death and everyone played games of Blindman's Gambit by moonlight in the deserted barracks yard.

Tobin was hiding behind a hayrack when he happened to glance up at the tower. A faint glimmer of forbidden firelight showed through the shutters. He hadn't seen his mother in days and that suited him very well. All the same, a shiver danced up the knobs of his spine as he pictured her up there, peering out at him.

Suddenly something heavy knocked him to the ground and a burning pain blossomed in his right cheek, just below his eye. The invisible attacker vanished as quickly as it had come and Tobin blundered out from behind the rack, sobbing with fear and pain.

"What is it, pet?" Nari cried, gathering him into her arms.

Too shaken to answer, he pressed his throbbing cheek against her shoulder as she carried him into the hall.

"Someone strike a light!" she ordered.

"Not on Mourning Night . . ." the housemaid, Sarilla, said, hovering at her side.

"Then fetch the reserve coals and blow up enough flame to see by. The child's hurt!"

Tobin curled tightly against her, eyes shut tight. The pain was subsiding to a dull ache, but the shock of the attack still made him tremble. He heard Sarilla return, then the creak of the firepot lid.

"There now, pet, let Nari see."

Tobin lifted his head and let her turn his cheek toward the dim glow. Mynir and the others stood in a circle around them, looking very worried.

"By the Light, he's bitten!" the old steward exclaimed. "Go fetch a basin and a clean cloth, girl." Sarilla hurried off.

Tobin raised a hand to his cheek and felt sticky wetness there.

Nari took the cloth Sarilla fetched and wiped his fingers and cheek. It came away streaked with blood.

"Could it have been one of the hounds, Tobin? Perhaps one was sleeping in the hayrack," Mynir said anxiously. Dogs couldn't abide Tobin; they growled and slunk away from him. There were only a few old ones left at the keep now, and Nari wouldn't let them in the house.

"That's no dog bite," Sarilla whispered. "Look, you can see—"

"It was the demon!" Tobin cried. There had been moonlight enough to see that nothing with a proper solid body had been behind that rack with him. "It knocked me down and bit me!"

"Never mind that," Nari said soothingly, turning the rag to a clean side and sponging away his tears. "Never you mind. We'll talk about it in the morning. Come to bed now, and Nari will keep that old demon away."

Tobin could hear the others still whispering to each other as she led him toward the stairs.

"It's true, what they say!" Sarilla was whimpering. "Who else does it attack like that? Born cursed!"

"That's enough, girl," Mynir hissed back. "There's a cold, lonesome road outside for those who can't keep their mouths shut."

Tobin shivered. So, even here, people whispered.

He slept deeply with Nari close beside him. He woke alone, but well tucked in and could tell by the slant of the sun through the shutters that it was midmorning.

Disappointment swept away all the terror of the night before. At the dawn of Sakor's Day he and Mynir always woke the household to the new year, beating on the shield gong by the shrine. The steward must have done it without him this year and he hadn't even heard.

He padded barefoot across the cold floor to the small bronze mirror above his washbasin and inspected his cheek. Yes, there it was; a double line of red tooth marks, curved like the outline of an eye. Tobin bit his forearm just hard enough to leave an impression in the skin and saw that the two marks looked very much the same. Tobin looked back at the mirror, staring into his own blue eyes and wondering what sort of invisible body the demon had. Until now it had only been a dark blur he sometimes saw from the corner of his eye. Now he imagined it as one of the goblins in Nari's bedtime tales—the ones she said looked like a boy burned all over in a fire. A goblin with teeth like his. Was that what had been lurking at the edges of his world all this time?

Tobin glanced nervously around the room and made the warding sign three times over before he felt brave enough to get dressed.

He was sitting on the bed tying the leather lacings over his trouser legs when he heard the door latch lift. He glanced up, expecting Nari.

Instead, his mother stood framed in the doorway with

the doll. "I heard Mynir and Cook talking about what happened last night," she said softly. "You slept late this
Sakor's Day."

This was the first time in more than year that they'd
been alone together. Since that day in the tower.

He couldn't move. He just sat staring, with the leather
lacing biting into his fingers as she walked to him and
reached to touch his cheek.

Her hair was combed and plaited today. Her dress
was clean and she smelled faintly of flowers. Her fingers
were cool and gentle as she smoothed his hair back and
examined the swollen flesh around the bite. There were
no shadows in her face today that Tobin could see. She
just looked sad. Laying the doll aside on the bed, she cradled his face in both hands and kissed him on the brow.

"I'm so sorry," she murmured. Then she pushed his
left sleeve back and kissed the wisdom mark on his forearm. "We're living in an ill-starred dream, you and I. I
must do better by you, little love. What else do we have
but each other?"

"Sarilla says I'm cursed," Tobin mumbled, undone by
such tenderness.

His mother's eyes narrowed dangerously, but her
touch remained gentle. "Sarilla is an ignorant peasant. You
mustn't ever listen to such talk."

She took up the doll again, then reached for Tobin's
hand. Smiling, she said, "Come, my dears, let's see what
Cook has for our breakfast."

Chapter 8

Since that strange Sakor's Day morning, his mother ceased to be a ghost in her own household.

Her first acts were to dismiss Sarilla and then dispatch Mynir to the town to find a suitable replacement. He returned the following day with a quiet, good-natured widow named Tyra who became her serving maid.

Sarilla's dismissal frightened Tobin. He hadn't cared much for the girl, but she'd been a part of the household for as long as he could remember. His mother's dislike of Nari was no secret, and he was terrified that she might send the nurse away, too. But Nari stayed and cared for him as she always had, without any interference.

His mother came downstairs nearly every morning now, properly dressed, with her shining black hair braided or combed in a smooth veil over her shoulders. She even wore some scent that smelled like spring flowers in the meadow. She still spent much of the day sewing dolls by the fire in her bedchamber, but she took time now to look over the accounts with Mynir and came out to the kitchen yard with Cook to meet the farmers and peddlers who called. Tobin came along, too, and was surprised to hear of famine and disease striking in nearby towns. Before now, those were things that always happened far away.

Still, as bright as she was during the day, as soon as the afternoon shadows began to lengthen the light seemed to go out of her, too, and she'd retreat upstairs to the forbidden third floor. This saddened Tobin at first, but he was never tempted to follow. The next morning she would reappear, smiling again.

The demon seemed to come and go with the daylight, too, but it was most active in the dark.

The tooth marks it had left on Tobin's cheek soon healed and faded, but his terror of it did not. Lying in bed beside Nari each night, Tobin could not rid himself of the image of a wizened black form lurking in the shadows, reaching out with taloned fingers to pinch and pull, its sharp teeth bared to bite again. He kept the covers pulled up to his eyes and learned to drink nothing after supper, so that he wouldn't have to get up in the dark to use the chamber pot.

The fragile peace with his mother held, and a few weeks later Tobin walked into his toy room to find his mother waiting for him at a new table.

"For our lessons," his mother explained, waving him to the other chair.

Tobin's heart sank as he saw the parchments and writing materials. "Father tried to teach me," he said. "I couldn't learn."

A small frown creased her forehead at the mention of his father, but it quickly passed. Dipping a quill into the inkpot, she held it out to him. "Let's try again, shall we? Perhaps I'll be a better teacher."

Still dubious, Tobin took it and tried to write his name, the only word he knew. She watched him struggle for a few moments, then gently took back the quill.

Tobin sat very still, wondering if there would be an outburst of some sort. Instead, she rose and went to the windowsill, where a row of his little wax and wooden carvings stood in a row. Picking up a fox, she looked back at him. "You made these, didn't you?"

Tobin nodded.

She examined each of the others: the hawk, the bear, the eagle, a running horse, and the attempt he'd made at modeling Tharin holding a wood-splinter sword.

"Those aren't my best ones," he told her shyly. "I give them away."

"To who?"

He shrugged. "Everyone." The servants and soldiers had always praised his work and even asked for particular animals. Manies had wanted an otter and Laris a bear. Koni liked birds; in return for an eagle he'd given Tobin one of his sharp little knives and found him soft bits of wood that were easy to shape.

As much as Tobin loved pleasing them all, he always saved his best carvings for his father and Tharin. It had never occurred to him to give one to his mother. He wondered if her feelings were hurt.

"Would you like to have that one?" he asked, pointing to the fox she still held.

She bowed slightly, smiling. "Why, thank you, my lord."

Returning to her chair, she placed it on the table between them and handed him the quill. "Can you draw this for me?"

Tobin had never thought to draw anything when it was so easy to model them. He looked down at the blank parchment, flicking the feathered end of the quill against his chin. Pulling the shape of something from soft wax was easy; to make the same shape real this way was something else again. He imagined a vixen he'd seen in the meadow one morning and tried to draw a line that would capture the shape of her muzzle and the alert forward set of her ears as she'd hunted mice in the grass. He could see her as clearly as ever in his mind, but try as he might he couldn't make the pen behave. The crabbed scrawl it drew looked nothing like the fox. Throwing the quill down, he stared down at his ink-stained fingers, defeated again.

"Never mind, love," his mother told him. "Your carvings are as good as any drawing. I was just curious. But let's see if we can make your letters easier for you."

Turning the sheet over, she wrote for a moment, then sanded the page and turned it around for Tobin to see. There, across the top, were three As, written very large. She dipped the pen and gave it to him, then rose to stand behind him. Covering his hand with hers, she guided it to trace the letters she'd drawn, showing him the proper strokes. They went over them several times, and when he tried it alone he found that his own scrawls had begun to resemble the letter he was attempting.

"Look, Mama, I did it!" he exclaimed.

"It's as I thought," she murmured as she drew out more practice letters for him. "I was just the same when I was your age."

Tobin watched her as she worked, trying to imagine her as a young girl in braids who couldn't write.

"I made little sculptures, too, though not nearly as nice as yours," she went on, still writing. "Then my nurse taught me doll making. You've seen my dolls."

Thinking of them made Tobin uncomfortable, but he didn't want to seem rude by not answering. "They're very pretty," he said. His gaze drifted to her doll, slumped in an ungainly heap on the chest beside them. She looked up and caught him staring at it. It was too late. She knew what he was looking at, maybe even what he was thinking.

Her face softened in a fond smile as she took the ugly doll onto her lap and arranged its misshapen limbs. "This is the best I ever made."

"But— Well, how come it doesn't have a face?"

"Silly child, of course he has a face!" She laughed, brushing her fingers across the blank oval of cloth. "The prettiest little face I've ever seen!"

For an instant her eyes were mad and wild again, as they had been in the tower. Tobin flinched as she leaned forward, but she simply dipped the pen again and went on writing.

"I could shape anything with my hands, but I couldn't

write or read. My father—your grandfather, the Fifth Consort Tanaris—showed me how to teach my hand the shapes, just as I'm showing you now."

"I have a grandfather? Will I meet him someday?"

"No, my dear, your grandmama poisoned him years ago," his mother said, busily writing. After a moment she turned the sheet to him. "Here now, a fresh row for you to trace."

They spent the rest of the morning over the parchments. Once he was comfortable with tracing, she had him say the sounds each letter represented as he copied them. Over and over he traced and repeated, until by sheer rote he began to understand. By the time Nari brought the midday meal up to them on a tray, he'd forgotten all about his grandfather's curious fate.

From that day on, they spent part of each morning there as she worked with surprising patience to teach him the letters that had eluded him before. And, little by little, he began to learn.

Duke Rhius stayed away the rest of the winter, fighting in Mycena beside the king. His letters were filled with descriptions of battles, written as lessons for Tobin. Sometimes he sent gifts with the letters, trophies from the battlefield: an enemy dagger with a serpent carved around the hilt, a silver ring, a sack of gaming stones, a tiny frog carved from amber. One messenger brought Tobin a dented helmet with a crest of purple horsehair.

Tobin lined the smaller treasures up on a shelf in the toy room, wondering what sort of men had owned them. He placed the helmet on the back of a cloak-draped chair and fought duels against it with his wooden sword. Sometimes he imagined himself fighting beside his father and the king. Other times, the chair soldier became his squire and together they led armies of their own.

Such games left him lonesome for his father, but he

knew that one day he would fight beside him, just as his father had promised.

*T*hrough the last grey weeks of winter Tobin truly began to enjoy his mother's company. At first they met in the hall after his morning ride with Mynir. Once or twice she even went with them and he was amazed at how well she sat her horse, riding astride with her long hair streaming free behind her like a black silk banner.

For all her improvement with him, however, her attitude toward the others of the household did not change. She spoke seldom to Mynir and almost never to Nari. The new woman, Tyra, saw to her needs and was kind to Tobin, too, until the demon pushed her down the stairs and she left without even saying good-bye. After that, they made do without a maid.

Most disappointing of all, however, was her continuing coldness toward his father. She never spoke of him, spurned any gifts he sent, and left the hall when Mynir read his letters by the hearth each night to Tobin. No one could tell him why she seemed to hate him so, and he didn't dare ask his mother directly. All the same, Tobin began to hope. When his father came home and saw how improved she was, perhaps things might ease between them. She'd come to love him, after all. Lying in bed at night, he imagined the three of them riding the mountain trails together, all of them smiling.

Chapter 9

Tobin and his mother were at his lessons one cold morning at the end of Klesin when they heard a rider approaching the keep at a gallop.

Tobin ran to the window, hoping to see his father on his way home at last. His mother followed and rested a hand on his shoulder.

"I don't know that horse," Tobin said, shading his eyes. The rider was too muffled against the cold to recognize at a distance. "May I go see who it is?"

"I suppose so. Why don't you see if Cook has anything nice for us in the larder, too? I could do with an apple. Hurry back now. We're not done for today."

"I will!" Tobin called, dashing off.

There was no one in the hall, so he went through to the kitchen and saw with delight that it was Tharin being greeted by Nari and the others. His beard had grown long over the winter. His boots were filthy with mud and snow, and he had a bandage wrapped around one wrist.

"Is the war over? Is Father coming home?" Tobin cried, throwing himself into the man's arms.

Tharin lifted him up, nose to nose. "Yes to both, little prince, and he's bringing some guests with him. They're just behind me." He set Tobin back on his feet. He was trying to smile, but Tobin read something else in the lines around the man's eyes as he glanced at Nari and the steward. "They'll be here soon. You run along and play now, Tobin. Cook doesn't need you underfoot. There's much to do."

"But—"

"That's enough," Nari said sharply. "Tharin will take you out for a ride later. Off with you now!"

Tobin wasn't used to being dismissed like this. Feeling sulky, he dawdled back toward the hall. Tharin hadn't even said who Father was bringing. Tobin hoped it was Lord Nyanis or Duke Archis. He liked them the best of all his father's liegemen.

He was halfway across the hall when he remembered that his mother had asked for an apple. They couldn't very well scold him for coming back for that.

The kitchen door was open and as he approached, he heard Nari say, "What is the king doing coming here, after all these years?"

"For the hunting, or so he claims," Tharin replied. "We were on our way home the other day, nearly in sight of Ero, when Rhius happened to mention the fine stag hunting we have here. The king took it into his head for an invitation. He's struck with these strange whims more often now—"

The king! Tobin forgot about apples as he scurried back upstairs, thinking instead of the little wooden figure in the box—The Present King, Your Uncle. Tobin wondered excitedly if he'd be wearing his golden crown, and if he'd let Tobin hold Ghërilain's sword.

His mother was still by the window. "Who was that on the road, child?"

Tobin ran to the window but couldn't see anyone coming yet. He flopped down in his chair, panting for breath. "Father sent Tharin ahead— The king— The king is coming! He and Father are—"

"Erius?" Ariani shrank back against the wall, clutching the doll. "He's coming here? Are you certain?"

The demon's cold, angry presence closed in around Tobin, so strong it felt hard to breathe. Parchments and inkpots flew from the table and scattered across the dusty floor.

"Mama, what's wrong?" he whispered, suddenly afraid of the look in his mother's eye.

With a choked cry, she lunged for him and half dragged, half carried him from the room. The demon raged around them, blowing up the dry rushes into whirling clouds and knocking the lamps from their hooks. She paused in the corridor, looking wildly around as if seeking some way to escape. Tobin tried not to whimper as her fingers dug into his arm.

"No, no, no!" she muttered. The rag doll's blank, dingy face peeped out at Tobin from under her arm.

"Mama, you're hurting me. Where are we going?"

But she wasn't listening to him. "Not again. No!" she whispered, pulling him toward the third-floor stairs.

Tobin tried to pull away, but she was too strong for him. "No, Mama, I don't want to go up there!"

"We must hide!" she hissed, gripping him by both shoulders now. "I couldn't last time. I would have. By the Four, I would have, but they wouldn't let me! Please, Tobin, come with Mama. There's no time!"

She pulled him up the stairs and along the corridor to the tower stairs. When Tobin tried to pull away this time, unseen hands shoved him forward from behind. The door flew open before them, slamming back against the wall so hard that one of the panels splintered.

Panicked birds flapped and screeched around them as she wrestled Tobin up the stairs to the tower room. This door slammed shut behind them and the wine table flew across the room, narrowly missing Tobin's shoulder as it smashed across the doorway, blocking his escape. Dusty tapestries flew from the walls and the shuttered windows banged wide. Sunlight flooded in on all sides, but the room remained dim and deathly cold. Outside they could hear a great company of riders now, coming up the road.

Ariani released Tobin and paced frantically around the room, weeping with one hand pressed over her mouth.

Tobin cowered by the broken table. This was the mother he knew best—hurtful and unpredictable. The rest of it had all been a lie.

"What are we to do?" she wailed. "He's found us again. He can find us anywhere. We must escape! Lhel, you bitch, you promised me . . ."

The jangle of harness grew louder outside and she dashed to the window overlooking the front court. "Too late! Here he is. How can he? How can he?"

Tobin crept up beside her, just close enough to peek down over the sill. His father and a group of strangers in scarlet cloaks were dismounting. One of them wore a golden helmet that shown in the sun like a crown.

"Is that the king, Mama?"

She yanked him back, clutching him so close that his face was pressed against the doll. It had a sour, musty smell.

"Mark him," she whispered, and he could feel her trembling. "Mark him, the murderer! Your father brought him here. But he won't have you this time."

She dragged him to the opposite window, the one that overlooked the mountains to the west. The demon overturned another table, spilling mouthless dolls across the floor. His mother whirled at the noise, and Tobin's head hit the corner of the stone sill hard enough to daze him. He felt himself falling, felt his mother pulling at him again, felt sunlight and wind on his face. Opening his eyes, he found himself hanging out over the still, looking down at the frozen river.

Just like the last time she'd brought him here.

But this time she was crouched on the sill beside him, tear-stained face turned to the mountains as she grasped the back of Tobin's tunic and tried to pull him out.

Overbalancing, he thrashed back wildly, grasping for anything—the window casing, his mother's arm, her clothing—but his feet were already tipping up over his head. He could see the dark water moving like ink beneath the ice. His mind skittered on ahead; would the ice break when he landed on it?

Then his mother screamed and tumbled past him, skirts and wild black hair billowing around her as she fell. For an instant they looked one another straight in the eye and Tobin felt as if a bolt of lightning passed between them, joining them just for a second eye to eye, heart to heart.

Then someone had Tobin by the ankle, dragging him roughly back into the room. His chin struck the outer edge of the sill and he spun down into darkness with the taste of blood in his mouth.

Rhius and the king were about to dismount when they heard a shriek echo behind the keep.

"By the Flame! Is it that demon of yours?" Erius exclaimed, looking around in alarm.

But Rhius knew the demon had no voice. Pushing past the other riders, he ran out the gate, seeing already in his mind's eye what he should have anticipated, what he would see again and again in his dreams for the rest of his life: Ariani at an upper window that should have been tightly shuttered, catching the glint of her brother's golden helm at the bottom of the meadow, imagining—

He stumbled along the riverbank, following the keep wall around a final corner. There he stopped, and let out an anguished cry at the sight of bare white legs splayed awkwardly between two boulders at the river's edge. He ran to her and tugged down her skirts, which had blown up around her head as she'd fallen. Looking up, he saw the tower bulking over them. There were no other windows on this side but the single square one directly overhead. The shutters were open.

A rock had broken her back, and her head had struck the ice and split. Black hair and red blood spread out around her face in a terrible corona. Her beautiful eyes were open and fixed in an expression of anguish and outrage; even in death she accused him.

Recoiling from that gaze, Rhius staggered back into the arms of the king.

"By the Flame," Erius gasped, staring down at her. "My poor sister, what have you done?"

Rhius clutched his fists against his temples, resisting the urge to pull back and strike the man in the face.

"My king," he managed, sinking down beside her. "Your sister is dead."

$\mathcal{T}$obin remembered falling. As consciousness gradually returned he became aware of a hard floor under him and instinctively pressed his belly to it, too terrified to move. Somewhere nearby echoing voices were talking all at once, but he couldn't understand the words. He didn't know where he was or how he had gotten there.

Opening his heavy eyelids at last, he realized that he was in the tower room. It was very quiet here.

The demon was with him. He'd never felt it so strongly. But there was something different about it, though he couldn't say just what.

Tobin felt very strange, like he was in a dream, but the pain in his chin and mouth told him he wasn't. When he tried to remember how he'd gotten up here his mind went all fuzzy and loud, as if his head was full of bees.

His cheek hurt where it was pressed to the stone floor. He turned his head the other way and found himself looking into the blank face of his mama's doll, which lay just inches from his outstretched hand.

Where could she be? She never left the doll behind, not ever.

Father won't let me keep it, he thought. But suddenly he wanted it more than anything in the world. It was ugly and he'd hated it all his life, but he reached out for it anyway, remembering his mama saying so fondly, *This one is the best I ever made.* It was almost as if she'd just spoken the words aloud.

Where is she?

The buzzing in his head grew louder as he sat up and hugged the doll. It was small and coarse and lumpy, but solid and comforting all the same. Looking around dizzily, he was surprised to see himself squatting by a broken table across the room. But this Tobin was naked and filthy and angry and his face was streaked with tears. This other self held no doll; he still covered his ears with both hands to block out something neither of them wanted to remember.

Nari cried out once then clamped a hand over her mouth as the duke staggered into the hall with Ariani's broken body in his arms. Nari could see at once that she was dead. Blood ran from the woman's ears and mouth; her open eyes were fixed as stones.

Tharin and the king followed close behind. Erius kept reaching out to touch his sister's face, but Rhius wouldn't let him. He got as far as the hearth before his knees buckled. Sinking down, he gathered her closer and buried his face in her black hair.

It was probably the first time since Tobin's birth that he'd been able to embrace her, thought Nari.

Erius sat heavily on one of the hearth benches, then looked up at her and those of his entourage who'd followed. His face was grey and his hands shook.

"Get out," he ordered, not focusing on anyone in particular. He didn't have to. Everyone scattered except Tharin. The last Nari saw of him, he was still standing a little way off, watching the two men with no expression at all.

Nari was halfway up the stairs before it occurred to her that Tobin had been at lessons with his mother that morning.

She took the remaining stairs two at a time and ran

down the corridor. Her heart skipped a painful beat as she took in the smashed lamps on the floor. Tobin's bedchamber and toy room were both empty. The writing things they'd been using were strewn across the floor and one of the chairs lay on its side.

Fear closed a fist around Nari's heart. "O Illior, let the child be safe!"

Rushing back into the corridor, she saw the door leading to the third floor standing open.

"Maker's mercy, no!" she whispered, hurrying up.

Upstairs, torn hangings were strewn around the dank corridor. They seemed to catch at Nari's feet as she ran to the broken tower door and on up the narrow stairs beyond. She hadn't been welcome here when Ariani lived; even now she felt like a trespasser. What she saw as she reached the top of the stairs drove out all such doubts.

The tower room was choked with broken furniture and dismembered dolls. All four windows stood open, but the room was dark and fetid. She knew that smell.

"Tobin, are you here, child?"

Her voice hardly seemed to penetrate the small space, but she heard clearly enough the sound of ragged breathing and followed it to the corner furthest from the fatal window. Half hidden under a fallen tapestry, Tobin sat curled against the wall, his thin arms locked around his knees, staring wide-eyed at nothing.

"Oh, my poor pet!" Nari gasped, falling to her knees beside him.

The child's face and tunic were streaked with blood, making her fear at first that Ariani had tried to cut his throat, that he would die here in her arms, that all the pain and lies and waiting had been for nothing.

She tried to pick him up, but Tobin pulled away and curled tighter into his corner, his eyes still vacant.

"Tobin, pet, it's me. Come now, let's go down to your room."

The child didn't move or acknowledge her presence.

Nari settled herself closer beside him and stroked his hair. "Please, pet. This is a nasty cold place to be. Come down to the kitchen for a nice cup of Cook's good soup. Tobin? Look at me, child. Are you hurt?"

Heavy footsteps pounded up the tower stairs and Rhius burst in with Tharin on his heels.

"Did you—? O, thank the Light!" Rhius stumbled over shattered furniture to kneel beside her. "Is he badly hurt?"

"No, just very frightened, my lord," Nari whispered, still stroking Tobin's hair. "He must have seen . . ."

Rhius leaned in and cupped Tobin's chin gently, trying to raise the boy's head. Tobin jerked away.

"What happened? Why did she bring you here?" Rhius asked softly.

Tobin said nothing.

"Look around you, my lord!" Nari stroked Tobin's black hair back from his face to examine the large bruise blossoming there. The blood on his face and clothes came from a crescent-shaped cut on the point of his chin. It wasn't large, but it was deep. "She must have seen the king ride in with you. It's the first time since . . . Well, you know how she was."

Nari looked more closely into Tobin's colorless face. No tears, but his eyes were wide and fixed, as if he were still watching whatever had happened here.

He didn't resist when his father lifted him in his arms and carried him down to his bedchamber. But he didn't relax either, and remained curled in a tight ball. There was no question of getting his soiled clothing off yet, so Nari took off his shoes, bathed his face, and tucked him into bed with extra quilts. The duke knelt beside the bed and took one of Tobin's hands in his, murmuring softly to him and watching the pale face on the pillow for any response.

Turning, Nari saw Tharin standing just inside the door, pale as milk. She went to him and took his cold hand in hers.

"He'll be fine, Tharin. He's just badly frightened."

"She threw herself from the tower window," Tharin whispered, still staring at Rhius and the boy. "She took Tobin with her— Look at him, Nari. Do you think she tried—?"

"No mother could do such a thing!" In her heart, however, she wasn't so certain.

They remained there for some time, still as a mummer's tableau. At last Rhius got to his feet and ran a hand absently down the front of his bloodied tunic. "I must attend the king. He means to take her back to the royal tomb at Ero."

Nari knotted her hands angrily in her apron. "For the child's sake, shouldn't we wait—?"

Rhius gave her a look so filled with bitterness that the words withered on her tongue. "The king has spoken." Wiping again at his tunic, he left the room. With a last sad look at the sleeping child, Tharin followed.

Nari pulled a chair up next to the bed and patted Tobin's thin shoulder through the quilts. "My poor dear little one," she sighed. "They won't even let you mourn her!"

Stroking the sleeping child's brow, she imagined what it would be like to bundle him up and carry him far away from this house of misery. Closing her eyes, she imagined raising him as her own in some simple cottage, far from kings and ghosts and madwomen.

Tobin heard wailing and huddled up more tightly as it grew louder. Gradually, the sobbing voice changed to the sound of a strong east wind buffeting itself against the walls of the keep. He could feel the weight of heavy blankets pressing down on him, but he was still so cold.

Opening his eyes, he blinked at the small night lamp guttering on the stand by his bed. Nari was asleep in a chair beside it.

She'd put him to bed in his clothes. Slowly uncurling

his cramped body, Tobin rolled to face the wall and pulled the rag doll out of his tunic.

He didn't know why he had it. Something bad had happened, something so bad that he couldn't make himself think what it was.

My mama is—

He squeezed his eyes shut and hugged the doll tightly.

If I have the doll, then my mama is—

He didn't recall hiding the doll under his clothes, didn't recall anything really, but now he hid it again under the covers, pushing it all the way down the bed with his feet, knowing he must find a better place very soon. He knew it was wicked to want it, shameful for a boy who was going to be a warrior to need a doll, but he hid it all the same, full of shame and longing.

Perhaps his mama had given it to him, after all.

Slipping back into a broken doze, he dreamed over and over again of his mother passing the doll to him. Every time she was smiling as she told him that it was the best she ever made..

Chapter 10

Tobin was made to stay in bed for two days. At first he slept much of the time, lulled by the sound of the rain pelting steadily against the shutters and the groan and grumble of the river ice breaking up.

Sometimes, half awake, he thought his mama was in the room with him, standing at the foot of his bed with her hands clasped tight the way she had when she saw the king riding up the hill. He'd be so certain she was there that he could even hear her breathing, but when he opened his eyes to look, she wasn't.

The demon was, though. Tobin could feel it hovering around him all the time now. At night he pressed closer to Nari, trying to pretend he didn't feel it staring at him. Yet powerful as it was, it didn't touch him or break anything.

By afternoon on the second day he was awake and restless. Nari and Tharin sat with him during the day, telling stories and bringing him little toys as if he were a baby. The other servants came too, to pat his hand and kiss his brow.

Everyone came except Father. When Tharin explained at last that he'd had to go back to Ero with the king for a little while, Tobin's throat ached, but he couldn't find the tears to cry.

No one spoke of his mother. He wondered what had happened to her after she'd gone to the tower, but he couldn't bring himself to ask. In fact, he didn't feel like speaking at all, and so he didn't, not even when the others coaxed him. Instead, he played with his wax or burrowed under the blankets, waiting for everyone to go away. The few times that he was left to himself, he took the rag doll from its new hiding place behind the wardrobe and just held it, looking down at the blank circle of cloth where its face should be.

Of course he has a face. The prettiest—

But it wasn't pretty at all. It was ugly. Its stuffing was lumpy and clumped inside and he could feel little sharp bits like splinters in the uneven legs and arms. Its thick muslin skin was dingy and much patched. He did discover something new, though; a thin, shiny black cord tied tightly around its neck, so tight that it didn't show unless he bent the head sharply back.

Ugly as it was, though, Tobin thought he could smell the flower scent his mother had worn during those last happy weeks on it, and that was enough. He guarded the doll jealously and, when he was finally allowed up on the third day, he moved it to the bottom of the old chest in the toy room.

The weather had turned cold again and sleet was hissing down outside. The toy room was dim and dreary in this light. There was dust on the floor and on the flat roofs of the city's wooden block houses; the little wooden people lay scattered about the Palatine like the plague victims his father had written of. In the corner, the Plenimaran chair warrior seemed to mock him and he took it apart, throwing the cloak into the empty wardrobe and putting the helmet away in the chest.

Wandering over to the writing table by the window, Tobin gingerly touched the things he and his mother had shared—the parchments, sand shaker, scraping blades, and quills. They'd labored through almost half the alphabet. Sheets of new letters in her bold, square hand lay waiting for his practice. He picked one up and sniffed it, hoping to catch her scent here, too, but it only smelled of ink.

The sleet had given way to early spring rain when his father came back a few days later. He looked strange and sad and no one seemed to know what to say to him, not even Tharin. After supper that night Rhius sent everyone out of the hall, then took Tobin onto his lap by the fire. He was quiet for a long time.

After a while he raised Tobin's bruised chin and looked into his face. "Can't you speak, child?"

Tobin was shocked to see tears trickling down into his father's black-and-silver beard. *Don't cry! Warriors don't cry,* he thought, frightened to see his brave father weeping. Tobin could hear the words in his head, but he still couldn't make any sounds come out.

"Never mind, then." His father pulled him close and Tobin rested his head against that broad chest, listening to the comforting thump of his father's heart and grateful not to have to watch those tears fall. Perhaps that's why his father had sent everyone away; so they wouldn't see.

"Your mother . . . She wasn't well. Sooner or later, you'll hear people say she was mad, and she was." He paused and Tobin felt him sigh. "What she did in the tower . . . It was the madness. Her mother had it, too."

What had happened in the tower? Tobin closed his eyes, feeling strange all over. The bees had started buzzing in his head again. *Did making dolls drive you mad?* He remembered the toy maker he'd seen in town. He hadn't noticed anything wrong with her. *Had his grandmama made dolls? No, she'd poisoned her husband—*

Rhius sighed again. "I don't think your mama meant to hurt you. When she was in her bad spells, she didn't know what she was doing. Do you understand what I'm telling you?"

Tobin didn't understand at all, but he nodded anyway, hoping that would satisfy his father. He didn't like thinking about his mother now. When he did, he seemed to see two different people and that made him feel afraid. The mean, distant woman who had the "bad spells" had always been frightening. The other—the one who had shown him how to trace letters, who rode astride with her hair flying in the wind and smelled like flowers—she was a stranger who'd come to visit for a little while, then abandoned him. In Tobin's mind, she had disappeared from the tower like one of her birds.

"Someday you'll understand," his father said again. He pulled Tobin up and looked at him again. "You are very special, my child."

The demon, who'd been so quiet, snatched a tapestry from the wall across the room and ripped it violently up the middle, snapping the wooden rod that held it. The whole thing fell to the floor with a clatter, but his father paid it no mind. "You're too young yet to think about it, but I promise you that you will be a great warrior when you're grown. You'll live in Ero and everyone will bow to you. Everything I've done, Tobin, I've done for you, and for Skala."

Tobin burst into tears and pressed his face against his father's chest again. He didn't care if he ever lived in Ero or any of the rest of it. He just didn't want to see this strange new look on his father's face. It reminded him too much of his mother.

The one with bad spells.

The next day Tobin gathered up the parchments and quills and inkpots and put them away in an unused chest in his bedroom, then placed the doll under them, hidden in an old flour sack he found in the kitchen yard. It was risky, he knew, but it made him feel a little better to have the doll close by.

After that he could look into his own shadowed eyes in the mirror by his washstand and mouth *my mama is dead* without feeling anything at all.

Whenever his mind strayed to why she was dead or what had happened that day in the tower, however, his thoughts would scatter like a handful of spilled beans and a hot red ache would start under his breastbone, burning so badly that he could hardly breathe. Better not to think of it at all.

The doll was a different matter. He didn't dare let anyone know about it, but he couldn't leave it alone. The need to touch it woke him in the middle of the night and drew him to the chest. Once he fell asleep on the floor and woke just in time to hide it from Nari as she awakened the next morning.

After that he sought out a new hiding place for it, settling at last on a chest in one of the ruined guest chambers upstairs. No one seemed to care anymore if he came up there. His father spent most of his time shut away in his chamber. Now that most of the servants had run away or been dismissed, Nari did more work around the keep during the daytime, cleaning and helping Cook in the kitchen. Tharin was there as always, but Tobin didn't feel like riding or shooting, or even practicing at swords.

His one companion during the long, dreary days that spring was the demon. It followed him everywhere and lurked in the shadows of the dusty upstairs room when he visited the doll. Tobin could feel it watching him. It knew his secret.

*T*obin was pushing a little stick person around the streets of his city a few days later when Tharin appeared in the doorway.

"How goes life in Ero today?" Tharin sat down beside him and helped set some of the clay sheep back on their feet in their market enclosure. There were raindrops in his short blond beard, and he smelled like fresh air and leaves. He didn't seem to mind that Tobin said nothing. Instead, he carried on the conversation for both of them, just as if he knew what Tobin was thinking. "You must be missing your mother. She was a fine lady in her day. Nari tells me she brightened up these past few months. I hear she was teaching you your letters?"

Tobin nodded.

"I'm glad to hear it." Tharin paused to arrange a few sheep more to his liking. "Do you miss her?"

Tobin shrugged.

"By the Flame, I do."

Tobin looked up in surprise and Tharin nodded. "I watched your father court her. He loved her then, and she him. Oh, I know it must not have seemed so to you, but that's how it was before. They were the handsomest pair in all Ero—him a warrior in his prime, and her the fair young princess, just come into womanhood."

Tobin fiddled with a toy ship. He couldn't imagine his parents acting any differently toward one another than they ever had.

Tharin got up and held out a hand to Tobin. "Come on, then, Tobin, you've moped around inside long enough. The rain's stopped and the sun's shining. It's fine shooting weather. Go fetch your boots and cloak. Your weapons are downstairs where you left them."

Tobin let himself be pulled up and followed the man out to the barracks yard. The men were lounging in the sun and greeted Tobin with false heartiness.

"There he is at last!" grey-bearded Laris said, swinging Tobin up on his shoulder. "We've missed you, lad. Is Tharin putting you back to your lessons?"

Tobin nodded.

"What's that, young prince?" Koni chided playfully, giving Tobin's foot a shake. "Speak up, won't you?"

"He will when he's ready," said Tharin. "Fetch the prince's sword and let's see how much he remembers."

Tobin saluted Tharin with his blade and took his position. He felt stiff and clumsy all over as they began the forms, but by the time he reached the final set of thrusts and guards, the men were cheering him on.

"Not bad," said Tharin. "But I want to see you out here every day again. The time will come when you'll be glad of all these exercises. Now let's see how your bow arm is."

Ducking into the barracks, he returned with Tobin's bow and practice arrows, and the sack of shavings they used for a target. He tossed the sack out into the middle of the yard, about twenty paces away.

Tobin checked his string, then fitted an arrow to it and pulled. The arrow flew high and awry and landed in the mud near the wall.

"Mind your breathing and spread your feet a little," Tharin reminded him.

Tobin took a deep breath and let it out slowly as he drew again. This time the arrow struck home, skewering the bag and knocking it several feet.

"That's the way. And again."

Tharin only allowed him three arrows at practice. After he shot them all, he was to think about how to improve his shooting as he collected them.

Before he could do so this time, Tharin turned to Koni. "Do you have those new arrows fletched for the prince?"

"Right here." Koni reached behind the barrel he was sitting on and brought out a quiver with half a dozen new shafts fletched with wild goose feathers. "Hope they bring you luck, Tobin," he said, presenting them to the boy.

Pulling one out, Tobin saw that it had a small round stone for a head. He grinned up at Tharin; these were hunting arrows.

"Cook has a hankering to cook some rabbit or grouse," Tharin told him. "Want to help me find supper? Good. Laris, go ask the duke if he'd like to join a hunting party. Manies, get Gosi saddled."

Laris hurried off, only to return alone a few moments later shaking his head.

Tobin hid his disappointment as best he could as he rode up the muddy mountain road with Tharin and Koni. The trees were still bare, but a few green shoots were already pushing up through last year's leaves. The first hint of true spring was on the air, and the forest smelled of rotting wood and wet earth. When they reached what Tharin judged to be a promising stretch of woods, they dismounted and set off along a faint, winding trail.

This was the first time Tobin had ever traveled so far into the forest. The road was soon lost from sight behind them and the trees grew thicker, the ground rougher. With only their own careful footsteps to break the quiet, he could hear the eerie squeak of trees rubbing together, and the patter of little creatures in the undergrowth. Best of all, the demon hadn't followed. He was free.

Tharin and Koni showed him how to call the curious grouse into the open, mimicking its funny *puk puk puk* call. Tobin pursed his lips as they did, but only a faint popping sound came out.

A few birds answered Tharin's call, poking their heads from the undergrowth or hopping up on logs to see what was going on. The men let Tobin shoot at all of them and he finally hit one, knocking it off a fallen tree.

"Well done!" said Tharin, clapping him on the shoulder proudly. "Go on and gather your kill."

Still clutching his bow, Tobin hurried to the tree and peered over it.

The grouse had fallen over on its breast, but it wasn't dead. Its striped head was twisted to the side and it stared up at him with one black eye. Its tail fan beat weakly as he bent over it, but the bird couldn't move. A drop of bright blood welled at the tip of its beak, red as—

Tobin heard a strange buzzing, like bees, but it was too early in the year. The next thing he knew, he was lying on the damp ground, looking up into Tharin's worried face as the man chafed his wrists and chest.

"Tobin? What's wrong with you, lad?"

Puzzled, Tobin sat up and looked around. There was his bow lying on the damp ground, but no one seemed upset about that. Koni was sitting on the fallen tree beside him, holding the dead grouse up by its feet.

"You got him, Prince Tobin. You knocked old Master

Grouse right off his log. What did you go and faint for, eh? Are you sick?"

Tobin shook his head. He didn't know what had happened. Reaching for the bird, he spread its tail and admired the fan of barred feathers.

"It was a fine shot, but I think perhaps that's enough for today," said Tharin.

Tobin shook his head again, more vigorously this time, and jumped up to show them how well he was.

Tharin hesitated a moment, then laughed. "All right then, if you say so!"

Tobin shot another grouse before dusk, and by the time they started down the road everyone had forgotten all about his silly faint, even Tobin.

Over the next few weeks the days grew longer and they spent more time in the forest. Spring came to the mountains, clothing the trees in fresh new green and pulling tender shoots and colorful mushrooms up through the brown loam. Does came out into the forest clearing to teach their spotted fawns to graze. Tharin would not shoot at them, just grouse and rabbits.

They stayed out all day sometimes, cooking their kills on sticks over a fire when the hunting was good, eating the bread and cheese Cook sent along when it wasn't. Tobin didn't care either way, so long as it meant being outdoors. He'd never had so much fun.

Tharin and Koni taught Tobin how to keep his bearings in the trees using the sun's position over his shoulder. They came across a nest of wood snakes in a rock pile, still sluggish from their winter sleep, and Koni explained how to tell if they were vipers or not by the shape of their heads. Tharin showed him the tracks and spoor of the creatures that shared this forest. There were mostly signs of rabbits and fox and stag. As they walked along a game trail one day, however, Tharin suddenly bent down next to a patch of soft earth.

"See that?" he said, pointing out a print broader than his hand. It looked something like a hound's, but rounder. "That's a catamount. This is why you play in the court-yard, my lad. A big she cat with cubs to feed would con-sider you a good day's catch."

Seeing Tobin's look of alarm, he chuckled and ruffled the boy's hair. "You're not likely to see one in daylight, and as summer comes they'll move back up into the mountains. But you don't ever want to be out here alone at night."

Tobin took in all these lessons eagerly, and made a few observations of his own: the inviting gap beneath a fallen tree, a sheltered circle of rocks, a shadowy hole be-neath a boulder—all fine hiding spots, big enough for the troublesome doll. For the first time, he wondered what it would be like to walk here alone and explore these hid-den places by himself.

His father hunted with them now and then, but he was too quiet for Tobin to feel comfortable around him. Most days he stayed shut up in his room, just as Tobin's mother had.

Tobin would steal to his father's door and press his ear to it, aching for things to be the way they had been. Before.

Nari found him there one afternoon and knelt down, putting her arms around him. "Don't fret," she whispered, stroking his cheek. "Men do their grieving alone. He'll soon be right again."

But as wildflowers burst out to carpet the new grass in the meadow, Rhius remained a shadow in the house.

By the end of Lithion the roads were dry enough to drive the cart to market. On market day, Cook and Nari took Tobin with them into Alestun, thinking it would be a treat for him to ride Gosi beside the cart. He shook his head, trying to tell Nari that he didn't want to go, but she clucked her tongue at him, insisting he'd enjoy the ride.

There were a few new lambs and kids in the meadows around the town, and the fields of young oats and barley looked like soft woolen blankets thrown on the ground. Wild crocus grew thickly at the edges of the road and they stopped to gather handfuls of these for the shrine.

Alestun held no charm for Tobin now. He ignored the other children and never allowed himself to look at any dolls. He added his flowers to the fragrant piles around the pillar of Dalna and waited stoically for the adults to finish their business.

They arrived home that evening to find Rhius and the others in the courtyard, packing their horses to leave. Tobin slid off Gosi's back and ran to his father.

Rhius took him by the shoulders. "I'm needed at court. I'll come back as soon as I can."

"So will I, little prince," Tharin promised, looking sadder than his father did to be leaving.

I need you here! Tobin wanted to cry out. But words still would not come, and he had to turn away so they wouldn't see his tears. By nightfall they were gone, leaving him lonelier than ever.

Chapter 11

Iya and Arkoniel spent the late winter months just outside Ilear, guesting with a wizard named Virishan. This woman had no vision except her own, which drove her to seek out and shelter god-touched children among the poor. She had fifteen young students, many of them already severely crippled or battered by the ignorant folk they'd been born to. Most of them would never amount to much as wizards, but what humble powers they'd retained were cherished and coaxed forth under Virishan's patient tutelage. Iya and Arkoniel gave what help they could in return for shelter, and Iya left Virishan one of her pebbles when they departed.

When the weather cleared they made their way to Sylara, where Iya had arranged passage south. They reached it just before sundown and encountered an unusual number of people on the road, all streaming into the little port.

"What's going on?" Arkoniel asked a farmer. "Is it a fair?"

The man eyed their silver amulets with distrust. "No, a bonfire stoked with your kind."

"The Harriers are there?" asked Iya.

The man spat over his shoulder. "Yes, Mistress, and they've brought a gang of traitors who dared speak against the king's rule. You'd do best to steer clear of Sylara today."

Iya reined her horse to the side of the road and Arkoniel followed. "Perhaps we should take his advice," he muttered, looking nervously around at the crowd. "We're strangers here, with no one to vouch for us."

He was right, of course, but Iya shook her head. "The Lightbearer has put an opportunity in our path. I want to see what they do, while we're still unknown to them. And that's something we should make certain of, too. Take off your amulet."

Leaving the road, she led him to a small oak grove on a nearby hill. Here, protected by a circle of stones and sigils, they left their amulets and every other accouterment that marked them as wizards except the leather bag.

Trusting that their plain traveling garb would excite no suspicion, they rode on to Sylara.

Even without his amulet, Arkoniel couldn't help glancing around nervously as they entered the town. Could these Harriers recognize a wizard merely by his powers? Some of the rumors they'd picked up invested the white-clad wizards with powers beyond the normal range. If so, they'd chosen an odd place to show them off. Sylara was nothing but a rambling, dirty harbor town.

The waterfront was already crowded with spectators. Arkoniel could hear jeers and catcalls echoing across the water as they made their way down the muddy street to the shore.

The crowd was too thick to get through, so Iya paid a taverner to watch from a squalid little upper room that overlooked the waterfront. A broad platform had been set up here, built between two stone jetties. Soldiers wearing dark grey tabards with the outline of a flying hawk stitched in red across the breast stood two deep on the landward side. Arkoniel counted forty in all.

Behind them stood a long gibbet and a knot of wizards by two large wooden frames. These last looked like upended bedframes, but larger.

"White robes," Iya muttered, looking at the wizards.

"Niryn's fashion. He had on a white robe the night Tobin was born."

Six people already dangled from the horizontal pole

of the gibbet. The four men hung limp at the end of their halters; one still wore the robes of a priest of Illior. The remaining two, a woman and a boy, were so small that their weight was not enough to break their necks. Bound hand and foot, they bucked and twisted wildly.

Fighting for life, or death? Arkoniel wondered, horrified. They reminded him perversely of a butterfly he'd watched emerge from its winter chrysalis—suspended beneath a branch by a bit of silk, it had twitched and jiggled inside the shiny brown casing. These two looked like that, but their struggle would not end in wings and color.

At last some soldiers grabbed their legs and hauled down to snap their necks. A few cheers went up among the crowd, but most of the onlookers had fallen silent.

Arkoniel clutched the window frame, already nauseated, but there was worse to follow.

The wizards had remained motionless near the wooden frames all this time. As soon as the last of the hanged went still, they spread out in a line across the platform, revealing the two naked, kneeling men they'd been shielding with their circle. One was an old man with white hair; the other was young and dark. Both wore thick iron bands around their necks and wrists.

Arkoniel squinted down at the Harrier wizards and let out a gasp of dismay. He couldn't make out faces at this distance, but he recognized the forked red beard of the man standing closest to the frames.

"That's Niryn himself!"

"Yes. I didn't realize there were so many, but I suppose there would have to be. . . . Those prisoners are wizards. See those iron bands? Very powerful magic, that. They cloud the mind."

Soldiers pulled the prisoners to their feet and bound them spread-eagled on the frames with silver cables. Now Arkoniel could see the complex spell patterns that covered each man's chest. Before he could ask Iya what these signified, she let out a groan and clutched his hand.

When the victims were secured, the wizards flanked them in two rows and began their incantations. The old man fixed his gaze stoically on the sky, but his companion panicked, screaming and imploring the crowd and Illior to save him.

"Can't we do—" Arkoniel staggered as a blinding ache struck him behind the eyes. "What is it? Do you feel it?"

"It's a warding," Iya whispered, pressing a hand to her brow. "And a warning to any of us who might be watching."

The crowd had gone completely silent now. Arkoniel could hear the chanting growing louder and louder. The blur of words was unintelligible, but the throbbing in his head grew stronger and spread to his chest and arms until his heart felt as if it was being squeezed between heavy stones. He slowly slid down to his knees in front of the window but could not look away.

Both prisoners began to shake violently, then shrieked as white flames sprang from their flesh to engulf them. There was no smoke. The white fire burned with such intensity that within a few moments nothing was left on the frames but shriveled black hands and feet dangling from the silver bonds. Iya was whispering hoarsely beside him, and he joined her in the prayer for the dead.

When it was over, Iya slumped down on the narrow bed and wove a spell of silence around them with shaking fingers. Arkoniel remained where he was under the window, unable to move. For a long time neither could speak.

At last Iya whispered, "There was nothing we could have done. Nothing. I see their power now. They've banded together and joined their strength. The rest of us are so scattered—"

"That, and the king's sanction!" Arkoniel spat out. "He's his mad mother's son after all."

"He's worse. She was insane, where he is ruthless, and intelligent enough to turn wizards against their own kind."

Fear kept them in the tiny room until nightfall, when the tavern keeper shooed them out to make way for a whore and her cully.

The taverns were open and there were still many people on the street, but none ventured out onto the platform. Torches had been left burning there. Arkoniel could see the bodies on the gibbet swinging in the night breeze. The frames, however, were gone.

"Should we go see if there's anything to be learned?"

"No." Iya drew him hastily away. "It's too dangerous. They might be watching."

Slipping out of town by the darkest alleys, they rode back to the grove and gathered their tools. But when Arkoniel reached for the amulets, Iya shook her head. They left them where they lay and rode on without speaking until the town was far behind them.

"Eight wizards could do that, Arkoniel, just eight!" Iya burst out at last, voice shaking with fury. "And there was nothing we could do against them. I begin to see more clearly now. The Third Orëska the Oracle revealed to me in my vision—it was a great confederation of wizards in a shining palace of their own at the heart of a great city. If eight are enough to carry out the evil we witnessed here, what could a hundred accomplish for good? And who could stand against us?"

"Like in the Great War," said Arkoniel.

Iya shook her head. "That union lasted only as long as the war, and in the face of the most horrible conflict and upheaval. Think what we could do with peace and time enough to work! Imagine—the knowledge you and I have collected in our travels combined with that of a hundred other wizards. And think of Virishan's poor children. Imagine them saved sooner and brought up in such a place, with dozens of teachers instead of one, and whole libraries of wisdom to draw from."

"But instead, that same power is being used to divide us against ourselves."

Iya stared into the distance, her face unreadable in the starlight. "Famine. Disease. Raiders. Now this. Sometimes, Arkoniel, I see Skala like a sacrificial bull at Sakor-tide. But instead of a clean stroke of the sword to kill it, it's being stuck over and over with little knives until it weakens and falls to its knees." She turned grimly to Arkoniel. "And there's Plenimar just across the water, scenting blood like a wolf."

"It's almost as if Niryn has had the same vision, but turned it on its head," Arkoniel murmured. "Why would the Lightbearer do that?"

"You saw the priest on the gibbet, my boy. Do you really think it's Illior who guides him?"

Chapter 12

Spring turned to summer and the meadow below the keep was thick again with daisies and willow bay. Tobin longed to go riding, but Mynir was ailing and there was no one else left to go out with, so he had to be content with walks with Nari.

He was too old now to be content playing in the kitchen under the women's watchful eyes, but Nari wouldn't let him go out to the barracks yard to practice unless one of the servants was free to go with him. Cook was the only one in the house who knew anything of shooting or swordplay, and she was too old and fat to do more than advise him.

He still had the parchments and ink his mother had given him, but they brought too many dark memories. He began to spend more time shut up in the third-floor chamber, with only the doll and the demon for company. He sometimes whittled with the sharp little knife Koni had given him, using chunks of soft pine and cedar purloined from the kindling pile. The wood was fragrant under his hands and seemed to hold shapes for his blade to discover. Caught up in puzzling out how to coax out a leg or fin or ear, he forgot for a while how lonely he was.

Often, however, he would sit with the doll on his lap the way his mama had, wondering what to do with it. It wasn't useful like a sword or bow. Its blank face made him sad. He remembered how his mama used to talk to it, but he couldn't even do that, for his voice had not come back. Sitting there, squeezing his fingers into the stuffed limbs to find the mysterious lumps and sharp bits inside, he still couldn't remember why his mama had given him the strange, misshapen toy. All the same, he clung to the solid reality of it and the notion that she had loved him a little after all, at the last.

Someone had replaced the door to the tower with a stout new one and Tobin was glad of this without knowing quite why. Whenever he went upstairs, he always made certain it was tightly locked.

Standing in front of it one day, he suddenly had the oddest sense that his mother was just on the other side, staring at him through the wood. The thought sent a thrill of longing and fear through him, and this fancy grew stronger each day, until he was certain he could hear her inside the tower, walking up and down the stone steps with her skirts swishing behind her, or sliding her hands across the wooden panels of the door in search of the latch. He tried hard to imagine her kind and happy, but more often it seemed to him that she was angry.

This darker vision took root and grew like nightshade in his imagination. One night he dreamt that she reached out under the door and pulled him underneath to her side like a sheet of parchment. The demon was there, too, and they dragged him up the stairs to the open window overlooking the mountains to—

He woke thrashing in Nari's arms, but couldn't speak to tell her what the trouble was. But he knew that he didn't want to go upstairs anymore.

The following afternoon he crept to the third floor one last time, heart hammering in his chest. He didn't go near the tower door this time. Instead, he snatched the doll from its hiding place and dashed downstairs as fast as he could, certain he could hear his mother's ghost trying to claw her way under the tower door to catch him.

Never again, he vowed, making certain the door at the bottom of the stairs was shut tight. Running to the toy room, he curled up in the corner beside the wardrobe, cradling the doll in his arms.

𝒯obin spent the next few days fretting over a new hiding place but couldn't find anywhere that seemed safe. No matter how safely he thought he'd tucked it away, he couldn't stop worrying about it.

At last, he decided to share his secret with Nari. She loved him more than anyone now and perhaps, being a woman, wouldn't think so badly of him.

He decided to show the doll to her when she came up to fetch him for supper. He waited until he heard her step in the corridor, then took the doll from its latest hiding spot beneath the toy room wardrobe and turned to the door.

For an instant he thought he saw someone standing in the open doorway. Then the door slammed shut and the demon went into a frenzy.

Tapestries flew from the walls and leaped at him like living things. Dust choked him as layers of heavy fabric knocked him to his knees and shut out the light. He dropped the doll and managed to struggle out from beneath them just in time to see the wardrobe topple forward with a crash, landing just inches from where he lay. The chest upended, spilling toys and inkpots out over the floor. The seal on one of the larger pots broke and a pool of sticky black fluid spread out across the stone floor.

Like Mama's hair on the ice—

The thought came and went like a dragonfly skimming the river's surface.

Then the demon attacked his city.

It tore wooden houses from their places and threw them into the air. People and animals flew at the wall. Tiny ships scattered as if a gale was driving them.

"No! Stop it!" Tobin shrieked, fighting his way free of the fallen tapestries to protect the cherished toy. A flock of clay sheep flew past his head and shattered to bits against the wall. "Stop it! That's *mine!*"

Tobin's vision seemed to narrow to a long, dark tunnel, and all he could see at the end of it was his most cherished possession being torn to pieces. He struck out wildly, flailing with his fists to drive the hateful spirit away. He heard a loud pounding from somewhere nearby and fought harder, blind with fury, until his hand connected with something solid. He heard a startled cry. Strong hands grabbed him and wrestled him down to the floor.

"Tobin! Tobin, stop that!"

Gasping for breath, Tobin looked up at Nari. Tears were streaming down her plump cheeks and blood trickled from her nose.

A red droplet on a grouse's beak—the same bright red on river ice—

Tobin's vision went completely black. Pain blossomed like a flower of fire in his chest, pressing a ragged wail from his lungs.

His mother's birds beating themselves against the tower walls behind him as he looked down on her—

No, don't think—

—broken body at the river's edge.

Black hair and red blood on the ice.

The fiery ache disappeared, leaving him cold and empty.

"Oh Tobin, how could you?" Nari wept, still holding him down. "All your pretty things! Why?"

"I didn't," he whispered, too tired to move.

"Oh, my poor love— Maker's mercy, you spoke!" Nari gathered Tobin into her arms. "Oh, my love, you've found your voice at last."

She carried him next door to his bed and tucked him in, but he hardly noticed. He lay limp as the doll, remembering.

He remembered why he'd been in the tower.

He remembered why his mama was dead.

Why he had the doll.

She hadn't given it to him.

Another swift, sharp stab of pain pierced Tobin's chest, and he wondered if it was what Nari meant in her bedtime stories when she spoke of someone's heart breaking.

She lay down beside him and held him close through the covers, stroking his hair the way she always did. It made him drowsy.

"Why?" he managed at last. "Why did Mama hate me?" But if Nari had an answer for this, he fell asleep before he heard it.

Tobin woke with a start in the night, knowing he'd left the doll lying somewhere in the toy room.

He slipped out of bed and hurried next door in his nightshirt, only to find that the room had been put right already. The tapestries were back on the walls. The wardrobe and chest were in their places. The ink was gone, and all the scattered toys. His city lay in ruins in the middle of the floor and he knew he must fix it before his father came home and saw.

But the doll was nowhere to be seen. Leaving the room, he searched the house, room after room, even the barracks and the stables.

There was no one else in the house. This frightened him terribly, for he'd never been so alone. Worse yet, he knew that the only place left to look was upstairs in the tower. He stood in the courtyard, looking up at the shuttered windows above the roofline.

"I can't," he said aloud. "I don't want to go up there."

As if in answer, the courtyard gate swung open with a creak of hinges, and Tobin caught a glimpse of someone small and dark slipping away across the bridge.

He followed but as soon as he was through the gate he found himself deep in the forest, following a path that ran along the riverbank. Far ahead, half hidden by branches, he caught movement again and knew it was the demon.

He followed it to a clearing but it disappeared. The moon was up now and he could see two does grazing on the silvery, dew-covered grass. They pricked up their ears at his approach, but didn't spring away. Tobin went to them and stroked their soft brown muzzles. They bowed their heads under his hand, then sidled away into the dark forest. There was a hole in the ground, like the entrance to a fox's burrow, where they'd been grazing. It was just big enough for him to crawl into, and he did.

Wiggling through, he found a room below very much like his mother's tower chamber. The windows were open, but blocked by packed earth and roots. It was bright all the same, though, lit by a cheerful fire on the hearth in the center of the room. A table beside it was set with honey cakes and cups of milk, and next to that was a chair. It was turned away from him, but he could see that someone was sitting there, someone with long black hair.

"Mama?" Tobin asked, caught between joy and terror. The woman started to turn—

And Tobin woke up.

He lay there a moment, blinking back tears as he listened to Nari's soft snoring beside him. The dream had been so real, and he'd wanted to see his mother again so badly. He wanted her to be smiling and kind. He wanted for them to sit at the table by the fire and eat the honey cakes together, as they never had on any of his name days.

He burrowed deeper beneath the blankets, wondering if he could slip back into the dream. Suddenly a fragment of it brought him fully awake again.

He *had* left the doll in the toy room.

Slipping out of bed, he took the night lamp from its stand and went into the next room, wondering if it would all be the way it had been in his dream.

But the room was still a shambles. Everything lay where it had fallen. Trying not to look at the broken city, he hauled the heavy tapestries aside, looking for the doll where he must have dropped it.

It wasn't there.

Crouched miserably with his arms around his knees, he pictured someone—Nari or Mynir perhaps—finding it and shaking their head in disapproval as they carried it away. Would they tell his father? Would they give it back?

Something struck him on the head and he toppled sideways, choking back a cry of alarm.

There was the doll on the floor beside him, where it most certainly had not been the moment before. Tobin couldn't see the demon but he could feel it, watching him from the far corner.

Slowly, cautiously, Tobin picked up the doll and whispered, "Thank you."

Chapter 13

Not daring to risk losing the doll again, Tobin moved it back to his room, tying it up in the flour sack and burying it deep in the unused clothes chest under his parchments, some old toys, and his second-best cloak.

He felt a little easier after that, but the dream of going into the forest came to him three more times over the next week, always ending before he could reach the woman in the chair.

It was the same each time in every detail except one. In these dreams he was bringing the doll back to his mother, knowing she would keep it safe for him in her room under the ground.

Another week passed, and the dream came again, growing so real in his mind that he knew at last that he must go see for himself if there really was such a place. This meant disobeying everyone and going out by himself, but the dream was too strong to be denied.

He bided his time and saw his chance one washing day in mid-Gorathin. Everyone would be busy in the kitchen yard all day. He worked with them in the morning, hauling buckets of water in from the river to fill the wash cauldron and dragging bundles of branches from the woodshed to start the fire. The eastern sky, so clear at dawn, was darkening ominously over the treetops and everyone was in a hurry to finish before the rain came.

He ate his midday meal with the others, then asked to be excused.

Nari pulled him close and kissed him on the top of his head. She always seemed to be hugging him these days.

"What will you do with yourself, pet? Stay and keep us company."

"I want to work on my city." Tobin pressed his face against her shoulder so she wouldn't see that he was lying. "Do you . . . do you think Father will be angry when he sees?"

"Of course not. I can't imagine your father ever being angry with a boy as good as you. Isn't that right, Cook?"

The woman nodded over her bread and cheese. "You're the moon and sun to him."

The ash shovel by the hearth jumped off its nail with a loud clatter, but everyone pretended not to notice.

Freeing himself from Nari's embrace, Tobin ran upstairs and waited by his window until he could hear everyone out in the yard again. Then, hiding the doll beneath his longest cloak, he crept downstairs again and slipped out the front gate. He half expected to be magically transported to the forest, as he always was in the dream, but simply ended up outside the wall. As the gate swung shut behind him, he froze for a moment, overcome by the enormity of what he was about to do. What if Nari found him gone? What if he met with a catamount or a wolf?

A rising breeze stroked his face with the scent of rain as he crept between the courtyard wall and the riverbank toward the forest. Robins were singing of the storm somewhere nearby, and doves called mournfully to each other in the trees.

The gate of the kitchen yard was still open. He could see Nari and Cook at work there as he passed, laughing as they stirred the wash pot with their wooden paddles. It felt very odd, standing out here looking in.

He continued on, following the wall past the base of the tower. He kept his eyes down as he passed the boulders where his mother had died.

He reached the cover of the trees at last, and only now did it occur to Tobin that he had no idea where to go; in his dreams, he'd had the demon to guide him. But there had been a river in the dream and he had a river here, so he decided to follow it and hope for the best. He paused to check the sun's position over his shoulder the way Tharin had taught him. It wasn't so easy today. The sun was little more than a bright blur behind the haze.

The river is as good as a path, he thought. *All I have to do is follow it home.*

He'd never been this way before. The riverbank was steep and the trees grew down close to the water. To follow it, he had to clamber over rocks and wriggle through thick stands of willow and alder. In low places he found animal tracks in the mud and scanned these nervously for signs of prowling catamounts. He found none, but still wished he'd thought to bring his bow.

The sky grew darker as he toiled on, and the wind began to toss the branches around overhead. There were no doves or robins calling now, just some ravens croaking nearby. Tobin's arm cramped from carrying the doll. He thought of all the hiding places he'd seen on his rides, but the few holes he found here were all too wet. Even if he did find a dry hiding place, he wasn't sure if he'd dare come out and visit it very often. On the heels of that thought came the realization that he did not want to be parted from it at all.

Better to keep going and look for that hidden room, he told himself.

But nothing looked the way it had in his dream. There was no clearing, no friendly deer waiting for him, just rocks and roots that caught his feet, little biting flies that buzzed in his ears, and mud that soaked his shoes. He was almost ready to give up when he struck a clear trail leading up to a pine grove on higher ground.

The way was much easier here. Fragrant rust-colored needles lay thick underfoot and his feet hardly made a sound as he walked. He followed this path eagerly, certain it would lead him to the clearing and the deer. Instead, it gradually grew fainter until it disappeared altogether beneath the thick, straight trunks of the pines. Turning around, he couldn't see his way back. His feet had left no impression in the thick needles. He couldn't even hear the sound of the river anymore, just the first patter of rain through the boughs. No matter what direction he turned, it all looked the same. The bit of sky he could see through the thick branches was an even blanket of grey with no hint of the sun.

The breeze had died and the day had turned close. Flies with big green eyes joined the clouds of tiny midges buzzing around him, biting him on the neck and behind his ears. The grand adventure was over. Tobin was hot, frightened and lost.

He cast around frantically to find the path but it was no use. At last, he gave up and sat on a rock, wondering if Nari had noticed that he was gone yet.

It was quiet here. He heard a red squirrel's angry trill and the sounds of small creatures creeping in the undergrowth around him. Little black ants toiled in the needles around his feet, carrying their eggs and bits of leaves. Exhausted, he leaned forward to watch them. One had a shiny beetle's leg in its pinchers. A long black snake as thick as Tobin's wrist emerged from a hole under a nearby tree and slithered past his foot, paying no attention to him at all. Rain fell softly through the branches, and he could hear the different sounds the drops made, striking dead leaves, plants, rocks, and the needles on the ground. Tobin wondered uneasily what catamount's feet sounded like on pine needles, or if they made any sound at all.

"I thought you come today maybe."

Tobin nearly toppled off his rock as he whirled around. A small, black-haired woman sat on a mossy log just a few yards away, hands clasped in her lap. She was very dirty and wore a ragged brown rag of a dress decorated with animal teeth. Her hands and bare feet were stained, and there were sticks and bits of leaf tangled in her long, curly hair. She grinned at him, but her black eyes held no mockery.

Tobin thrust the doll behind him, shamed at being caught with it, even by a stranger. He was scared, too, noting the long knife sheathed at her belt. She didn't look like one of his father's tenants, and she spoke strangely.

She gave him a broad smile that lacked several teeth. "Look what I got, *keesa*." She moved her hands and he saw that she held a young rabbit on her lap. She stroked its ears and back. "You come see?"

Tobin hesitated, but curiosity overcame caution. He rose and slowly walked over to stand before her.

"You rub her," the woman said, showing him how to pat the rabbit. "She like."

Tobin stroked the rabbit's back. Its fur was soft and warm under his hand and, like the deer in his dream, it wasn't the least bit skittish.

"She like you."

Yes, thought Tobin, this woman didn't speak like anyone he'd met in Alestun. He was close enough now to tell that she didn't smell very good, either, but for some reason he wasn't afraid anymore.

Keeping the doll hidden under his cloak, he knelt and patted the rabbit some more. "She's soft. Dogs don't let me pet them."

The woman clicked her tongue against her teeth. "Dogs don't understanding." Before Tobin could ask what she meant, she said, "I waiting for you long time, keesa."

"My name isn't Keesa. It's Prince Tobin. I don't know you, do I?"

"But I knowing you, keesa called Tobin. Knowing your poor mama, too. You got one was her thing."

So she had seen the doll. Blushing, Tobin slowly brought it out from under his cloak. She took it and passed him the rabbit to hold.

"I Lhel. You don't be scared me." She held the doll on

her lap, smoothing it with her stained fingers. "I know you born. Watch for you."

Lhel? He'd heard that name somewhere before. "How come you never come to the keep?"

"I come." She winked at him. "Not be see."

"How come you don't talk right?"

Lhel touched a finger playfully to his nose. "Maybe you teach? I teach, too. I wait be your teaching, all this time out in trees. Lonesome time, but I wait. You ready learn some things?"

"No. I was looking for—for—"

"Mama?"

Tobin nodded. "I saw her in a dream. In a room under the ground."

Lhel shook her head sadly. "Don't her. Be me. That mama don't be need now."

Sadness overwhelmed Tobin. "I want to go home!"

Lhel patted his cheek. "Not so far. But you don't come just get lost, no?" She patted the doll. "This give you some troubles."

"Well—"

"I know. You come, keesa."

She got up and walked off through the trees with the doll. Tobin had little choice but to follow.

*T*he washing didn't take as long when Rhius and the men were away. With rain threatening, Nari and Cook made quick work of the clothing and linens while Mynir strung lines up in the hall for drying.

They were finished in time to start a proper supper.

"I'll do the bread," Nari said, surveying the lines of dripping linen with satisfaction. "Just let me go see if Tobin wants to help."

The truth was, she didn't feel easy in her mind leaving the child alone so much, not since the mess in the toy room. It could have been the spirit that tore the room up— the thought of Tobin heaving over that heavy wardrobe scared the liver out of her—but it had been Tobin she'd seen throwing toys and torn tapestries around, and he who'd attacked her, bloodying her nose before she could hold him. It was getting harder to tell when to blame the spirit, and when Tobin was in one of his fits. He'd been so strange since the death, keeping to himself and always acting as if he had some great secret he was keeping.

Nari sighed as she climbed the stairs. Ariani had never been much use as a mother, except perhaps for those last quiet months. And Rhius? Nari shook her head. She'd never been able to puzzle that one out, and all the more so since his wife's death. If Tobin was a bit strange—well, who was to blame for that?

She found Tobin kneeling beside his toy city, his black hair hanging in a tangled mess around his face as he worked on a broken ship.

"Would you like to help with the baking, pet?" she asked.

He shook his head, struggling to fit the tiny mast back into place.

"Want some help with that?"

He shook his head again and turned away, reaching for something beside him.

"Suit yourself, then, Master Silence." Giving him a last, fond look, Nari headed back for the kitchen, already pondering what sort of bread they ought to have tonight.

She didn't hear the sound of the little ship falling to the floor in the empty room behind her.

*T*obin cradled the rabbit in his arms as he followed Lhel deeper into the forest. There was no path that he could see, but she picked her way through the trees as swiftly as if she could see one. The forest grew darker, and the trees here were larger than any Tobin had seen before. Soon they were walking between huge oaks and hemlocks. Wide swaths of yellow lady slippers, wintergreen, and foul-smelling purple trillium covered the ground like a colorful rag quilt.

Tobin studied Lhel as he followed her. She wasn't much taller than he was. Her hair was black like his mama's, but coarse and curly, with thick locks of silver mixed in.

They went on for a very long time. He didn't want to go this deep in the woods, not with her, but she had the doll and she didn't even look back to see if he was following. Blinking back fresh tears, he promised himself he would never come out alone again.

She stopped at last by the largest oak tree Tobin had ever seen. It towered over them as high as the tower and its trunk was nearly as thick. It was festooned with animal skulls, antlers, and hides tacked up to cure. A few small fish hung on drying racks beside it, and there were baskets made of woven grass and willow. Just beyond these a spring welled up in a clear, round pool that sent a trickling streamlet down the hill. They drank from their hands at the pool, and then Lhel led him back to the great tree.

"My house," she said, and vanished into the trunk.

Tobin gaped, wondering if the tree had eaten her, but she peeked out at him from its side and beckoned him to follow.

Coming closer, he saw that there was a crack in the trunk large enough for him to walk through without stooping. Inside the ancient tree was a hollow place almost as big as Tobin's bedchamber, with a floor of packed, dry earth. The smooth silvery wood of the walls went up into darkness, and a second crack a few yards above the door let in enough light for Tobin to make out a pallet bed piled with furs, a firepit, and a small iron pot beside it. The pot looked just like the ones Cook used.

"Did you make this place?" he asked, forgetting his fear again as he gazed around. This was even better than a room under the ground.

"No. Old grandmother trees open up hearts, make good place inside." She kissed her palm and pressed it to the wood as if she was thanking the tree.

Lhel settled Tobin on the pallet and kindled a small blaze in the firepit. He put the rabbit down, and it settled beside him and began cleaning its whiskers with its paws. Lhel reached into the shadows near the door and brought out a basket of wild strawberries and a braided loaf of bread.

"That looks like the bread Cook made the other day," Tobin observed.

"She good maker," Lhel replied, setting the food down in front of him. "Tell you I go your home."

"You stole the bread?"

"I earn it, wait for you."

"How come I've never seen you there, then?" Tobin asked again. "How come I've never heard of you, living so close?"

The woman scooped a handful of berries into her mouth and shrugged. "I don't want folks be see me, they don't see. Now, we fix this *hekka*, yes?"

Before Tobin could object, Lhel drew her knife and cut the shiny black cord from the doll's neck. Once severed, the cord unwound into a thin hank of black hair.

"Mama's." Lhel tickled Tobin's cheek with it, then cast it into the fire. Using her knife again, she picked open a seam on the doll's back and shook some brown, crumbling flakes into the fire, then replaced them with sprigs of herbs from a basket. Among them Tobin recognized the spiky tips of rosemary and rue.

Producing a silver needle and some thread from the pouch at her belt, she held out her hand to Tobin. "Need bitty of you red, keesa, hold the charm. Make this you hekka."

"It's already mine," Tobin protested, shrinking back.

Lhel shook her head. "No."

Not knowing what else to do, Tobin allowed her to prick his finger and squeeze a drop of his blood into the body of the doll. Then she stitched it all up again, set it upright on her knee, and wrinkled her nose into a comic grimace. "Need face, but you maker for that. I done last thing now. Little thing."

Humming to herself, Lhel cut a lock of Tobin's hair, rubbed the strands with wax like a bowstring, and twisted them into a new neck cord for the doll. Tobin watched her fingers as she secured it with a fancy knot that seemed to knit the ends of the strand together. "Are you a wizard?"

Lhel snorted and handed him the finished doll. "What you think this be?"

"Just—just a doll?" Tobin replied, already suspecting it wasn't. "Is it magic now?"

"Always be magic," Lhel told him. "My folk call this *hekkamari*. Got spirit in it. You know the one."

"The demon?" Tobin stared down at it.

Lhel gave him a sad smile. "Demon, keesa? No. Spirit. Ghost. This be your brother."

"I don't have a brother!"

"You do, keesa. Born with you but die. I teaching your mama be make this for his poor *mari*. He be wait, too. Long time. You say—" She paused, pressing her palms together beneath her chin as she thought. "You say, 'Blood, my blood. Flesh, my flesh. Bone, my bone.' "

"What will that do?"

"Bind him to you. You see then. He need you. You need him."

"I don't want to see it!" Tobin cried, thinking of all the monsters he'd conjured up trying to put a form to the presence that had overshadowed his life.

Lhel reached out and cupped his cheek in her rough palm. "You being scared long enough. Be brave now like warrior. You got things coming of you, you don't know. You always being brave, all the time."

Always being brave, like a warrior, thought Tobin. Feeling anything but brave, he closed his eyes and whispered, "Blood, my blood. Flesh, my flesh . . ."

"Bone, my bone," Lhel prompted softly.

"Bone, my bone."

He felt the demon enter the oak and come so close to him he could reach out and touch it if he dared. Lhel's cool hand covered his.

"Keesa, see."

Tobin opened his eyes and gasped. A boy who looked just like him crouched a few feet away. But this boy was dirty and naked, and his dull black hair was tangled around his face in filthy clumps.

I saw him that day when Mama . . . Tobin shoved the thought away. He didn't think of That Day. Not ever.

The other boy glared at Tobin with eyes so black the pupils didn't show.

"He looks like me," Tobin whispered.

"He you. You he. Look-likes."

"Twins, you mean?" Tobin had seen twins in Alestun.

"Twins, yes."

The demon bared its teeth at Lhel in a soundless hiss, then scuttled to squat on the far side of the fire. The rabbit hopped back into Tobin's lap beside the doll and went on washing.

"He doesn't like you," Tobin told Lhel.

"Hates," Lhel agreed. "You mama have him. Now you have him. Keep hekkamari safe or he be lost. He need you, help you some."

Unnerved by the demon's unblinking glare, Tobin huddled closer to Lhel. "Why did he die?"

Lhel shrugged. "Keesa die sometime."

The ghost crouched lower, ready to spring at her. She ignored it.

"But—but how come he didn't go to Bilairy?" Tobin demanded. "Nari says we go to Bilairy at the gates when we die and he takes us to Astellus, who guides us to the dead lands."

Lhel shrugged again.

Tobin squirmed in frustration. "Well, what's its name?"

"Can't name on dead."

"I have to call it something!"

"Call him Brother. That he is."

"Brother?" The ghost just stared at him and Tobin shivered again. This was worse than when it was something he couldn't see at all. "I don't want him looking at me all the time. And he hurts me, too. He broke my city!"

"He don't be do that no more, now you keep hekkamari. You tell him 'go way!' he go way. You call him back, too, with words I teaching you. You say, so I know you know them."

"Blood, my blood. Flesh, my flesh. Bone, my bone."

The spirit boy flinched, then crept closer to Tobin, who scrambled back, dropping the rabbit.

Lhel hugged him and laughed. "He don't be hurt you. Tell him go way."

"Go away, Brother!"

The spirit vanished.

"Can I make him go away forever?"

Lhel gripped his hand, suddenly serious. "No! You need him, I tell you." She shook her head sadly. "Think how lonesome he be? He miss mama, like you miss. She make this hekka, care for him. She die. No care. You care now."

Tobin didn't like the sound of that. "What do I do? Do I have to feed him? Can I give him some clothes?"

"Spirits eat with they eye. Needs be with folk. Way you see him, that's how your mama keep him. All she could, so sick in the heart. You call him sometime, let him look around with you so he don't be so lonesome and hungry. You do that, keesa?"

Tobin couldn't imagine calling a ghost on purpose,

but he understood all too well what Lhel said about Brother being lonesome and lost.

He sighed, then whispered the words again. "Blood, my blood. Flesh, my flesh. Bone, my bone."

Brother reappeared beside him, still glowering.

"Good!" Lhel said. "You and spirit—" She linked her forefingers together.

Tobin studied the sullen face, so like his own, and yet not. "Will he be my friend?"

"No, just do as he do. Be a lot worse before you mama make hekkamari." She made the joining sign with her fingers again. "You kin."

"Will Nari and Father be able to see him when I call him?"

"No, 'less they got eye. Or he want."

"But you can see him."

Lhel tapped her forehead. "I got eye. You, too, yes? You see him a little?" Tobin nodded. "They know him, without seeing. Father. Nari. Old man at door. They know."

Tobin felt like someone had squeezed all the air out of him. "They *know* who the demon is? That I have a brother? Why didn't they tell me?"

"They don't be ready. 'Til then, you keep your secret tight." She tapped him over the heart. "They don't know hekkamari. Just your mama and me. You keep it tight, just you. Don't show it no *one*!"

"But how?" This brought Tobin right back to his original dilemma. "I keep putting it places to hide it, but—"

Lhel stood up and went to the door. "Yours, keesa. You carry it. Go home now."

Brother moved along with them as they started back, sometimes ahead, sometimes behind. It appeared to walk, but it didn't look quite right, though Tobin couldn't say exactly why.

In a surprisingly short time, he caught sight of the watchtower roof above the treetops.

"You're not very far from us at all!" he exclaimed. "Can I come see you again?"

"Some while, keesa." Lhel stopped beneath a drooping birch. "Your father, he don't like you know me. You have a new teaching, soon." Reaching out, she cupped his cheek again and drew a design on his forehead with her thumb. "You be great warrior, keesa. I see. You remember then I help you, yes?"

"I will," he promised. "And I'll take care of Brother."

Lhel patted his cheek, not quite smiling, and her lips didn't seem to move when she said, "You will do all that must be done."

She turned and strode away, disappearing so quickly Tobin wasn't even certain which direction she'd gone. Brother was still with him, though, watching him with that same frightening stare. Without Lhel there, all the old fears flooded back.

"You go away!" Tobin ordered hastily. "*Blood my blood, flesh my flesh, bone my bone!*" To his relief, the spirit obeyed, winking out of sight like a snuffed candle. All the same, Tobin was sure he could feel it dogging his steps as he hurried home.

Using the watchtower as a guide, he found the riverbank again and hurried along it to the back wall of the keep. The usual evening sounds came from the kitchen and yard as he slipped in through the gate but there was no one in the hall. He dashed through and made it all the way to his room without meeting anyone.

The whole house smelled nicely of baking. Hiding the doll in the chest again, he shoved his ruined shoes under the wardrobe, washed his hands and face, and went downstairs for supper.

Home safe at last, he quickly forgot how frightened he'd been. He'd been gone for hours, had an adventure, and no one had even noticed. Even if he had been frightened, even if Brother wasn't going to be his friend, or even much less scary, he somehow felt older, and closer to being the warrior who would wear his father's armor someday.

Nari and Mynir were laying out spoons on the kitchen table while Cook tended something savory in a pot over the fire.

"There you are!" Nari exclaimed as he came in. "I was just coming up to fetch you. You've been so quiet this afternoon I hardly knew you were here!"

Tobin took a warm bun from the pile cooling on the sideboard and bit into it, smiling to himself.

Lhel would like these.

Chapter 14

Tobin sat beside his toy city the next day, holding the doll on his lap. Nari had gone to town with Mynir, and Cook could be counted on not to come upstairs looking for him.

The pungent aroma of fresh herbs rose in Tobin's nostrils as he stared down into its blank face, wondering again what his mama had seen when she looked at it. Had she seen Brother? He hooked a finger under the hair cord around the doll's neck and tugged idly at it, thinking, *My hair. My blood.*

And his responsibility, Lhel said, but one he wanted no part of. It had been bad enough, calling Brother when she was with him. To do it now? Here? His heart beat faster just thinking about it.

Instead, he fetched ink and a quill from the chest and carried the doll to the window where the light was better. Dipping the quill, he tried to draw a round eye on the blank cloth face. The ink bled through the muslin and he ended up with a spidery black blotch instead. Sighing, he flicked a few drops of ink from the quill tip and tried again with a drier point. This worked better and he drew around the blotch, smoothing the edges in to make a large dark iris, and framing it with two curved horizontal lines for lids. He drew the other eye to match, and found himself looking into large black eyes not unlike Brother's. He made an attempt at the nose and dark brows. When he reached the mouth, however, he drew it smiling. That didn't look right at all; the eyes still looked angry, but there was no changing it now. It wasn't a very good face, but it was still an improvement over the blank one he'd known all his life.

It made the doll seem more like his now, too, but it didn't make it any less daunting to summon Brother. Tobin carried it to the corner furthest from the door and sat down with his back pressed to the wall. What if Brother attacked him? What if it broke the city again, or flew off to hurt someone?

In the end it was what Lhel had said about Brother being hungry that forced Tobin to utter the summons. Pressing back into the corner as far as he could, he squinted his eyes half shut and whispered, "Blood my blood. Flesh my flesh. Bone my bone."

At the oak yesterday the spirit had crouched like a wild beast at his very feet. This time, however, Tobin had to look around to find it.

Brother stood by the door as if he'd just walked in like a living person. He was still thin and dirty, but he had on a plain, clean tunic like the one Tobin wore. He didn't look so angry today, either. He just stood there, staring at Tobin with no expression at all, as if he was waiting for something.

Tobin stood up slowly, never taking his eyes off the ghost. "Would—would you like to come over here?"

Brother didn't walk across the room. He was just suddenly there beside him, staring at him with those unblinking black eyes. Lhel had said to feed him by letting him look at things. Tobin held out the doll. "See? I drew a face."

Brother showed no sign of interest or understanding. Tobin warily studied the strange face. Brother had all his features except for the crescent-shaped scar on his chin, yet he didn't really look like Tobin at all.

"Are you hungry?" he asked.

Brother said nothing.

"Come on, then. I'll show you things. Then you can go." Tobin felt a little silly as he walked around the room showing his favorite possessions to a silent ghost. He held up his little sculptures and carvings, and the treasures his father had sent. Would Brother be jealous? Tobin wondered. He picked up a Plenimaran shield boss and held it out to him. "Would you like to have this?"

Brother accepted it with a hand that looked solid, but where their fingers appeared to touch Tobin felt only a wisp of cold air.

Tobin squatted down beside the city and Brother did the same, still holding the boss. "I'm fixing all the things you broke that day," he told him, letting a little resentment creep into his voice. He picked up a boat and showed Brother where the mast had been mended. "Nari thinks I broke it."

Brother still said nothing.

"It's all right, I guess. You were afraid I'd show Nari the doll, weren't you?"

You must keep it.

Tobin was so startled he dropped the ship. Brother's voice was faint and expressionless, and his lips didn't move, but there was no question that he'd spoken.

"You can talk!"

Brother stared at him. *You must keep it.*

"I will, I promise. But you talked! What else can you say?"

Brother stared.

Tobin was stumped for a moment, wondering what you could say to a ghost. Suddenly, he knew exactly what he wanted to ask. "Do you see Mama in the tower?"

Brother nodded.

"Do you visit her?"

Another nod.

"Does—does she want to hurt me?"

Sometimes.

A knot of sorrow and fear lodged in Tobin's chest. Hugging himself, he searched the ghost's face. Did he see a hint of satisfaction there? "But why?"

Brother either could not or would not tell him.

"Go away then! I don't want you here!" Tobin cried.

Brother disappeared and the brass boss clattered to the floor. Tobin stared at it a moment, then threw it across the room.

Several days passed before Tobin could summon the courage to call Brother again. When he finally did so, however, he found he wasn't as afraid of him.

He was curious to know whether Nari could see Brother, so he ordered him to follow him into the bed-chamber where Nari was changing the linens. The woman looked right at Brother without seeing him.

No one else saw him that night, either, when Tobin brought him to the kitchen briefly, thinking that looking at food might help Brother not to look so very hungry.

Alone in his bedroom that night, Tobin summoned him again to see if there was any change. There wasn't, though. Brother looked as famished as ever.

"Didn't you eat the food with your eyes?" Tobin asked him as Brother stood motionless at the end of his bed.

Brother tilted his head slightly, as if he were consider-ing the question. *I eat everything with my eyes.*

Tobin shivered as Brother looked at him. "Do you hate me, Brother?"

A long pause. *No.*

"Then why are you so mean?"

Brother had no answer for this. Tobin couldn't tell if he even understood what he'd said.

"Do you like it when I call you?"

Again, no comprehension.

"Will you be nice to me if I let you come out every day? Will you do as I say?"

Brother blinked slowly at him, like an owl in the sun.

That would have to do for now. "You mustn't break things or hurt people anymore. That's very bad. Father wouldn't let you act so if you were alive."

Father . . .

The cold, hissing whisper raised the hairs on Tobin's arms. Ordering Brother away, Tobin pulled the covers around his head like a hood and stared at the flickering night lamp until Nari came to bed. After that, he only summoned Brother in the daytime.

Chapter 15

Iya and Arkoniel spent the summer in the southernmost provinces, and here Iya searched out an ancient wizard named Ranai, who lived in a little fishing village north of Erind. As a girl Ranai had fought beside Iya's master in the Great War and been badly wounded there. Iya had prepared Arkoniel to meet her, but he still cringed inwardly at his first sight of her face when she answered their knock on her cottage door.

She was a frail, stooped woman. A necromancer's demon had crippled her left leg and raked the left side of her head with claws of fire; the skin clung to her skull in pale waxlike ridges that did not move when she smiled or spoke.

Perhaps this was why she'd chosen to immure herself in this tiny hamlet, thought Arkoniel. The power in the woman made the hairs on the young wizard's arms prickle.

"Greetings, Mistress Ranai," Iya said, bowing to the old woman. "Do you remember me?"

Ranai squinted at her for a moment, then smiled. "Why, you're Agazhar's girl, aren't you? But not a girl any longer. Come in, my dear. And I see you have a student of your own now. Come in and welcome, young man, and share my hearth."

Rain pattered cozily down on the thatched roof as the old woman limped from table to hearth and back, serving them bread and soup. Iya contributed cheese and a skin of good wine they'd bought in the village. The night breeze carried the smell of wild roses and the sea through the cottage's single window.

They spoke of small matters as they ate, but after the dishes had been cleared away Ranai fixed Iya with her good eye and said, "You've come here for a reason, I think."

Arkoniel settled back with his wine, knowing by heart the conversation that would follow.

"Do you ever wonder, Ranai, what we wizards might accomplish if we put our heads together?" Iya asked.

This is the two hundred and thirteenth time, Arkoniel thought. He'd kept count.

"Your master and I saw what wizards are capable of, for good and for evil," Ranai replied. "Is that why you came all the way down here, Iya? To ask me that?"

Iya smiled. "I wouldn't say this straight out to many, but I will to you. Where do you stand regarding the king?"

The sound portion of Ranai's face took on a familiar look of wonder and hope. She waved a hand and the window shut itself tight. "You've been dreaming of her!"

"Who?" Iya asked quietly, but Arkoniel sensed her excitement. They'd found another.

"The Sad Queen, I call her," Ranai whispered. "The dreams started about twenty years ago, but Illior sends them more often now, especially on the nights between the moon's two crescents. Sometimes she's young, sometimes old. Sometimes a victor, others a corpse. I never see her face clearly, but there's always a sense of deep sorrow about her. Is she real?"

Iya did not answer her question directly. She never did, any more than she would ever show the bowl she carried in the worn leather sack. "I was granted a vision at Afra. Arkoniel will bear witness to that. In it I saw the destruction of Ero, and then a new city and a new age of wizards. But a queen must rule that new city. You know Erius will never let that happen. He follows Sakor of the Four, but it is Illior who protected Skala in the Great War and since. It's Illior's hand over wizards, as well. Have we served the Lightbearer well, standing idly by all these years while the great prophecy given to Thelátimos is trampled and ignored?"

Ranai drew designs in a dribble of wine on the table-top. "I've wondered that myself. But compared to his mother, Erius hasn't been a bad ruler, and he won't live forever. I might even outlive him. And that business with the female heirs? It's not without precedent. Ghërilain's own son Pelis seized the throne from his sister—"

"And the land was struck with a plague that killed him and thousands of others within the year," Arkoniel reminded her.

Ranai raised an eyebrow and he saw a flash of the great woman she had been. "Don't lecture me on history, young man. I was there. The gods struck down Pelis swiftly. But King Erius has ruled for over two decades now. Perhaps he's right about the Oracle being misinter-preted. You know as well as I that his mother, descendent of Thelátimos though she was, was no fit ruler."

"Perhaps she was sent to test us," Arkoniel replied, trying to maintain a respectful tone with the elder wizard. He'd had ten years and thousands of miles to ponder the point. "King Pelis suffered one terrible plague. Since Erius took the throne, there have been dozens, if on a smaller scale. Perhaps these have been warnings. Perhaps the Lightbringer's patience is running out. What Iya saw at Afra—"

"Have you heard of the Harriers, young man?" Ranai snapped. "Do you know that the king's wizard serves by hunting down his own kind?"

"Yes, Ranai," said Iya, intervening. "We've seen their work."

"Have you seen them kill anyone you knew? No? Well, I have. I had to stand by helplessly while a dear friend of mine, a wizard who served four queens, was burned on a yew frame for merely speaking aloud of a dream very sim-ilar to my mine; and yours, too, I've no doubt. Burned alive for speaking of a *dream*! Imagine, if you can, what the power of the Harriers must be, to be able to kill so cruelly. And it's not just us they persecute, either, but anyone who dares speak against the male succession. Illiorans in particular. By the Four, if he'd kill his own sister—"

The cup fell from Arkoniel's hand, splattering wine across the table. "Ariani is dead?"

Nari's letters had continued to arrive at the appointed places at regular intervals. How could she not have sent word?

"Last year, I think," Ranai was saying. "Did you know her?"

"We did," Iya replied, sounding calmer than Arkoniel would have believed possible.

"Then I'm sorry that you had to hear of it this way," Ranai said.

"The king killed her?" Arkoniel rasped out, hardly able to get his breath.

Ranai shrugged. "I'm not certain of that, but by all reports he was there when she died. So you see, that's the last of them, and Prince Korin will inherit the throne. Perhaps he will sire our Sad Queen."

"Perhaps," Iya murmured, and Arkoniel knew she would speak no more of her vision to this woman.

An uneasy silence fell over the room. Arkoniel fought back tears and avoided Iya's watchful eye.

"I served Illior and Skala well," Ranai said at last, sounding defeated and old. She touched a hand to her ruined face. "All I ever asked was a bit of peace."

Iya nodded. "Forgive us for disturbing you. If the Harriers come here, what will you tell them?"

The elder wizard had the good grace to look ashamed. "I have nothing to say to them. You have my word on it."

"Thank you." Iya reached to cover Ranai's damaged hand with her own. "Life is long, my friend, and shaped of smoke and water, not stone. Pray we meet again in better days."

A terrible suspicion took root in Arkoniel's heart as they left the wizard's cottage and set off along the muddy track leading away from the village. He couldn't speak of it yet; he didn't know if he could bear the answer.

They made camp beneath a huge fir beside the sea. Iya sang a spell to keep out the damp, and Arkoniel coaxed his newly perfected spell, a sphere of black fire, into being and fixed it in the air at their feet.

"Ah, that's nice." Iya pulled off her sodden boots and warmed her feet. "Well done."

They sat for a while listening to the rain and the rhythmic wash of the waves on the ledges. He tried to speak of Ariani, needing to hear from Iya's lips that his dark suspicion was wrong, but he couldn't seem to shape the words. Sorrow stuck in his throat like a stone.

"I knew," Iya said at last, reducing his heart to ashes.

"For how long?"

"Since it happened. Nari sent word."

"And you didn't tell me?" Unable to look at Iya, he stared up through the branches overhead. All these years he'd been haunted by memories of that terrible night, of the strange child they'd created and the lovely woman they'd betrayed. They had not been back to Ero since—Iya still forbade it—yet he'd always imagined that one day they would go back to make things right again somehow.

Arkoniel felt her hand on his shoulder. "How could you not tell me?"

"Because there was nothing to be done. Not until the child is of age. Erius didn't kill his sister, at least not directly. Ariani threw herself from a tower window. Apparently she tried to kill the child as well. There is nothing we can do there."

"That's what you always say!" He wiped angrily at the tears welling in his eyes. "I don't question that what we're doing is Illior's will. I never have. But are you so certain this is *how* we're meant to do it? It's been nearly ten years, Iya, and not once have we been back to see if she's well or fit, or to help with the mess Lhel left. The child's own mother kills herself and still you say we have more-important work?"

Too upset to sit still, he scrambled from the shelter and strode down to the water's edge. The tide was high, the water smooth beneath the shifting pattern of rain. In the distance, the glow of a ship's lantern cast a thread of light across that glassy surface. Arkoniel imagined himself swimming out to the ship and begging a berth among the sailors. He'd heave cargo and pull sheets until his hands bled and never think of magic or spirits or women falling from towers again.

O Illior! he prayed silently, turning his face up to the moon's pull beyond the clouds as he strode along the water's edge. *How can this be your will if my heart is breaking? How can I love and follow a teacher who can look unblinking upon such acts and keep such silence between us?*

In his heart, he knew that he still loved and trusted Iya, yet some crucial balance was lacking between means and end that only he seemed to sense. And how could that be? He was only her student, a wizard of no account.

He stopped and sank down on his heels, cradling his face in his hands. *Something is wrong. Something is missing, if not for Iya, then for me.*

Since Afra.

It sometimes seemed that his life had begun anew that fateful summer day. Resting his forehead on his knees, he summoned the brightness of the sun, the taste of dust, the hot smoothness of the sun-warmed stele beneath his hand. He thought of the cool darkness of the Oracle's cavern, where he'd knelt to receive the strange answer that had been no answer at all; a vision of himself holding a dark-haired boy in his arms. . . .

A strange stillness stole over him as he remembered. *The child. Which child?*

Now it was the chill of the murdered child's angry spirit that gripped him, stiffening his hands and making his bones ache. For an instant it seemed he was standing under that chestnut tree again, watching the tiny body sink down into the earth.

The witch's magic had not been enough to hold the angry spirit down.

The vision grew brighter in his mind's eye, taking on new shape and form. A child rose from the earth at his feet, fighting the grip of the roots and hard earth. Arkoniel grasped his hands and pulled, looking down into dark blue eyes, not black. But the roots still held the child, pulling at his arms and legs. One had pierced his back and came out of the wound in his chest where Lhel had sewn a strip of skin with stitches finer than eyelashes. The tree was drinking the child's blood. Arkoniel could see him withering before his eyes. . . .

The unnatural chill still gripped him, making Arkoniel shake and stagger like an old man as he slowly made his way back to the fir.

Wizards see well enough in the dark, but what Iya sensed as Arkoniel came lurching back made her strike a light.

His face was ashen beneath his thin beard, his eyes red-rimmed and staring.

"At Afra!" he gasped, falling to his knees beside her. "My vision. The one I didn't— Tobin's my path. That's why— Oh, Iya, I must go! We have to go!"

"Arkoniel, you're babbling! What is it?" Iya cradled his face in both hands and pressed her brow to his. He was shaking like a man with spring plague, but there was no hint of fever. His skin was icy. She reached out cautiously to his mind and was immediately presented with a vision: Arkoniel stood on a high cliff looking west over a dark blue sea. Just ahead of him, much too close to the edge, stood Ariani's twins, grown tall and slender now. Strands of golden light connected the young wizard to the children.

"You see?" Pulling back, Arkoniel clasped her hands and told her of the darker vision he'd had at the shore. "I must go to the child. I must see Tobin."

"Very well. Forgive me for not telling you. My vision—" She held out her empty hands, palm up. "It's so clear and yet so dark before me. So long as the child lives, I have other things I must do. I forgot, I suppose, how much time has passed since Ariani died, how much faster it passes for you than for me. But you must believe me when I tell you that I have not forgotten the child. It was for Tobin's sake that we've kept our distance all these years, and now it seems to me even more crucial to be careful not to draw Erius' attention to that house, now that he distrusts all wizards but his own."

She paused as a new thought struck her. Twice she'd had a glimpse of the Lightbearer's hand on Arkoniel and, while he appeared in her visions, she did not appear in his. The realization brought sadness and a twinge of fear.

"Well, it seems you must go," she told him.

He kissed both her hands. "Thank you, Iya. I won't be away long, I promise. I only want to make certain the child is safe and try to discover what it is that Illior is trying to say to me. If I can find a ship tomorrow, I'll be back in a week. Where should I meet with you?"

"There's no need for such haste. I'll go on to Ylani as we planned. Send word to me there when you've seen the child. . . ." There it was, that sadness again. "Then we shall see."

Chapter 16

Arkoniel looked back over his shoulder as he set off the next day. Iya stood by the fir, looking very small and ordinary. She waved and he waved back, then turned his face for the village, trying to ignore the sudden lump in his throat. It felt strange, walking alone after all these years.

The wizardly accouterments he carried were stowed safely out of sight in the bedroll slung over his shoulder. Hopefully anyone looking at him would see nothing more than a traveler in muddy boots and a dusty, broken-brimmed hat. All the same, he planned to heed Iya's warning to avoid priests and other wizards, and to keep the usual cautious eye out for men wearing the hawk badge of the Harriers.

He found a fisherman willing to take him up the coast as far as Ylani, where he boarded a larger vessel bound north for Volchi. Leaving the ship there two days later, he bought a sturdy sorrel gelding and set off for Alestun and whatever tasks the Lightbearer had set for him there.

He knew from Rhius and Nari's letters that the duke had moved his family from Ero to the keep the spring following Tobin's birth; by then tales of the "demon" had already spread around the city. The spirit, it was said, threw things at visitors, hit them, and spirited away jewels and hats. And beautiful Ariani with her stained dress and strange doll, wandering the corridors in search of her child—that was still remembered, too.

The king had apparently been content to let Rhius go.

The same had not been so for the "demon," which had somehow followed them to the keep.

A chill ran up Arkoniel's spine as he tried to imagine it. Unquiet spirits were fearsome, shameful things, and any dealings with them were normally left to the priests and drysians. He and Iya had learned what they could from such folk, knowing that sooner or later they would have to face the ghost they'd helped create. He'd never expected to have to face it alone.

Arkoniel reached Alestun on the third day of Shemin. It was a pleasant, prosperous little market town nestled in the foothills of the Skalan Range. A few miles further west, a line of jagged peaks loomed against the cloudless afternoon sky. It was cooler here than it had been on the coast, and the fields showed no sign of drought.

He stopped in the square to ask directions of a woman selling fresh cheeses from a cart.

"Duke Rhius? You'll find him up at the old keep on the pass," she told him. "He's been back the better part of a month now, though I hear he's not to stay long. He'll be at the shrine tomorrow to hear petitions, if that's what you need."

"No, I'm looking for his home."

"Just keep on the main road through the woods. If you're peddling, though, I'll save you the trip. They'll set the watch on you, 'less they know you. They do no business with strangers up there."

"I'm not a stranger," Arkoniel told her. He bought some of her cheese and walked away smiling, pleased to have been taken for a vagrant.

Riding on, he passed golden barley fields and meadows filled with shorn sheep and fat pigs, and on into the dark forest beyond. The road she'd sent him on showed less travel than the one leading into town. Sere grass stood thick between the wheel ruts, and he picked out more tracks of deer and pigs in the mud than of horses. The shadows were lengthening quickly now and he pushed his sweating mount into a gallop, wishing he'd thought to ask how far it was to the keep.

He came out into the open again at last beside a river at the bottom of a steep meadow. At the top of the rise stood a tall grey keep backed by a single square watchtower.

Threw herself from a tower window—

Arkoniel shuddered. As he turned his horse to continue up the road, he saw a little peasant boy hunkered down in the weeds by the road, not twenty feet from where he sat.

The boy's ragged tunic left his skinny arms and legs bare. His skin was streaked with mud and his dark hair was matted with burrs and leaves.

Arkoniel was about to call out to him when he remembered that there was only one child in this house—a child with black hair. Shocked at the prince's condition, he urged his horse forward at a walk to greet him.

Tobin had his back to the road, staring intently at something in the long grass above the riverbank. He didn't look up as Arkoniel approached. The wizard started to dismount, then remained in the saddle. Something in Tobin's stillness warned him to keep his distance.

"Do you know who I am?" he asked at last.

"You're Arkoniel," the boy replied, still looking down at whatever had engaged his attention.

"Your father won't like you being so far from the house all by yourself. Where's your nurse?"

The child ignored the question. "Will it bite, do you think?"

"Will what bite?"

Tobin thrust a hand into the grass and plucked out a shrew, holding it up by one hind leg. He watched it struggle for a moment, then snapped its neck, neat as a poacher. A drop of blood welled at the tip of the creature's tiny snout.

"My mama is dead." He turned to Arkoniel at last, and the wizard found himself staring down into eyes as black and deep as night.

Arkoniel's voice died in his throat as he realized what he'd been conversing with.

"I know the taste of your tears," the demon said.

Before he could make any warding sign against it, it leaped up and flung the dead shrew in his horse's face. The gelding reared, throwing Arkoniel into the tall grass. He came down awkwardly on his left hand and felt a sickening snap just above his wrist. Pain and the fall knocked the wind out of him, and he lay in a tight ball, fighting back nausea and fear.

The demon. He'd never heard of one appearing so clearly or speaking. Arkoniel managed to lift his head, expecting to find it squatting beside him, watching him with its dead black eyes. Instead, he saw his gelding tossing its head and kicking in the meadow across the river.

He sat up slowly, cradling his injured arm. His left hand hung at a bad angle and felt cold to the touch. Another wave of nausea burned his throat and he eased himself back down in the grass. The sun beat down on his upturned cheek, and insects investigated his ears. He watched the green rye and timothy dancing against the sky and tried to imagine himself walking the rest of the way up the steep road to the keep.

Failing that, he returned to the demon. Only now did its words really register.

My mama is dead.

I know the taste of your tears.

This was not the racketing poltergeist he'd expected. It had matured like a living child and come to some sort of awareness. He'd never heard of such a thing.

"Lhel, you damned necromancer, what did you do?" he groaned.

What did we do?

He must have drifted off for a time, because when he

opened his eyes again he found a man's head and shoulders blocking the sun.

"I'm not a peddler," he mumbled.

"Arkoniel?" Strong hands reached under his shoulders and helped him to his feet. "What are you doing here all by yourself?"

He knew that voice, and the weathered, bearded face that went with it, although it had been more than a decade since he'd last laid eyes on the man. "Tharin? By the Four, I'm glad to see you."

Arkoniel swayed and the captain got an arm around his waist, holding him upright.

Blinking, he tried to focus on the too-close face. Tharin's fair hair and beard had faded with age, and the lines around his eyes and mouth were deeper, but the man's quiet, easy manner was just the same and Arkoniel was grateful for it. "Is Rhius here? I must—"

"Yes, he's here, though you're lucky to catch us. We're leaving for Ero tomorrow. Why didn't you send word?"

Arkoniel's legs buckled and he staggered.

Tharin hoisted him upright again. "Never mind, then. Let's get you up to the house."

Helping him over to a tall grey, Tharin got him up into the saddle. "What happened? I saw you sitting down here looking at the river, then your horse just threw you off. Looked like it went crazy. Sefus is having a hell of a time over there trying to catch him for you."

Out in the meadow, Arkoniel could see a man trying to calm his runaway gelding, but it shied and kicked every time he reached for the bridle. He shook his head, not yet ready to speak of what he'd seen. Clearly Tharin hadn't seen the demon. "Skittish beast."

"Apparently. So, how shall we get you up to the house? Slow and painful or fast and painful?"

Arkoniel managed a wretched grin. "Fast."

Tharin mounted behind him and reached around

Arkoniel for the reins, then kicked the horse into a canter. Every pounding hoofbeat sent a hot stab up Arkoniel's arm. He fixed his eyes on their destination and held on as best he could with his good hand.

At the top of the hill they rode across a wide wooden bridge and on through a gate into a paved yard. Mynir and Nari were there, with a large-boned woman in the stained apron of a cook.

Nari had aged, too. She was still plump and ruddy, but there were streaks of grey in her thick brown hair.

They helped him down and Tharin supported him through a dim, echoing hall to the kitchen.

"Whatever are you doing here?" Nari asked as Tharin eased him down onto a bench beside a scrubbed oak table.

"The child," he croaked, resting his spinning head on his good hand. "Come to see the child. Is he well?" Tharin gently took his swelling wrist in both hands. Arkoniel gasped as the man felt for damage.

Nari raised an eyebrow at him. "Of course he's well. What makes you think he isn't?"

"I just—" He caught his breath again as Tharin probed deeper.

"That's lucky," he told Arkoniel. "It's just the outer bone, and a clean break. Once it's set and bound it shouldn't trouble you too badly."

Mynir fetched a slat and some strips of cloth.

"Best have this first," the cook said, giving him a clay cup.

Arkoniel downed the contents gratefully and felt a numbing heat spread quickly through his belly and limbs. "What is this?"

"Vinegar, brandywine, with a little poppy and henbane," she told him, patting his shoulder.

It still hurt like hell when Tharin set the bone, but Arkoniel was able to bear it without complaint.

Tharin bound the slat in place with the cloth and a leather thong. When he was done he sat back and grinned at Arkoniel.

"You're tougher than you look, boy."

Arkoniel groaned and took another gulp from the cup. He was beginning to feel quite sleepy.

"Did Iya send you?" Nari asked.

"No. I thought I should come pay my—"

"So one of you could finally spare us a visit, could you?" a harsh voice snapped.

Jarred back to alertness, Arkoniel found Rhius scowling at him from the kitchen doorway.

Tharin rose and stepped toward the duke as if he expected violence. "Rhius, he's hurt."

The duke ignored him as he crossed the kitchen to glare down at Arkoniel. "So you've finally come back to us, have you? Where's your mistress?"

"She's still in the south, my lord. I came to pay our respects. We were both so sorry to hear of your lady's death."

"So sorry that it took a year for you to come?" Rhius sat down across from him and glanced at the wizard's bound wrist. "But I see you won't be leaving us anytime soon. I leave for Ero tomorrow, but you may stay until you're fit to ride."

It was a far cry from the welcome they used to enjoy under Rhius' roof, but Arkoniel suspected that he was lucky the duke didn't toss him into the river.

"How is the king?" he asked.

Curdled anger curled Rhius' lip. "Very well, thank you. The Plenimaran raids have ceased for the harvest season. The crops are ripening. The sun continues to shine. It seems the Four smile on his reign." Rhius spoke quietly, his voice devoid of inflection, but Arkoniel read betrayal in those hard, tired eyes. Iya would have talked of patience and visions, but Arkoniel didn't know where to begin.

Just then an eerily familiar face peered in around the corridor doorway. "Who's that, Father?"

All the harshness left Rhius' face as he held out his hand to the boy, who came and pressed close to his father's side, looking at Arkoniel with shy blue eyes.

Tobin.

There was nothing of the hidden girl child in this plain, skinny lad. Lhel had done her work too well. But Tobin's eyes were the same striking blue as his mother's and, unlike his demon twin, Tobin looked well cared for except for the fading pink scar that marred his pointed chin. Arkoniel stole a quick glance at the triangle of smooth pale skin that showed at the unlaced neck of the child's tunic, wondering what Lhel's stitching looked like after all these years.

The child's long black hair was shiny and, though no one would have taken him for the son of a princess in such garb, his simple tunic was clean and well made. Looking around at the others in the room, Arkoniel recognized a love for this solemn child that made his heart ache with a strange burst of compassion for the demon, an abandoned child shut out from the warmth of hearth and family while its double grew up in comfort and warmth. It was aware. It must know.

Tobin didn't smile or come forward to greet him; he just stared at Arkoniel. Something in his stillness made him seem as strange as his ghostly twin.

"This is Arkoniel," Rhius explained. "He's a—friend I haven't seen in a very long time. Come now, introduce yourself properly."

The boy made Arkoniel a stiff formal bow, left hand on his belt where a sword would someday hang. There was the wine-colored faver mark on the outside of his forearm, like the print of a rosebud cut in half. Arkoniel had forgotten about that, the only outward sign left of the girl's true form.

"I am Prince Tobin Erius Akandor, son of Ariani and Rhius." The way he moved reinforced Arkoniel's initial impression. There was nothing of a normal child in his manner. He had his father's dignity, but not the stature or years to carry it off properly.

Arkoniel returned the bow as best he could seated. The cook's draught seemed to work more strongly the longer it was in him, making him dizzy. "I am most honored to make your acquaintance, my prince. I am Arkoniel, son of Sir Coran and Lady Mekia of Rhemair, fostered to the wizard Iya. Please accept my humble service to you and all your house."

Tobin's eyes widened. "You're a wizard?"

"Yes, my prince." Arkoniel held up his bandaged wrist. "Perhaps when this feels a bit better, I can show you some of the tricks I've learned."

Most children greeted such an offer with exclamations of delight, or at least a smile, but Tobin seemed to retreat without moving a muscle.

I was right, Arkoniel thought, looking into those dark eyes. *Something is very wrong here.*

He attempted to rise and found that his legs and head would not cooperate in the effort.

"That draught of Cook's isn't done with you," Nari said, pressing him back onto the bench. "My lord, he must lie down somewhere, but none of the guest chambers are fit to sleep in."

"A pallet here by the fire is all I need," Arkoniel mumbled, nauseated again. Despite the brandy burning his belly and the warmth of the day, he felt chilled all over.

"We could set up a bed in Tobin's second room," Mynir suggested, ignoring Arkoniel's much simpler solution. "It wouldn't be such a climb for him."

"Very well," Rhius replied. "Have some of the men fetch whatever you think necessary."

Arkoniel sagged against the table, wishing they'd just let him curl up here by the hearth so he could get warm.

The women went to fetch linens. Tobin went out with Tharin and the steward, leaving the wizard alone with Rhius.

For a moment neither man said anything.

"The demon frightened my horse," Arkoniel told him. "I saw it clearly in the road at the bottom of the meadow."

Rhius shrugged. "It's here with us now. I see the gooseflesh on your arms. You feel it, too."

Arkoniel shivered. "Yes, I feel it, but I *saw* it in the meadow, as clearly as I see you now. Tobin looks just like it."

Rhius shook his head. "No one has ever seen it, except perhaps for—"

"Tobin?"

"By the Four, no!" Rhius made a sign against bad luck. "He's been spared that much, at least. But I think Ariani did. She made a doll to replace the dead child, and sometimes spoke to it as if it were real. But I often had the feeling that it wasn't the doll she was seeing. Illior knows, she paid little enough attention to her living child, except at the end."

Arkoniel's throat tightened again. "My lord, words cannot express how sorry—"

Rhius slammed a hand down on the table, then leaned forward and snarled, "Don't you *dare* weep for her! You have no right, no more than I!" Lurching to his feet, he strode from the room, leaving the startled wizard alone in the demon-haunted kitchen.

The chill pressed in around him and Arkoniel was certain he felt a child's cold hands on the back of his neck. Thinking of the dead shrew, he whispered, "By the Four—Maker, Traveler, Flame, and Lightbearer—I command you! Lie down, Spirit, until Bilairy guides you to the Gate."

The cold intensified around him and the bright room darkened as if a thunderhead had covered the sun. A large clay pot flew from a shelf and shattered against the opposite wall, narrowly missing his shoulder. A basket of onions followed, then a wooden bowl of dough and a platter. Arkoniel slid hastily under the table, broken bones forgotten for the moment.

Scant yards away, an iron poker scraped across the stone hearth in his direction. He tried to dive away toward the door, but came down on his bad wrist and collapsed with a strangled scream, eyes screwed shut in agony.

"No!" A boy's high clear voice.

The poker clattered to the floor.

Arkoniel heard whispering and footsteps. Opening his eyes, he found Tobin kneeling beside him. The room was warm again.

"It doesn't like you," Tobin said.

"No—I don't think it does," Arkoniel panted, content for the moment to stay where he was. "Is it gone?"

Tobin nodded.

"Did you send it away?"

Tobin gave him a startled look, but said nothing. He was a few months shy of his tenth birthday, but looking into that face now, Arkoniel could not have put an age to it. Tobin looked at once too old and too young.

"It listens to you, doesn't it?" he asked. "I heard you speaking to it."

"Don't tell Father, please!"

"Why?"

Now Tobin looked like any frightened little boy. "I—it would make him sad. Please, don't tell him what you saw!"

Arkoniel hesitated, recalling the duke's violent outburst. Crawling out from beneath the table, he sat on the floor next to Tobin and rested his hand in his lap. "I take it all this—" He looked around at the broken crockery. "It isn't going to surprise anyone?"

Tobin shook his head.

"Very well, then, my prince, I'll keep your secret. But I'd very much like to know why the demon obeys you."

Tobin said nothing.

"Did you tell it to throw the dishes at me?"

"No! I'd never do that, on my honor."

Arkoniel studied that strained, earnest little face and knew Tobin spoke the truth, and yet there was some great secret behind those eyes. *Another house of closed doors,* he thought, but here at least he sensed the chance of finding the keys.

Voices came from the direction of the hall. "Go on, then," he whispered.

Tobin slipped out the courtyard door without a sound.

Thank you, Illior, for sending me here, Arkoniel thought, watching him go. *Whatever darkness surrounds this child, I'll make it right, and stand by her until I see her crowned in her rightful form.*

Chapter 17

Arkoniel staggered a bit as Nari and Tharin helped him upstairs. The sun had fallen behind the peaks, casting the whole house into dusky gloom. Tharin carried a clay hand lamp and by its light Arkoniel made out the faded, flaking colors of the painted pillars in the great hall, the tattered banners from long-forgotten battles hanging in shreds from the carved beams overhead, and the tarnished brass lamps festooned with cobwebs. Despite the fresh strewing herbs among the rushes on the floor, there was an underlying odor of damp and mice.

The upstairs corridor was darker still. They brought Arkoniel into a dusty, cluttered chamber on the right. A lamp on a stand shed enough light to see what appeared to be a miniature city taking up one side of the room. A few other toys lay scattered in the corners, but they had an abandoned look.

A few old chests and a wardrobe with a cracked door stood against the bare stone walls. An ornate oak bed-stead had been set at an awkward angle near the window. It was a handsome piece, carved with vines and birds, but bits of cobwebs still clung to it here and there.

Tharin helped Arkoniel to the bed and pulled off his boots and tunic. The wizard couldn't suppress another groan as he slid the sleeve over his broken wrist.

"Go fetch him more of Cook's brew," Nari said. "I'll get him settled."

"I'll have her make it strong enough to help you sleep," Tharin told him.

The scents of cedar and lavender rose from the eiderdown as Nari drew it over him and propped his arm on a cushion. The blue silk cover still showed fresh creases from being packed away. "You don't get many guests here, I gather," Arkoniel said, sinking gratefully into the deep, musty-smelling bed.

"The duke entertains his guests elsewhere, mostly." She smoothed the coverlet over his chest. "You know it's best this way. Tobin's safe."

"But not happy."

"That's not for me to say. He's a good boy, our Tobin. I couldn't ask for better. And his father dotes on him, or did. . . . The way he was today?" She shook her head. "It's been hard on him since the princess . . . Her dying like that—by the Light, Arkoniel, I fear it's broken him."

"How did it happen? I've heard only rumors."

Nari pulled a chair over and sat down. "The king came here to hunt. She saw him on the road from a window and dragged poor Tobin up to the tower. Well, Tobin won't speak of it, but he had a cut on his chin, and I found blood on the windowsill."

"The scar?"

"Yes, that's when he got it."

"You think she meant to kill him?"

Nari said nothing.

Muzzy as he was from the draught, Arkoniel stared at her, trying to fathom her silence. "You don't think— Nari, he's scarcely ten years old and undersized at that! How would he push a grown woman out a window?"

"I'm not saying he did! But there have been times when he seems to be possessed with the demon. He tore this room to pieces one day. I caught him at it! And the tower room when we finally found him? It was just the same."

"That's absurd."

Nari folded her hands and frowned down at them. "I'm sure you're right. Believe me, I don't want to think ill of the child. But he does talk to it now."

"To the demon?" Arkoniel thought of the whispering he'd heard in the kitchen and Tobin's plea to keep his secret.

"He thinks I don't hear, but I do. Sometimes it's at night, sometimes when he's in here playing alone. Poor thing. He's so lonely he'll talk to a ghost just for someone to play with."

"He has you and his father. And Tharin and the others seem very fond of him."

"Oh yes. But it's not the same for a child, is it? You're young enough to remember. What would you have done, shut away in an old house like this with nothing but servants and soldiers? And the men not even here most of the time? I'll bet you come from a house full of children."

Arkoniel chuckled. "I had five brothers. We all slept in the same bed and fought like badgers. When Iya took me on, I still found children to play with everywhere we traveled until it began to show that I was different."

"Well, our Tobin's as different as they come, and never has known what it is to play with another child. It's not right. I've said so all along. How is he supposed to know what folks are really like, shut away here?"

How, indeed? thought Arkoniel. "What does he do with his days?"

Nari snorted. "Works like a peasant child and trains to be a great warrior. You should see him at it with the men, like a puppy going at bears. He'll be lucky if he gets through the summer without another broken finger. Tharin and his father do say he's quick, and he shoots as well as some of the grown men."

"That's all?"

"He rides when someone can take him, and makes his little carvings—oh, but he's good at that!" She reached over to the windowsill and placed several little wax and wooden animals on the coverlet for him to see. They were quite good.

"And he plays in here." She pointed to the city, smiling fondly. "The duke made that for him years back. They spend hours with it. It's meant to be Ero, you know. But he's not allowed outside alone to ramble or fish as we did. As any child should! Noble boys his age are serving as pages at court by now. He can't do that, of course. But Rhius won't even allow any of the village children to visit. He's that terrified of being found out."

"He's right in that. Still . . ." Arkoniel pondered a moment. "What about the rest of the household. Does anyone else know?"

"No. Sometimes even I forget. He's our little prince. I can't think what it will be like when the change comes. Just imagine being told, 'Oh, by the by, pet, you're not . . .' "

She broke off as Tharin returned with the cup for Arkoniel. The captain said his good nights and left again, but Nari lingered a moment. Bending close to the wizard's ear, she whispered, "It's a pity Iya wouldn't let Rhius tell him. There's not a better friend to this family. Secrets. We're all about secrets here."

The second draught had the promised effect. Arkoniel slept like a stone, and dreamt of playing fox and geese with his brothers in his father's orchard. At some point he noticed Tobin watching them, but couldn't find the words to invite the child to join them. Then he was sitting in his mother's kitchen and the demon was there with him.

"I know the taste of your tears," it told him again.

He woke late the next morning with a full bladder and a nasty taste in his mouth. His left side was bruised from the fall and his arm throbbed from wrist to shoulder. Holding it against his chest, he found a chamber pot under the bed and was in the midst of using it when the door inched open. Tobin peeked in.

"Good morning, my prince!" Arkoniel slid the pot away and eased himself back onto the bed. "I don't suppose

you'd be so good as to tell Cook I need another of her po-
tions?"

Tobin disappeared so suddenly that Arkoniel wondered if he'd understood.

Or if that really was Tobin I was talking to.

But the boy soon returned with a mug and a small
brown loaf on a napkin. There was no hint of the previous night's shyness now, but he was still unsmiling and
reserved. He gave Arkoniel the food, then stood there
staring at him with those too-old eyes as he ate.

Arkoniel took a bite of the dense, warm bread. Cook
had split it and slipped a thick slice of well-aged cheese
inside. "Ah, that's wonderful!" he exclaimed, washing it
down with the brandy draught. It tasted weaker this time.

"I helped with the baking," Tobin told him.

"Did you? Well, you're a fine baker."

This won him not so much as a hint of a smile.
Arkoniel began to feel like a mediocre player before a
very critical audience. He tried another tack. "Nari tells me
you shoot very well."

"I brought home five grouse last week."

"I used to shoot quite well myself."

Tobin raised an eyebrow, just as Iya might have when
she was about to disapprove of something he'd said or
done. "Don't you anymore?"

"I went on to other studies and never seemed to find
the time."

"Wizards don't need to shoot?"

Arkoniel smiled. "We have other ways of getting
food."

"You don't beg, do you? Father says it's shameful for
any able-bodied man to beg."

"My father taught me the same. No, my teacher and I
travel and earn our bread. And sometimes we are guests,
like I am now with you."

"How will you earn your bread here?"

Arkoniel fought down the urge to chuckle. This child

would be checking his mattress next to see if he was steal-ing the spoons. "Wizards earn their keep with magic. We make things and fix things. And we entertain."

He stretched out his right hand and concentrated on the center of his palm. An apple-sized ball of light took shape there and resolved itself into a tiny dragon with transparent, batlike wings. "I saw these in Aurënen—"

Looking up, he found Tobin backing slowly away, eyes wide with fear.

This was hardly the reaction he'd hoped for. "Don't be scared. It's only an illusion."

"It's not real?" Tobin asked from the safety of the doorway.

"It's just a picture, a memory from my travels. I saw lots of these fingerlings at a place called Sarikali. Some of them grow to be larger than this keep, but they're very rare and live on mountains. But these little ones scamper everywhere. They're sacred creatures to the Aurënfaie. They have a legend about how the first 'faie were created—"

"From eleven drops of dragon blood. My father told me that story, and I know what the 'faie are," Tobin said, cutting him off as tersely as his father might have. "Some came here once. They played music. Did a dragon teach you?"

"No, a wizard named Iya is my teacher. You'll meet her someday." He let the dragon illusion fade away. "Would you like to see something else?"

Still poised for escape, Tobin glanced over his shoul-der into the corridor, then asked, "Like what?"

"Oh, anything, really. What would you most like to see?"

Tobin considered this. "I'd like to see the city."

"Ero, you mean?"

"Yes. I'd like to see my mother's house in Ero where I was born."

"Hmmm." Arkoniel quashed a stirring of disquiet. "Yes,

I can do that, but we'll have to use a different sort of magic. I need to hold your hand. Will you let me do that?"

The boy hesitated, then slowly came back to him and held out his hand.

Arkoniel took it in his and gave him a reassuring smile. "This is quite simple, but you may feel a little odd. It's going to be like having a dream while you're awake. Close your eyes."

Arkoniel could feel tension in the boy's thin, hard little hand, but Tobin did as he was asked.

"Good, now imagine that we're two great birds flying over the forest. What sort of bird would you like to be?"

Tobin pulled his hand away and took a step back. "I don't want to be a bird!"

Fear again, or was it just distrust? "It's just pretending, Tobin. You pretend when you play, don't you?"

This was met with a blank stare.

"Pretending. Imagining things that aren't really there." That was another misstep. Tobin cast a nervous look at the door.

Arkoniel looked around at the toys available. With any other child, he would have made the little ships in the city's harbor sail across the floor, or had the dusty wooden horse on wheels take a turn about the room, but something warned against it. Instead, he slid off the bed and limped over to the city. Seen at closer range, there was no mistaking the layout of streets and major buildings, even though it had seen some rough handling. Part of the western wall was missing, and there were holes in the clay base where some of the wooden houses had been lost. Those that remained varied from simple cubes of plain wood to fancy carved and painted ones recognizable as some of the principal houses and temples on the Palatine. The New Palace was done in detail, with rows of stick columns along the sides and tiny gilt emblems of the Four along its roof.

Little stick people lay scattered in the markets and on the roof of the wooden box that served as the Old Palace. He picked one up.

"Your father must have worked very hard to make all this. When you play with it, don't you imagine that you're one of these little fellows walking around the town?" He took his stick person by the head and marched it around the central market. "See, here you are in the great marketplace." He changed to a comic falsetto. " 'What shall I buy today? Think I'll see what Granny Sheda has for sweets at her booth. Now I'll run down to Fletcher Street and see if they have a new hunting bow just my size.' "

"No, you're doing it wrong." Tobin squatted down beside him and picked up another figure. "You can't be me. You have to be you."

"I can pretend to be you, can't I?"

Tobin shook his head emphatically. "I don't *want* anyone else to be me."

"Very well, I'll be me and you be you. Now, what if you stay you but change form." Covering Tobin's hand with his own, Arkoniel transformed the figure Tobin held into a small wooden eagle. "See, it's still you, but now you look like an eagle. You can do the same thing in your mind. Just imagine yourself with a different shape. It's not magic at all. My brothers and I spent hours being all sorts of things."

He'd half expected Tobin to drop the toy and flee, but instead, he was inspecting the little bird closely. And he was smiling.

"Can I show you something?" he asked.

"Of course."

Tobin ran from the room, still holding the bird, and returned a moment later with both hands cupped in front of him. Squatting down beside Arkoniel again, he spilled a dozen little carvings and wax figures on the floor between them, similar to the ones Nari had shown him earlier.

These were even better, though. There was a fox, several horses, a deer, and a pretty little wooden bird about the same size as the one he'd conjured.

"You made all these?"

"Yes." Tobin held up his bird and Arkoniel's. "Yours is better than mine, though. Can you teach me to make them your way?"

Arkoniel picked up a wooden horse and shook his head in wonder. "No. And yours are better, really. Mine are just a trick. These are the products of your hands and imagination. You must be an artist like your father."

"And my mama," Tobin said, looking pleased at the praise. "She made carvings, too, before the dolls."

"I didn't know that. You must miss her."

The smile disappeared. Tobin shrugged and began lining the animals and people up in phalanxes across the painted harbor. "How many brothers do you have?"

"Two now. I had five, but two died of plague and the oldest was killed fighting the Plenimarans. The others are both warriors, too."

"But not you."

"No, Illior had other plans for me."

"Have you always been a wizard?"

"Yes, but I didn't know it until my teacher found me when I was—" Arkoniel paused as if surprised. "Well, since I was just a bit younger than you are now."

"Were you very sad?"

"Why would I be sad?"

"Not to be a warrior like your brothers. Not to serve Skala with heart and sword."

"We all serve in our own way. Did you know that wizards fought in the Great War? The king has some in his army now."

"But you're not," Tobin pointed out. This clearly lowered Arkoniel in his eyes.

"As I said, there are many ways to serve. And a country doesn't just need warriors. It needs scholars and builders and farmers." He held up Tobin's bird. "And artists! You can be an artist and a warrior, too. Now, how would you like to see the great city you'll be protecting, my young warrior? Are you ready?"

Tobin nodded and held out his hand again. "So I should pretend that I'm a bird, but I'm still me?"

Arkoniel grinned. "You'll always be you, no matter what. Now relax and breathe like you're asleep, very gently. Good. What kind of a bird will you be?"

"An eagle."

"Then I'll be one, too, or I won't be able to keep up."

This time Tobin relaxed easily and Arkoniel silently wove the spell that would project his own memories into Tobin's mind. Careful to avoid any sudden transitions, he began the vision with them both perched in a tall fir that overlooked the meadow outside. "Can you see the forest and the house?"

"Yes!" Tobin replied in an awed whisper. "It is like dreaming."

"Good. You know how to fly, so spread your wings and come with me."

Tobin did with surprising readiness. "I can see the town now."

"We're going to fly east now." Arkoniel summoned an image of trees and fields passing rapidly below them, then conjured Ero and poised them high above the Old Palace, trying to give the boy a recognizable view. Below them, the Palatine Circle looked like a round green eye atop the crowded hill.

"I see it!" Tobin whispered. "It's just like my city, only lots more houses and streets and colors. May I see the harbor, and ships?"

"We'll have to fly to it. The vision is limited." Arkoniel smiled to himself. So there was a child behind that stern face, after all. Together, they swooped down to the harbor and circled the round-bellied carracks and longboats moored there.

"I want to sail on ships like that!" Tobin exclaimed. "I want to see all the Three Lands, and the 'faie, too."

"Perhaps you can sing with them."

"No . . ."

The vision dimmed as something distracted the boy. "You must concentrate," Arkoniel reminded him. "Don't let any worries bother you. I can't do this for very long. Where else would you like to go?"

"To my mother's house."

"Ah, yes. Back up to the Palatine we go." He guided Tobin to the warren of walled houses that lay between the Old and New Palaces.

"Mama's is that one," Tobin said. "I know it by the golden griffins along the roofline."

"Yes." Rhius had taught his son well.

As they circled closer, the vision faltered again, but this time the problem did not lie with the boy. Arkoniel felt a growing uneasiness as the shape of the house and its grounds became more distinct. He could pick out the yards and outbuildings, and the courtyard where the tall chestnut tree stood, marking the dead twin's grave. As they drew closer, however it withered before his eyes. Gnarled bare branches reached up to snare him like clawed fingers, just as the roots had held Tobin in his vision by the sea.

"By the Light—!" he gasped, trying to end the vision before Tobin saw. It was ended for him as a blast of cold buffeted them both. The vision collapsed, leaving him reeling and momentarily blind.

"No, no!" Tobin cried,

Arkoniel felt the boy's hand yanked from his. Something struck him a stinging blow on the cheek and the pain broke the last of the magic, clearing his mind and his eyes.

The entire room was shaking. The wardrobe doors

banged open, then slammed again with a crash. Chests jittered against the walls, and objects flew through the air in all directions.

Tobin knelt by the city, holding down the roof of the Palace with both hands. "Stop it!" he cried. "Go away, Wizard. *Please!* Get out!"

Arkoniel stayed where he was. "Tobin, I can't—"

Nari rushed in and ran to the boy. Tobin clung to her, pressing his face to her shoulder.

"What are you doing?" she cried, giving Arkoniel an accusing glare.

"I was just—" The roof of the Palace spun up into the air and he caught it with his good hand. "We were looking at the city. Your demon didn't care for that."

He could see enough of Tobin's face to know that the boy's lips were moving, forming quick, silent words against the dark fabric of Nari's loose gown.

The room went still, but an ominous heaviness remained, like a lull in a thunderstorm. Tobin struggled free of his nurse and fled the room.

Nari looked around at the mess and sighed. "You see what it's like for us? No telling what it will do, or why. Illior and Bilairy shield us from angry spirits!"

Arkoniel nodded, but he knew exactly why the thing had chosen the moment it did this time. He thought again of bending over a small, still body beneath that chestnut tree, weeping as it sank out of sight, his tears sinking into the hard earth. Yes, it knew the taste of his tears.

Tobin wanted nothing to do with him after that, so Arkoniel spent the rest of the day quietly exploring the keep. The pain in his arm required several draughts of Cook's infusion, and its dulling effects left him feeling like he was walking about in a dream.

His original impression of the keep was borne out in daylight; it was only partially inhabitable. The upper floor was in total disrepair. Once-handsome chambers lay in ruin, overrun by rats and rot. Leakage from the roof or attics above had destroyed the fine murals and furnishings.

Strangely enough, there was evidence that someone had continued to frequent these gloomy rooms. Several sets of footprints were visible in the dust that covered the bare floors. One room in particular had had a frequent, small-footed visitor, though the footprints had a new layer of fine grit in them now. This room lay halfway along the corridor and was sounder than its neighbors, and better lit thanks to the loss of a shutter on one of the tall, narrow windows.

Tobin had come here on numerous occasions, and always went to the back corner of the room. A cedarwood chest of Mycenian design stood here, and the dust on its ornate painted lid continued the tale. Arkoniel summoned a small orb of light and bent to examine the smudges and finger marks there. Tobin had come here to open this chest. Inside Arkoniel found nothing but a few tabards of ancient cut.

Perhaps it had been a game of some sort? Yet what game would a child play alone, a child who did not know how to pretend? Arkoniel looked around the dirty, shadowed room, imagining Tobin here all by himself. His small footprints crossed and recrossed each other for however many days the game had lasted. Another pang of compassion pierced the young wizard's heart, this time for the living twin.

Equally intriguing were the sets of tracks that led to the far end of the corridor. The door here was new, and the only one that was locked.

Placing his hand over the bronze key plate, he examined the intricacies of its mechanism. It would have been a relatively easy matter to trick it open, but the unwritten laws of guesting forbade such a coarse trespass. He already suspected where it led.

Threw herself from the tower window—

Arkoniel rested his forehead against the door's cool surface. Ariani had fled here, fled to her death taking her child with her. Or had Tobin followed? It had been too long and too many others had come and gone here since for him to read the tale of their tracks.

Nari's vague suspicions still nagged at him. Possession was rare, and he did not believe Tobin would have hurt Ariani himself. But Arkoniel had felt the demon's rage three times now; it possessed both the strength and will to kill. But why kill his mother, who'd been as much a victim of circumstance as he and his twin?

Downstairs, he crossed the gloomy hall and went outside. The duke was nowhere to be seen, but his men were busy packing horses and stacking arms for the journey back to Ero.

"How's the arm today?" asked Tharin, coming over to him.

"I think it will mend very well. Thank you."

"Captain Tharin keeps us all mended," a young sandy-haired man remarked, swaggering by with a handful of tools. "So you're the young wizard who can't manage a gelded two-year-old?"

"Mind yourself, Sefus, or he'll turn you into something useful," an older man snapped from a lean-to workshop built against the courtyard wall. "Get over here and help with the harness, you lazy pup!"

"Don't mind Sefus," another young soldier told him, grinning. "He gets irritable when he's away from the brothels too long."

"I don't imagine any of you enjoy being so far from the city. This doesn't seem a very cheerful place."

"Took you all morning to figure that one out, did it?" Tharin replied with a chuckle.

"Are the men good to the boy?"

"Do you think Rhius would tolerate anyone who wasn't? The sun rises and sets on that child, as far as he's concerned.

Far as any of us are concerned, for that matter. It's not To-bin's fault." He gestured at the house. "Not any of it."

The defensiveness with which he declared this was not lost on Arkoniel. "Of course not," he agreed. "Does anyone say it is?"

"Tongues always wag. You get something like a de-mon haunting the king's own sister and you can imagine what the gossips do with that. Why else do you think Rhius stuck his poor wife and son out here, so far from proper society? A princess, living here? And a prince? No wonder . . . Well, that's enough said about that. There's enough ignorant gossip in the town. Back in Ero, even."

"Perhaps Rhius is right. Tobin might not be happy in the city with all those wagging tongues. He's old enough to understand now."

"Yes. And it would break his father's heart. Mine too, for that matter. He's a good boy, our Tobin. One of these days he'll come into his own."

"I don't doubt it."

Leaving Tharin to his preparations, Arkoniel made a circuit of the outer walls.

Here, too, he saw sad evidence of neglect and de-cline. There had been gardens here once. A few bush roses ran wild against the remains of crumbling stone en-closures, and he could see the brown dry seed heads of rare peonies here and there, fighting to hold their ground amidst the wild native blooms of willow bay, daisy, milk-weed, and broom. Ariani had had banks of peonies in her garden at Ero, he recalled. In the early months of summer, huge vases of them had scented the entire house.

Only a kitchen garden between a back gate and the river's edge was still tended here now. Arkoniel plucked a sprig of fennel and chewed it as he let himself in the back gate.

This let onto a rear court. Entering by an open door, he found himself back in the kitchen. Cook, who seemed to have no other name, was busy preparing the evening meal with the help of Tobin, Nari, and Sefus.

"I don't know, pet," Nari was saying, sounding annoyed. "Why do you ask such things?"

"Ask what things?" Arkoniel joined them at the table. As he sat down, he saw what Tobin had been doing and grinned. Five white turnip sheep were being stalked by a pair of beet root bears and a carroty something that looked vaguely like the dragon Arkoniel had shown him that morning.

"Cook used to be an archer and fight the Plenimarans with Father like Tharin does," Tobin said. "But she says the king doesn't like women to be in his army anymore. Why is that?"

"You were a soldier?" asked Arkoniel.

Cook straightened from stirring a kettle and wiped her hands on her apron front. Arkoniel hadn't paid much attention to her before, but now he saw a flash of pride as she nodded. "I was. I served the last queen with Duke Rhius' father, and the king after her for a time. I'd be serving still—my eye and arm are still true—but the king don't like seeing women in the ranks." She gave a shrug. "So, here you find me."

"But *why*?" Tobin insisted, starting work on another turnip.

"Maybe girls can't fight proper," Sefus said with a smirk.

"I was worth three of you, and I wasn't even the best!" Cook snapped. Snatching up a cleaver, she set to work on a joint of mutton as if it were a Plenimaran foot soldier.

Arkoniel recognized Sefus' smug attitude. He'd seen plenty of it in recent years. "Women can be fine warriors, and wizards, too, if they have the heart and the training," Arkoniel told Tobin. "Heart and training; that's what it takes to be good at anything. Remember how I told you this morning that I don't shoot anymore? Well, I wasn't very good to begin with, or at swordplay, either. I wouldn't have been much use to anyone as a warrior. Why, if Iya hadn't made a wizard of me, I'd probably be a scullion instead of a scholar!" He cast a sidelong glance at Sefus. "Not too long ago, I met an old woman who'd been both warrior and wizard in the wars. She fought with Queen Ghërilain, who won the war because she was such a good warrior herself. You do know about the warrior queens of Skala, don't you?"

"I have them in a box upstairs," Tobin replied, still engrossed in his carving. In a singsong voice, he recited: "There's King Thelátimos, who got told by Oracle to give his crown to his daughter, then Ghërilain the Founder, Tamír the Murder, Agnalain who isn't my grandmama, Ghërilain the Second, Iaair who fought the dragon, Klia who killed the lion, Klie, Markira, Oslie with six fingers, Marnil who wanted a daughter so much but Oracle gave her a new husband instead, and Agnalain who is my grandmama. And then the king my uncle."

"Ah, I see." Arkoniel paused, trying to unravel the garbled litany. Clearly, Tobin had little understanding of what he'd just rattled off, beyond a few odd or interesting facts. "Agnalain the First, you mean. And Queen Tamír, who was murdered."

Tobin shrugged.

"Well, you have the names right, but do—"

Nari cleared her throat loudly and gave Arkoniel a warning look. "Duke Rhius sees to Tobin's education. He'll instruct the boy about such things when he thinks fit."

He needs a proper tutor, Arkoniel thought, then blinked at the resonance the notion struck in his mind: teacher, friend, companion. Guardian. "When is the duke leaving?" he asked.

"First light tomorrow," Sefus told him.

"Well then, I'd best pay my respects tonight. Will he and the men be dining in the hall?"

" 'Course," Tobin mumbled. Under his knife, a turnip was changing into another dragon.

Excusing himself, Arkoniel hurried upstairs to compose his thoughts, hoping that the idea that had come clear so suddenly was indeed an inspiration sent by the Lightbearer.

He needed very much to believe that, for that's what he was going to tell Rhius.

And Iya.

Chapter 18

Arkoniel found himself seated on Rhius' right at the evening meal, and served by Tharin and several of the men. The food, though well seasoned, was shockingly simple and sparse. This only strengthened the wizard's concerns. In Ero and Atyion, Rhius had hosted lavishly. There were always color and music there; feasts of twenty courses, and a hundred guests all glittering with jewels, silks, and furs. The life Tobin knew here was little different than that of a landless backcountry knight.

Rhius himself was severely dressed in a short dark robe accented with a bit of fox and gold. His only jewel was a large mourning ring. Tobin could have passed for a serving boy in his plain tunic. Arkoniel doubted the boy owned more than two suits of clothes, and this was probably his best.

The duke paid Arkoniel little attention during the meal, focusing instead on Tobin, telling him stories of court and the wars. Listening quietly, Arkoniel thought the exchange seemed hollow and forced. Tobin looked miserable. Seated far down the table, Nari caught the wizard's eye and silently shook her head.

When the meal was finished Rhius moved to a large chair by the open hearth and sat staring into the small fire laid there. Neither dismissed nor invited, Arkoniel settled uncomfortably on the hearth bench beside him and waited, listening to the crackle of the flames as he searched for words to broach his request.

"My lord?" Arkoniel ventured at last.

Rhius didn't look up. "What is it you want of me now, Wizard?"

"Nothing but a word in private, if you please."

He thought the duke might refuse, but Rhius stood and led Arkoniel outside to a path into the meadow. They followed it down the hillside to the riverbank.

It was a cool, pleasant evening. The sun's last rays lit the sky behind the peaks, stretching their shadows over the keep and meadow. Swallows flitted after their supper overhead. Frogs tuned their throats under the riverbank.

They stood watching the roiling water in silence for a time, and then Rhius turned to Arkoniel. "Well? I've given you a child and a wife. What would your mistress have of me now?"

"Nothing, my lord, except the safety and well-being of your remaining child."

Rhius let out a derisive laugh. "I see."

"I don't think you do. If Tobin is to be—what we wish him to be, he must understand the world he will inherit. You did right, protecting him here, but he's older now. He needs to learn the ways of dress and manner, and the courtly arts. He must have teachers. He also needs friends of his own age, other children—"

"No! You've seen the demon that haunts him, thanks to the fumbling of your filthy witch that night. Mothers from here to Ero scare their brats with tales of the 'haunted child at the keep.' Didn't you know? Oh, but how could you, since neither you nor your mistress deigned to come back to us until now? Shall I send Tobin and his demon to court, present them to the king? Just how long would it be before one of Erius' creatures saw through the veil with their sharp eyes and killing spells?"

"But that isn't possible. That's why we brought the witch—"

"I won't take that risk! Erius may still wear a mourning ring for his sister, but how sentimental will he be if he learns that her surviving child is—" He caught himself and lowered his voice to a scathing hiss. "A true heir? If you imagine that *any* of us whom he saw there that night in the birthing chamber would be spared, then you are a fool. As much as I might welcome death, think of the child. Have we come this far to throw it away on the whim of . . ." He paused, waving a hand at Arkoniel. "Of a half-trained apprentice wizard?"

Arkoniel ignored the insult. "Then let me bring children here, my lord. Children from another province who haven't heard the tales. Tobin is a prince; by right he should join the Prince Royal's Companions soon, or have a company of Companions of his own. What will the nobles at Ero say about the king's own nephew, the child of a princess and a high lord, growing up like a peasant? Tobin must be prepared."

Rhius gazed out at the river, saying nothing, but Arkoniel sensed he'd struck his mark.

"Tobin is still young, but soon his absence at court will be noted—perhaps even by the king's wizards. And then they'll come here looking for him. No matter what we do, you'll have to present him at court sooner or later. The less odd he seems—"

"One, then. One child here, as a companion. But only if you agree to my terms." He turned bleak eyes on Arkoniel. "First: should this other child discover our secret, you will kill him yourself."

"My lord—"

Rhius leaned closer, speaking very low. "My own child had to die. Why should a stranger's child live to jeopardize our plans?"

Arkoniel nodded, knowing that Iya would exact the same promise. "And your second requirement?"

When Rhius spoke again, the anger was gone. In the gathering gloom, he looked stooped and old—a sad, hollow effigy of the man he'd once been. "That you will remain here and be Tobin's tutor. You're of noble birth and know something of the court. I won't chance bringing another stranger into my house. Stay and guard my child until the world is set right."

Arkoniel felt dizzy with relief. "I will, my lord. By my hands and heart and eyes, I will." This was the fulfillment of the vision he'd been given at Afra, and Rhius himself had proposed it.

"But if you will permit me, my lord," he said, proceeding gingerly with his own elaborations. "You're a very wealthy man, yet your child is being raised in a tomb. Couldn't you make this place a proper home for him? I'll need chambers of my own, too, for sleeping and study. The rooms on the third floor could be repaired. And we'll need a room for Tobin's lessons—"

"Yes, very well!" Rhius snapped, throwing up his hands. "Do what you will. Hire workmen. Fix the roof. Have gold chamber pots cast if you like, so long as you protect my child." He stared at the keep for a moment.

The barracks windows glowed warmly and they could hear men singing around the watch fire. Beyond it, the keep looked abandoned except for a thin sliver of light showing at a second-level window.

Rhius let out a long sigh. "By the Four, it has become a tomb, hasn't it? This was a handsome house once, with gardens and fine stables. My ancestors hosted hunts and feasts here in the autumn and queens guested. I—I always hoped that Ariani would be well again and help me make it fine again."

"A future queen calls this home. Make it beautiful for her. After all, Tobin is an artist and for such people the eye feeds the soul."

Rhius nodded. "Do what you will, Arkoniel. But leave the tower as it is. No one is to go there. The shutters are nailed down and the doors have no keys."

"As you will, my lord."

The swallows had gone to roost and little brown bats had come out to hunt moths. Fireflies flashed in the long grass, turning the darkened meadow into a mirror of the starry sky above.

"There'll be a real war again soon, I think," Rhius said. "It's been skirmishes and sword rattling for years now, but Plenimar is chafing harder against her borders every year."

"War?" Arkoniel asked, surprised by this abrupt change of subject. "Then you don't think Plenimar will uphold the Treaty of Kouros?"

"I stood beside the king when Overlord Cyranius put his seal to it. I watched his face. No, I don't think he will keep the treaty. He wants the Three Lands as an empire again, as they were under the hierophants. But this time he'll sit on the throne, not a priest king. He wants the lands of Mycena, and he wants the wizards of Skala."

"I suppose so." Aurënen had long ago cut off trade with Plenimar; there were no longer the necessary intermarriages to maintain the wizard bloodlines in Plenimar. In his travels he'd heard rumors of Plenimaran pirates attacking Aurënfaie ships and carrying off prisoners for forced breeding, like animals.

"These past few years they've been testing us, feinting in and out of the islands and raiding our shores," Rhius went on. "I only hope Tobin is old enough when the time comes."

"We must make him ready in every way we can."

"Indeed. Good night, Arkoniel." Rhius bowed and started back up the path, still looking bowed and old.

The wizard remained by the river, listening to the quiet sounds that filled the warm summer night and wondering what a battle sounded like. He'd left his father's house before he could carry a sword. He smiled, recalling Tobin's disdainful reaction to his choice of vocation.

As he started up the hill the tower caught his eye again, and he thought he saw one of the shutters move.

He thought again of casting, but Rhius' order stopped him. It had probably only been a bat.

*T*obin had watched the two men in the meadow from his window. He knew who they were; Brother had told him.

The wizard will stay, Brother whispered in the shadows behind him.

"Why?" Tobin demanded. He didn't want Arkoniel to stay. He didn't like him at all. There was something wrong behind his smile, and he was too tall and too loud and had a long face like a horse. Worst of all, though, he'd surprised Tobin with his magic and expected him to like it.

Tobin hated surprises. They always ended badly.

"Why is he staying?" he asked again, then turned to see if Brother had heard him.

The flame of the little night lamp by his bed was hardly more than a fuzzy patch of light now. This was Brother's doing. Since Lhel had bound them together with the doll, Tobin could see the darkness Brother sometimes made, especially at night. Some nights Tobin could hardly see at all.

There you are, he thought, catching sight of a slither of shadow along the far wall. "What are they saying down there?"

Brother slipped away, saying nothing.

Tobin often wished he hadn't kept the ugly doll, that it had fallen out the window with his mama. He'd even slipped away from the house again a few weeks ago, hoping to find Lhel and make her take her magic back, but he didn't dare leave the riverbank this time and she didn't hear him calling.

So he'd gone on obeying her instructions, summoning Brother every day and letting the spirit follow him around. He couldn't tell if Brother enjoyed this or not; he still leered at Tobin sometimes and twitched his fingers, as if he wanted to pinch him or pull his hair the way he used to. But Brother didn't hurt him anymore, not since Lhel had put his blood and hair on the doll.

Almost without realizing it, Tobin had begun to call for Brother more often lately, even inviting him to play with the city. Brother just watched while Tobin moved his wooden people about the streets and sailed the little ships, but it was better than being alone.

Tobin searched the dark corners of the room for movement. Even when he sent Brother away, he didn't go very far. The servants still complained of his antics. The only person he'd seriously hurt, however, was Arkoniel.

As much as Tobin disliked the wizard, he was angry with Brother for that. He'd had to do the calling spell right in front of the man and Arkoniel had seen something, perhaps even heard the words. If he told Tobin's father, then sooner or later they'd find out about the doll, and then his father would be ashamed and the men would laugh like the people in the town and he would never be a warrior.

Tobin's belly cramped painfully as he turned back to the window; perhaps that's what his father and the wizard were talking about out there. Arkoniel had promised not to tell but Tobin didn't trust him. He didn't trust anyone anymore, really, except maybe Tharin.

When it got too dark to see his father in the meadow, Tobin crawled into bed and lay rigid between the sweaty sheets, waiting for angry voices.

Instead, Nari came to bed presently looking very pleased.

"You'll never guess what's happened!" she exclaimed as she began unlacing the sleeves of her gown. "That young wizard is to stay on and be your tutor. Not only that, but you're to have a companion! Arkoniel is going to write to his teacher, asking her to find a suitable boy. You'll have a proper playfellow at last, pet, just as a young prince should! What do you think of that?"

"What if he doesn't like me?" Tobin mumbled, thinking again of the way the townspeople looked at him and gossiped behind their hands.

Nari clucked her tongue and climbed in beside him. "Who wouldn't like you, pet? And to be companion to a prince, the king's only nephew? Any boy would be thrilled with such an honor!"

"But what if he's not nice?" Tobin insisted.

"Why, then I'll send the little fool packing myself," Nari declared. Then, more gently, "Don't you fret, love. Don't you worry about a thing."

Tobin sighed and pretended to go to sleep. There was a great deal to worry about, as far as he was concerned, not the least of which was being saddled with ill-tempered ghosts and loud, laughing, sharp-eyed wizards.

Chapter 19

Iya read Arkoniel's brief letter over several times while the duke's courier waited outside in the inn yard for her reply. Pressing the little parchment to her heart, she gazed at the crowded harbor outside her window and tried to sort out her warring emotions.

Her initial response was much like the duke's; to bring in the child of another noble put both houses at risk. Yet in her heart she knew Arkoniel was correct. She looked down at the letter again.

I know you will disapprove of my decision, perhaps even be angry at my presumption, but I believe I am right in this. The child is nearly ten, and already so strange in his ways that I fear he'll fare poorly at court when he is grown. The household is overbearingly protective. This child has never gone swimming on a hot day or had an afternoon to himself in the meadow outside the gates. For the sake of his mother's memory and her line, we must do what we can—

"Him, indeed," Iya murmured, pleased that Arkoniel had been so careful. Letters too often fell into the wrong hands, by mistake or design.

I leave the choice of companion to you, of course. Yes, here he tried to placate her after he'd already gone his own way. *The boy should be cheerful, brave, light of heart, and much interested in the arts of war and hunting, for he finds me sorely lacking in those regards. Since the keep is so lonely and the prince does not attend court yet, perhaps you might find a boy who will not be too dearly missed by*

his family, if he should be long away. He should not be a
first-born son.

She nodded to herself, understanding the implication
all too well; this must be an expendable boy.

She tucked the letter away, already making her plans.
She'd visit some of the country lords who had small holdings here in the southern mountains. They ran to large
families.

Such concerns helped fend off the deeper implication
of his proposal: Arkoniel was going to stay with Tobin. He
was far enough along in his training to leave her for a
time, of course, or even to strike out on his own. Other
students had left her, contented with less. Arkoniel knew
enough already to be entrusted with the bowl when the
time came.

All the same, she hated to be without him. He was the
finest pupil she had ever had, capable of learning far more
than he had as yet. Far more than she knew to teach him,
come to that. But a few years apart would not unmake
him as a wizard.

No, it was the memory of his visions that haunted her,
the visions in which she had no part. She was not ready to
be without him, the son of her heart.

Chapter 20

As Tobin had feared, the wizard began changing things almost at once, though not quite in the way he'd expected.

Arkoniel remained in the toy room for the time being, but within a week of Father's departure workers began arriving by the cartload and set up a small village of tents in the meadow. A steady stream of wagons followed, laden with materials of every sort. Soon the courtyards and empty barracks were stacked with lumber, stone, mixing troughs, and heavy sacks. Tobin wasn't allowed to go out among the strangers, so he stood at his window instead and watched them bustling about.

He'd never realized how quiet the keep was until now. Banging and clanging came from every direction all day long, and with it the loud voices of the workers, shouting directions or singing songs.

A crew of masons clattered about on the roof with slates and pots of hot lead and tar, so that by night and day it looked like the roof was on fire. Another gang came into the house and took over the third level and the great hall all at once, shoving the furniture about and filling the house with the exciting new smells of wet lime and sawdust.

Arkoniel gained a little in Tobin's favor when he insisted that Tobin be allowed to watch the craftsmen at work. One night, after Nari had tucked him into bed, Brother came and led Tobin to the top of the stairs to listen to an argument going on below. Nari and Arkoniel were standing by the hearth.

"I don't care what you or Duke Rhius says," Nari sputtered, balling her hands in her apron front the way she did when she was upset. "It's not safe! What's the sense of being out here in the midst of nowhere—"

"I'll stay by him," the wizard interrupted. "By the Light, woman, you can't keep him wrapped in fleece his whole life. And there's so much he can learn. He's clearly got an aptitude for such things."

"Oh, so you'd have him grow up to wear a mason's apron rather than a crown, would you?"

Tobin chewed his thumbnail thoughtfully, wondering what they meant. He'd never heard that a prince could wear a crown. His mother hadn't that he knew of, and she'd lived at the palace when she was little. But if wearing a mason's apron meant he'd be able to use a trowel and mortar to build walls, then he wouldn't mind that. He'd spied on the crew working upstairs that day when Nari wasn't looking, and it had been interesting. He guessed it would be far more fun than his other lessons with Arkoniel, learning verse by heart and memorizing the names of the stars.

Before he could learn who was going to win this argument, Brother whispered to him to hurry back to bed. He made it to his room and got the door shut before Mynir passed by, whistling happily and rattling his keys on their iron ring.

Fortunately, Arkoniel won, and he and Tobin spent the next day watching the workmen.

The tools of the plasterers and stonecutters, and the ease with which they wielded them, fascinated Tobin. Whole walls went from dirty grey to sugar white in a morning's time.

But it was the wood-carver he admired most. She was a slight, pretty woman with ugly hands, who shaped wood with her chisels and knives like it was butter. The broken newel post in the hall had been torn out the day before and Tobin watched with rapt attention as she carved a new one out of a long block of dark wood. It seemed to Tobin that she was digging into the wood to find the pattern of fruited vines that already existed inside. When he shyly told her this, she nodded.

"That's just how I see it, Your Highness. I take a piece of fine wood like this in my hands and ask it, 'What treasure are you holding inside for me?' "

"Prince Tobin does the same with vegetables and lumps of wax," Arkoniel told her.

"I carve wood, too," Tobin said, waiting for the artist to laugh at him. Instead, she whispered to Arkoniel, then went to a pile of scrap lying nearby and brought him a piece of pale yellow wood about the size of a brick. She handed him two of her sharp carving blades, too, and asked, "Would you like to see what's inside this piece?"

Tobin spent the rest of the afternoon sitting on the ground beside her, and at the end of the day presented her with a fat otter that was only a little lopsided. She was so pleased that she traded him the knives for it.

When they weren't watching the workmen, Tobin and Arkoniel took long rides or walks on the forest roads. These turned into lessons, too, without Tobin even noticing. Arkoniel might not know how to fight or shoot properly, but he knew a great deal about herbs and trees. He began by letting Tobin show him the ones he knew, then taught him others, together with their uses. They picked wintergreen and dug wild ginger in shaded forest glades, and gathered wild strawberries and bunches of goosegrass, sorrel, and dock in the meadow for Cook's soups.

Tobin still distrusted the wizard, but found he could tolerate him. Arkoniel wasn't so loud now, and never did any magic. Even though he wasn't a hunter, he knew as much as Tharin did about tracking and traveling the forest.

They ranged far up the mountainside, and now and then came across a trail or clearing that seemed familiar to Tobin. But he saw no sign of Lhel.

Unbeknownst to Arkoniel, Brother was often with them, a silent, watchful presence.

As soon as the masons finished their work in the great hall, the painters began scratching out their designs on the fresh plaster. As a long band of design took shape along the top of one wall, Tobin cocked his head and remarked, "That looks a little like oak leaves and acorns, but not quite."

"It's not meant to be a picture of anything," Arkoniel explained. "Just a pattern that pleases the eye. He'll do rows and rows of different patterns and paint them with bright colors."

They climbed the rickety scaffolding and Arkoniel had the artist show Tobin how he used a brass straightedge and calipers to mark out the shapes and keep the lines even.

When they came down again, Tobin ran upstairs to the toy room and took the neglected writing materials from the chest. Laying them out on the table in his room, he began a row of patterns, using his fingers for calipers and a piece of broken practice blade for a straightedge. He had half a row done when he noticed Arkoniel watching from the doorway.

Tobin kept working to the edge of the page, then sat back to inspect his effort. "It's not very good."

Arkoniel came over and looked at it. "No, but it's not bad for a first effort, either."

That was his way. While Nari praised whatever Tobin did, whether it was good or not, Arkoniel was more like Tharin—finding the good in an effort without praising it more than it deserved.

"Let's see if I can do it." Arkoniel took a sheet of

parchment from the pile and turned it over, then stood there with a strange sick expression on his face. This side of the sheet was covered with lines of small words Tobin's mother had written one day while he traced his letters. Tobin couldn't read it, but he could see that it upset Arkoniel.

"What does it say?" he asked.

Arkoniel swallowed hard and cleared his throat, but Brother tore the page from his hand and sent it sailing across the room before he could read it.

"It was just a bit of verse about birds."

Tobin retrieved the sheet and stuck it at the bottom of the pile so Brother wouldn't get more upset. The uppermost parchment had several lines of practice letters on it, all smudged and blurred from his tracing.

"Mama was teaching me my letters," he said, running a finger over them.

"I see. Would you like to show me what you've learned so far?" Arkoniel tried to smile as if nothing were wrong, but his gaze kept straying to the parchment Brother had taken and he looked sad.

Tobin laboriously wrote out the eleven letters he knew. He hadn't drawn them in months and they came out very crooked. Some were even upside down again. He'd forgotten most of their names and sounds, too.

"You're off to a good start. Would you like me to make you some more to trace?"

Tobin shook his head, but the wizard was already scratching away with the pen.

Soon Tobin was so busy that he forgot all about the verse Arkoniel had not read to him, and Brother's small tantrum.

Arkoniel waited until Tobin was engrossed in his work, then carefully pulled at the edge of the parchment the demon had snatched away, tugging it out just far enough to see the lines Ariani had written:

Only in my tower can I hear the bird's song
My prison is my freedom. My heart sings only there
With the dead for company
Only the dead speak clearly, and the birds

Tobin had secretly fretted over the impending arrival of the promised companion, but when none immediately arrived he happily forgot about it, assuming his father had changed his mind.

There were far too many people in the house as it was. For as long as he could remember, the house had been shadowy and peaceful. Now workers tramped in and out at all hours. When he wearied of watching the craftsmen, he retreated to the kitchen with Nari and Cook, both of whom seemed absurdly pleased with all the commotion, despite what Nari had said about Tobin mixing with the workers.

But no one was more pleased than old Mynir. Even though it appeared to be the wizard's fault that all the changes were being made, Mynir was in charge, and he'd never looked happier than when he was instructing the workmen on the colors and designs to use. He met with merchants in the hall, too, and soon polished plate appeared on the bare shelves and bright new hangings arrived by the cartload.

"Ah, Tobin, this is what I used to do at Atyion!" he said one day as they inspected the new hangings. "Your father is letting me make this into a proper house at last!"

As much as he enjoyed watching the workers, however, as the repairs progressed Tobin began to feel uneasy about the results. The more the house changed, the harder it was for him to think of his father or mother living there. When Mynir began to talk of changes to his own bedchamber, Tobin slammed the door and pushed a chest against it, refusing to come out until the steward promised him through the latch hole that it would be left alone.

And so the work continued around him. Sometimes,

at night, before Nari came up to join him, he crept to the top of the great stairway and stared down into the bright, colorful new hall, imagining it as it had been before his father began staying away so much. Perhaps if they changed it too much, Father wouldn't want to come back at all.

Chapter 21

Finding a suitable companion for Tobin proved to be a more difficult task than Iya had expected.

She wasn't especially fond of children in general. For decades the only ones she'd anything to do with were the wizard born. None of her students were ordinary to start with, and training and time soon brought out the bright flashes of ability. With these children she relived her own tentative first steps, early frustrations, and glories; and she exulted with them as they claimed the power of their own unique natures. No two were alike in power or ability, but that made no difference. The joy was in finding a vein of talent in a novice and following it to its core.

But this . . . As her search stretched dismally from weeks to a month, her opinion of ordinary children was not much improved. She found children enough among the country nobles, but not one who struck her as any more interesting than a turnip.

Lord Evir, whose house she had visited first, had six fine boys, two of them of an age and ability to serve, but they were thick, heavy-footed bullcalves, dull as moles.

She went to Lady Morial's great holding next, recalling that some number of babes had been born there. The good widow had a son just turned ten who seemed lively enough, but when Iya brushed his mind with hers, she found it already stained with greed and envy. One could not well serve a prince, or a queen, if one coveted their station.

So she traveled on, moving slowly up the spine of

Skala, encountering yet more turnips, moles, and vipers-to-be. She was within a week's ride of Ero when the first rains of Rhythin came. She wandered on through the cold, misty drizzle, searching for the estate of Lord Jorvai of Colath, whom she'd known as a youth.

Two days later, with the afternoon waning and no sign of estate or shelter in sight, the muddy road she'd been following ended abruptly at the bank of a swollen stream. She tried to urge her mare on, but the beast shied and sidestepped.

"Damnation!" Iya shouted, looking around at the empty barrens that surrounded her on every side. She couldn't wade the flood and there was no inn nearby if she turned back. She had passed a side road an hour or so earlier, she recalled, wrapping her sodden cloak more closely around her. That had to lead somewhere.

She'd backtracked less than half a mile when a small band of riders appeared out of the mist, leading a string of fine horses. They were a hard-bitten lot, either soldiers or bandits by the look of their gear. Iya put on a brave face to meet them. As they drew up ahead of her, she noted that one of the riders was a woman, though she looked as rough and grim as any of the others.

Their leader was a tall, gaunt old man whose long grey moustaches framed a mouth full of broken teeth. "What's your business on this road, woman?" he challenged.

"And who might you be to ask?" Iya retorted, already weaving a blinding spell at the back of her mind. There were only seven of them. From the dark looks she was getting, the horses they led were probably stolen.

"I'm Sir Larenth of Oakmount Stead, a tenant of Lord Jorvai, whose lands you're on." He jerked a thumb at the woman and two of the others. These are my sons, Alon and Khemeus, and my daughter Ahra. We guard Jorvai's roads."

"I beg pardon, then. I'm Iya of Maker's Ford, a free

wizard of Skala. And as it happens, I was seeking your lord myself, but I believe I've lost my way."

"By a good mark, too. His manor is half a day's ride back the way you came," Larenth replied, still brusque. "You may claim hospitality at my hearth tonight, if you've nowhere else to go."

Iya had little choice. "Many thanks, Sir Larenth. I do claim it, and gratefully."

"What business do you have with my lord?" Larenth asked as she fell in with them.

"I'm charged with seeking a companion for a nobleman's son."

The old knight snorted. "I've a houseful of whelps— four wives' worth—and plenty of bastards. Good as any you'll find in the capital. I could do with a few less mouths to feed. I suppose I'd be paid for the loss of labor?"

"The customary boon fee would be paid, of course." Iya eyed the dour offspring present and doubted there was much chance of loosening her purse strings under his roof. All the same, he had a girl trained to arms, a rare and welcome sight these days. "Your daughter serves with you. That's rather out of fashion these days, I hear."

The young woman straightened in the saddle, looking offended.

"Fashion be damned, and the king, too, with his airs and laws," Larenth snapped. "My mother earned her keep by the sword, and her mother before her. I won't have my girl done out of a good living, by the Light I won't! All of my children are trained to arms soon as they can walk. You'll find Lord Jorvai is of a like mind, and not afraid to say so. You're a wizard; you must hold with the old ways, too?"

"I do, but these days it's not always wise to say so too loudly."

Larenth blew out his moustaches with another snort. "Mark my words, Mistress. There'll come a day when the king will be glad enough of my girl in his ranks, and all the others like her he's pushed out. Those bastards across the water won't be content with raiding forever."

Sir Larenth's steading proved to be nothing but a small, sparse-looking bit of land with a few outbuildings and corrals surrounding a rude stone house inside a stockade. A pack of barking hounds greeted their arrival and milled around their legs as they dismounted. Half a dozen muddy young children came running to do the same, hanging on their father and older siblings.

Larenth's harsh face softened a little as he tossed a little girl up on his shoulder and ushered Iya into the damp, smoky hall with rough courtesy.

There was little in the way of comfort to be found here. Even with the doors open, the room was cramped and malodorous. The furnishings were plain and few, with no hangings or plate in sight. Sides of meat and ropes of sausages dangled from the rafters below the smoke hole in the roof, curing in the smoke of the fire that blazed in the center of the packed earth floor. Beside it a thin, pregnant young woman in a sack of a gown sat twirling a distaff. She was introduced as the old knight's fourth lady, Sekora. With her were a few women, and an idiot stepson of about fourteen. Four bare-bottomed little children scrambled among the hounds at the women's feet.

The rest of Larenth's brood soon came straggling in for the evening meal. Iya lost count at fifteen. It was impossible to distinguish trueborn from bastard; in country households like this, where only the eldest stood to inherit the father's rank, it didn't much matter. The rest would have to make their own way.

Supper was a disorganized affair. Trestles were set up and pots hung on tripods over the hearth. Trenchers were brought in from a bake house and everyone sat where they could find space to eat. No one stood on ceremony here; more children arrived and elbowed the others out of the way to reach the hearth. It was not an elegant household, or a particularly friendly one, and the food was vile, but Iya was grateful to be off the road. The drizzle had turned into a downpour and lightning lit the yard outside.

The meal was nearly over before Iya noticed the trio of boys standing by the open doorway. Judging by their wet clothes and small portions, they'd arrived late during the chaos of the meal. One of them, the muddiest of the lot, was laughing over something with his brothers. He was as wiry and sun-browned as all the others, with thick dark hair that was probably a good brown under the dirt and twigs. She wasn't certain at first why she noticed him at all. Perhaps it was something in the tilt of his smile.

"Who is that?" she asked her host, trying to make herself heard over the chatter and the rain pounding on the thatch.

"That one?" Larenth frowned a moment. "Dimias, I think."

"That's *Ki*, Father!" Ahra chided.

"Is he trueborn or bastard?" asked Iya.

Stumped again, Larenth consulted his daughter. "Trueborn, of my third wife," he said at last.

"May I speak with him?" asked Iya.

Larenth gave her knowing wink. "All you like, Mistress, but remember there's other pups in the litter, if that one don't suit you."

Iya made her way over dogs and legs and babes to the trio in the doorway. "Are you called Ki?" she asked the boy.

Caught in midchew, he swallowed hastily and bowed. "Yes, Lady. At your service."

Though he was not striking in any particular way, Iya knew at once that this was no turnip. His eyes, the color of chestnut hulls, shone with good nature and intelligence.

Iya's heart skipped a beat; could he be wizard born? Taking his dirty hand in greeting, she touched his mind out of habit and found with a twinge of disappointment that he was not.

"Is that all there is to your name?" she asked.

He shrugged. "It's all I'm ever called."

"It's *Kirothius*," one of the older boys reminded him, giving him a poke in the back. "He just don't like it 'cause he can't say it."

"I can so!" Ki told Iya, blushing under the dirt that streaked his cheeks. From the smell of him, he'd spent his day tending pigs. "I like just Ki better. And it helps Father remember, with so many of us to keep track of."

Everyone within hearing laughed, and Ki of the shortened name flashed a buck-toothed grin that seemed the brightest thing in this wretched hovel, or the whole wretched day.

"Well now, Ki, how old are you?"

"Eleven summers, Lady."

"And are you trained to the sword?"

The boy's chin rose proudly. "Yes, Lady. And the bow."

"Trained to the pig-whacking stick, more like it," the poking brother chimed in.

Ki turned on him angrily. "You just shut your mouth, Amin. Who broke your finger for you last month?"

Ah, so the pup has cut some teeth, too, Iya noted approvingly. "Have you ever been to court?"

"I have, Lady. Father takes us to Ero for the Sakor festival most years. I seen the king and his son in their golden crowns, riding with the priests to the temple. I'll serve at court one day, myself."

"Tending the king's pigs!" teasing Amin put in.

Outraged, Ki jumped on his brother and knocked him down onto a circle of children sitting on the floor behind them. Iya retreated hastily as the discussion devolved into a loud free-for-all involving an increasing number of children and dogs and wailing babies. A few minutes later, she spotted Ki and the offending brother perched in the rafters overhead, grinning at the mayhem they'd created. The current mother waded into the fray, wielding a ladle.

Iya knew she'd found her boy, but was surprised by a twinge of conscience. If the worst happened, there could be no hesitation, no mercy. Yet surely it was worth the risk. What future did the poor child have here? No land, no title; at best, he'd end up a foot soldier or mercenary and die on the end of a Plenimaran lance. This way, he at least had a chance to realize his dream of court and some title of his own.

After the children were asleep that night in scattered piles on the floor, Sir Larenth bound the boy over for a boon fee of five gold sesters and a packet of charms to keep his well sweet and his roof sound.

No one thought to ask Ki what he thought of the matter.

By the light of day, Iya worried that she might have acted rashly. Ki had cleaned up well enough, and even had on a clean suit of faded hand-me-down clothes. His hair, tied back with a thong today, was the same warm brown as his eyes. He came armed, too, with a knife at his belt and a decent bow and quiver over his shoulder.

But he showed none of the previous night's sparkle as he bid his family good-bye and set off on foot beside Iya's horse.

"Are you well?" she asked, watching him march doggedly along.

"Yes, Lady."

"You mustn't call me 'lady.' You're more nobly born than I am. You may call me Mistress Iya and I shall call you Ki, just as you like. Now, would you like to come up and ride behind me?"

"No, Mistress."

"Did your father tell you where we're going?"

"Yes, Mistress."

"Are you glad to be the companion of the king's nephew?"

He said nothing and Iya noted the grim set of his jaw. "Does the prospect displease you?"

Ki shrugged his little bundle higher on his shoulder. "I'll do my duty, Mistress."

"Well, you might be a bit happier about it. I should think you'd be glad to leave that wretched place back there. Nobody will expect you to tend pigs or sleep under a table in Duke Rhius' house."

Ki's spine stiffened visibly, just as his half sister's had the day before. "Yes, Mistress."

Wearying of this strange, one-sided conversation, Iya let him be and Ki trudged along behind her in silence.

By the Light, perhaps I have made a mistake after all, Iya thought.

Glancing back at him, she saw that he was limping now.

"Do you have a blister?"

"No, Mistress."

"Then why are you limping?"

"I got a stone in my shoe."

Exasperated, she reined her horse to a halt. "Then why in the world didn't you say so? By the Light, child, you have a voice!"

He met her gaze squarely, but his chin was trembling. "Father said I was to speak only when spoke to," he told her, trying desperately to keep up a brave front as the words spilled out. "He said if I give you any back talk or stepped wrong, you'd turn me back to him and make him give the gold back and he'd flay the skin off me and turn me out on the road. He said I must do my duty to Prince Tobin and never come home again."

It was quite a speech, and boldly stated except for the tears spilling down his cheeks. He swiped at them with his sleeve, but kept his head up proudly as he waited to be sent home in disgrace.

Iya sighed. "Wipe your nose, boy. No one's going to send you home for having a rock in your shoe. I don't have a lot of experience of ordinary boys, Ki, but you strike me as a good sort, over all. You're not going to hurt Prince Tobin or run away, are you?"

"No, La— Mistress!"

"Then I doubt there'll be any need to send you home. Now empty your shoe and come up here."

When he'd finished with his shoe she gave him a hand up and gave his knee an awkward pat. "That's settled. We'll get along just fine now."

"Yes, Mistress."

"And perhaps we can have a more interesting conversation. It's a long ride to Alestun from here. You may speak freely, and ask me questions whenever you like. You won't learn much in life if you don't, you know."

Ki shifted his knee against the leather sack, which hung against his leg. "What's in here? You carry it around with you all the time. I seen you sleep with it, last night."

Startled, she snapped, "Nothing you need to know of, except that it's very dangerous and I *will* send you home if you ever meddle with it."

She felt the boy cringe and let out a slow breath before she spoke again. He was only a child, after all. "That wasn't a very good start, was it? Ask me another."

There was a long moment of silence, then, "What's the prince like?"

Iya thought back to Arkoniel's letter. "He's a year or so younger than you. I'm told he likes to hunt and he's training to be a warrior. He might make you his squire if you're a good boy."

"How many brothers and sisters he got?"

"'Does he *have*,'" Iya corrected. "By the Light, we must work on your grammar."

"How many does he have?"

"Not a one, nor any mother, either. That's why you're going to keep him company."

"Did his mother die?"

"Yes, a year ago last spring."

"A year? And the duke ain't got hisself a new woman yet?" Ki asked.

Iya sighed. "'Duke Rhius hasn't gotten himself—' Illior's

Fingers! 'Hasn't remarried' is how it's said, not that it's any concern of yours! And no, he has not. I believe you'll find this household rather different from what you're used to."

Another pause, then, "I heard some folks claim there's a ghost at this prince's castle."

"Are you afraid of ghosts?"

"Yes, Mistress Iya! Aren't you?"

"Not especially. And you mustn't be, either, because there *is* a ghost at the keep."

"Bilairy's balls!"

Suddenly Ki was no longer behind her. Turning, Iya found him standing in the road with his bundle in his arms, staring miserably back toward home.

"Get back up here, boy!"

Ki wavered, evidently uncertain which he was more afraid of, ghosts or his formidable father.

"Don't be ridiculous," she chided. "Prince Tobin has lived his whole life with it and it hasn't done him any harm. Now come along or I will send you back. The prince needs no cowards around him."

Ki swallowed hard and squared his shoulders, just as she'd guessed he would. "My father sired no cowards."

"I'm pleased to hear it."

When he was safely mounted again, she asked, "How did you know of the ghost?"

"Ahra told me this morning after she heard who Father bound me off to."

"And how did she know of it?"

She felt a shrug. "Said she heard it among the ranks."

"And what else did your sister hear?"

Another shrug. "That's all she told me, Mistress."

Ki was polite in a glum sort of way the rest of the day, and that night he wept very quietly after he thought Iya was asleep. She half expected to find him gone in the morning. When she opened her eyes just after dawn, however, he was still there, watching her from across a freshly laid fire. There were dark circles under his eyes, but he'd fixed a cold breakfast for both of them and looked much more the bright fellow she'd taken him for that first night.

"Good morning, Mistress Iya."

"Good morning, Ki." Iya sat up and stretched the stiffness from her shoulders.

"How long 'til we get there?" he asked as they ate.

"Oh, three or four days, I think."

He bit off another mouthful of sausage and chewed noisily. "Could you learn me to talk proper on the way, like you said?"

"For a start, don't speak with your mouth full. And don't chew with your mouth open." She chuckled as he hastily swallowed. "There's no need to choke on my account. Let's see, what else? Don't curse or swear by Bilairy's body. It's coarse. Now, say 'could you please teach me to speak properly?' "

"Could you please teach me to speak properly?" he repeated, as carefully as if it were some foreign tongue he was mastering. "And could you please learn—teach me about ghosts?"

"I'll do both, as best I can," Iya replied, smiling at him. She'd judged rightly after all. This boy was no turnip.

Chapter 22

Sitting on the roof with Arkoniel one afternoon in late Rhythin, Tobin looked out over the blazing colors of the forest and realized it was only a few weeks until his name day. He hoped no one remembered.

He hadn't wanted to come up here for their morning lesson, and made certain they sat as far as possible from the base of the tower.

Arkoniel was trying to teach him mathematics, using dried beans and lentils to work through the problems. Tobin wanted to pay attention, but his thoughts kept straying to the tower. He could feel it looming behind him, cold like a shadow even though the sun was warm on his shoulders. The tower shutters were closed tight, but Tobin was sure he could hear noises behind them; footsteps, and the soft brush of long skirts across stone floors. The sounds scared him the way his visions of his mother's ghost behind the tower door did.

He didn't tell Arkoniel about the sounds, or about the dream he'd had the night before; he'd made that mistake several times already and everyone, even Nari, had started to look at him strangely when the ones he told came true.

In this one, he and Brother went outside again, but this time the demon led him to the bottom of the meadow, where they stood waiting for someone. In the dream, Brother started crying. He cried so hard that dark blood ran from his nose and mouth. Then he pressed one hand over his heart and the other over Tobin's, and leaned so close their faces were almost touching.

"She's coming," Brother whispered. Then he flew

through the air like a bird back to the tower, leaving Tobin to wait alone, watching the road.

He'd woken up with a start, still feeling Brother's hand pressing on his chest. *Who's coming,* he thought, *and why?*

Sitting here in the sunshine now, Tobin didn't tell Arkoniel any of that. He hadn't been scared in the dream, but when he thought of it now, listening to the noises in the tower, he was overcome with a strange sense of dread.

An especially loud bump sounded overhead and Tobin stole a quick glance at the wizard, thinking he must have heard *that*, that perhaps Arkoniel was just choosing not to say anything.

In their first days together Arkoniel had asked him many questions about his mother. He never mentioned the tower or what had happened there, but Tobin could see in his eyes that he wanted to.

Tobin let out a sigh of relief when Tharin appeared in the courtyard below. Father and the others were still away, but Tharin had come home to be his weapons master.

"It's time for my practice," he said, jumping up.

Arkoniel raised an eyebrow at him. "So I see. You know, Tobin, there's more to being a noble than arms. You have to understand the world and how it works. . . ."

"Yes, Master Arkoniel. May I go now?"

A familiar sigh. "You may."

Arkoniel watched the child scamper eagerly away over the slates. He doubted Tobin had heard half the lesson. Something about the tower had distracted him; he'd twisted around to stare at it every time he thought Arkoniel wasn't looking.

The wizard stood and looked up at it. Something about those closed shutters always sent a chill down his spine. When the duke returned, Arkoniel meant to get his permission to see that room. Perhaps if he could stand there, breathe the air, touch the things she'd left behind, then he could gain some sense of what exactly had happened that day. He certainly wasn't going to learn it from Tobin. The few times Arkoniel had broached the subject the child had gone blank and silent in the most disquieting way.

Arkoniel gave no credence to Nari's wild talk of possession, or her fear that Tobin had somehow caused his mother's fall. But the longer Arkoniel remained here, the more keenly aware he was of the dead child's permeating presence. He could feel its chill. And he'd heard Tobin whispering to it, just as Nari had said, and found himself wondering what sort of replies Tobin heard.

What if Tobin had fallen that day? For an instant he imagined the two children watching him from behind those peeling shutters, united in death, as they should have been in life.

"I'll go mad here," he muttered, scattering the lentils for the birds.

Hoping to shake off his dark mood, he made his way down to the practice yard and watched Tharin working with Tobin. Here was a man who knew how to teach a boy.

Both of them were grinning as they moved back and forth with their wooden blades. No matter how hard Tharin worked Tobin, the boy strove to please him, worshiping the big warrior with an openness that Arkoniel envied. Tobin had put on a battered leather tunic and tied back his hair with a thong; a dark miniature of fair-skinned Tharin.

Arkoniel had come to accept that these lessons captured the boy's interest in a way that his own lame attempts could not. He'd never meant to be a tutor and suspected he was making a poor job of it.

Part of the problem was Tobin's distrust. Arkoniel had

felt it since the day he arrived, and things had not changed much for the better. He was certain that the demon had something to do with this. It remembered the events of its birth; had it told Tobin? Nari didn't think so, but Arkoniel remained certain the demon had somehow set Tobin against him from the start.

In spite of all these obstacles, however, he found himself growing increasingly attached to the child. Tobin was intelligent and perceptive when he chose to be, and around anyone else except Arkoniel he was pleasant and well mannered.

Recently, however, something new had given the wizard pause and filled him with a mix of wonder and unease. The boy had shown a few flashes of what appeared to be foreknowledge. A week earlier Tobin had claimed that a letter was coming from his father, and waited all afternoon by the gate until a rider appeared with the message that Duke Rhius was not coming home in time for Tobin's name day after all.

Stranger still, a few nights ago he had frantically woken Nari and Tharin, begging them to go into the woods to find a fox with a broken back. They'd tried to reassure him that it had only been a dream but he grew so upset that Tharin had finally taken a lantern and gone out. He'd returned within the hour with a dead vixen. Tharin swore the fox had been too far from the house for Tobin to hear its cries and, when asked how he'd known, Tobin had mumbled that the demon had told him, but wouldn't say any more.

This morning he'd had a furtive air and Arkoniel guessed he'd had another vision, and that it might have something to do with the way Tobin had squirmed so inattentively through the aborted lesson in mathematics.

While foreknowing in a future ruler was an undoubted advantage, what if it presaged the first blossoming of a wizard's gifts? Would the people accept a wizard queen, unable for all her power to bear a successor?

Leaving Tobin and Tharin to their practice, Arkoniel crossed the bridge and wandered down the road into the forest.

As the keep disappeared from sight behind him, Arkoniel felt his spirits lift. The crisp autumn air cleansed him of the tainted atmosphere he'd been breathing for the past month, and he was suddenly grateful to be away from that strange house and its haunted people. No amount of repair and fresh paint could mask its underlying rot.

"That baby still sit heavy on you heart," an unmistakable voice said behind him.

Arkoniel whirled around to find the road as empty as before. "Lhel? I know it's you! What are you doing here?"

"Be scared, Wizard?" Now the mocking voice came from a thick stand of yellow-leafed poplar on his right. He couldn't make out anyone hidden there, but just then a small brown hand appeared—not from behind the trees but out of thin air just in front of them. The forefinger crooked, beckoning, then disappeared as if it had been pulled back through an invisible window frame. "You come here, I take your fear away," the voice wheedled, almost at his ear.

"By the Light, show yourself!" Arkoniel demanded, intrigued in spite of his surprise. "Lhel? Where are you?"

He stared into the trees, looking for telltale shadows, listening for stealthy footsteps. Nothing came to him but the patter of leaves in the wind. It was as if she had opened a portal in the air and spoken to him through it. And put her hand through it.

It's a trick. You're seeing what you want to see.

But what if it wasn't?

The more important question right now was what she was doing here at all after all these years?

"Come to me, Arkoniel," Lhel called to him from behind the screen of poplars. "Come into the woods."

He hesitated just long enough to summon a protective

core of power deep in his mind, strong enough—he hoped—to keep away any creatures of darkness she might summon. Gathering his courage, he pushed through the screen of branches, following the voice into the forest beyond.

The light was muted here, and the ground rose gently before him. Laughter came from up the hillside and he looked up to see the witch floating beside a large oak tree a dozen yards from where he stood. Lhel smiled at him, framed by a long oval of soft green light. He could see rushes and cattails swaying around her, bathed in the rippling shimmer of light reflected from unseen water. The vision was so clear he could even make out the exact demarcation between the illusion and the surrounding forest, like a painting hung on the air.

She beckoned coyly, then the entire apparition collapsed like a washday soap bubble.

He ran to where she had appeared and felt the tingle of magic in the air there. He breathed it in, and felt a long-forgotten memory stir.

Years earlier, while still a child apprentice, Arkoniel had thought he'd seen a similar miracle. Half asleep in some noble's hall, he'd awakened in the early light to see men appearing silently out of thin air at the far end of the room. The sight had both frightened and excited him.

When he told Iya of it later that morning, however, he was heartbroken to learn that it had simply been a clever trick of the eye, using a painted wall and the placement of a tapestry in front of a servant's entry.

"No such spell has ever existed in Orëska magic," Iya had told him. "Even the Aurënfaie have to walk from place to place, just as we do."

The disappointment had faded, but not the inspiration. There were spells aplenty that could move objects like locks or doors or stones; surely there must be some way of translating these. He'd toyed with the notion for years, but had come no closer to making it a reality. He could push a pea across a carpet with ease, but he could not make it pass through a solid door or wall, no matter how he meditated and envisioned the act.

Arkoniel shook off the reverie with suspicion. This was some witch trick, coupled with the memory his mind had fastened onto in the shock of the moment.

Lhel's faint call drifted down to him again, leading him to a trail that wound off to his right through a thick stand of fir. The ground fell away sharply from here and he came out at last at the edge of a marsh.

Lhel stood waiting for him at the water's edge, surrounded by cattails and faded marshworts, just as he'd seen her earlier. He stared hard at her, trying to pierce whatever new illusion she was practicing on him, but her shadow fell across the wet ground just as it should, and her bare feet sank into the soft mud as she took a step toward him.

"What are you doing here?" he demanded.

"I be here, waiting for you," she replied.

This time it was Arkoniel who stepped closer. His heart was racing, but he felt no fear of her now.

She looked smaller and more ragged than he recalled, as if she'd been hungry for a long time. There were thicker streaks of white in her hair, too, but her body was still rounded and ripe, and she moved with the same challenge in her hips that had so unnerved him. She took another step toward him, then tilted her head and set her hands on her hips like a fishwife, regarding him with a combination of heat and wry disdain in her black eyes.

He was close enough to smell herbs and sweat and moist earth, with something else mixed in that made him think of mares in heat.

"When—when did you arrive?" he asked.

She shrugged. "I be here always. Where *you* be, all these times? How you take care what we make, be gone so long?"

"You mean you've been *here*, near the keep, all these years?"

"I help the lady. I follow and keep watch. Help that spirit not be so angry."

"You haven't done much of a job of that," Arkoniel retorted, holding out his splinted wrist for her to see. "Tobin's life has been a misery because of it."

"It be worse, I don't do as the Mother show," she retorted, shaking a finger at him. "You and Iya, you don't know! A witch make a spirit, she . . ." She held her wrists up, crossed, as if she were bound. "Iya say, 'You go home, witch. Don't come back.' She don't know." Lhel tapped her temple. "That spirit call out for me. I *tell* her, but she don't listen."

"Does Rhius know you're here?"

Lhel shook her head and an earwig squirmed loose from a tendril of hair and skittered away down her bare arm. "I close always, but not to be see." She smiled slyly, then faded from sight before his eyes. "You do that, Wizard?" she whispered, behind him now and close enough to his ear for him to feel her breath. She'd made no sound as she moved, nor left any mark on the ground.

Arkoniel flinched away. "No."

"I show you," she whispered. An invisible hand stroked his arm. "Show you what you dream."

The memory of the men emerging from the air intruded on his thoughts again.

She was doing this.

Arkoniel jerked back, caught between the water and the invisible hands that tried to stroke his chest. "Stop that! This is no time for your petty teasing."

Something struck him hard in the chest, knocking him backward into the mud at the water's edge. A weight settled on his chest, holding him down, and Lhel's musky unwashed scent overwhelmed him. Then she was visible again, squatting naked on top of him.

His eyes widened in wonder. The three-phase moon—a circle flanked by two outfacing crescents—was tattooed on her belly, and concentric serpent patterns covered each full breast. More symbols covered her face and arms. He had seen such marks before, carved into the walls of caves on the sacred island of Kouros, and on rocks along the Skalan coastline. According to Iya, such marks had been old long before the Hierophant came to the Three Lands. Had Lhel somehow hidden these markings before, he wondered, unable to move, or were they another illusion? There was certainly considerable magic of some sort involved. Strength greater than her small body could account for held him flat as she took his face between her hands.

You and your kind dismiss my people, and my gods. Her true voice intruded into his mind, devoid of accent or stumbling grammar. *You think we are dirty, that we practice necromancy. You are strong, you Orëska, but you are often fools, too, blinded by pride. Your teacher asked me for a great magic, then treated me with disrespect. Because of her I offended the Mother and the dead.*

For ten years I have guarded that spirit, and the child it is bound to. The dead child could have killed the living one and those around her if I had not bound it. Until its flesh is cut free from the one you call Tobin, it must be so bound and I must remain, for only I can do both unbindings when the time comes.

Arkoniel was amazed to see a tear roll down the witch's cheek. It fell and struck his face.

I have waited alone all these years, cut off from my people, a ghost among yours. There's been no full moon priest for me, no harvest sacrifice or spring rites. I die inside, Wizard, for the child and for the goddess who sent you to me. My hair turns white and my womb is still empty. Iya put gold in my hands, not understanding that a great magic must be paid for with the body. When she first came

to me in my visions, I thought you were for me, my pay-
ment. But Iya sent me away empty. Will you pay me now?

"I—I can't." Arkoniel dug his fingers into the earth as
the meaning of her words dawned on him. "It . . . such in-
tercourse . . . it takes away our power."

She leaned over him and brushed her heavy breasts
across his lips. Her skin was hot. A hard brown nipple
brushed the corner of his mouth and he turned his head
away.

You are wrong, Orëska, she whispered in his mind. *It
feeds the power. Join with me in flesh and I will teach you
my magic. Then your power will be doubled.*

Arkoniel shivered. "I can't give you a child. Orëska
wizards are barren."

But not eunuchs. Slowly, sinuously, she slid back until
she was straddling his hips. Arkoniel kept silent, but his
body answered for him. *I need no child from you, Wizard.
Just your heat and your rush of seed. That is payment
enough.*

She pressed against him and pleasure bordering on
pain blossomed through his groin as her heat seeped
through his tunic. He closed his eyes, knowing she would
take him if she chose. There was no way to prevent it.

But then the pressure, the heat, the hands were gone.
Arkoniel opened his eyes and found himself alone.

It had been no vision, though; he could still taste her
salt on his lips, smell her scent on his clothes. In the mud
on either side of him the prints of small bare feet slowly
filled with water.

He sat up and rested his head on his knees, drawing
in the musky woman smell that clung to him. Cold,
aching, and strangely ashamed, he groaned aloud as he
conjured her warmth pressing against him.

I thought you were for me.

The words made the breath catch in his throat and his
groin pound. He forced himself up to his feet. Mud and

pond slime oozed from his hair and dripped down inside the front of his tunic like cold little fingers seeking his heart.

Illusions and lies, he thought desperately, but as he made his way back toward the rotting keep, he could not forget what she'd shown him, or the whispered invitation; *Join with me, Wizard—your power will be doubled.*

Chapter 23

Tobin's head started to hurt during his sword practice. It ached so badly it made him sick to his stomach, and Tharin sent him up to bed in the middle of the day.

Brother came without being called and crouched on the end of Tobin's bed, one hand pressed to his chest. Curled on his side, cheek pressed to the soft new coverlet Father had sent from Ero, Tobin stared at his baleful mirror self, waiting for Brother to touch him or weep as he had in the dreams. But Brother didn't do anything, just stayed there gathering darkness around himself. Queasy from the headache, Tobin slipped into a doze.

He was riding Gosi up the forest road toward the mountains. Red and gold leaves swirled around him, bright in the sunshine. He thought he could hear another rider just behind him, but he couldn't see who it was. After a moment he realized that Brother was sitting behind him with his arms wrapped around Tobin's waist. In the dream Brother was alive; Tobin could feel the other boy's chest pressing warm and solid against his back, and Brother's breath against his neck. The hands clasped at his waist were brown and callused, with dirt under the nails.

Tobin's eyes filled with happy tears. He had a real brother! All the rest of it—demons and wizards and strange women in the forest—it had just been one of his bad dreams.

He tried to look at Brother, to see if his eyes were blue like his own, but Brother pressed his face to Tobin's back and whispered, "Ride faster, she's almost here!"

Brother was afraid, and that made Tobin feel scared, too.

They rode further into the mountains than Tobin had ever gone before. Huge snow-capped peaks surrounded them on every side. The sky grew dark and a cold wind whipped around them.

"What will we do when it gets dark? Where will we sleep?" Tobin asked, looking around in dismay.

"Ride faster," whispered Brother.

But when they rounded a bend in the road, they found themselves at the bottom of the meadow below the keep, heading for the bridge at a gallop. Gosi would not take the rein and stop—

Tobin woke with a start. Nari stood over him, rubbing his chest. It was nearly dark and the room was very cold.

"You've slept the day away, pet," she told him.

It was only a dream! Tobin thought, heartbroken. He could feel Brother somewhere nearby, cold and strange as ever. Nothing had changed. He wanted to roll over and escape back into the dream, but Nari hustled him out of bed.

"You have visitors! Get up now, and let's change that tunic."

"Visitors? For me?" Tobin blinked up at her. He knew he should send Brother away, but it was too late now, with Nari fussing over him.

She pressed the backs of her fingers to his forehead and clucked her tongue. "You're like ice, pet! Ah, look— the window's been open all day, and you with no covers. Let's get these clothes changed so you can come down to the hall and warm yourself."

Tobin's head still hurt. Shivering, he let Nari pull off his rumpled tunic, then wiggled into the stiff new one with the embroidery on the hem. This had come in the same package as the coverlet, along with another suit of good clothes, better than anything Tobin had ever worn, and other fancy things for the house.

He caught sight of Brother in a dark corner as he

turned to leave the room; the demon was wearing the very same new clothes, but his face was paler than Tobin had ever seen it.

"Stay here," he whispered. Following Nari downstairs, he wondered what it would feel like to have a living brother walking beside him.

The hall was dark except for the hearth fire and a few torches. Still beyond the reach of the light, Tobin could see the people standing by the hearth without being seen. Arkoniel, Cook, Tharin, and Mynir were all there, speaking softly with an old woman in a plain, travel-stained gown. She had a brown, wrinkled face and wore her thin grey hair in a braid over one shoulder. Was this the "she" Brother had spoken of? She looked like a peasant.

Mistaking his hesitation for fear, Nari took his hand. "Don't be afraid," she whispered, leading him down. "Mistress Iya is a friend of your father's, and a great wizard. And look who she's brought with her!"

As Tobin came closer, he saw that there was another stranger hanging back in the shadows behind the old woman. Iya said something over her shoulder and this one came forward into the light.

It was a boy.

Tobin's heart sank. This must be the companion they'd promised him. They hadn't forgotten about that after all, even though he had.

The boy was taller than he was, and looked older. His tunic was embroidered, but frayed at the hems and patched under one arm. His shoes were stained and his trousers were bound from ankle to knee with twine. Nari would have scolded Tobin for being so poorly turned out. The boy looked Tobin's way just then, and the firelight struck his face. His skin was ruddy from the sun, and his thick brown hair fell in ragged bangs over his forehead. His dark eyes were wide now with trepidation as he looked around the hall. Tobin braced for the worst as Nari urged him into the light. Did this boy already know he was odd?

As soon as the boy noticed him, however, he made Tobin a quick, clumsy bow.

Tharin gave him a reassuring smile. "Prince Tobin, this is Kirothius, son of Sir Larenth of Oakmount Stead at Colath. He's come to be your companion."

Tobin returned the bow, then held up his hand for the warrior's clasp as his father had taught him. Kirothius managed a small smile as he gripped it. His palm felt like a soldier's: hard and callused.

"Welcome to the house of my father," said Tobin. "I am honored—" It took a moment to summon the rest of the host's ritual greeting; he'd never had to offer it by himself before. "I am honored to offer you the hospitality of my hearth, Kirothius, son of Larenth."

"I am honored to accept, Prince Tobin." Kirothius ducked his head again in a half bow. His front teeth were big and stuck out a little.

Tharin gave him a wink and Tobin felt a stab of jealousy. His friend already seemed to approve of this newcomer.

"And this is Mistress Iya," said Arkoniel, introducing the old woman. "I've told you a little about her, my prince. She is my teacher, just as I am yours."

"I am most glad to make your acquaintance, Prince Tobin," Iya said, bowing. "Arkoniel had written me many good things about you."

"Thank you, Mistress." Tobin felt held by her eyes and voice. She might dress like a peasant, but there was an air of power about her that made him tremble a little.

All the same, when she smiled he saw kindness and a hint of amusement in her colorless eyes as she placed a hand on the new boy's shoulder. "I hope that young Kirothius here will serve you well. He prefers to be called Ki, by the way, if you have no objection?"

"No, Mistress Iya. Welcome to the house of my father," Tobin replied, bowing again.

The instant the words left his lips the room went cold

and Brother came down the stairs like a hurricane, whipping new tapestries from the walls and scattering sparks from the hearth across the rushes in great swirling clouds. Ki cried out as an ember struck his cheek, then jumped to stand between Tobin and the fire.

With the wind came a deep, slow throbbing sound, like the beating of a huge drum. Tobin had never heard such a sound; it went through him and shook his heart in his chest. A loud buzzing noise filled his ears—it reminded him of something bad but he couldn't quite recall what.

The wizard woman stood calmly in the midst of it all with nothing but her lips moving. Brother, no more than a dark blur of motion, flung a bench at her, but it veered away and toppled over on its side.

Brother whirled on Ki then and yanked on his cloak, trying to pull him into the fire. Tobin grabbed at the older boy's arm as Ki fought to untie the lacings at his throat. They came free and both boys tumbled backward as the cloak pulled free and disappeared into the rafters.

As Tobin righted himself he caught the look of terror in Ki's eyes and the sight burned him with shame.

Now he's sure to hate me! he thought, knowing it was his fault for being so careless. He never should have gone to sleep without sending Brother away. Turning away from the others, he whispered, "Blood my blood, flesh my flesh, bone my bone. Go away, Brother. Leave them alone!"

The wind dropped instantly. The furniture stopped moving and silence fell over the room. The beautiful new newel post at the bottom of the staircase split down the middle with a loud crack that made them all jump, then Brother was gone.

When Tobin turned around again, both wizards were watching him as if they knew what he'd been doing. Iya stared at him for a long moment, then said something to Arkoniel, too low for Tobin to hear.

Ki got up and offered Tobin a hand. "Are you hurt, Prince Tobin?" A blister was already rising on his cheek.

"No."

Ki was staring at Tobin, too, but he didn't look angry. "So that was your ghost?"

"He does that sometimes. I'm sorry." Tobin wanted to say something more, something to keep that warm, amazed smile aimed at him. "I don't think he'll hurt you again."

"We were not expecting guests, Mistress," Mynir was saying to Iya, as if nothing had happened. "I hope you will not think poorly of our house. We'd have readied a feast if we'd known."

Iya patted the old steward's arm. "We're no strangers to the duke's hospitality. Whatever you have will please us very well. Is Catilan still running the kitchen?"

They all chattered on like they were old friends and had known each other for a long time. Tobin didn't like this at all. Nothing had felt right since the first wizard had arrived. Now there were two of them, and Brother hated Iya even more than Arkoniel. Tobin had felt that during the brief attack.

He was certain that this was the "she" of his dreams, the one who'd made Brother weep blood. Yet Nari had claimed Iya was a friend of his father's, and treated her like an honored guest. He was tempted to call Brother back, just to see what would happen.

Before he could, however, he noticed the other boy watching him. Ki looked away quickly and so did Tobin, embarrassed without knowing why.

The steward insisted that Cook serve dinner in the hall at the high table, even though Tobin's father was not at home. Brother had knocked down the new canopy, but that was soon put right. Tobin had to sit in his father's place, between Iya and the new companion, and Tharin served as carver and butler for them. Tobin wanted to talk to Ki and put him at ease, but found himself completely tongue-tied. Ki was silent, too, and Tobin saw him stealing uneasy glances around the hall and at him during each successive course. Tobin kept one eye out for Brother through the meal, but the spirit heeded his command.

The adults didn't seem to notice his discomfort, chattering on among themselves. Nari, Arkoniel, and Iya were talking about people Tobin had never heard his nurse mention before, and he felt another pang of jealousy. As soon as the last fruit tart had been dispatched, he excused himself, intending to retreat upstairs. But Ki rose, too, clearly meaning to follow. Perhaps this was what companions were supposed to do. Tobin changed direction and went outside into the front courtyard instead, with the older boy tagging along behind.

A ruddy autumn moon was climbing the sky, bright enough to cast shadows in the courtyard.

Alone with this stranger, Tobin felt more awkward than ever. He wished he'd stayed in the hall now, but knew it would look too silly to go back in so soon with Ki trailing him like a duckling.

They stood there awhile in silence. Then Ki looked up at the keep and said, "Your house is very grand, Prince Tobin."

"Thank you. What's yours like?"

"Oh, about like your barracks here."

The frayed edges on the boy's tunic caught his eye again. "Is your father a poor man?" The words were out of his mouth before it occurred to him that this might be taken as an insult.

But Ki just shrugged. "We're not rich, that's for certain. My great-great-grandmother was married to one of Queen Klie's kin and had lands of her own. But there's been so many of us since that no one has claim to that anymore. That's the trouble in my family, Father says; we're too hot in our passions. Those of us that don't get killed in battle breed like conies. In our house the young ones sleep in a big pile on the floor like puppies, there's so many of us."

Tobin had never heard of such a thing. "How many of you are there?"

"Fourteen brothers and twelve sisters living, counting all the bastards."

Tobin wanted to know what a bastard was and why they would be counted differently than the rest, but Ki was still talking. "I'm one of the younger ones, from the third wife, and our new mama is kindling again. The five oldest fight in your uncle's army now, with our father," he added proudly.

"I'm going to be a warrior, too," Tobin told him. "I'll be a great lord like my father and fight the Plenimarans on land and sea."

"Well, of course! You being a prince and all."

"I suppose you could come with me and be my squire. You'd be a knight, like Tharin."

The older boy stuck his hands under his belt like a grown man and nodded. "Sir Ki? I like the sound of that. Not much chance of that back home."

There was that smile again, making Tobin feel all funny inside. "Why do you prefer being called Ki?" he asked.

"That's what everyone calls me back home. Kirothius is too damn long—" He stopped, looking embarrassed. "Begging your pardon, Tobin! I mean prince—! That is, my prince. Oh hell!"

Tobin giggled with guilty delight. He wasn't allowed to curse and swear; Nari said it was common. But Tharin's men did when they thought he wasn't listening. "You can just call me Tobin. Everyone else does most of the time."

"Well—" Ki looked around nervously. "I better call you Prince Tobin when anyone else is around. Father said he'd make sure I got a beating if he got word I was disrespectful."

"I wouldn't let him!" Tobin exclaimed. No one ever struck Tobin except Brother. "We'll just tell him that I gave you my permission. Since I'm a prince, he'll have to obey me. I think."

"That's all right then," Ki said, relieved.

"Do you want to see my horse?"

In the stable Ki climbed the side of Gosi's stall and let out a whistle of appreciation. "He's a beauty, all right. I seen lots of these Aurënfaie at the Horse Fair at Ero. What kind of 'faie did you get him from?"

"How do you mean?"

"Well, there's all kinds of them, depending on what part of Aurënen they're from. The people, I mean, not the horses. You can tell 'em apart by the colors of their *sen'gai*."

"Their what?"

"Those colored head cloths they wear."

"Oh, those. I saw some Aurënfaie wizards once," Tobin told him, glad at last to seem a little worldly. Ki was only a poor knight's son, but he'd been to Ero and knew about horses. "They did magic and played music. And they had marks on their faces. Designs."

"That'd be Khatme or Ky'arin clan, I bet. They're the only ones that do that, far as I know."

They wandered back out to the barracks yard, where Tobin spied the wooden swords he and Tharin had used earlier in the day. "I think you're supposed to practice with me. Want to try now?"

With some common ground established at last, they saluted each other and started in. But Ki didn't fight in careful drills like Tharin did. He swung hard and moved in aggressively, as if they were really fighting. Tobin fought back as best he could until Ki caught him a sharp blow across the hand. Tobin yelped and stuck his fingers in his mouth without thinking to call "hold."

Ki lunged in and poked him in the belly. "I call a kill!"

Tobin grunted and grabbed at his middle with his wounded hand, trying not to let on how embarrassed he was. "You're much better than I am."

Ki grinned and clapped him on the shoulder. "Well, I had all them brothers and sisters to teach me, and Father, too. You should see me after a practice with them! Bruises all over. My sister Cytra split my lip wide open last year. I bawled like a cut shoat when my stepmother sewed it up. Look, you can still see the scar over on the left side."

Tobin leaned close and squinted at the small white line that crossed Ki's upper lip.

"That's a nice one, too." Ki touched his thumb to the scar on Tobin's chin. "It looks just like Illior's moon. Bet that makes it lucky. How'd you get it?"

Tobin jerked back. "I—I fell."

He wished that Ki was right about the scar being lucky, but he was certain it wasn't. Just thinking about it made him feel bad.

"Well, don't fret yourself," said Ki. "You're just not used to my way of fighting. I'll learn—ah, teach you, if you like. I'll go slow, too. Promise." He touched his sword to his brow and gave Tobin a bucktoothed grin. "Shall we go again, my prince?"

The bad feeling quickly passed as he and Ki began again. This boy was different than anyone he'd ever met, except maybe Tharin. Even though he was older and obviously knew more of the world than Tobin, there was nothing behind his eyes or smile that didn't match what he said. Tobin felt all strange inside when Ki grinned at him, but it was a good feeling, like the way he'd felt in his dream where Brother was alive.

Ki kept his word, too. He went more slowly this time, and tried to explain what he was doing and how Tobin could defend himself. In this way, Tobin saw that he was using the same thrusts and guards that Tharin had taught him.

They started slow, stepping through the positions, but soon Tobin found himself having to work to keep his guard up. Their wooden blades clacked together like a heron's beak, and their shadows jumped and darted like moths in the moonlight.

Ki was the more aggressive fighter, but he didn't have

the control that Tharin had instilled in Tobin. Ducking a wild swing, Tobin lunged forward and struck Ki across the ribs. The older boy dropped his sword and collapsed in an ungainly heap at his feet.

"I'm slain, Your Highness!" he gasped, pretending to hold his guts in. "Send my ashes home to my father!"

Tobin had never seen anything like this, either. It was so absurd that he laughed, hesitantly at first out of surprise, then louder because it felt so good when Ki joined in.

"Damn your ashes!" Tobin giggled, feeling giddy and wicked.

This started Ki laughing again and their voices echoed together off the courtyard walls. Ki made faces, screwing up his eyes and hanging his tongue out of the side of his mouth. Tobin laughed so hard his sides hurt and his eyes watered.

"By the Four, what a racket!"

Tobin turned to find Nari and Tharin watching them from the gateway.

"You haven't hurt him, have you, Tobin?" Nari demanded.

Tharin chuckled. "What do you say, Ki? Will you live?"

Ki scrambled to his feet and bowed. "Yes, Sir Tharin."

"Come along, you two," Nari said, shooing them toward the door. "Ki's had a long ride and you've been feeling ill, Tobin. It's time you were both off to bed."

Tobin stifled the sudden urge to shout, "Damn your bed!" settling instead for an exchanged smirk with Ki. As they headed back into the house, he heard Tharin chuckle again and whisper to Nari, "You have been exiled too long, girl, if you don't recognize play when you see it!"

It wasn't until they reached Tobin's door that he realized Ki was to share both his chamber and his bed. Ki's small traveling bundle lay on the disused chest where Tobin had the doll hidden, and an unfamiliar bow and quiver leaned in the corner next to his own.

"But, he can't!" Tobin whispered, tugging Nari back out into the corridor. What would Brother do? And what if Ki found the doll or saw him with it?

"Now, now. You're too old for a nurse," Nari murmured. "A boy your age should have been sharing a room with a companion long since." She rubbed at her eyes, and Tobin saw she was trying not to cry. "I should have told you, I know, pet, but I didn't think he'd get here so soon and— Well, this is the way it must be." She was using her firm voice now, the one that warned there was no use in arguing. "I'll sleep down in the hall now, with the others. Just call down if you need me, like you always do when you're in bed before me."

Ki must have heard them. When Tobin and Nari came back in, he was standing in the middle of the room looking uncertain again. Nari bustled over to the bed and went to put his bundle away in the chest. "We'll just stow your things in here. Tobin doesn't—"

"No!" Tobin cried. "No, you can't put that in there."

"Tobin, shame on you!"

Ki had his head down now, looking as if he wanted to sink into the floor.

"No, it's just— I have ink jars in there," he explained hastily. The words came easily, being true. The doll was hidden in the flour sack under a heap of parchments and his drawing tools. "There's ink and pens and wax and things. They'd soil his clothes. There's lots of room in the wardrobe, though. Put your things in with mine, Ki. We can share. Like—like brothers!"

He felt his face go hot. Where had those last words come from? But Ki was smiling again and Nari looked pleased.

Nari put Ki's few belongings into the wardrobe and made them wash their teeth and faces. Tobin stripped down to his shirt and climbed into bed, but Ki seemed hesitant again.

"Go on, lad," Nari urged. "Strip off and get in. I put a warm brick down the end to take the chill off."

"I don't strip off to sleep," Ki told her.

"That's all well and good for country folk, but you're in a noble house now, so the sooner you learn our ways, the better for you."

Ki mumbled something else as his cheeks flamed.

"What's the matter, boy?"

"I don't have a shirt," Ki told her.

"No shirt?" Nari clucked her tongue. "Well now, I'll go find you one. But see that you skin out of those dusty things before I get back. I don't want your road dirt in the clean linens."

She lit the night lamp and blew out the others. Then she kissed Tobin soundly on the cheek, and Ki, too, making him blush again.

He waited until the door had closed behind her, then pulled off his tunic and trousers and hurried under the covers to keep warm. As he got in, Tobin saw that Ki's slender body was almost as brown as his face, except for a band of pale skin around his hips and privates.

"How come you're only white there?" asked Tobin, whose own body was fair as new butter summer and winter.

Shivering, Ki snuggled in next to him. "We wear clouts, swimming. There's snapper turtles in the river and you don't want them biting off your diddler!"

Tobin giggled again, though more at the oddness of having a stranger in Nari's place than what Ki had said. Nari returned with one of Tharin's old shirts and Ki struggled into it under the covers.

Nari kissed them both again and went out, shutting the door softly behind her.

Both boys lay quiet for a while, watching the play of lamplight on the carved beams overhead. Ki was still shivering.

"Are you cold?" asked Tobin, shifting away from a sharp elbow.

"You're not?" Ki said through chattering teeth. "Well, I guess you're used to it."

"Used to what?"

"Sleeping bare, or almost, with just one person for warmth. Like I told you before, my brothers and me sleep all together in our clothes. It's nice, mostly, especially in winter." He sighed. " 'Course, Amin gets the farts, which makes it that much warmer."

Both boys dissolved into laughter again, shaking the bed.

"I've never heard anyone talk like you!" Tobin gasped, wiping his eyes on the edge of the sheet.

"Oh, I'm a bad character. Ask anyone. Hey, what's that?" He pushed back Tobin's left sleeve to inspect the birthmark. "Did you burn yourself?"

"No, I've always had it. Father says it's a sign I'm wise."

"Oh, yeah? Like this." Ki hauled down the covers and showed Tobin a brown spot on his right hip the size of a man's thumbprint. "Bad luck mark, a soothsayer told my mam, but I been lucky so far. Look at me, here with you. That's luck! Now, my sister Ahra's got one of them red ones like yours on her left tit. A wizard she showed it to down in Erind claimed it means she's feisty and sharp-tongued, so I guess he must have known how to read marks better. She's got a voice can curdle vinegar when she's riled up." He pulled the covers up again and sighed. "She treated me good, though, mostly. That's her old quiver I come with. It's got cuts on it from Plenimaran swords, and a stain she claims is blood!"

"Really?"

"Yeah. I'll show you tomorrow."

As they drifted off to sleep at last, Tobin decided that having a companion might not be such a bad thing after all. Caught up in thoughts of sisters and battles, he didn't notice the dark shape lurking unbidden in the far corner.

Brother woke Tobin sometime later with a cold touch on his chest. When Tobin opened his eyes, the ghost was standing next to the bed, pointing across the room at the chest where the doll was hidden. Tobin could feel Ki's warm, bony back pressed against his own, but he also saw him kneeling in front of the chest.

Tobin shivered as he watched the boy open the lid and take out a few things, examining them with curiosity. Tobin knew this was a vision. Brother had shown him things before, like the dying fox, and they were never nice. When Ki found the doll, his expression changed to one Tobin knew all too well.

Then the scene shifted. It was daylight now; Iya and Arkoniel were there with Ki, and Father, too. They put the doll down on the chest and cut it open with long knives, and it bled. Then they took it away, looking back at him with expressions of such sadness and disgust that his face burned.

The vision vanished, but the fear remained. As much as the thought of losing the doll terrified him, the look on everyone's faces—especially his father's and Ki's—filled him with grief and desperation.

Brother was still there beside the bed, touching his chest and Tobin's, and Tobin knew he'd shown him a true thing. Nari had never bothered with the old chest before. Ki was going to find the doll and everything would be ruined.

He lay very still, his heart beating so loudly in his ears he could hardly hear Ki's soft breathing behind him. What could he do?

Send him away, hissed Brother.

Tobin thought about what it had felt like to laugh with Ki and shook his head. "No," he replied, barely making a sound with his mouth. He didn't have to. Brother always heard him. "And don't you ever try to hurt him again! I have to hide it somewhere else. Somewhere no one will find it."

Brother disappeared. Tobin looked around and found him by the chest, motioning to him.

Tobin slid out of bed and crept across the cold floor, praying Ki wouldn't wake up. The lid rose by itself as he reached for it. For an instant he imagined Brother slamming it down on him for spite as he reached in, but he didn't. Tobin eased the flour sack out from under the rustling parchments and tiptoed into the corridor.

It was very late. No light showed at the staircase leading to the hall. The corridor lamp had gone out, but patches of moonlight gave him enough light to see by.

Brother wasn't showing himself now. Tobin hugged the doll to his chest, wondering where to go. Arkoniel was still sleeping in the toy room next door, and would soon occupy the newly repaired rooms upstairs, so that was no good. There was nowhere downstairs that someone wouldn't look, either. Perhaps he could get outside again into the forest and find some dry hole nearby? But no, the doors would all be barred and besides, there might be catamounts in the forest at night. Tobin shivered miserably. His bare feet ached with cold and he had to piss.

A creak of hinges came from the far end of the corridor as the door to the third floor swung open, shining like silver in the moonlight. The doorway beyond was a black mouth waiting to swallow him up.

Yes, there *was* one place, a place no one could go except Brother. And him.

Brother appeared in the open doorway. He looked at Tobin, then turned and disappeared up the dark stairs. Tobin followed, stubbing his bare toes on steps he could not see.

In the upstairs corridor moonlight streamed in through

the new rosette windows, casting pools of black and silver lace on the walls.

It took all his courage to approach the tower door; he thought he could feel his mother's angry spirit standing just on the other side, glaring at him right through the wood. He stopped a few feet away, heart beating so hard it hurt to breathe. He wanted to turn and run away but he couldn't move, not even when he heard the lock give. The door swung slowly open to reveal—

Nothing.

His mother was not standing there. Neither was Brother. It was dark inside, so dark that the lacy moonlight faded to a murky glow just a few inches inside. A current of cold, stale air crawled around his ankles.

Come, Brother whispered from the darkness.

I can't! Tobin thought, but somehow he was already following that voice. He found the first worn stone step with his toes and put his foot on it. The door closed behind him, shutting out the light. The spell that held Tobin broke. He dropped the doll and scrabbled for the door handle. The metal was so cold it burned his palm. The wooden door panels felt as if they were covered with frost as he beat his hands against them. The door wouldn't budge.

Upstairs, Brother urged.

Tobin slumped against the door, breathing in panicky sobs. "Flesh my flesh," he managed at last. "Blood my blood, bone my bone," and there was Brother at the base of the stairs, dressed in a ragged nightshirt and holding out his hand for Tobin to follow. When he didn't move, Brother squatted down in front of him, peering into his face. For the first time, Tobin saw that Brother had the same little crescent-shaped scar on his chin that Tobin did. Then Brother opened the neck of his shirt, showing Tobin that he had another scar, as well. Tobin could see two thin vertical lines of stitching on Brother's chest, very close

together, perhaps three inches long. It reminded Tobin of
the seams on his mother's dolls, but the stitches were even
finer, and the skin was puckered and bloody around
them.

That must hurt, Tobin thought.

It does, all the time, whispered Brother, and one
bloody tear fell down his cheek before he disappeared
again, taking all illusion of light with him.

Feeling his way blindly, Tobin found the bag and slid
his feet across the stone floor until he found the first step
again. The darkness made him dizzy, so he crawled up
the stairs on his hands and knees, dragging the bag beside
him. His bladder was so full it hurt, but he didn't quite
dare let go here in the darkness.

As he climbed higher he realized that he could see a
few stars through the arrow slits above. This gave him his
bearings and he hurried up the last few steps to find the
upper door standing open for him, just as he'd expected.
All he had to do now was hide the doll. Then he could
find a chamber pot or even an open window and go back
to bed.

The room was full of moonlight. Brother had opened
the shutters. The few times Tobin had let himself think of
this room, he remembered a cozy little chamber with tapestries on the walls and dolls on a table. This was a shambles. His memories of his last visit here were still
fragmentary, but the sight of a broken chair leg stirred
something dark and hurtful deep in his chest.

*His mother had brought him up here because she was
scared of the king.*

*She had jumped out the window because she was so
scared.*

She'd wanted him to jump, too.

Tobin inched inside and saw that only the window
facing west toward the mountains was open.

The same window—

That's where the light came from. He moved to stand

before it, as if the moon's white glow could protect him from all the shadowy fears building around him. His foot struck a broken chair back, then trod on a soft lump. It was a doll's arm. He'd watched his mother make hundreds. Someone—

Brother

—had strewn his mother's things all over the floor.

Bolts of cloth were thrown into a corner and mice had chewed holes in the little bales of stuffing wool. Turning slowly, he searched in vain for her fine boy dolls among the wreckage, but he couldn't see any, just bits and lumps and rags.

Something, a spool of thread perhaps, tinkled to the floor and Tobin jumped.

"Mama?" he croaked, praying she was there.

Praying she wasn't.

Not knowing which face she would show now that she was dead.

He heard another little thud and a rat scampered across the floor with a mouthful of wool.

Tobin slowly eased his aching grip on the flour sack. Brother was right. This was the best place.

Nobody came here.

Nobody would look.

He carried the sack to a moonlit corner across from the door. Placing it on the floor, he pulled the chair back over it and then piled some of the musty cloth over that. Dust motes rose in firefly clouds to choke him.

There. That's done.

The task had held his fear at bay, but as he got to his feet again he felt it flooding back. He turned hastily for the door, trying not to think about having to go down those steep stairs in the dark.

His mother stood silhouetted in the open window. He knew her by the shape of her shoulders and the way her hair fell loose around them. He could not see her face to read her eyes or the lines around her mouth. He didn't know if this was the good or the frightening mother taking a step toward him, holding out her arms.

For an instant Tobin hung suspended in time and horror.

She threw no shadow.

She made no sound.

She smelled of flowers.

That was the window she had tried to throw him out of. She had dragged him there, sobbing and cursing the king. She *had* pushed him out, but someone else pulled him back and he'd banged his chin on the sill—

The memory tasted like blood.

Then somehow he was in motion, dashing out the door, blundering down the stairs, one hand pressed to the rough stone wall, feeling the dry crusts of bird droppings and parched lichen flaking off beneath his fingers. He heard a sob and a slam behind him but refused to look back. He could see all the way to the bottom of the stairs now, guided by a rectangle of moonlight where the tower door stood open. He rushed headlong through it and flung it shut, not waiting to see if the latch caught, not caring if anyone heard. He fled downstairs, deafened by the ragged rush of his own frantic lungs, only dimly aware that his nightshirt and legs were wet. The realization that he'd wet himself halted him just outside his own room. He didn't even remember doing it.

He fought back fresh tears, berating himself for such weakness. Slipping in, he listened to be certain Ki was still sleeping, then pulled off the soiled shirt and used a sleeve and the cold water left in the basin to clean himself. He found his other shirt in the wardrobe, then carefully climbed back into bed. He tried not to shake the mattress, but Ki jerked awake with a frightened gasp, staring wide-eyed down the bed.

Brother stood there, glaring back at him.

Tobin gripped the older boy's shoulder, trying to keep him from crying out. "Don't be scared, Ki, he won't—"

Ki turned to him with a shaky little laugh. "Bilairy's balls, it's only you! For a minute I thought it was that ghost of yours crawling into the bed. You're cold enough to be one."

Tobin glanced at Brother, then back at Ki. He couldn't see Brother standing there hating him. He didn't have the eye.

Even so, Ki looked as scared as if he had as he asked, "Can I tell you something, Prince Tobin?"

Tobin nodded.

Ki fiddled with the edge of the quilt. "When old Iya told me about the ghost, I almost ran for home, even though I knew my father'd beat me and put me on the road. I almost did. And then, when the ghost started throwing things around downstairs tonight? I nearly pissed myself I was so scared. But you just stood there, like it didn't even matter. . . ." He hugged his arms around his drawn-up knees. "I guess what I'm trying to say is that my father didn't raise any cowards. I'm not feared of anything, except ghosts, and I can stand that to serve someone as brave as you. If you'll still have me."

He thinks I'm going to send him away. In that instant of recognition, Tobin nearly blurted it all out, about Brother and the doll and his mother and the wet nightshirt in a heap by the door. But the worshipful look in the older boy's eyes sealed the words behind his teeth.

Instead, he just shrugged and said, "Everyone's afraid of him, even Arkoniel. I'm used to him, that's all." He wanted to promise Ki that Brother wouldn't hurt him again, but he wasn't sure of that yet and didn't want to lie.

Ki got up on his knees and touched his forehead and heart in the soldier's salute. "Well, I still say you're brave, and if you'll accept my service, then I swear by Sakor and Illior that I'm your man until death."

"I accept," Tobin replied, feeling silly and proud at the same time. Ki had no sword to offer him, so they clasped hands on it and he flopped back down beside Tobin and burrowed under the covers.

Young as he was, Tobin understood that something important had passed between them. Until death, Ki had said. This conjured images of them riding side by side under his father's banner on some distant battlefield.

So long as the doll stayed hidden. So long as no one ever found out what was up there in the tower.

Mama is up there, locked in the tower.

The night's horror closed in around him again and he turned his back against Ki's, glad not to be alone. He would never go there again. She was there, waiting to catch him. But the tower was locked and Brother wouldn't let anyone else in.

Brother had warned him and his secret was safe. Now he would never see Ki looking at him with the face Brother had shown him in the vision.

"Tobin?" A sleepy mumble.

"What?"

"You say that ghost of yours is a he?"

"Yes. I call him Brother."

"Huh. . . . I'd heard tell it was a girl."

"Huh."

Ki's soft snore lulled Tobin to sleep, and he dreamed of riding east with Ki to find Ero and the sea.

Chapter 24

After the household had settled for the night, Arkoniel took Iya outside to walk in the meadow, just as he and Rhius had two months before. There had been bats and fireflies that night, and the song of frogs.

Tonight the meadow and forest were silent except for the hunting cries of owls in the moonlight. It was very cold, and the wizards' shadows fell sharp-edged across frost-coated grass as they followed one of the paths the workers had worn along the riverbank. The forest and peaks glimmered white around them. In the distance, a few fires still glowed in front of the handful of tents left at the bottom of the meadow. Most of the workmen had finished their tasks. The rest would soon be gone, as well, anxious to return to the city before the snow fell.

Arkoniel's encounter with Lhel earlier in the day weighed heavily on his mind. As they walked he tried to find the proper words to explain what had happened.

"What do you think of your new occupation?" she asked before he could broach the subject.

"I don't think I'm much of a teacher. Tobin cares nothing for learning or me, as far as I can tell. It's all warcraft and hunting with him. All he talks of is being a warrior." Even alone here they were careful to refer to Tobin as "he" and "him."

"So you dislike him?"

"Not in the least!" Arkoniel exclaimed. "He's intelligent, and a wonderful artist. You should see the little figures he makes. I think we're the happiest together when we're watching the craftsmen and builders."

Iya chuckled. "Then it's not 'all warcraft and hunting' after all? A clever teacher would find a way to make use of such interests. There's a great deal of mathematics in building a sound arch or planning a mural. The compounding of colors is practically alchemy. And to create the shapes of living things, one ought to have a sound knowledge of them."

Arkoniel raised his hands in surrender. "Yes, I see I've been a complete mole. I'll try to make a fresh start with him."

"Don't judge yourself too harshly, my boy. This isn't a young wizard you're training, after all, but a noble. Even as ruler, Tobin will never need the sort of education that we do. Half the Palatine can't write much more than their names. I must say I admire Rhius' stand on the matter; you still hear a good many fine lords and ladies calling it scribe's work. Teach them all to read for themselves and you'll put half the well-bred merchants' daughters out of an occupation. No, you keep on with that, and give him what you can of the disciplines he might find useful later on. Geography and history—you're well versed in those. He should learn something of music, and dancing, too, before he's summoned to court—"

"Have you heard something? Do you think he will be summoned soon?"

"No, but it must come eventually, unless Rhius is willing to paint him as an utter idiot to the king. And that will make our task a great deal more difficult when the moment arrives. No, I think we must assume that it will be necessary in the due course of time. He's just turning ten now. I'd say three years is the best we can hope for—perhaps less, being Royal Kin." She paused, frowning. "I pray he has time to grow up to his role before he has to step into it. There's no way of knowing."

Arkoniel shook his head. "He's so young, so—" He groped for the word. "Unworldly. It's difficult to imagine the fate that weighs on those narrow little shoulders."

"Take what the Lightbearer sends," Iya replied. "Whatever happens, we must make the best of what we are given to work with. For now, your task is to keep him safe and happy. You'll be my eyes here from now on. And if anything—untoward should happen with Ki . . . Perhaps you shouldn't allow yourself to get too attached."

"I know. Rhius made that a condition. It makes poor Ki sound like the pet lamb being fattened for the Solstice feast."

"He is here at your insistence, Arkoniel. Don't ever let that gentle heart of yours blind you to the reality of our situation."

"I've felt the god's touch, Iya. I never forget that."

She patted his arm. "I know. Now tell me more of Tobin."

"I'm concerned about his fear of magic."

"He fears you?"

"Not me, exactly, but— Well, he takes the oddest turns! When I first arrived, for instance, I tried to entertain him with a few pretty spells. You know, the sort of illusions that we'd do to amuse the children of any host?"

"And he was not amused?"

"You'd think I'd cut off my head and thrown it at him! The one time I did manage to please him with a vision of Ero, the demon nearly tore the room down. I haven't dared try anything more with him since."

Iya raised an eyebrow. "He must be cured of this if we are to realize our goal. Perhaps Ki can be of some help to you there. He liked the little tricks and illusions I showed him as we traveled." She smiled up at him. "You haven't yet said what you think of my choice."

"Judging by what I saw tonight, you chose very well. I was watching him when the demon attacked. He was terrified, but still went to Tobin instead of running away. He already understands his duty, without even knowing his lord."

"Rather exceptional for one so young. Now, as for the demon, was that unusual, what happened?"

"Not really, though it was more severe than anything I've seen since my arrival. I got something of the same kind of reception when I first arrived. It said it remembered me, so it must have known you, as well. That doesn't explain its attack on Ki, though. Has he any magic in him?"

"No, and it's a shame, for he might make an interesting wizard. He should do very nicely for Tobin. Now that I've seen the child, I must admit you were correct. He desperately needs some semblance of normal society." Iya turned back toward the keep and a frown creased her brow. "I only hope Ki influences him, rather than the other way around. I expected better of Rhius."

"I gather it's been difficult for him, with the demon and Ariani's madness. None of us foresaw that."

"Illior brings madness, as well as insight." In the cold, pale light, Iya suddenly looked like a statue made of iron. The image struck Arkoniel through with sadness. For the first time since he'd known her, he admitted to himself how hard she could be, how removed from the common flow of humanity. He'd seen this in other wizards, a detachment from what seemed to him normal feeling. It came of living so long, she'd once told him, but he'd tried hard to not see it in her.

Then she turned to him with a sad smile and the dark fancy retreated. She was again his patient teacher, the woman he loved as a second mother.

"Did you see anything when the demon was present?" he asked.

"No, but I felt it. It does remember me and it does not forgive. But I gathered from your letter that you saw it?"

"Only once, but as clearly as I see you now. The day I arrived here it was waiting for me down there where the road comes out of the trees. It looked exactly like Tobin, except for the eyes—"

"You're wrong there." Iya plucked a stalk of dead

grass and twirled it between her fingers. "It doesn't look like Tobin. Tobin looks like it, or at least as the dead boy would have looked, had he lived. That was the purpose of Lhel's magic, after all, to give the girl child the semblance of her brother. Illior only knows what Tobin actually looks like." She paused, tapping the dry stalk against her chin. "I wonder what name he will choose, after the change?"

The thought was somewhat disorienting, but it also jarred him back to what he'd come out here for in the first place.

"I saw Lhel today. From what I could gather, I'd say she's been here all along."

"The witch is here? By the Light, why didn't Nari or Rhius say something?"

"They don't know. No one does. I don't know how, Iya, but it seems she followed the child here and lives somewhere nearby."

"I see." Iya gazed around at the forest that hemmed in the keep. "Did she say why?"

Arkoniel hesitated, then slowly explained what had happened between the two of them. When he reached the point where Lhel had overpowered him, however, he faltered to a halt. The temptation had been so great; just thinking of it now stirred the dark, thrilling guilt in him. It had been Lhel who had stopped short of coupling, not he.

"She—she wanted me to break celibacy, in return for learning what she had to teach. And as payment for watching over Tobin."

"I see." Arkoniel caught another glimpse of iron in her. "Is it your impression that she will abandon the child if you don't comply with her demand?"

"No, she must make amends to her own gods somehow for creating the demon. I don't think she could go against that. Short of killing her, I doubt we could force her away."

"Nor should we." Iya stared at the river, lost in thought.

"I've never told anyone this before," she said softly, "but my own master studied the Old Magic. It's more powerful than you know."

"But it's forbidden!"

Iya snorted. "So is what we are attempting, dear boy. And why do you suppose I sought her out in the first place? Perhaps it's the fate of the wizards of our line to do what is forbidden when necessary. Perhaps it is what Illior intends for you."

"You mean I *should* learn from her?"

"I believe I can undo the magics she wove on Tobin. But what if I'm wrong? What if I die before the time comes, as Agazhar did with me? Yes, it might be best if you learn from her what must be done, and in her way."

"But her price?" Arkoniel's chest tightened at the thought. He tried to believe it was purely revulsion.

Iya's lips pressed into a thin line of disapproval. "Offer her something else."

"What if she refuses?"

"Arkoniel, I taught you what my master taught me; that celibacy preserves our power. I have practiced it since I undertook the craft. There are those who stray, however, and not all of them have been weakened by the experience. Many, but not all. . . ."

Arkoniel felt as if the earth were opening up under his feet. "Why didn't you ever tell me this before?"

"Why would I? As a child you didn't need to know. And as a young man in your prime? It was too dangerous, the temptation too real. I was nearly as old as you are now when I began my training, and no virgin. The tides of the flesh are strong, make no mistake, and we all feel their pull. Once a wizard gets past the first life and feels his power strong in him, it becomes easier to bear. The carnal pleasures pale in comparison, I promise you."

"I *will* refuse her, Iya."

"You will do what you will do, dear boy." Iya took his

hands between her own and looked into his face; her skin was cold as ivory. "There's so much more I'd hoped to teach you. Before Afra I imagined that we had the rest of my life together. You are my successor, Arkoniel, and the finest student I've ever had. We've known that for some time, Illior and I." She patted the bag hanging over her shoulder. "But Illior has other plans for you just now, as we've both seen. For the time being you must take what lessons you can find and make of them what you can. If Lhel can teach you, then learn from her. Barring all else, you must keep watch and learn if she has any ill intent toward the child."

"Your answer is no answer at all!" Arkoniel groaned, more confused than ever.

Iya shrugged. "You're not a child anymore, or an apprentice. There comes a time when a wizard must learn to trust his own heart. You've been doing just that for some time now, though you don't seem to have noticed yet." Smiling, she tapped him on the chest. "Listen to this, my dear. I believe it to be a good, true guide."

Arkoniel felt a sudden chill of premonition. "That sounds almost like a farewell."

Iya smiled sadly. "It is, but only to the boy who was my student. The man who's stolen into his place needn't fear losing me. I like him too much for that, and we've a great deal of work to do together."

"But—" Arkoniel groped for words. "How will I know the right things to do, to help Tobin and protect him?"

"Do you think Illior would have sent you here unless you were worthy of the task? Now, then. Are you going to keep an old woman outdoors all night or may we go in now?"

"Old woman, eh? When did that happen?" Arkoniel asked, slipping his arm through hers as they walked up the hill.

"I've been wondering that myself."

"How long can you stay?"

"Not long, judging from the demon's reception. How has it treated you since it broke your arm?"

"Surprisingly well. It knocks the furniture around now and then, but Tobin appears to have some control over it. According to Nari, it has been much quieter since Ariani's death."

"Very odd. You'd think it would be just the opposite. In all my years, Arkoniel, I've never seen a spirit quite like this one. It makes one wonder . . ."

"What?"

"Whether it will surprise us again when we try to break its bond with Tobin."

They returned to the keep, intending for Iya to share Arkoniel's room for the night. As soon as they set foot inside the hall, however, they could feel the demon's malevolence closing in around them. The air thickened perceptibly and the hearth fire guttered and burned pale.

Nari and the others of the household gathered around the hearth looked up in alarm.

"Be careful, Iya. There's no telling what it will do," Tharin warned.

The ominous weight of silence drew out, and then they heard something clatter loudly to the floor at the far end of the room near the high table. Another clatter followed and Iya cast a light in the air, illuminating the room enough to see the silver plate being knocked from the shelves of the sideboard. One by one, platters and bowls slid off with a thud or clank onto the rushes. Each object moved by itself, but Arkoniel could easily imagine the wild, surly child he'd encountered at the bottom of the meadow, watching them over its shoulder and smiling spitefully as it reached for the next salver or cup.

The strange performance continued, and each successive dish flew a little further from the sideboard, veered a little more in their direction.

"That's quite enough of that!" Iya muttered. Striding down the hall, she stopped just short of the sideboard and sketched a circle of white light on the air before her with her crystal wand.

"What's she doing?" asked Nari.

"I'm not certain," Arkoniel said, trying to read the sigils Iya was inscribing into the circle. It looked something like a banishing spell a drysian had tried to teach them, but the sigils taking shape in the circle were not what he recalled.

Perhaps Iya was mistaken in her weaving, for just then a heavy silver platter flew from its shelf and collided with the circle. Pattern and wand exploded in a sudden burst of blue-white fire. Iya cried out, clutching her hand to her side.

Blinking black spots from his vision, Arkoniel ran to her and pulled Iya away as the demon scattered the remaining silver around the room, then began overturning benches. Arkoniel wrapped his arms around her and pulled her head down, trying to shield her. Then Tharin was there, doing the same for both of them.

"Outside!" Iya gasped, trying to push them off.

They staggered out into the courtyard with the rest of the frightened servants, then looked back in through the open doorway to see tapestries flying through the air. One landed on the open hearth.

"Fetch water!" Mynir shouted. "It means to set the house afire!"

"Go to the barracks. You can sleep there," Tharin ordered, then dashed back into the house to aid the others.

Arkoniel helped Iya to the dark barracks house. A brazier stood just inside the door and he snapped a finger over it, kindling a small blaze. Narrow pallets lined the walls and Iya sank down on the closest one. Arkoniel gently took her wounded hand and examined it in the flickering light. A long red burn marked where the crystal wand had laid against her palm. Small cuts and fragments of the wand peppered her fingers and knuckles.

"It's not as bad as it looks," Iya said, letting him pick out the shards of crystal.

"Yes, it is. Lie down. I'll go get a few things and come right back."

He ran back into the hall and found Cook and the others flailing at a smoking tapestry and kicking smoldering rushes onto the hearth.

"Douse!" Arkoniel ordered, clapping his hands sharply and spreading his palms over the floor. The last of the sparks fizzled out, leaving a stinking cloud in their wake. "Iya's hurt. I need simples for a burn, and clean rags for binding."

Cook fetched what he needed, and Tharin followed him out to the barracks to oversee the binding of Iya's hand.

"What happened?" the captain demanded. "What was it you were trying to do?"

Iya winced as Arkoniel bathed her hand in a basin. "Something rather unwise, it would seem."

Tharin waited, giving her the opportunity to elucidate. When she didn't, he nodded and said, "You'd best stay out here tonight. I'll sleep in the hall."

"Thank you." She looked up from Arkoniel's work. "What are you doing here, Tharin? Rhius is at Atyion, isn't he?"

"I'm Prince Tobin's swordmaster. I've stayed behind to continue his training."

"Indeed, Tharin?"

Something in the way Iya said this made Arkoniel pause and look up.

"I've known you since you and Rhius were boys together. Tell me how Rhius fares. I've been away too long and feel like a stranger."

Tharin rubbed a hand over his short beard. "He's had a rough time of it, as you might imagine. It was hard before, and losing Ariani in such a way—not just her death, but having her mad all those years after the birth, and hating him." He shook his head. "I can't for the life of me understand why she blamed him for that child dying, or why she took it so hard. I don't mean to speak ill of the dead, Iya, but I think there was more of her mother in her than anyone ever guessed. Some say that's why the dead child haunts the living one, though I don't put any stock in that."

"What else do people say?"

"Oh, all sorts of things."

"For the sake of the child, tell me. You know it will go no further with us."

Tharin looked down at his scarred hands. "There are those who say that Rhius found out he wasn't the father and killed one of the babes before anyone could stop him; that that's why the dead child haunts, and why he keeps Tobin away from court."

"What nonsense! How is the duke managing at court?"

"The king keeps him close, as always. He calls Rhius 'brother,' but— Things have been a bit strained between them since she died, though a good deal of that seems to be on Rhius' side. He's cleared out of his rooms at the New Palace and gone back to Atyion. He can't even bear to be here anymore."

"That's not fair to the child."

Tharin looked up at them and, for the first time, Arkoniel saw a shadow of pain and guilt there. "I know that and I told him so. That's part of the reason I was sent back, if you must know. I haven't told anyone here at the keep, for fear it would get back to Tobin. It would break his heart and it's about broken mine."

Iya took his hand in her good one. "You've always spoken to Rhius like a brother, Tharin. I can't imagine that you've fallen too far out of his graces. I'll speak to him about it when I meet him."

Tharin rose to go. "You don't need to. This will pass. Good night to you."

Iya watched him go, then shook her head. "I've often regretted not telling him."

Arkoniel nodded. "I feel it more strongly the longer I'm here."

"Let's leave things as they are for now." Iya flexed her bandaged hand and winced. "I can ride with this. I think I'll be off tomorrow. I want to see Ero again, and have a word with Rhius."

"Ero? That's walking into the wolves' own den. You're sure to meet with Harriers there."

"No doubt, but they need looking into. I wish Illior had given us a glimpse of *them* when this whole thing started. Don't fret, Arkoniel. I'll be careful."

"More careful than you were in the hall just now, I hope. What happened?"

"I don't know, exactly. When I first arrived tonight and it attacked I felt the circle of protection I'd cast bow like a tent wall in a high wind. Just now I thought something stronger was called for and attempted to push it from the room and seal the hall against it until morning."

"Did you make an error in the pattern?"

"No, the spell was laid out properly. But it didn't work, as you saw. As I said earlier, this spirit is unlike anything I've ever encountered. I wish I had more time to study it, but as things stand it would be too disruptive for the children. I don't even dare go back in the house. I would like to see Tobin again before I go, though. Will you bring him to me in the morning? Alone, this time."

"Of course. But I wouldn't expect it to be a long conversation if I were you. He's not easily drawn."

Iya lay down on the pallet and chuckled. "I could see that much at a glance. By the Light, you do have your work cut out for you!"

Chapter 25

Ki was at the open window when Tobin woke the next morning. He stood with his chin on one hand, picking absently at a patch of lichen on the sill with long, restless fingers. He looked younger in daylight, and sad.

"Do you miss your family?"

Ki's head jerked up. "You must be a wizard, too. You can read thoughts." But he smiled as he said it. "It's awful quiet here, isn't it?"

Tobin sat up and stretched. "Father's men make a lot of noise when they're here. But they're all at Atyion now."

"I've been there." Ki hitched himself up on the sill, bare legs dangling under the hem of his shirt. "At least I've ridden past it on the way to the city. Your castle is the biggest in Skala, outside of Ero. How many rooms does it have?"

"I don't know. I've never been there." Seeing Ki's eyebrows shoot up, he added, "I've never been anywhere except here and Alestun. I was born at the Palace but I don't remember it."

"You don't go visiting? We have family all over the place and go guest with them. If my uncle were the king, I'd want to go to Ero all the time. There's music there, and dancing, and players in the street and—" He broke off. "Oh, because of the demon?"

"I don't know. Mama didn't like to go anywhere. And Father says there's plague in the cities." It occurred to Tobin that Ki had survived his travels well enough. He shrugged. "I've always just been here."

Ki twisted around to look out the window. "Well,

what do you do for fun? I bet you don't have to mend walls or tend pigs!"

Tobin grinned. "No, Father has tenants to do those things. I train with Tharin and go hunting in the forest. And I have a toy city my father made for me, but Arkoniel's in that room now so I'll have to show you later."

"All right then, let's go hunting." Ki slid off the sill and began looking under the bed for his clothes. "How many hounds do you have? I didn't see any in the hall last night."

"Just a few old ones in the yard. But I don't hunt with them; dogs don't like me. But Tharin says I'm a fine archer. I'll ask if he can take us hunting."

Brown eyes peered at him over the edge of the bed. "*Take* us? You mean you don't go by yourself?"

"I'm not to go away from the keep alone."

Ki disappeared again and Tobin heard a sigh. "All right then. It's not too cold to swim, or we could fish. I saw a good spot at the bottom of the meadow."

"I've never fished," Tobin admitted, feeling very awkward. "And I can't swim."

Ki rose up and rested his elbows on the edge of the bed, regarding Tobin quizzically. "How old are you?"

"I'll be ten come the twentieth of Erasin."

"And they don't let you have any fun on your own? Why not?"

"I don't know, I—"

"You know what?"

Tobin shook his head.

"Before I left home, after Iya bought me off my father, my sister told me she'd heard of you."

Tobin's heart turned to stone in his chest.

"She said that some folk at court say you're demon cursed, or simple in the head, and that that's why you live clear out here instead of in Ero or Atyion. You know what I think?"

This was it, then. Last night hadn't meant a thing after all. It was going to be just the way he'd feared. Tobin kept his chin up and made himself look Ki in the eye. "No. What do you think?"

"*I* think the folks who say that have shit between their ears. And I think the folks raising you are the ones simple in the head if they won't let you outside on your own— not meaning any disrespect to Duke Rhius, mind you." Ki gave him a teasing grin that swept away every shadow and fear. "And I think it's well worth a beating to get out on a day as fair as this is making up to be."

"Do you, now?" asked Arkoniel, leaning against the door frame. Ki sat up, blushing guiltily, but the wizard laughed. "So do I, and I don't think it has to come to beatings. I've been talking with Nari and Tharin. They agree that it's time Prince Tobin began following proper boy's pursuits. With you here to accompany him, I don't think any reasonable request will be refused so long as you don't stray too far."

Tobin stared at the man. He knew he ought to be grateful for this sudden change in the household rules, but he resented it coming from the wizard. Who was Arkoniel to make such decisions, as if he was the master of the house?

"Before you go off on any adventures, though, my prince, Iya would like to speak with you," Arkoniel told him. "She's at the barracks. Ki, why don't you go see what Cook has to eat? I'll meet you in the hall, Tobin."

Tobin glared angrily at the door as it closed behind the wizard, then began yanking on his clothes. "Who do they think they are, these wizards, coming here and ordering me about?"

"I don't think he was doing that," said Ki. "And don't worry about Iya. She's not so frightening as she seems."

Tobin shoved on his shoes. "I'm not scared of her."

Iya was enjoying her breakfast in a sunny corner of the barracks yard when Arkoniel arrived with Tobin.

Daylight bore out the brief impression she'd formed the night before. The child was thin and rather pale from too much time spent indoors, but otherwise unmistakably male in appearance. No spell known to the Orëska could have done more than create a glamour around the girl, too easily detected or broken. Lhel's cruel stitching had held perfectly. The magics sewn in with that bit of flesh had held sinew and flesh in solid form, real as the female frame that lay hidden beneath it.

Sadly, Tobin hadn't inherited his parents' handsome looks except for his mother's eyes and well-shaped mouth, and even these were spoiled at the moment by a sulky, guarded expression. Clearly, he wasn't pleased to see her, but he made her a proper bow all the same. Too proper, really. As Arkoniel had observed, there was little that was childlike about this child.

"Good morning, Prince Tobin. And how are you liking your new companion?"

Tobin brightened a little at that. "I like him very much, Mistress Iya. Thank you for bringing him."

"I must leave today, but I wanted to speak with you before I go to visit your father."

"You're going to see Father?" Yearning so plain it made her heart ache showed on the child's face.

"Yes, my prince. May I take him a greeting from you?"

"Would you please ask him when he's going to come home?"

"I plan to speak to him about that. Now come and sit beside me so I may know you better."

For a moment she thought he would refuse, but manners won out. He settled on the stool she'd placed beside her chair, then looked curiously at her bandaged hand. "Did you hurt yourself?"

"Your demon was very angry with me last night. It burned my hand."

"Just as it made my horse throw me when I first arrived," added Arkoniel.

"It shouldn't have done that." Tobin's cheeks colored hotly as if he'd done these things himself.

"Arkoniel, I'd like to speak privately with the prince. Would you excuse us?"

"Of course."

"It wasn't your fault, my dear," Iya began after Arkoniel had gone, wondering how to draw out this strange child. When Tobin said nothing, she took his thin, callused hand between her own and looked deeply into his eyes. "You've had too many sorrows and frights already in your young life. I won't tell you that there are no more to come, but I hope things will be easier for you for a time."

Still holding his hand, she asked him about simple things at first: his horse, his carvings, and his studies with Arkoniel and Tharin. She did not read his thoughts, simply let the impressions come to her through their clasped hands. Tobin answered each question she put to him, but volunteered nothing more.

"You've been very frightened, haven't you?" she ventured at last. "Of your mother and the demon?"

Tobin shuffled his feet, drawing twin arcs in the dust with the toes of his shoes.

"Do you miss your mother?"

Tobin didn't look up, but a jolt passed between them and she caught an image of Ariani as Tobin must have seen her that last terrible day, clear as if Iya was standing in the tower room with them. So it had been terror that had driven the princess up to that tower, rather than hatred of the child. But with this image came something else: a fleeting twinge of something else associated with the tower, something the child had pushed further from his mind than she'd imagined possible in one so young. She saw him glance up at it.

"Why are you so frightened of it now?" she asked.

Tobin pulled back and clasped his hands in his lap, not looking at her. "I—I'm not."

"You mustn't lie to me, Tobin. You are mortally afraid of it."

Tobin sat mute as a turtle, but a torrent of emotion was building up behind those stubborn blue eyes. "Mama's ghost is there," he said at last, and again he looked strangely ashamed. "She's still angry."

"I'm sorry she was so unhappy. Is there something more you'd like to tell me about her? You can, you know. I must seem like a stranger to you, but I have served your family for many years. I've known your father all of his life, and his mother and grandfather before him. I was a good friend to them. I want to be your friend, as well, and serve you as best I can. So does Arkoniel. Did he tell you that?"

"Nari did," Tobin mumbled.

"It was his idea to come here and be your teacher, and to bring Ki here, too. He was worried that you were lonely without any friends of your own age. He also told me that you don't seem to like him."

This earned her only a sidelong glance and more silence.

"Did the demon tell you not to like him?"

"It's not a demon. It's a ghost," Tobin said softly. "And it doesn't like you, either. That's why it hurt you last night."

"I see." She decided to gamble, knowing she had little to lose in the way of trust. "Did Lhel say that the ghost doesn't like me?"

Tobin shook his head, then caught himself and looked up at her with startled eyes. Here was one secret revealed.

"Don't be scared, Tobin. I know she's here. So does Arkoniel. Did she speak to you about us?"

"No."

"How did you meet her?"

Tobin squirmed on the stool. "In the woods, after Mama died."

"You went into the forest alone?"

He nodded. "Are you going to tell?"

"Not if you don't want me to, so long as you tell me the truth. Why did you go into the woods, Tobin? Did she call you?"

"In dreams. I didn't know it was her. I thought it was Mama. I had to go see, so I stole out one day. I got lost but she found me and helped me get back home."

"What else did she do?"

"She let me hold a rabbit, and she told me how to call Brother."

"Brother?"

Tobin sighed. "You *promise* you won't tell?"

"I'll try not to, unless I think your father should know to keep you safe."

Tobin looked at her directly for the first time and the hint of a smile quirked the corner of his mouth. "You could have lied, but you didn't."

For an instant Iya felt like she'd been stripped naked. If she hadn't already known otherwise, she'd have looked for magic in him. Trying to cover her surprise, she replied, "I'd rather we be honest with each other."

"Brother is what Lhel said to call the spirit. She said you can't give the dead a name if they never had one before they died. Is that true?"

"She knows about such things, so it must be true."

"Why didn't Father or Nari tell me about him?"

Iya shrugged. "What do you think of him, now that you know?"

"He still does mean things, but I'm not as scared of him anymore."

"Why did Lhel teach you to call him?"

He looked away, guarded again. "She said I'm to take care of him."

"You made him stop throwing things in the hall last night, didn't you? Does he always do what you tell him to do?"

"No. But I can keep him from hurting people." He looked at her hand again. "Usually."

"That's very good of you." Another child might just as easily have done the opposite. She would speak to Arkoniel about this before she left. Outside the sheltered confines of the keep, it might occur to Tobin to use his power differently. "Will you show me what she taught you?"

"You mean call Brother here?" Tobin looked less than enthusiastic at the prospect.

"Yes. I'll trust you to protect me."

Still Tobin hesitated.

"Very well. What if I close my eyes and put my fingers in my ears while you do what she showed you? Just touch me on the knee when I can look."

"You promise not to look?"

"By my hands and heart and eyes, I swear it. That's the most solemn and binding oath a wizard can give." With that, she squeezed her eyes shut and plugged her ears, then turned her back for good measure.

She kept her promise not to look or listen. She didn't have to, for she felt clearly enough the spell that rippled briefly in the air nearby. It was a summoning of some sort, but not any she recognized. The air around her went deathly cold. She felt a tap on her knee and opened her eyes to find two boys standing before her. Perhaps it was Tobin's proximity, or the spell itself. Perhaps the unquiet spirit had simply chosen to show itself to her, but the one called Brother looked as solid as his twin, except that he cast no shadow. Even without this, however, there was no confusing the two.

Brother was completely still, but Iya sensed a wild black rage in him. His mouth did not move, but she heard the words, *You will not enter* as clearly as if he'd put those pale lips to her ear. The hair rose on the back of her neck, for the words had the bitter tang of a curse.

Then he was gone.

"You see?" said Tobin. "Sometimes he just does what he wants to."

"You kept him from attacking me. He would have if you weren't here. Thank you, my prince," said Iya.

Tobin managed a smile, but Iya felt more disturbed than ever. A young child, especially a child with no magic, should not have been able to do what she had just witnessed.

She nearly laughed aloud when this bold little tamer of spirits replied, "You won't tell, will you?"

"I'll make you a bargain. I won't tell your father, or anyone else, if you let me tell Arkoniel, and if you promise to try to be his friend and go to him for help whenever you need it." She hesitated, weighing her words. "You must tell him if Lhel asks anything of you that scares you, anything at all. Will you promise me that?"

Tobin shrugged. "I'm not scared of her."

"Keesa don't should be, Wizard," a familiar voice said from the barracks doorway. "I help her." Iya turned and found Lhel regarding her with a scornful smile. "I help you. Help that boy wizard of yours, too." She raised her left hand and showed Iya the crescent moon tattooed there. "By Goddess, I swear you not make me go this time. When Brother go on, then I go. You leave me to work until time I can go. You got own work, Wizard, to help this child and the spirit."

"What are you looking at?" asked Tobin.

Iya glanced at him, then back. Lhel was gone.

"Nothing. A shadow," Iya said, distracted. Even looking straight at the woman, she'd been unable to sense what manner of magic the witch had used. "Now, give me your hand, my prince, and promise me you'll try to be Arkoniel's friend. He'll be very sad if you refuse."

"I'll try," Tobin muttered. Pulling his hand free, he walked away, but not before she'd seen the betrayed look in his eyes. He might not have seen Lhel, but he'd known she'd lied.

Iya watched him out of sight, then sank her face into her good hand, knowing the witch had surprised her into a serious misstep, perhaps even intentionally.

Like it or not, she had misjudged Lhel all those years ago and now their fates were twined together too tightly to risk any rash action.

The deathly coldness washed over her again. Brother crouched at her feet now, staring at her with gloating, hate-filled eyes.

You will not enter, he whispered again.

"Enter where?" she demanded.

But Brother kept his own secrets and took them with him when he vanished.

Iya sat for some time, pondering the spirit's ominous words.

After Tobin left with the wizard, Ki found his way back down to the hall. He still couldn't believe that this grand place was to be his home. Haunted it might be, but to live among royalty and wizards seemed well worth the risk in daylight.

Young as he was, however, he'd seen enough of the world to know how strange a household this was. A prince belonged in the fine palaces Ki had glimpsed over the Palatine walls at Ero, not in a backwater keep like this one. Then again, Prince Tobin was damned strange himself. A pinched-up, dark little thing with eyes like an old man. Ki had been a little scared of him the first time he'd seen him. But after they'd gotten to laughing, Ki saw something else. Odd Tobin might be, but not like people said. Ki thought again of how the younger boy had stood up to the demon's rage, not even twitching an eyelid, and his heart swelled with pride. What would a living enemy be to someone like that?

He continued on and met Captain Tharin coming into the hall by another door behind the high table. The lanky blond man had on a rough shirt and tunic like a common soldier's, and shared the men's barracks here, even though Ki knew from Iya that he was the son of a rich knight at Atyion. Here was another person he had a good feeling about, and this one from first look last night.

"Good morning, lad. Looking to break your fast? Come on, then, the kitchen's through here."

Tharin led him through another door and into a large warm kitchen where the cook was at work over a kettle.

"How does the place suit you so far?" Tharin asked, settling down by the hearth to repair a buckle on his scabbard.

"Very well, sir. I hope I'll suit the prince and Duke Rhius."

"I've no doubt of that. Mistress Iya wouldn't have chosen you otherwise."

Cook brought them some broth and stale bread. Ki sat down on a bench and watched Tharin work with his awl and waxed thread. Tharin had a nobleman's fine hands, but the skill of a craftsman in them.

"Will the duke be coming here soon?"

"That's hard to say. The king keeps him busy in the city these days." He made short work of the buckle and laid his tools aside.

Ki dipped his bread in the broth and took a bite. "How come you're not with him?"

Tharin raised an eyebrow at him, but looked more amused than annoyed. "Duke Rhius has entrusted me with Tobin's training at arms. Until we go off to fight again, I'm honored to serve him here. From what I saw last night, you're going to be quite a help to me. Tobin needs someone matched to him for practice." He reached for his own cup and took a sip. "That was a fine thing you did last night."

"What did I do?" asked Ki.

"You stepped in to protect Tobin when the demon was racketing about in the hall." Tharin said, as nonchalantly as if they were discussing the weather or crops. "I don't believe you even thought about it. You just did it, even though you'd scarcely met him. I've seen a lot of squires—I was with Rhius in the Royal Companions in our youth—and I can tell you there aren't many, even the best, who'd have thought to do that under such conditions. Well done, Ki."

Tharin set his cup aside and ruffled Ki's hair. "Tobin and I will take you up the road later and show you some good hunting. I've got a craving for Cook's good grouse pie."

Struck speechless by this unexpected praise, Ki could only nod as the man went outside again. As Tharin had said, he'd acted without thinking and so had thought nothing of it. His own father seldom took note when Ki tried to do well, only when he'd failed.

He sat for a moment, then tossed the rest of his bread into the fire with a prayer to Sakor to always be worthy of this man's regard.

By the time Arkoniel came back to the barracks yard, Iya had reached an uneasy decision.

"Are you ready to go?" he asked.

"Yes, but there's one last thing we must speak of before I leave."

Rising, she took his arm and led him inside. "We're likely to be separated for some time, you know." Reaching behind the narrow pallet she'd used, she pulled out the leather bag and placed it in his arms. "I think it's time I passed this on to you."

Arkoniel stared at her in alarm. "This is passed on when the old Guardian dies!"

"Don't go scattering my ashes just yet!" She did her best to sound annoyed. "I've been thinking about what you said before. The Harriers will be more vigilant in Ero, and perhaps more likely than most to notice something like this. It's safer here with you for the time being." When he remained dubious she gripped his arm firmly. "Listen to me, Arkoniel. You know what happened to Agazhar. What do you suppose I've been doing all these years but training you for this? You're as much the Guardian now as I am. You know all the spells to hide and mask it. You know the history, what little there is left. There's nothing left to teach you. Say you'll do this for me. I'm ready to be free of it. I must concentrate on Tobin now."

Arkoniel clasped the bag in both hands. "Of course I will. You know that. But— You are coming back, aren't you?"

Iya sighed, determined not to make the same mistake with him she had with Tobin just now. "I certainly plan to, my dear, but these are dangerous times. If one of us falls, the other must be ready to carry on with the task Illior has set for us. The bowl is safer here, just as Tobin is."

She stood to go and he embraced her, something he hadn't done since he was a child. Her cheek came just to his shoulder now. She hugged him back, thinking, *What a fine man you've grown into.*

Chapter 26

Iya dressed as a merchant to enter the city. She hadn't worn an amulet since that night in Sylara and wanted no undue attention now. She was soon glad of her decision.

A few miles out from Ero, she came upon a gibbet by the side of the road. The body of a naked man still hung there, swinging gently in the wind that blew in from the sea. The face was too black and swollen to make out, but as she came closer she could see that in life he'd been young and well fed, not a laborer.

She reined in. A large "T" for "traitor" was branded into the center of the dead man's chest. Uneasy memories of Agnalain stirred in her heart. This road had once been lined with such sights as this. She was about to ride on when the wind caught the body again and swung it around so she caught a glimpse of his palms. The center of each was covered with a circle of black tracery.

This poor fellow had been a novice at the Temple of Illior.

Wizards and priests, she thought bitterly. *The Harriers hunt the children of Illior at the gates of the capital itself and hang them out like a farmer would a dead crow.*

She made a blessing sign and whispered a prayer for the young priest's spirit, but as she rode on she was haunted by Brother's parting words to her.

You will not enter.

She steeled herself as she approached the guards at

the gate, waiting for some challenge or outcry, but none came.

She took a room in a modest inn near the upper market and spent the next few days listening in high places and low, trying to gauge the mood of the people. She was careful to avoid anyone who might recognize her, nobles and wizards alike.

Prince Korin and his Companions were a common sight around the city, galloping about with their guards and squires. Korin was a fine, strong lad of thirteen now, the image of his father with his ruddy dark coloring and laughing eyes. Iya felt a pang of regret the first time she watched him ride past; if Tobin was who he appeared to be, and if a better ruler sat upon the throne, he'd have soon been of age to claim his place in this happy band, not hidden away with a landless knight's unwanted brat as his only companion. With a sigh, she put such thoughts aside and resolved to concentrate on what she'd come here to do.

Years of intermittent drought and sickness had left their mark even here. The warren of tenements that ringed the city was less crowded now. Many doors were still nailed shut and bore the lead circles used to mark plague houses, remnants of the previous summer's outbreak. One house in Sheepshead Street had been burned; the epithet "Plague Bringer" was still scrawled on one charred wall.

In the wealthier wards up the hill such reminders were usually taken down as soon as the illness passed and the bodies had been burnt, but many fine houses were still boarded up, and shops, too. Weeds growing in the doorways showed that there was no one left inside to clean them away.

A strange, unhealthy gaiety reigned in the wake of death. The clothing of the wealthy was dyed brighter colors, and made gaudier still with patterned borders and jewels. Many mourners had their lost loved ones' likenesses embroidered on their coats or skirts, with maudlin verses stitched beneath. Sleeves, caps, and mantles were ornate even among the merchant classes, and cut to exaggerated lengths.

The strange hysteria was not limited to fashion. Every masker, mummer, and puppeteer company who plied their trade in the streets now featured a gaudy new persona in their repertoire—Red and Black Death. Red ribbons fluttered gaily from this character's mask and tunic, signifying the blood that seeped through the afflicted's skin like sweat, and poured from their mouth and nose in the final agony. He also sported an exaggerated black codpiece and lumpy armlets, mimicking the dark pustules that swelled in groin and armpits. His fellow maskers delighted in abusing this strutter and donned beaked masks to chase him off.

Nosegays and pomanders of purifying herbs said to fend off the foul humors that caused the plague were worn by folk of every class. In these times, one never knew when the real Red and Black would come for a return engagement.

Another noticeable difference was the scarcity of wizards about on the streets. In the old days conjurers and fortune readers plied their trade in every market. Wizards with noble patrons lived like lords and ladies themselves. Now she saw few except the occasional white-robed Harrier accompanied by patrols of grey-uniformed guards. Iya turned aside quickly when she saw them coming, but watched the faces of those around her.

Many people paid the patrols little mind, but others watched with poorly concealed fear or anger. Grey-backs, the boldest called them, well out of hearing. Grey-back was common parlance for "louse."

Iya was standing at the booth of an Aurënfaie goldsmith when one such patrol marched past. The gold-

smiths' faces were inscrutable beneath the intricate tattooed patterns of Khatme clan, but there was no mistaking
the outrage in their grey eyes, or the implicit curse as the
eldest woman spat over her left shoulder at their backs.

"You don't think much of them," Iya remarked quietly
in their language.

"Wizard killers! They spit in the Lightbearer's face!"
The 'faie were monotheists, worshipping only Illior, whom
they called Aura. "We expect such things in Plenimar, but
never here! No wonder your land suffers."

That evening Iya was watching a mummer's show in the
great marketplace near the Palatine when she felt a touch
on her sleeve. Turning, she found herself face-to-face with
a young Harrier flanked by a dozen or more grey-backs.
The red birds on their tunics seemed to circle her like vul-
tures as they closed ranks around her.

"Good day, Mistress Wizard," the young wizard
greeted her. He had a round, cheerful face and innocent
blue eyes that she distrusted the moment she looked into
them. "I haven't had the pleasure of your acquaintance."

"Nor I yours," she replied. "I haven't been in the city
for years."

"Ah, then perhaps you did not know that all wizards
entering the capital are required to register with the Grey
Guard, and to display their symbols openly?"

"No, young man, I did not. There was no such law
when I was last here and no one troubled to inform me."
Iya's heart was hammering in her chest, but she summoned up the dignity of her years, hoping to overawe
him. In truth, however, it had shaken her badly to be discovered by one so young. She had used no magic to mask
herself, but he'd still had to make a conscious effort to
identify her. "If you'd be so kind as to direct me to the
proper officials, I will make myself known to them."

"In the king's name, I must ask you to accompany me.
Where are you lodged?"

Iya felt his mind brush hers, seeking out her thoughts. He must have mistaken her for a lower order wizard to make so bold. Age and experience were proof against such clumsy attempts, but she suspected he would recognize an outright lie.

"I'm lodged at the Mermaid, in Ivy Lane," she told him.

The wizard motioned for her to follow him. Several of the soldiers split off from the rest, presumably to search her room.

She suspected she was more than a match for this wizard and his men, but to resist or disappear could only be construed as provocation. She dared not cause any stir, especially now that they knew her face.

They conducted her to a tall stone and timber building not far from the Palatine Gate. She knew the place. It had once been an inn; now it was full of soldiers and wizards.

In the great room she was made to sit in front of another wizard at a table and place her hands on two plaques made of ebony ringed with silver and iron. There were no markings on them that she could make out, but the touch of the combined metals stung her wrists where they brushed it. What the purpose of these might be, she could only guess.

The wizard behind the table had a thick ledger in front of him, open to the middle pages.

"Your name?"

She gave it.

He glanced at her hand. "I see you've injured yourself."

"A mishap with a spell," she replied, looking chagrined.

With a condescending little smile he returned to his ledger, asking her about her business in the city and noting her responses word for word in his book. Beside it was a covered basket, not unlike the ones traveling performers carried trained snakes and ferrets in.

"I'm simply here to renew old acquaintances," she assured him. The words held no lie, should anyone here be a truthknower. Perhaps that was the purpose of the plaques, she thought, pressing the polished wood with her fingertips.

"How long have you been in the city?"

"Four days."

"Why did you not register upon your arrival?"

"As I told the young man who brought me here, I had no idea there was such a law."

"When was the last time you were in—"

They were interrupted just then by the sound of a scuffle outside.

"I've done nothing wrong!" a man cried out. "I wear the symbol. I've professed my loyalty! What right have you to lay hands on me? I am a free wizard of the Orëska."

A pair of grey-backs dragged in a disheveled young wizard, followed by an older man in white. The prisoner's hands were bound with shining silver bands and there was blood running down his face from a cut over his right eye. As he threw back long, dirty hair from his face, Iya recognized him as a vain but mediocre student of one of Agazhar's friends. He hadn't amounted to much, as Iya recalled, but he still wore the silver amulet.

"This fellow spat at the person of a King's Harrier," the white-robed wizard told the one behind the ledger.

"Your number, young man?" the recording wizard asked.

"I refute your numbers!" the young prisoner snarled. "My name is Salnar, Salnar of Scop's Rest."

"Ah yes. I remember you." The wizard thumbed back through the ledger and carefully noted something down. When he'd finished he motioned for the prisoner to be taken upstairs. Salnar must have realized the implication of this, for he began to scream and struggle as the guards rushed him through an inner door. His cries continued loudly until they were cut off by the slam of a heavy door somewhere overhead.

Unruffled, the recording wizard returned to Iya. "Now, where were we?" He glanced down at his notes. "Ah, yes. When was the last time you visited the city?"

Iya's fingers twitched against the dark wood. "I—I can't think of the exact date. It was around the time the king's nephew was born. I visited Duke Rhius and his family." This was dangerous ground, but what choice did she have?

"Duke Rhius?" The name had a better effect than she'd hoped. "You are a friend of the duke's?"

"Yes, he's one of my patrons, though I haven't seen him in some time. I travel and study."

The wizard noted this information next to her name. "Why do you not wear the symbol of our craft?"

This was more difficult to evade. "I did not wish to draw attention to myself," she told him, allowing an old woman's quaver to creep into her voice. "The executions have made people suspicious of our kind."

This answer seemed to satisfy her interrogator. "There have been outrages, as you say." He reached into the basket beside him and took out a crudely molded copper brooch inset with the silver crescent of Illior. He turned it over, read the number inscribed there, and jotted this into his ledger. "You must wear this at all times," he instructed, holding it out for her to take.

Iya removed her hands from the plates to accept it and was not ordered to replace them. She turned the ugly brooch over and her heart skipped a beat. A number was engraved below the crown-and-eagle imprint of the Harriers.

222

The number she'd seen in her vision at Afra, in numerals of fire.

"If you wish to have a more attractive piece fashioned, you may," he went on. "There are a number of jewelers specializing in such commissions now. But take care that any you have made bear this same number, and that it is sent here to be struck with the king's mark before it is delivered to you. Is that quite clear?"

Iya nodded as she fastened it to the front of her gown.

"I promise, no harm will come to you because of it," he told her. "Show it to the gate wardens whenever you leave or enter a city. Do you understand? Any wizard who refuses is subject to further interrogation."

Iya wondered what "further interrogation" meant to someone like poor Salnar.

It took a moment to realize that she'd been released. She could hardly feel her legs as she stood and walked out into the autumn sunlight. She half expected someone to call out, seize her, drag her back to whatever terrors lay beyond the slamming of a door.

At no time during the interview had anyone openly threatened her, or even been rude. Yet the implications of the encounter left her so shaken that she entered the first tavern she came to and sat for nearly an hour at the table furthest from the door, sipping vile sour wine and fighting back tears. Then, with shaking fingers, she undid the brooch and placed it on the table in front of her, studying it back and front.

Silver was Illior's metal. Copper and all the other sun-colored metals of weapons and armor belonged to Sakor. These two of the Four had long been the principal patrons of Skala, but since the days of Ghërilain, Illior had been the most highly revered. Now Iya was made to wear the Lightbearer's symbol like a criminal's brand, the beautiful silver bow held thrall against the copper disk.

The king dares to number the free wizards, she thought as fear gave way to anger. *As if we are beasts of his flock!*

And yet they'd given her the number ordained by Illior.

A shadow fell across her table, and renewed fear scattered her thoughts. She looked up, expecting to find the

Harriers surrounding her with their silver and iron bonds, but it was only the taverner.

He sat down across from her and handed her a small brass cup. Pointing to the brooch, he gave her a wry smile and said, "Drink up, Mistress. I imagine you need fortifying."

"Thank you." Iya downed the strong liquor gratefully and wiped her lips with fingers that still trembled. The taverner was a big, comfortable fellow with kind brown eyes. After the icy cordiality of the Harriers, even a stranger's kindness was welcome. "I suppose you've seen a lot like me in here, being so close to—that place?"

"Every day, sometimes. Took you by surprise, did they?"

"Yes. Has this been going on long?"

"Just started last month. I hear it was that Niryn's idea. I don't imagine your kind thinks much of him these days."

Something in the taverner's manner suddenly rang false. Looking into his eyes again, she saw the same disarming innocence she'd seen in the young Harrier's.

Taking up her wine cup, she gave him a wide-eyed look over its rim. "He frightens me, but I suppose he is only doing his duty to our king." She did not dare touch this man's mind; instead she gently sought out any magic about his person, and found it. Under his tunic he wore a charm that warded against thought reading. He was a spy.

It had taken less than the blink of an eye to learn this, but Iya retracted her seeking quickly lest there was someone else lurking to catch her at it.

The taverner plied her with more brandy and questions about herself and the burnings, perhaps trying to coax her into some admission that could be turned against her. Iya meekly persisted in lukewarm platitudes until he must have decided she was a very minor wizard, and not a very smart one to boot. After extending an offer of future hospitality he bid her farewell. Iya forced herself to

finish the wretched wine, then walked back to her lodg-
ings to see what the grey-backs had left of it.

The frightened look the Mermaid's host gave her was
enough to confirm that they had been here. Iya hurried up
the stairs, expecting to find her chamber turned upside
down.

Except for the missing glyph she'd left on the door
latch, however, nothing appeared to have been disturbed.
Her pack lay as she had left it on the bed. Whoever had
searched this room had not used their hands to do so. Iya
closed the door and fixed the latch, then sprinkled a sand
circle on the floor and set about inscribing the necessary
chart of wards inside it to create a safe casting space.
Once this was done, she sat down inside and cautiously
opened her mind, seeking some echo of the searchers and
their methods. Gradually a murky scene took shape behind her closed eyelids: a woman and a man, with Harrier
guards. The woman was robed in white and had carried a
short wand of polished red obsidian. Sitting on Iya's narrow bed, she had held its ends between her palms and
cast a spell of—

Iya concentrated on the vision, trying to see the patterns of light and color in the space between the woman's
hands. As the glimpses became clearer Iya's breath caught
in her throat. It was a powerful seeking for signs of something . . . someone . . .

Iya concentrated harder, trying to see the woman's
lips as they formed words around the spell.

When the answer came Iya had to choke down a cry
of alarm.

The woman was seeking a girl child.

She was seeking Tobin.

The vision collapsed and Iya slumped forward, resting
her face in her hands.

"Be calm," she whispered to herself, but fragments of
the vision she'd had at Afra danced in the vault of her

memory: a queen old, young, ragged, crowned, dead with a halter around her neck, garlanded and victorious. So many of the other wizards she'd talked to over the years had said the same. The myriad strands of fate were still unspliced, despite the guidance of Illior. The king's creatures had some inkling of the threat to his throne and even now they were seeking her out.

Then again, she told herself, if they were searching and questioning every wandering wizard who passed through, then they had no idea of the truth. Lhel's strange magic still shielded Tobin.

Iya weighed the hated broach in her palm, thinking how the recording wizard had simply reached into a basket and pulled this out at random.

222

Two—the number of twins, of duality—repeated thrice like a summoning spell. Two parents. Two children.

Two wizards—herself and Arkoniel—with different visions of how to protect this child.

A knowing smile curved her lips. Two wizards—herself and Niryn—with different visions of how to unite the wizards of Skala and serve the throne.

The Harriers might intend their numbers as instruments of control or shame, but for Iya they were a call to arms.

Chapter 27

The castle town of Atyion dominated the fertile plain north of Ero. The castle itself had been built in the embrace of an oxbow in the meandering Heron River, in sight of the Inner Sea. The castle's two huge round towers were visible for miles around and could easily shelter a thousand men or more in time of siege.

Duke Rhius' family had earned their place by war and honor, but their great wealth flowed out of the acres of vineyards, groves, and lush, well-watered pastures full of horses that covered the plain. What had once been a village nestled in the castle's protective shadow had grown into a prosperous market town. The few plague markers found here were weathered white; Atyion had not been touched by disease for a decade.

Not since Tobin's birth.

Iya rode through the muddy streets and across the lowered drawbridge that spanned the castle moat. Inside the curtain walls lay more land, enough to pasture sizeable herds, and ranks of barracks and stables for the duke's armies. Many of these were deserted today; the duke's ally lords and vassals had gone home to tend their own lands.

The soldiers who remained moved at their leisure, practicing at arms or lounging around the corrals. Armorers and farriers were noisily at work over their smoky forges along the inner wall. A few saddlers sat beneath an awning, cutting leather and mending harnesses. Out of deference for the king, Rhius had no women soldiers among the ranks of his guard, but there were a number of them among the castle household who had once served his father with sword and bow. Cook, back at the keep, was such a one, too. They all still knew how to fight, and would gladly do so if given the order.

Iya left her horse with a stable hand and hurried up the broad stair to the arched portal that let into the main hall. The doorway was flanked by rows of columns supporting a pointed arch. A painted relief of the Cloud Eye of Illior had decorated the peak of this arch since Atyion was built, but today Iya saw that a carved oak panel had been fitted over it. This bore one of the more martial symbols of Sakor: a gloved hand holding up a flaming sword garlanded with laurel and rue. It had been fitted by a master craftsman; anyone unfamiliar with the house would never guess that another image lay hidden below.

It's like the brooch, she thought, saddened and angered. *How has it come to this, that we have set the very gods against one another?*

An ancient fellow with a paunch beneath his blue livery greeted her in the hall.

"How long has Sakor guarded the entrance, Hakone?" she asked, giving him her cloak.

"Nearly nine years, my lady," the porter told her. "It was a gift from the king."

"I see. Is the duke at home today?"

"He is, Mistress. He's in the open gallery. I'll bring you to him."

Iya looked around as they passed through the great vaulted hall and on through a series of rooms and inner galleries. Atyion was still magnificent, but the glory of the house seemed tarnished, as if the structure itself lay under the same pall as its master. A few servants were at work, polishing and scrubbing, but the furnishings and hangings, even the brightly painted walls, were more faded than she recalled.

There used to be music and laughter here, she thought.

And children running thorough the hall. Tobin had never seen this house.

"Is Lord Rhius well?"

"He grieves, Mistress."

They found Rhius walking in a pillared gallery overlooking the castle gardens. Judging by the dusty leather boots and jerkin he wore, he'd spent the day in the saddle and only recently returned. A young page trailed after him, ignored.

As a boy Rhius had always run to meet Iya. Now he dismissed the servants and stood regarding her in bleak silence.

Iya bowed and looked out over the deserted gardens. "Your aunts and uncles used to play blind beggars with me in that stand of walnut trees."

"They're dead now, too," Rhius told her. "All but Uncle Tynir. He lost his wife in the plague and his daughter to the king. He's carved a new estate for himself in the northern territories."

A pair of gardeners came into view below them, pulling a cartload of rotted manure. A tall, bald man in a jeweled robe wandered out from a rose maze to watch them at their work.

Rhius' mouth tightened with distaste at the sight of him. "Come, let's speak inside."

Iya glanced back at the stranger, trying to make out who it was. "You have a guest?"

"Several."

Rhius led the way to an inner room lit by several lamps. He shut the door and Iya cast a seal to keep out prying eyes and ears.

"That man in the garden is Lord Orun, Chancellor of the Treasury. Surely you remember him?" Rhius asked, circling a round table that stood at the center of the room.

Iya remained near the door, watching him pace like a cornered wolf. "Ah yes, he often guested here in your father's day. I remember Tharin always detested him."

"Yes, that's him. He's risen high and serves the king closely now as the royal ear. Not a man to cross. Thank Illior, Erius has kept Hylus on as Lord Chancellor. He's able to keep most of the nobles from eating one another alive."

"But why is Orun here?"

"He knew my father, and now he makes it his business to know me. This time he's brought me some young cousin of his and asks me to take him on as an equerry."

"Spreading his spies around, is he?"

"I'm surrounded by them. He's gifted me with several pages and a very pretty court minstrel whom I think he intends for my bed. She's away for the day, or I'd introduce you and do away with the mystery."

He sat down and turned a weary eye on her. "So, you've come back, as well? You took your time."

Iya let that go for the moment. "I've just come from visiting your child, my lord. Prince Tobin sends you his regards and a message. He misses you."

"By the Four, if you knew how much I miss him!"

"Tharin gave me to believe otherwise."

An angry flush rose in the duke's cheeks. "Lies breed like maggots on a dead horse, as they say. All these years I've kept my secret from Tharin. Now that lie has festered between us and driven him away."

"How so?"

Rhius waved a hand around at the room, the house, perhaps the entire estate. "King Erius prefers to keep me close by him, now that his sister's life no longer binds me. This is as far from Ero as I'm allowed to venture. Should I bring Tobin here now, where Erius and his wizards come to guest whenever the whim takes them? No, instead I drive away a man who loves me better than any brother, send him back to be the father to Tobin that I can't be." He rubbed his hands over his face. "Another sacrifice."

Iya went to him and clasped his hand. "You know Tharin better than that. He loves you still and keeps you close in your child's heart. Surely the king would not begrudge you the occasional visit?"

"Perhaps not, but I'm so—fearful." The word seemed to choke him. "We both know what Tobin is, and is to be, but she's also my beloved child and all I have left of Ariani. No sacrifice is too great to keep her safe!"

"Then perhaps you can find a little forgiveness in your heart for me; you know perfectly well that's why I've stayed away." She took the Harrier's brooch from a pouch at her belt and tossed it onto the table. "I was given this in Ero."

Rhius eyed it with distaste. "Ah yes. Niryn's badges."

It was Iya's turn to pace as she told him of her visit to the city, ending with the search made of her room at the inn and the spell the wizard had cast for the unknown girl.

Rhius let out a bitter bark of a laugh. "You've been too long away. Niryn has turned oracle and claims to dream of a usurper who'll unseat Erius from the throne—a false queen raised by necromancy. It wasn't enough to slaughter the innocents of royal blood. They go on looking for signs and wonders now."

"I think he's been sent the same vision that I was given, but he misinterprets it. Or chooses to. It wasn't enough to slaughter the royal girls; none of them was the one and so the dream continues. Fortunately, he hasn't yet seen Tobin clearly. I think we may thank Lhel's magic for that. All the same, Niryn has an inkling of what's coming, and the wizards of Skala are to be numbered and divided against themselves."

"By the Light! If they discover Tobin before she's old enough to fight, to lead—"

"I don't believe there is any danger of that just yet. Clearly, however, they've had some inkling of wizardly protection, otherwise why should they have scoured my room looking for her?"

"Are you certain they found no clue there?"

"I saw no sign of it. Sooner or later, though, the king's spies will recall the connection between your family and myself. I only hope that Arkoniel's presence at the keep won't bring undue attention on the household."

"I've said nothing of him. Keep him away from the city and unnumbered."

"I plan to. Has Niryn shown any interest in the child recently?"

"None at all. Of course, he's had the Harriers and their work to occupy his attention. Quite a powerful little cabal he's building up."

"How so?"

Rhius laced his fingers together around one knee and stared down the black mourning ring on his left hand. "There are rumors of secret meetings being held somewhere outside the city."

"And Erius says nothing to this? I can't imagine even the rumor of such a thing going unchallenged."

"They serve him, or so he believes. For all his caution about rivals, Erius has a true blind spot when it comes to Niryn and his followers."

"Or has been given one. Tell me, how does the king seem to you these days? Do you see any of his mother's madness growing in him?"

"On the face of it, he's nothing like her. The business with the girl children—" He made a weary, dismissive gesture. "He's not the first to take such ruthless measures to ensure a succession. For years now Niryn has filled his head with fears of traitors and rivals, then earned favor by rounding up people for execution. Mad Agnalain had no use for wizards; her son keeps his by him day and night. Niryn brags openly about his "visions," but rages against Illiorans and wizards and anyone who might rise up and proclaim the Prophecy of Afra again."

"How many Harrier wizards are there now?"

"Twenty, perhaps. Many of them are very young and he keeps them on a tight rein. But there are others at court

who recognize power when they see it and support him—
Lord Orun among them. Tell me, Iya, in all your wandering, how many wizards can you claim to our cause?"

Iya held a finger to her lips. "More, but leave that to
me until the moment arrives. And you know wizards
alone won't put Tobin on the throne. We must have
armies. Are you still prepared to take the risk?"

Rhius' face set like a grim mask. "What have I to lose
that hasn't already been taken from me? Tobin can't remain hidden forever. He must reveal—" He rubbed at his
eyelids and sighed. "*She* must reveal herself eventually
and either take the throne or die. If she's discovered before that, then none of us will survive Erius' rage. Where
there's such certainty, a warrior sees no risk."

Iya covered his hand with her own and squeezed it.
"The Lightbearer chose you as much as Tobin. That trust
sits well on you. As you say, we must continue to be cautious. Even Illior's favor doesn't guarantee success." She
sat back and studied the duke's gaunt face. "If we had to
fight today, how many men could you bring to the field?
What nobles would back you?"

"Tharin, of course, and the men of his estate. Nyanis, I
think, and Solari. They'd stand with me. My uncle bears
the king no goodwill and has ships. Those who lost their
women and girls to him—many of those might be willing
to back a rightful queen in the field if they saw a chance
of winning. Five thousand, perhaps more. But not for a
child, Iya. I don't think they'd fight for Tobin yet. Erius is a
strong king, and a good one in many ways, and Plenimar
is still restless. It's the same as when his mother died and
Ariani was so young."

"Not entirely. Then they'd had a mad queen. Now
they've had years of plague and famine and war, and
whispers of prophecy. A sign will be given, my lord, and
when it comes, the people will recognize it."

Iya stopped, startled at how loud her voice had risen
in the little room, and how hard her heart was suddenly

pounding. At Afra she'd seen so many possible futures—was the sign she waited for among these?

She went to the table and sat down by Rhius. "The king keeps you close, yet not on Tobin's account. Why? What's changed between you?"

"I'm not certain. You know my marriage to Ariani was a one-sided love match. I loved her and her brother loved my lands. I expect he thought I'd die first and leave it all to her and the Crown. Now I think he means to do it through Tobin. Erius speaks often of bringing Tobin to court to join the Companions."

"He's not of age yet."

"But he soon will be, and even with the stories of Tobin being sickly and demon-cursed, Erius has always been anxious for the boys to know one another. Sometimes I honestly think that it is for love of his sister. All the same, once at court, Tobin will be little more than a hostage." Rhius frowned down at the brooch. "You've seen what it's like there; once he's at the Palace, can you still protect my child?"

"With all my heart, I will, my lord," Iya assured him, not daring to reveal the sudden doubt she felt at the prospect. Like a handful of unthrown dice, Tobin's future still encompassed all possibilities.

Chapter 28

The weeks following Ki's arrival were happy ones. Arkoniel never learned what Iya said to Rhius during her visit to Atyion, but the duke returned to the keep soon after and promised to stay until Tobin's name day in Erasin. Better still, Rhius seemed almost his old self again, praising the improvements to the house and inviting Arkoniel to game with him and Tharin in the evenings. Whatever rift had been between Rhius and his friend had healed. The two men appeared to be as close as ever.

The duke approved of Ki, as well, and praised Tharin's training when Ki served at table or matched Tobin at sword and bow practice. When Tobin knelt in the hall on his tenth name day and requested that Ki be made his squire, Rhius granted his permission readily and allowed the boys to pledge their oath to Sakor at the house shrine that same night. Tobin gave Ki one of his finest carved horse charms on a neck chain as a symbol of the bond.

Yet in spite of all this, Rhius maintained a certain aloofness with Ki that cost both boys some discomfort.

On Tobin's name day, Rhius had gifted Ki with a new suit of clothes and a fine roan horse named Dragon.

When Ki tried to thank him, Rhius said only, "My son should be well attended."

Ki already worshiped Tharin and was clearly prepared to accord Tobin's father the same regard; the man's coolness left him awkward and a little clumsy.

Tobin saw this, too, and hurt for his friend.

Only Arkoniel and Nari understood the reason for the

duke's distance and neither could offer the truth as comfort. Even among themselves they could not speak of the fatal possibility that hung by a spider's thread over Ki's young heart.

One bright cold afternoon a few weeks later Arkoniel found himself sharing the parapet with the duke as they watched the boys at play in the meadow below.

Tobin was attempting to track Ki, who lay hidden in a shallow depression surrounded by snow-dusted grass and weeds. Ki somehow managed to keep the white fog of his breath from rising, but in the end he gave himself away when his foot bumped a dead milkweed stalk. Several dry pods still clung to the stem and when he jarred them, their silky white seeds burst forth and rose like a battlefield signal.

Rhius chuckled. "Ah, he's done for now."

Tobin saw and dashed over to pounce on his friend. The resulting wrestling match sent up another thick cloud of milkweed fluff. "By the Light, that Ki is godsent."

"I believe he is," Arkoniel agreed. "It's amazing how they've taken to one another."

At first glance, no two boys could have been more different. Tobin remained quiet and serious by nature; bold Ki couldn't seem to sit still or keep quiet for more than a few minutes at a stretch. For him, talking seemed as necessary as breathing. He still spoke like a peasant and could be crude as a country tinker. Nari would have taken a switch to him a dozen times already if Tobin hadn't pleaded for leniency. Yet the substance of what he said was for the most part intelligent if unschooled, and invariably entertaining if not always seemly.

And if Tobin hadn't yet tried to emulate Ki's boisterous nature, Arkoniel could tell that he gloried in it. He glowed like a full moon in Ki's presence and delighted in the older boy's tales of his large and colorful family. It wasn't only Tobin who loved these, either. When the household gathered around the fire each night, Ki was often their principal entertainment and would soon have everyone holding their sides as he described the foibles and mishaps of his various siblings.

He also had a substantial store of garbled fables and myths learned at his father's hearth; stories of talking animals and ghosts, and fanciful kingdoms where men had two heads and birds shed golden feathers sharp enough to cut off the fingers of the greedy.

Endeavoring to follow Iya's advice, Arkoniel sent for richly illustrated texts of the more familiar tales, hoping these would coax the boys into their reading lessons. Tobin was still struggling with his letters and Ki was little help. The older boy had proven resistant to such learning in the proud, backward way of a country noble who'd never seen his own name written out and didn't care to. Arkoniel did not chide them; instead, he left a book or two open to particularly exciting illustrations, trusting curiosity to do his work for him. Only the other day, he'd caught Ki puzzling over *Gramain's Bestiary*. Meanwhile, Tobin had quietly set to work on a history of his famed ancestor, Ghërilain the First, a gift from his father.

Ki proved a better ally when it came to magic. The boy possessed a child's normal fascination with it, and his enthusiasm smoothed the way for Arkoniel to attempt to address Tobin's odd fears. The wizard began with small illusions and a few simple makings. But while Ki threw himself into such pastimes with all his usual carefree abandon, Tobin's reactions were less predictable. He seemed pleased with lightstones and firechips, but grew wary whenever Arkoniel suggested another vision journey.

*T*harin was well pleased with Ki, as well. The boy had an innate understanding of honor and took happily to a squire's training. He learned the rudiments of table service, though there was little formality at the keep, and eagerly strove to master the other arts of service, though

Tobin stubbornly resisted most efforts to be served. He refused any help in bathing or dressing, and much preferred to take care of his own horse.

In the end, it was at swordplay that Ki proved most useful. He was less than a head taller than Tobin, and had been fighting with his brothers and sisters since he could walk. He made a proper sparring partner, and a very demanding one, too. More often than not he emerged victorious, and Tobin bruised. To Tobin's credit, he seldom sulked about it and listened willingly as Tharin or Ki explained to him what he'd done wrong. It perhaps helped that Tobin was Ki's master at archery and horsemanship. Until he'd come here, Ki's backside had never had a proper saddle beneath it. A knight's son he might be in name, but he'd had the hard upbringing of a peasant. Perhaps because of this, he never balked at any task and was grateful for any favor. For his part, Tobin, who'd been kept too close to the women for too long, considered every new task a game and often insisted on helping out with chores that most noblemen's sons would have been insulted to consider. As a result, he grew brighter and browner by the day. The men in the barracks gave Ki all the credit and made pets of them both.

When Nari or Arkoniel fussed over Tobin raking stalls and mending wall beside Ki, Tharin simply shooed them back into the house.

"The demon has been quieter since he came," Rhius murmured aloud, interrupting Arkoniel's thoughts.

"Has it?" he asked. "I don't suppose I've been here long enough to judge."

"And it never seems to hurt Tobin anymore, not since—not since his poor mother died. Perhaps that was for the best, after all."

"You can't mean that, my lord!"

Rhius kept his gaze on the meadow. "You knew my

lady when she was happy and well. You didn't see what she became. You weren't here to see."

Arkoniel had no answer for that.

The boys had reached a truce now. Lying side by side in the snowy grass, they were pointing up at the clouds drifting across the blue winter sky.

Arkoniel looked up and smiled. It had been years since he'd thought to play at finding shapes in the clouds. He suspected that this might be the first time Tobin had ever tried.

Look," said Ki. "That cloud is a fish. And that one over there looks like a kettle with a pig climbing out of it."

Tobin was unaware of the wizard watching him, but his thoughts were running along similar lines. It seemed that everything had changed again since Ki's arrival, and this time for the better. Lying here with the sun on his face and the cold seeping up through his cloak, it was easy to forget about mothers and demons and all the other shadows that lurked at the corners of his memory. He could even almost ignore Brother crouched a few feet away, watching Ki with black, hungry eyes.

Brother hated Ki. He wouldn't say why, but Tobin could tell just by the way he watched the living boy that he wanted to pinch and slap and hurt him. Every time Tobin called Brother he warned him not to, but that didn't stop him from doing things that startled Ki, like pulling objects out of his hands or knocking over his mazer at table. Ki always jumped a little and hissed curses between his teeth, but he never ran or cried out. Tharin said that was a sign of real courage, to stand fast when you were scared. Ki couldn't see Brother, but after a while he claimed he could sometimes sense when he was there.

If it had been up to Tobin, he'd have sent Brother away and let him go hungry for a while, but he'd sworn to Lhel that he'd care for him and he couldn't go back on his word. So he called Brother every day and the baleful spirit lurked on the edges of their games like an unwelcome hound. He hovered in the shadows of the toy room, and went into the forest with them when they rode, somehow keeping up with their horses without ever running. Recalling his dream, Tobin once offered to let Brother ride behind him on his horse, but the spirit greeted this with his usual uncomprehending silence.

Ki pointed up at another cloud. "That one looks like the fancy cakes they sell at the Festival of Flowers back home. And there's a hound's head, with its tongue hanging out."

Tobin picked a few black beggars ticks from his hair and flicked the prickly seeds up at the sky shapes. "I like the way they change as they go. Your dog looks more like a dragon now."

"The great dragon of Illior, only white instead of red," Ki agreed. "When your father takes us to Ero I'll show you the painting of it in the temple in Goldsmith's Street. It's a hundred feet long, with jewels for eyes and the scales all outlined in gold." He searched the sky again. "And now the cake looks like our maidservant, Lilain, with Alon's bastard eight moons in her belly."

Tobin glanced over at his friend and could tell by the slant of Ki's grin that there was a story coming.

Sure enough, Ki went on. "We thought Khemeus would kill the pair of them, since he'd been panting over her since she come to us—"

"'Came to us,'" Tobin corrected. Arkoniel had tasked him with helping Ki learn to speak properly.

"Came to us, then!" Ki said, rolling his eyes. "But in the end the boys just had a fistfight out in the yard. It was pouring down rain and they fell in the manure heap. Then they went off and got drunk. When Lilain's baby finally did come it looked like Khemeus anyway, so it was probably his after all, and he and Alon had another fight over that."

Tobin stared at the cloud, trying to puzzle out the sense of this new exploit. "What's a bastard?"

"You know, a baby that comes when the man and woman haven't made contract together."

"Oh." That didn't really tell him anything. "How did it get in that girl's belly?"

Ki reared up on one elbow and stared at him in disbelief. "You don't know? Haven't you ever watched animals at it?"

"At what?"

"Why, *fucking*, of course! Like when a stallion climbs a mare's back, or a rooster treads a hen? Bilairy's balls, Tobin, you must have seen dogs fuck, at least?"

"Oh, that!" Tobin knew what Ki meant now, though he'd never heard anyone call it that. Suspecting it to be another of those words Nari and Arkoniel didn't approve of, he stored it away with delight. "You mean people do it, too?"

"Of course!"

Tobin sat up and wrapped his arms around his knees. The thought was intriguing and unsettling all at once. "But—how? Wouldn't they fall over?"

Ki fell back, whooping with laughter. "Not hardly! You never have seen anyone at it, have you?"

"Have you?" Tobin challenged, wondering if Ki was making fun of him.

"At our house?" Ki snorted. "Gods, all the time! Father's always on top of someone, and the older boys are at the maids or men, even, sometimes. It's a wonder any of us sleeps nights! Like I told you, in most houses everyone sleeps all in the same room. 'Least the ones I've been in."

When Tobin remained baffled as to the actual act, Ki found a couple of forked weed stalks and used them to illustrate a more detailed explanation.

"You mean it gets bigger?" Tobin asked, wide-eyed. "Doesn't it hurt the girl?"

Ki stuck one of the stalks in the corner of his mouth

and gave Tobin a wink. "From the sounds they make, I don't hardly think so."

He cocked an eye at the sun's height. "I'm cold. Come on, let's go riding before Nari decides it's too late. Maybe we'll find that witch of yours today!"

$\mathcal{T}$obin wasn't sure whether or not he'd done wrong in telling Ki about Lhel. He couldn't even remember exactly if she'd told him not to, but he had the guilty feeling that she had.

Ki had been spinning some yarn about a witch in his village one night as they lay in bed and Tobin blurted out that he knew one, too. Of course, Ki demanded details since his own story was only a made-up one he'd heard from a bard. In the end Tobin had told him about the dreams. He told him about getting lost, too, and about the hollow oak tree Lhel lived in, but he was careful to leave out any mention of the doll.

Since then it had been a secret quest between them to find her so Ki could meet her, too.

They went out riding nearly every day, but so far they'd found no sign of her. Tobin always came back from these searches with mixed feelings. As much as he wanted to see her again and find out what it was she meant to teach him, he was also relieved, in case she was angry with him for telling Ki.

Despite weeks of fruitless searching, Ki's faith remained unshakable and he delighted in sharing Tobin's secret.

That almost made up for those Tobin couldn't share.

$\mathcal{T}$he boys kept an eye on the sun's progress as they spurred their mounts up the road. The days were short now and storms blew down off the mountains fast.

Brother kept just ahead of them, moving with his usual stiff, unnatural walk that should have been too slow to keep up but wasn't. No matter how fast they rode, he stayed ahead of them.

Ki had other concerns. "How is this witch of yours going to live in a tree all winter?"

"She had a fire," Tobin reminded him.

"Yes, but the snow will cover the doorway, won't it? She must have to burrow out like a rabbit. And what will she eat?"

Pondering this, they left their mounts tied by the road and set off on foot to explore an untried game trail Tobin had spotted a few days earlier. Following it to a dead end used up their last margin of daylight. The sun was almost touching the peaks when they finally gave up and headed back; they'd have to lather their mounts to get back before Nari began to fret.

Ki had just mounted and Tobin had one foot in the stirrup when their horses shied. Gosi reared, throwing Tobin backward off his feet, then galloped away down the road. Tobin came down hard on his back with a grunt of surprise. Raising his head, he saw Ki trying to rein in Dragon as he careened away after Gosi. Both horses disappeared around a bend in the road, taking Ki with them.

"Damn!" he wheezed. He was halfway to his feet when a thunderous growl froze him in a crouch. Looking slowly to his right, he found himself facing a catamount that crouched at the edge of the trees across the road.

The great cat's tawny coat blended well with the winter cover, but its yellow eyes looked as big as the lids of nail kegs and they were fixed on him. It watched him, belly low to the ground, tail stirring the dead leaves and snow as it twitched this way and that. Then, like a nightmare, it glided out a step toward him, then two, muscles bunching and rippling across its shoulders.

It was stalking him.

There was no point in running. Tobin was too scared to even close his eyes.

The catamount took another step then stopped, ears pressed flat to its blunt head as Brother appeared between them.

The cat could see him. It crouched lower and snarled, showing cruel curved fangs as long as Tobin's thumbs. Beyond fear now, Tobin couldn't move.

The catamount screamed and lashed out at the ghost. The huge paw raked the air less than a yard from Tobin's chest, close enough for him to feel the air move and see the hooked claws rake through Brother's belly. Brother didn't move. The beast snarled again and gathered itself to spring.

Tobin heard someone running toward them. It was Ki, charging back on foot with his long hair flying around his head. He let out a fierce yell and ran straight at the catamount, brandishing nothing but a long, knobby stick.

"No!" Tobin screamed, but it was too late. The cat sprang and struck Ki full in the chest. Together they tumbled across the road and came to rest with the catamount on top.

For one awful moment Tobin felt time stop, just like it had when his mother was falling away from him down the side of the tower. Ki was on his back beneath the catamount; all Tobin could see were his friend's splayed legs and the catamount's hind foot braced against his belly, poised to gut him like a squirrel.

But neither Ki nor the cat moved, and now Brother was standing over them. Tobin was hardly aware that he was running until he threw himself on the catamount's back and grappled the huge head away from Ki's throat. The beast was limp, dead weight in his hands.

"Ki! Ki, are you dead?" Tobin cried, trying to wrestle the heavy carcass off his friend.

"I don't think so," came the faint reply. Ki began to struggle, and between the two of them they managed to heave the catamount aside. Ki emerged pale and shaking but unquestionably alive. The front of his tunic had several jagged tears and blood trickled down onto the lacings from a long scratch on his neck. Tobin dropped to his knees and stared at him, hardly able to believe what had just happened. Without a word, they turned to look at the huge she-cat lying beside them. The yellow eyes stared sightlessly into the ditch. Dark blood stained the snow under her gaping jaws.

Ki found his voice first. "Bilairy's hairy bag!" he croaked, his voice a full octave higher than normal. "What happened?"

"I think Brother killed her!" Tobin stared in wonder at the ghost crouching now over the dead cat. "He got between me and her and stopped her charge. But then you came running in with . . . What were you *thinking*, running at her with—with a *stick*?"

Ki pulled out the carved horse charm he wore around his neck. "I'm your squire. It was all I could find and—" Ki stopped, staring gape-mouthed over Tobin's shoulder.

The hair on Tobin's neck rose. Did catamounts hunt in pairs? Or packs? He twisted around quickly, lost his balance, and fell heavily on his backside.

Lhel stood a few feet away, looking as dirty and ragged as he remembered. She didn't seem at all surprised to find them here with a dead catamount.

"You be looking for me, keesas?"

"Well, yes. I—I hope you don't mind. I told my friend— He's never met a witch. And—and you said you were going to teach me things," he finished lamely, unable to tell in the failing light if she was angry or not.

"And instead you be find by big *maskar*." She nudged the dead cat with one rag-bound foot.

"Brother stopped it from catching me, then Ki came and drew it off and Brother killed—"

"I kill. Brother not make death."

Both boys gaped up at her. "You? But—but how?" asked Tobin.

She snorted. "I witch." She knelt and cupped Tobin's face between her rough palms. "You be hurt, keesa?"

"No."

"You?" She reached to touch Ki's neck.

Ki shook his head.

"Good." Lhel grinned, showing the gaps of missing teeth. "You Tobin's brave good friend. You got voice, keesa?"

Ki blushed. "I don't know what to say to a witch."

"Say 'hello, witch,' maybe?"

Ki got to his knees and made her a bow as if she were a lady. "Hello, Mistress Lhel. And thank you! I'm in your debt."

Lhel placed a hand on his head. For an instant Tobin thought he caught a fleeting look of sadness in her eyes and it sent an unpleasant chill coiling through his belly. But the look was gone when she turned and drew Tobin into a hug. He accepted the embrace stiffly; she still didn't smell very good.

Lhel held him tight for a moment and whispered, "This a good keesa. You be good to him? Be protecting him?"

"Protecting him? From who?"

"You know, comes the time." Lhel tapped a finger against his chest. "You hold that here, don't be forget."

"I won't."

Tobin pulled away. Brother stood close enough to touch now and he tried to, to thank him. As always, his hand found no purchase on that solid-looking form, only a patch of colder air.

"How did you know we were here?" Ki asked.

"I be seeing you many time to know what kind of good friend my Tobin be having. You be fine warriors together." She touched her forehead. "I see it here." She looked back at Tobin, then pointed to the keep. "You got another teacher. You like?"

"No. He does magic, but not like yours. Mostly he teaches us how to read and figure."

"He tried to teach us dancing, too, but he's like a big heron on ice," Ki told her. "Will you come to the house with us, Mistress? It's not my place to offer you hospitality, but you saved my life. It's a cold night and—and Cook is making a galantine pie."

She patted his shoulder. "No, they don't be know me. Not tell, yes?"

"I won't!" Ki promised, shooting Tobin a conspiratorial grin. The tale of a witch had been a fine secret; the witch herself was a treasure beyond all hopes.

"We have to get home." Tobin cast another worried look at the sky; it had darkened to purple-and-gold behind the black peaks. "Now that we've found you, can we come visit you again? You said you'd be my teacher, too."

"Time come. Not yet." She put two fingers in her mouth and let out a piercing whistle. The runaway horses came trotting up the road, dragging their loose reins in the snow. "You come visit times, though."

"Where? How will we find you?"

"You seek. You find." And with that she stepped lightly away and vanished into the gathering darkness.

"By the Flame!" Ki bounced up and down in excitement and punched Tobin on the arm. "By the Flame, she's just as you said! A real witch. She killed that catamount without even touching it. And she told our future, did you hear? Fine warriors!" He mimed a fierce blow at some future foe, then gasped at the pain in his side. It didn't slow him down much though. "The two of us together! Prince and squire."

Tobin raised his hand and Ki clasped it. "Together. But we can't tell," Tobin reminded him, all too familiar with Ki's tendency to blurt out whatever came into his head.

"By my honor, Prince Tobin, I shall obey. Torture wouldn't drag it out of me. Which is what we're in for when we get home! The sun's down for certain now." He looked ruefully at his torn tunic. "How are we going to explain this? If Nari finds out she'll never let us out of the house again!"

Tobin chewed at his lower lip a moment, knowing Ki was right. Even with Arkoniel's support, Nari still fretted and fussed over them if they were out of her sight for too long. The thought of losing a single day of their newfound freedom was intolerable. "We'll just tell her Dragon ran away with you. That's not even a lie."

Chapter 29

Rhius returned to Ero before the turn of the month, leaving Arkoniel and Tharin once more in charge of the boys.

Having defined his duties as tutor to his own satisfaction and that of his young charges, Arkoniel was pleased to find himself with a great deal of time to pursue his own studies. Iya had been content to wander, collecting ideas and practicing her craft for those who needed it and could pay. Arkoniel had always wished to create and study; now it seemed Illior had granted him both the means and the opportunity to do so.

By late Kemmin the rooms on the third floor were finally refurbished and he took possession of two of them: a small, comfortable bedchamber, and a large, high-ceilinged room adjoining it. In return for his guardianship of Tobin, the duke had granted the wizard a virtually unlimited allowance to pursue his own studies when not otherwise engaged.

For the first time in his well-traveled life, Arkoniel had both ample time and the means to pursue more complex magics. Long before the final coat of plaster was applied to the upstairs walls, he set about furnishing what he already thought of as his workroom. Over the next few months crates arrived almost daily, filled with books and instruments he'd seen in his travels with Iya. From the foundries and kilns of Ylani came the mortars, limbics, and crucibles for alchemical studies and the compounding of magical objects. At Alestun he found tables, braziers, and tools enough to fill another section of the room. He sent to the mines of the northern territories for fine, clear crystals and wrote to other wizards for herbs, ores, and other rare substances not available locally. He began to wonder if he dared ask for another room. In return for such largesse, he began crafting every household simple he knew how to make.

Since he dared commit little news of Tobin to writing, he filled long letters to Iya with his progress, plans, and hopes. In her infrequent replies he read approval and encouragement.

This is what a Third Orëska might be, she wrote, choosing her words carefully. *Not one wizard working alone, but many, sharing their knowledge with generations of students for the benefit of all. I expect you will have something new to show me, when next we meet.*

He fully intended to fulfill that expectation, and with something much more impressive than a new fire spell.

The year's first heavy snowstorm came on the fifth night of Cinrin. The following day the world was a startling palate of black and white under a sky of dazzling blue. The boys were absolutely incapable of sitting still for lessons with such a landscape waiting for them outside the window. Shaking his head, Arkoniel released them and retired to the workshop to pursue his current passion. Soon after, he heard laughter from outside. Going to the window, he saw Tharin and the boys building a snow fortress in the meadow. The slope around them looked like a sparkling white expanse of fine salt, unbroken except for the area they'd chowdered up with their building. Where they'd walked and rolled their snow boulders, the shadows showed blue. The road and bridge had disappeared beneath the snow. Only the river remained, flowing like a thick black serpent between its mounded white banks.

More laughter, and a bellow from Tharin. It appeared

Ki had taught Tobin of snowballs and their uses. Work on the snow fort halted as the battle raged. Arkoniel was tempted to go down and join them, but the warmth and quiet of his workroom won out.

The first step in creating magic, as Iya had taught him, was to envision the desired result. Casting a known spell began that way; if you wanted to make a fire, you envisioned a flame, then let form follow intent with focus.

Creating a new spell was simply a matter of finding out the steps in between to make that intent a reality.

At first, with the adjustment to his new role and home, and the excitement of setting up his own rooms occupying his mind, he'd toyed with alchemy and other known sciences, perfecting the skills he already possessed. However, with a routine established and winter settling in, he found himself thinking about his encounter with Lhel.

The startling power of her sexuality found its way into his dreams more and more often; he could feel her heat against him and smell her musky, feral scent.

He awoke each time with his heart pounding in panic, drenched in sweat. In the light of day he was able to discount all this as the raging of his young and unruly body. The thought of touching her as he did in those dreams made him sick with anxiety.

What drew him back to those memories today was not the carnality of their encounter, but what he thought he'd seen her do that day in the forest, and a dream.

The projection of one's image was a known magic; not easily mastered, but not uncommon, either. Iya could do it and Arkoniel himself had had a few minor successes, but by Orëska magic the resulting image was limited to the wizard's form alone, usually very clear and unnatural, like a specter seen in daylight. That day by the road, however, he'd seen Lhel as if through an oval window; the light that had struck her was daylight, and he'd been able to see the marsh around her before he'd had any idea that one existed in the area. His own mind could not have filled in such detail; Lhel had shown him where she was as clearly as if she had taken him there through a hole in the air.

A hole in the air.

The image had come to him just as he was waking up that morning. Up until now, he'd been relying on disappearance spells, trying to bend them into a combination of form and movement. Nothing had come even close to working.

But this morning he had a new idea, an inspiration left in the wake of a dream. In it, he'd again seen Lhel floating in that green-tinged light that did not match the sunlight where he stood. She was naked, beckoning him, as if she wanted him to step through the shining oval and join her without the trouble of walking up the hill. In this dream he perceived some sort of hole or tunnel connecting them by a tube of shifting green light. In the dream he'd known he was about to grasp the secret he needed, but the image of the naked witch intruded again and he woke with a full bladder and an aching groin.

As he sat here pondering all this, another long-forgotten and seemingly unrelated memory came to him. He and Iya had once explored echoing tunnels at the base of an ancient peak in the northern territories. The tunnels reminded him of enormous mole burrows, but the walls were glassy smooth and showed no sign of digging. Iya claimed that the mountain had created them itself somehow, and showed him chunks of obsidian that contained tiny holes, miniatures of the tunnels themselves, but these were as fine as ant holes in fine earth.

His member stirred again as he settled on a stool by his worktable and attempted to summon the details of the dream more clearly. He willed his body to behave and concentrated on the image: a hole in the air—no, a tunnel! Easy to visualize, but how to create such a thing when he didn't even understand how the mountain had achieved it?

Never in all their travels had Iya or he discovered any spell that resembled such a thing as he envisioned. Here, in his newfound solitude, he worked alone at devising some mechanism of mind that could encompass his vision.

As he had so often over the past few weeks, Arkoniel reached into a nearby bowl and took out a dried bean. It was half the size of his thumbnail and dark red with a smattering of white speckles, the sort his father's cook had called red hens. He rubbed it between thumb and forefinger, committing its weight and smoothness to memory.

Holding the image of the bean firmly in his mind, he placed it on the oak table in front of him, next to a lidded salt box Cook had grudgingly relinquished. Concentrating, he pushed the bean back and forth with his fingers a few times, then took his hand away and raised the bean with his mind until it hovered a foot off the table. Then he brought the full force of his concentration to bear on it, imagining the tunnel he'd dreamed of, willing the bean to find such a route into the closed box.

The bean certainly moved, but only in the usual prosaic manner. Flying against the box as if hurled from a sling, it struck the lid so hard it split in half. The pieces ricocheted in opposite directions and he heard them skitter away across the bare stone floor, no doubt to join their predecessors already scattered around the room.

"Bilairy's balls!" he muttered, resting his face in his hands. Over the past few weeks he'd used enough beans to make a pot of soup, and always with the same discouraging results.

He spent another hour trying to get his mind around the construct of an opening in the air, but ended up with nothing more than a thumping headache.

Leaving off, he turned to surer magics for the rest of the afternoon. Shaking out a newly made firechip from a covered crucible, he placed it on a plate and murmured, "Burn." The reddish brown chip flickered at his command to release a small tongue of pale yellow fire that would burn until he told it to stop.

He set a crucible full of rainwater to boil over it on an iron tripod, then went to his herb cabinet for the various simples he needed to concoct a sleeping draught for Mynir.

The initial mixture stank fiercely, but Arkoniel didn't mind. A feeling of satisfaction crept over him as he sat watching the first bubbles rise. He'd gathered the makings himself in the forest and meadow, and woven the spells from memory. Such melding of magic and material things calmed his nerves; it was pleasing to have a finished, useful product at the end of the incantations. The firechip was his work, as well. Remnants of the latest brick he'd fashioned still lay on a plank nearby, next to the stone hammer he'd used to smash it into usable pieces. This batch would keep the house supplied until spring.

The smell of the steeping herbs brought him back to memories of Lhel, this time as she'd been during their journey to Ero. She'd used every pause and rest break to seek out useful things in the earth or among the dry autumn leaves. His face burned again as he recalled how he'd dismissed her then, not realizing the power she possessed.

More recent memories of musky, tattooed skin and whispered promises crept up on him, making the wizard's heart skip a giddy beat.

Had she known his secret hope? Had she shown him a glimpse of that trick on purpose to snare him? During the long journey to Ero he'd caught her touching his mind so many times; how often had she stolen in unheeded?

He slid off the stool and went back to the window. Late afternoon shadows stretched themselves like long blue cats below the house and a three-quarter moon was rising. Tharin and the boys were gone. Their fort stood like a tiny outpost, surrounded by a welter of trampled footprints. Below it, a single track line of footprints crossed the smooth white flank of the hillside, leading down to the bend in the river.

In the forest the bare trunks and branches stood stark black against the blanket of new snow like hairs on a miller's arm. Soon the real storms would come and choke the roads and trails until spring. The keep was well stocked with provisions and fuel, but how would a barefoot little woman, even a witch, survive? How had she survived so long here already?

And where was she right now?

He stretched his arms out over his head, trying to ignore the fresh thrill of guilt-tainted longing that coursed through him at the thought.

Instead, he leaned far out the window, letting the cold air deal with the sudden flush that suffused his cheeks.

From here he could hear the clatter of cooking pots echoing from the kitchen and the muffled staccato of hooves on the road behind the keep. Arkoniel covered his eyes with one hand and sent a sighting spell up the mountain road. He was nearly as good at this spell as Iya now, and could see over a distance of several miles for short periods of time.

Looking down from a hawk's height, he spotted Tobin and Ki galloping for home, cloaks billowing behind them. They were still some distance away and riding hard to get home before sunset. They'd come in late a few weeks earlier and moped like caged bears when Nari had kept them inside the walls for two days as punishment.

Arkoniel smiled to himself as he watched them. As always, Ki was talking and Tobin was laughing. Suddenly, however, they both reined in so abruptly that their horses reared and wheeled, throwing up white bursts of snow. A third figure entered the wizard's field of vision and he let out a gasp of surprise.

It was Lhel.

She was wrapped in a long fur robe, her hair loose over her shoulders. Both boys dismounted and went to her, clasping her hands in greeting. Arkoniel did not have the power to hear their words at such a distance, but he could see their faces clearly enough. This was not a meeting of strangers.

The witch smiled fondly as she clasped hands with Ki. Tobin said something to her and she reached to touch his cold-reddened cheek.

Arkoniel shuddered, remembering those same fingers cutting, stitching, weaving souls together.

They talked for a few moments, then the boys mounted again and continued homeward. Arkoniel kept the sighting on the witch, but he could already feel the power of the spell waning. He pressed his fingers into his eyelids, straining to keep her in sight as his ability to focus slowly faded.

Lhel remained in the road, watching them ride away. He would have to break it off soon, but he wanted desperately to see where she would go. Just before he gave up, she raised her head slightly, perhaps looking up at the rising moon. For an instant she seemed to look directly at him.

Arkoniel knew he'd held the vision too long. Suddenly he was on his knees under the window, head pounding, and colored sparks dancing dizzily before his eyes. When the worst of it had passed, he pulled himself up and hurried down to the stables for his horse. Not bothering with a saddle, he climbed astride the sorrel and galloped up the road.

As he rode, he had time to wonder at the pounding of his heart and the furious sense of urgency that drove him on. He knew beyond all doubt that Lhel would not harm the children. What's more, he'd seen them part. Yet still he urged his horse on, desperate to find them—

Her.

And why not? he asked himself. She held secrets to magic he had only dreamed of. Iya wanted him to learn from her, and how could he do that without confronting her?

And why would she still be there, standing in the cold road with night coming on?

Tobin and Ki came around a bend and reined in to greet him. He pulled his gelding around so hard he had to cling to its mane to keep his seat.

"You met a woman on the road. What did she say to you?" He was surprised at how harshly the words came out. Ki shifted uneasily in the saddle, not looking at him. Tobin met his gaze squarely and shrugged.

"Lhel says she's getting tired of waiting for you," he replied, and for a moment he was again the dark, strange child Arkoniel had met that summer day. More than that; in the failing light, eyes shadowed to near black, he looked eerily like his demon twin. The sight sent a shiver up Arkoniel's back. Tobin pointed back up the road. "She says for you to hurry. She won't wait much longer."

Lhel. She. Tobin was speaking of someone he knew, not a stranger encountered by chance on the road.

Lhel was waiting for him, would not wait much longer.

"You'd best get home," he told them, and galloped on. He grasped for words to greet her with and found only demands. Where had she been all these months? What had she said to the child? But more than that, what magic had she used the first time she'd come to Arkoniel in the forest?

He cursed himself for not noting any landmarks in his vision, but in the end it didn't matter. A mile or so on and there she was, still standing in the road just as he'd last seen her, her shadow lying blue on the snow. The failing light softened her features, making her look like a young girl lost in the forest.

The sight drove every question from his mind. He reined his horse in and slid down to face her. Her smell came to him, hot on the cold air. It took away his voice and pulled a powerful ache of longing through him. She reached to touch his cheek, just as she had with Tobin, and the caress sent a jolt of raw desire through him, making it hurt to breathe. All he could think to do was to reach out for her, pull her close, and crush her warm body against his. She moaned softly as she pressed against him, rubbing a hard thigh against the answering hardness between his legs.

Thought fled, leaving only sensation and instinct. She must have guided him, he realized later, but at that moment he seemed to be moving in a dream filled with hands and warm lips moving over his skin. He wanted to resist, to summon the rectitude that had guided his life to this point, but all he could think of now was Iya's oblique permission to do exactly this; give Lhel what she wanted in return for the promise of knowledge.

Lhel wasted no time on niceties. Pulling him down on top of the fur robe, she dragged her skirt up to her waist. He fumbled his tunic out of the way, then he was falling onto her, into her, and she was pulling him deeper, so deep that he could scarely comprehend the hot grip of her body around his before he felt something like lightning strike him, pulling a raw cry of amazement from his throat. She shoved him over onto his back, and he felt the soft snow cradle him as she rode him beneath the first stars of evening. Head thrown back, she keened wildly, clenching his member with whatever strange inner muscles women possessed. Lightning struck again, harder and more consuming this time, and Arkoniel went blind, listening to his own cries and hers echoing through the forest like wolf song.

Then he was gulping air, too stunned to move. She leaned forward and kissed his cheeks, eyelids, and lips. His throat was sore, his body cold, and their mingled fluids were trickling in a chilly, ticklish stream over his balls. He couldn't have stirred if a whole regiment of cavalry had come thundering down the road at them. His horse nickered softly nearby, as if amused.

Lhel sat back and took his hand. Pressing it to one full

breast through her rough dress, she grinned down at him. "Make spell for me, Orëska."

He goggled stupidly up at her. "What?"

She kneaded his fingers into her firm, pliant flesh and her grin widened. "Make a magic for me."

The stars caught his eye again and he whispered a spell in their honor. A point of brilliant white light sprang to life above them, radiant as a star itself. The sheer beauty of it made him laugh. He spun the light into a larger sphere, then split it into a thousand sparkling shards and placed them in her hair like a wreath of frost and diamonds. Bathed in their ethereal light, Lhel looked like a wild spirit of the night masquerading in rags. As if reading his thoughts on his face, she grasped the neck of her dress and tore it down the front, revealing again the marks of power that covered her body. Arkoniel touched them reverently, tracing spirals, whorls, and crescents, then shyly reached down to where their bodies were still joined, flesh to flesh.

"You were right. Iya tried to tell me . . ." he managed at last, caught between wonder and betrayal. "It was all a lie, that this robs a wizard of power." He raised his hand to the crown of light glowing in her hair. "I've never made anything so beautiful."

Lhel took his hand again and pressed it to her heart. "Not lies for all, Orëska. Some can't serve the Goddess. But you? What you feel here . . ." She tapped his chest with her free hand. "That's what you make here." She touched his forehead. "Iya thinks this. She tried tell you."

"You heard us talking that day?"

"I hear a lot. See a lot. See you sleep with longing in your *raluk*." She squeezed him inside of her and gave him a playful wink. "I try send my words to you in dreams, but you stubborn one! Why you make me send children after you with all that heat in you?"

Arkoniel stared up at the sky, trying to summon the fear that had beset him less than an hour earlier. How had he come to be here, sated and laughing, without any memory of decision or consent? "Did you make me—?"

Lhel shrugged. "Can't make if desire don't be in you. Wasn't, that first time in the mud place. Now it is; I just call it out."

"But you could have had me easily in the—the 'mud place'!" Yet even as he said it, Arkoniel knew that something important had shifted in himself since that day at the marsh.

"I don't take," she said softly. "You give."

"But I didn't have any intention of—of—" He gestured weakly. "Of any of this until the moment I got here!"

"You did. In here." Lhel caught one of the light points on her fingertip and placed it on his chest. "Heart don't always tell head. But body know. You learn that."

"Yes, I learn that," Arkoniel agreed, surrendering to her logic.

Lhel rolled off him and stood up. Her feet were bound up with rags and strips of bark but she showed no sign of minding the cold. Pulling the torn dress and the robe around her, she said, "Too much in they head, you Orëskas. That why you need me for the *shaimari anan*. Why you need me put those keesas' shaimari back right."

"You'll teach me?"

Lhel looked down at him and raised an eyebrow. "You keep pay?"

Arkoniel got up and straightened his own clothing. "By the Four, yes, if that's your price. But can't you come to the keep?"

Lhel shook her head. "No, Iya right in that. I seen your king, read his heart. Nobody knows, is better."

Sudden doubt leeched up through Arkoniel's buoyant mood. "I saw you speak to Tobin and Ki in the road. They know you."

"Keesas knows not to say."

"You put Ki in danger, you know, revealing too much."

Lhel shrugged. "You don't be worry about Ki. Goddess send him, too."

This seemed to be the foundation of her reasoning. "She's a busy lady, your goddess."

Lhel folded her arms and stared at him until he felt uncomfortable, then turned abruptly and motioned for him to follow.

"Where are we going?"

A chuckle floated back to him as she melted into the shadow of the trees. "You want have all lessons in the road, Orëska?"

With a resigned sigh, Arkoniel reached for his horse's lead rein and followed her on foot.

Wizards saw well in the dark, and apparently so did witches. Lhel strode confidently through the trees with no path to guide her. Humming to herself, she seemed almost to dance ahead of him, brushing trees and stones with her hands as she went. Without the stars to sight by, Arkoniel soon lost track of the way and hurried to keep up with her.

She stopped at last under an enormous oak.

"Cama!" she said aloud, and a soft glow issued from an opening in its side.

Following her inside, he found himself in a comfortable shelter. A light similar to the one he'd conjured glowed softly some twenty feet overhead where the cleft in the oak ended. Iya and he had found shelters like this in their travels; ancient oaks often split without dying. Lhel had made herself nicely at home here. A fur-covered pallet lay against the far wall beside a rumpled pile of what might be clothing; there were a few pots and baskets, and the fire pit and upper walls of the tree were well blackened with smoke. Even so, he could not imagine living all these years in such a place.

Lhel pulled a deer hide across the entrance, then squatted by the firepit to strike a flame in the tinder stacked ready there.

"Here, a gift." Arkoniel took a small pouch of firechips from his tunic and showed her how to use them. Flames licked up and she fed the little blaze from a pile of twigs and broken branches next to it.

She looked into the pouch and smiled. "Is good."

"How have you survived here?" he asked, hunkering down beside her. In this light he could see how chapped her face and hands were, and the thick calluses and chilblains on her dirty bare feet under the wrappings.

Lhel looked at him over the fire. The flickering light sank deep shadows into the lines around her mouth and struck reddish glints in the silver streaks in her hair. As they'd rutted wildly in the road, she'd seemed so young; here she looked ancient as a goddess herself.

"This good place," she said, shrugging out of the cloak and letting the torn top of her dress slide off her shoulders to hang loose about her waist. Her full breasts glowed in the firelight, showing no sign of the symbols he'd seen there before. She reached into a basket and offered him a strip of dried meat. Arkoniel took it, still staring at her body as she found more food and began to eat. She was as filthy as ever, and had lost some teeth over the years. Those she had left were stained and worn. Yet as she turned to grin at him, she was still handsome, still deeply alluring. . . .

Without thinking, he leaned forward to kiss her shoulder, inhaling her odor and wanting her again. "How do you make me feel like this?" he whispered, genuinely mystified.

"How many year you be?" she asked around a mouthful of wizened caneberries.

Arkoniel had to stop and think. "Thirty-one," he said at last. It was nearly a life's span for some men; for a wizard he was hardly out of his youth.

Lhel raised her eyebrows in mocking surprise. "Thirty-one year no woman and now you don't know why you get hard?" She snorted and reached under his tunic to cradle his genitals in her hand. "You got *power* here!" Taking her hand away, she touched his belly, chest, throat, and brow. "Got power all places. Some can use. You can."

"And you'll teach me?"

"Some. For the keesa."

Arkoniel moved closer until his leg was pressed to hers. "That day at the marsh I saw you do something that I want to learn. I was on the road, and you appeared—"

Lhel smiled slyly and made a pinching motion with thumb and forefinger. "I see you with your *krabol.*"

Arkoniel stared at her a moment, then grinned sheepishly as he interpreted the hand gesture. "With the beans, you mean!"

"Beans." She repeated the word. "You think you move them—" Another less intelligible gesture, but he thought he understood.

"You've seen me trying to move them about. But how?"

Lhel held up her left hand and made a circle with thumb and forefinger. Rattling off a quick gabble of sounds that didn't quite seem to be words, she pursed her lips and blew through her fingers. When she took her hand away Arkoniel saw a small black hole in the air in front of them, no bigger than a horse's eye.

"Look," she offered.

Leaning over, Arkoniel peered into the spy hole and found himself looking at Tobin and Ki. They were sitting on the floor beside the toy city and Tobin was trying to teach Ki to carve. "Incredible!"

Lhel elbowed him sharply and closed the hole with a wave of her hand, but not before Arkoniel glimpsed two startled faces look up as one, trying to find the source of the voice that must have come out of thin air.

"I forgot that I could hear you through it, too," Arkoniel exclaimed. "By the Light, it *is* a tunnel in the air!"

"What 'tunnel'?" asked Lhel.

When Arkoniel tried to explain, she shook her head.

"No, it is—" She mimed what he finally understood to be opening a shuttered window. "Like that, with two side—" She pressed her palms tightly together.

Arkoniel pondered this with growing excitement. If a voice could go through so easily, then surely an object, or even a person, could as well? But when he tried to explain this to Lhel her eyes widened in alarm.

"No!" she warned, shaking his arm for emphasis. Placing her other hand on his brow, she spoke in his mind, as she had that day at the marsh. *No solid thing that goes into a seeing window comes out again, on the other side or anywhere else. They swallow up whatever is put into them.*

"Teach me," he said aloud.

Lhel took her hands away and shook her head. "Not yet. Other things more needful. You don't be knowing enough."

Arkoniel sat back on his heels, trying to swallow his disappointment. It was not the magic he'd hoped for, but one that would take him closer to his goal than anything else he knew of. He would bide his time. "What must I be knowing, then?"

Lhel produced a bone needle from somewhere in her skirts. She held it up for him to see, then pricked the pad of her thumb and squeezed out a bright red droplet. "First you learn the power of this, and flesh, and bone, and the dead."

"Necromancy?" Was he so blinded by a single rut that he'd forgotten the darker roots of her magic?

Lhel gazed at him with unfathomable black eyes, and again she looked ancient and powerful. "This word I know. Your people call us this when you drive us out of lands that be ours. You wrong."

"But it's blood magic—"

"Yes, but not *evil*. Necromancy is—" She struggled with the language. "Most worse dirty thing."

"Abomination," Arkoniel offered.

"Yes, abomination. But not this." She squeezed out

another drop and smeared it across her palm. "You have blood, flesh. I have. All people. No evil. *Power*. Evil come from heart, not blood."

Arkoniel stared at her palm, watching the thin smear dry into the lines of her palm. What she'd said went against everything he'd ever been taught as a Skalan in his father's house and as a wizard. Yet sitting here with this woman, feeling the aura of power that surrounded her, he sensed no evil in her. He thought of Tobin and the demon, and the lengths to which Lhel had gone to make things as right as she could. Grudgingly, fearfully, he listened to his heart and guessed that she spoke the truth.

Had he been gifted with future sight, he would have seen the course of Skalan and Orëska history shift ever so subtly in that moment of uneasy realization.

Chapter 30

Arkoniel found himself in the dual roles of teacher and pupil that winter, instructing his reluctant young charges each morning, then seeking out Lhel for his own lessons.

Tharin proved a stout ally in the former, for he refused to begin weapons practice until both boys had made an acceptable effort at Arkoniel's lessons. This system met with some resistance at first, but as Tobin finally mastered his letters and could read a little, he suddenly developed a taste for learning. His enthusiasm increased when Arkoniel offered to teach him to draw. As far as Arkoniel could tell, it was the only skill he possessed that impressed Tobin.

Ki still fidgeted and sighed a great deal, but Arkoniel saw improvements there, too, though he knew better than to flatter himself as to the reason. For Ki, the sun rose and set on Tobin and he would strive at any task his companion set value on. Whatever the young prince chose to apply himself to, Ki threw himself into with a will.

There was no arguing that he'd had the desired effect on Tobin, either. The prince laughed more now, and the daily rambles on the mountainside put color in his cheeks and lean muscle on his long bones.

Dispatch riders arrived every few weeks, carrying letters from Rhius filled with reports of the growing unrest across the sea.

The Plenimaran shipyards are too busy for comfort, he wrote in one letter, *and the king's spies send word of great numbers of Plenimarans massing along Mycena's eastern border. I fear they will not limit themselves to coastal raids, come spring. May Illior and Sakor grant that we fight on other shores this time.*

Arkoniel, who had no experience of war, found himself watching Tharin as these letters were read out in the hall.

Tharin listened carefully, brow furrowed in thought, then questioned the messenger in detail. How fared the garrisons at Atyion and Cirna? How many ships were anchored in Ero's harbor? Had the king raised another levy of soldiers, or provender from the countryside?

"I feel very green, listening to you," Arkoniel admitted one evening as he and Tharin sat up late over a game of bakshi. "For all my travels, I've led a sheltered existence compared to you."

"Wizards used to fight for Skala," Tharin mused, still focused on the gaming stones in front of them. "Now it seems the king is only willing to have you fight one another."

"I hope to see that change one day."

At such moments Arkoniel was uncomfortably aware of the secret that divided them. The more he grew to know the man, the more he regretted that Tharin did not know the truth.

"I wouldn't mind having you at my back," Tharin went on, gathering the stones for another toss. Firelight struck the polished carnelians, turning them to fire and blood in his fingers. "I'm no authority on wizards, but I know men. You've got steel in your spine. And I don't imagine old Iya would've taken you on if she didn't believe it, too. Or left that old bag of hers with you."

He looked up before Arkoniel could completely mask his surprise. "Oh, I'm not asking. But I'm not blind, either. If she trusts you, that should be good enough for anyone."

Neither said anything more about the matter, but Arkoniel was grateful to have the respect of this man.

He wished he were as certain of Lhel's opinion of him. Arkoniel burned for her. He dreamed of her body and awoke stiff and hot in the night with no recourse but his own hand, a remedy far less satisfying than it had once been.

But she remained obdurate; he was only allowed to find her at her whim. No seeking spell could locate her and he was never able to find his way to the oak on his own. When he wanted her, he rode into the forest and, if she wished, she would reveal herself. If not, he came home frustrated and fuming.

Sometimes when he did find her, the boys were with her. Then the four of them would tramp through the snow, exploring the forest together like some peasant family. It was pleasant and he smiled at the picture they made, for in daylight Lhel showed her age and he felt more akin to Tobin and Ki than he did to her.

When he and Lhel did manage to meet alone, however, it was quite another matter. They coupled each time—he never did equate her "price" with lovemaking, nor did she—and each time was as frenzied as the first. She asked no tenderness of him and gave none in return, only passion. Behind closed eyelids, Arkoniel saw visions of whirlwinds, thunderstorms, and earthquakes. When he opened his eyes he saw the power of Lhel's goddess blazing in her eyes and in the dark whorls on her skin that she showed him only then.

As they lay naked together on her pallet afterward, she showed him whatever she was moved to in the way of spellcraft. Much of it seemed designed to overcome his natural aversion to blood magic.

She began by teaching him to "read the blood," as she put it. She would hand him a bloodstained bit of cloth or bark; by touching it with fingers and mind, he soon learned to identify the creature that had shed it. As these lessons progressed, he learned to enter the mind of the creature if it was still living, and to see through its eyes. As a fox he padded through a meadow and dug sluggish mice from their tunnels in the brown, ice-rimed grass. As

an eagle, he circled the keep in search of stray hens. In
the strangest of these explorations, he entered a trout
swimming in the muted brown light under the river ice
and saw a woman's jeweled ring shining brightly among
the silky strands of slime that covered the rocks.

As a final test, Lhel gave him a bit of her own blood,
and he found himself inside her skin. The simple minds of
the beasts had given him nothing more than a few visual
images, cast in shades of grey. Settling in Lhel, however,
he felt the intimate weight of her body around him, as if
he wore her flesh as a garment over his own. He could
feel the sag of her breasts beneath her ragged dress, the
ache that plagued her left ankle, the heavy warmth of
their coupling between her thighs. After a moment's dis-
orientation, he realized that he was looking at himself
through her eyes. His body lay on the pallet next to the
fire, still as a corpse beneath the fur robe. With a mix of
chagrin and amusement he inspected his own long, bony
limbs, the jut of ribs under his white skin, the black pelt of
hair that covered his chest and back, arms and legs. The
expression on his face was ecstatic, like a temple Oracle's
when touched by the god.

For all that, however, he could not hear Lhel's
thoughts. That she would not share.

As his fear of her magic lessened, she began to impart
a few rudiments about spirits and ghosts.

"How did you make the change in Tobin?" he asked
one day as the wind moaned around the oak.

"You saw."

"I saw you trade a piece of skin between them. Does
it hold the magic?"

"It make skin one skin," she replied, casting about for
the right words. "When Tobin is to be a girl again, that
skin must come off."

He was not always the student with her. He helped Lhel
learn more of his language, and showed her all the ways

he knew to make fire. Comparing magics, they discovered that they could both call wind, and pass through any cover without leaving traces.

He taught her the Orëska method of wizard sighting, and in return she tried to teach him her "tunnel in the air" magic. However, this proved more difficult than he'd expected. It was not the whispered incantation, or even the patterned hand movements it required, but some odd twist of mind that he could not see and she did not have the language to explain.

"It will come to you," she assured him again and again. "It will come."

To Arkoniel's dismay, the one person at the keep whom he seemed to make the least progress with was Tobin. The child was civil and seemed determined to master what Arkoniel tried to teach him, but there was always a distance between them that seemed unbridgeable.

One thing Tobin did choose to share, much to Arkoniel's surprise, was the spell he used to summon Brother. Arkoniel attempted it, but with no result. Brother answered only to Tobin.

When he asked Lhel about it later, she shrugged and said, "They joined by flesh. That you cannot learn by magic."

Arkoniel was sorry to hear this, for the spirit often found its way into his workroom. He had not seen it with his eyes since that day it had fooled him and spooked his horse, but there was no mistaking its cold, hostile presence. It seemed to enjoy tormenting him, and often came close enough to raise the hairs on his neck. It did him no physical harm, but more than once it drove him downstairs in search of Tobin.

Spring came early with little rain. As expected, King Erius signed a pact with Mycena and launched a campaign against the Plenimaran invaders there, leaving his trusted minister, Lord Chancellor Hylus, to oversee the court in his absence. One of Iya's infrequent letters mentioned seemingly in passing that the king's wizard, Lord Niryn, had also remained behind.

Rhius was to accompany the king, of course, and Tharin could no longer be spared.

The duke came in early Lithion to make his farewells, and brought a band of minstrels and acrobats with him to perform. He stayed less than a week, but rode with the boys each day, and sat up late in the hall, gaming with Tharin and Arkoniel and listening to the minstrels. The wizard was delighted to see him acting so much more like his old self, and Tobin was ecstatic.

The only thing to mar the visit was the sudden passing of the old steward, Mynir. He failed to come down for breakfast one morning and Nari found the old man dead in his bed. The women drained and washed the body, wrapped it with spices, and sewed it into a shroud to be carried back to his people in Ero.

The old man had been beloved in the household and everyone wept around the body as it lay before the shrine—everyone except Tobin. Even Ki shed a few tears for the poor old fellow, but Tobin's eyes remained dry as he made his solemn offerings to Astellus. The sight chilled Arkoniel, though no one else seemed to remark on it.

The day of parting came too soon, and the household gathered in the courtyard to see Rhius and Tharin off. Arkoniel and Tharin had said their good-byes over wine the night before, but all the same the wizard felt a dull ache clutch his heart as he watched the tall swordsman saddle his mount.

Tobin and Ki helped glumly with the preparation, looking more subdued than Arkoniel had ever seen them.

When everything was ready and his father and Tharin were mounted to go, Tobin stood by his father's stirrup and looked up. "Ki and I will practice every day," he promised. "When can we come to join you?"

Leaning down, Rhius clasped hands with him, smiling proudly. "When my armor fits you, my child, and that day will come sooner than you think. When it does—" The man's voice caught roughly in his throat. "By the Four, then no general will be prouder than I to have such a warrior at my back." He turned to Ki then. "Do you have any message for your father, if I meet with him?"

Ki shrugged. "If I've served well here, my lord, you might tell him that. I can't think what else he'd want to know."

"I'll tell him that no prince has a more loyal squire. You have my thanks, Kirothius, son of Larenth."

Arkoniel would have been hard pressed to say whose eyes shone more brightly as they watched Rhius out of sight, Tobin's or Ki's.

Chapter 31

For weeks after his father left, Tobin watched for messengers on the Alestun road, but none came.

Arkoniel found him standing at his window one morning and guessed his thoughts. "Mycena's a long way off, you know. They may not even be there yet."

Tobin knew he was right, but he couldn't help watching the road, all the same.

When a rider finally did appear one warm spring day a month or so later, it was not with word of Rhius.

Tobin and Ki were fishing at the river bend when they heard the sound of hooves on the road. Scrambling up the bank, they peered over the edge. The horseman was a rough-looking character in leather with a mane of wild brown hair flying about his shoulders.

The rules for strangers had not changed since Ki's arrival: keep your distance and head for the keep. Ki knew this as well as Tobin did, but instead of obeying, he let out a whoop and leapt up to meet the rider.

"Ki, no!" Tobin shouted, catching at his ankle.

But Ki laughed. "Come on, it's only Ahra!"

"Ahra? Your sister?" Tobin followed, but hung back shyly. Ahra was often a rather formidable character in Ki's stories.

The rider saw them and reined in sharply. "That you, Ki?"

It was a woman after all, but not like any Tobin had ever seen. She wore the same sort of leather armor over mail that his father's men did, and a bow and longsword hung at her back. Her hair was dark brown like Ki's, and worn braided in front, wild behind. She didn't look much like him, otherwise, being only a half sister.

She swung down and grabbed her brother in a hug that lifted him off the ground. "It is you, boy! Skinny as ever, but you've grown two spans!"

"What're you doing here?" Ki demanded as she let him down.

"Come to see how you was faring." Ahra spoke with the same flat, country accent that Ki had had when he first came to the keep. "I met that wizard woman of yours on the road a few weeks back and she asked me to bring a letter to another wizard here—friend of hers. Said you'd worked in here well enough, too." She grinned at Tobin. "Who's this one with mud between his toes? Iya didn't say nothing about another boy sent to serve the prince."

"Mind your mouth," Ki warned. "That *is* the prince!"

Tobin stepped forward to greet her and the woman dropped to one knee before him, head bent. "Forgive me, Your Highness. I didn't know you!"

"How would you? Please, get up!" Tobin urged, embarrassed to have anyone kneel to him.

Ahra stood and shot Ki a dark look. "You mighta said."

"Didn't give me a chance, did you?"

"I'm glad to meet you," Tobin said, clasping hands with her. Now that his initial surprise had passed, he was very curious about her and delighted to finally meet one of Ki's kin. "My father's not here, but you're welcome to guest with us."

"I'd be most honored, Highness, but my captain only give me 'til nightfall. Rest of the company's back in Alestun buying supplies. We're bound for Ylani to fend off the summer raiders."

"I figured you'd be gone to Mycena with Jorvai and Father and all," said Ki.

She let out a snort and Tobin got a glimpse of her famous temper. "*They* went, all the boys right down to your mam's Amin, just year older'n you. Gone for a runner. But the king still wants no women in the ranks with him, by Sakor. Left us with the old men and cripples to watch the coastline."

Ahra gave Ki news of home as the three of them walked up to the house. Their fourth mother, who was only a year older than Ahra, had birthed twins soon after Ki left home and was pregnant again. Five of the younger children had been taken with fever, but only two had died. The house was quieter with the seven eldest gone; the war had come in time to save Alon from being taken up as a horse thief by a neighboring knight. Even though this was old news, Ki vigorously defended his brother's innocence in the matter all the same, outraged at the charge.

Tobin took all this in with mounting delight; he knew all these people through Ki's stories and here was one of them in the flesh. He liked Ahra, too, and decided Ki had exaggerated her bad points a bit. Like him, she was blunt and open, with no secrets behind her dark eyes. All the same, it was strange to see a woman carrying a sword.

Nari met them as they came across the bridge, and her scowl stopped all three in their tracks. "Prince Tobin, who's this and what's she doing here?"

"Ki's sister," he told her. "You know, the one who tried to leap her horse over the hog pen and fell in."

"Ahra, is it?" Nari softened at once.

Ahra glared at Ki. "You been telling tales on me, have you?"

Nari laughed. "That he has! You'll find you've no secrets with Ki about. Come in, girl, and eat with us. Cook will be glad to see a woman in armor again!"

They were listening to Cook trade stories with Ahra about her fighting days when Arkoniel came in with that smug, comfortable look he always had when he'd been with Lhel on his own.

That changed when he saw Ahra. He looked even less pleased than Nari until Ahra handed him Iya's letter.

"Well, if she sent you," he muttered. "I suppose I should have had Ki write to his mother before now."

"Wouldn't do no good if he did," Ahra told him with stiff dignity. "Can't none of *us* read."

Ki colored as if he'd been caught doing something shameful.

"What can you tell us of the war?" Tobin asked.

"Last news I had is a good month old. The king met up with the Mycenian Elders at Nanta and a fleet went down the coast to engage the Plenimarans at the frontier. I heard your father well spoken of, Prince Tobin. Word is he's at the front of every battle, the king's right hand."

"Have you been in the capital recently?" asked Arkoniel.

Ahra nodded. "We come through there a week back. Two ships were burned at anchor when the harbormaster found plague aboard. When it turned out that some of the sailors had got ashore already and gone into a tavern, the deathbirds come and nailed it up with them in it and burned 'em for plague bringers."

"What are deathbirds?" Tobin asked.

"They're something like a healer," Arkoniel told him, though his look of distaste belied the explanation. "They go about the country trying to keep plague from coming in at the ports. They wear masks with long fronts on them that look like beaks. The beak part is filled with herbs to keep off the plague. That's why people call them deathbirds."

"There's plenty of Harriers about making trouble, too," Ahra told him, and again Tobin didn't know what she meant, except that she didn't think much of them.

"Have there been any more executions in the city?"

Ahra nodded. "Three more, one of them a priest. People don't like it much, but no one dares speak against them, not since the arrests a few months back."

"That's enough about that," said Cook. "I think the boys might like to see how a woman fights, don't you? You're the first Prince Tobin has ever met still in armor."

They finished the visit with a bout of swordplay in the barracks yard. Ahra fought hard and dirty, and showed the boys a few new ways of tripping up and backhanding an opponent.

"That's no way to be teaching the king's nephew!" Nari objected, watching from a safe distance.

"No, let them have at it," said Cook. "No one pays attention to titles or birthrights in battle. A young warrior can do with a few tricks up his sleeve."

Arkoniel remained in the kitchen, committing Iya's letter to memory so he could burn it. To anyone else, it would appear to be nothing more than a rambling account of people Iya had met in her recent travels. However, when Arkoniel muttered the correct words over it, the spell silvered a few letters here and there, revealing the true message. It was still cryptic, but clear enough to send a nasty jolt of dread through him.

Three more friends lost to flames. The hounds still hunt but have not struck a scent. Come White or Grey, flee. I keep my distance. Illior watch over you.

Grey or White. Arkoniel imagined a column of such riders coming up through the meadow and shivered. He tossed the letter into the fire and watched until it was completely consumed.

"Illior watch over you, too," he whispered, knocking the ashes to bits with the poker.

Chapter 32

Messengers from Mycena began to arrive by early Gorathin. From then on, all through the summer and the long winter that followed, the boys lived from dispatch to dispatch. The duke wrote infrequently; each letter was read and reread until the parchment was limp and dog-eared. The king returned to Ero for the winter, but left the bulk of his force on the frontier. As one of his most valued commanders, Rhius remained, camped with his armies on the western bank of the Eel River. The Plenimarans did the same on their side of the water and when spring came the fighting broke out anew.

The summer that followed was hotter than any even Cook could recall. Arkoniel kept the boys at their lessons as best he could while they fretted that the war was passing them by.

Ki turned thirteen on the fourth of Shemin. His voice cracked wildly at odd moments now and he proudly showed off a faint line of downy black hair on his upper lip.

Tobin would soon be twelve, and though his cheeks and lip remained bare, he now matched Ki in height. Both boys were still rangy and coltish in build, but endless days of riding, chores, and arms practice had given them a wiry strength no town-bred boy could match.

Arkoniel continued to marvel at their bond. No two brothers could have been closer in love than these two. In fact, it seemed to the wizard that they got on with each other better than most brothers did. Despite the fact that they shared nearly every waking hour of the day and the same bed at night, Arkoniel seldom heard a harsh word pass between them. Instead, they challenged each other good-naturedly at all pursuits and shamelessly supported one another when caught in some prank around the house. Arkoniel suspected that Ki was behind most of the mischief, but it would have taken magic or torture to get the truth out of either of them.

Two years of careful tutelage had polished Ki up like a good gem. He spoke as fair as any country lord and managed not to swear most of the time. He still had a boy's unformed features, but he'd prove to be a comely fellow in time and Arkoniel suspected he had the wit to go far at court if he chose.

Or at least as far as a landless knight's middle son could go with the right patronage. His father's title was an empty one; it would be Rhius or Tobin who sent him higher, and even then it would not be an easy climb unless Rhius chose to adopt Ki—an unlikely prospect.

Had this been a normal household, the difference in the boys' stations might have made itself felt by now, but this was not a normal house by any measure. Tobin knew nothing of court life and treated everyone as his equal. Nari fretted over this, but Arkoniel advised her to let the boys be. Judged on his own merits, Ki was as worthy a companion as any young prince could ask for and Tobin was happy at last—for the most part, at least.

His strange bouts of foreknowing seemed to have passed, and with Lhel's help he'd reached some accord with Brother. The spirit had grown so quiet that Nari joked about missing its antics. Arkoniel asked Lhel if it was possible that the spirit might go to rest at last, but the witch shook her head and told him, "No, and you don't want for it to."

If Tobin thought at all of his mother's death, he said nothing. The only indication that it still haunted him was his aversion to the tower.

The only apparent clouds on the boy's youthful horizon were his father's absence and not being allowed to join him in Mycena.

Since Ahra's visit the previous summer, Tobin and Ki were painfully aware that boys younger than themselves had gone off to war. Arkoniel's assurances that no boy of Tobin's station, not even the Prince Royal himself, would be allowed in battle did little to assuage his wounded pride.

At least once a month since then, both boys tried on the armor Rhius had left behind and swore it nearly fit, though in truth the sleeves of the hauberk still hung well below their fingertips. They kept up their arms practice with grim determination and splintered enough practice blades to keep Cook in kindling through the winter.

Tobin capitalized on his hard-won writing skills and always had a thick packet of letters ready for his father's couriers. Rhius replied sporadically, and his letters made no mention of Tobin's pleas to join him. However, he did send a swordsmith to the keep. The man took their measure with his strings and calipers; within the month they each had proper swords to practice with.

Otherwise, life went on as it always had until one summer day when Arkoniel overheard them trying to guess the distance to Ero, and how they might present themselves to strangers on the road. That night he quietly fixed a small glyph on each of them as they slept, in case he had to track them down later.

Ki and Tobin didn't run away, but all through that long hot summer they grumbled and fretted and talked of war, and Ero.

In truth Ki had been to the city only a handful of times, but he relived each visit from memory for Tobin. Sitting by the dusty toy city at night, he would point here and there, painting a picture with his words, making a new section come alive in Tobin's imagination.

"Here's where Goldsmith Street lies, or thereabouts, and the temple," Ki would explain. "Remember I told you about the painted dragon on the wall there?"

Tobin questioned him closely about Aurënfaie horses and traders he'd seen at the Horse Fair, and repeatedly made him describe everything he could recall of the ships in the harbor, with their colored sails and banners.

It was Tobin, however, who taught Ki what lay inside the walls of the Palatine Circle, for Ki had never been there. Tobin had only his father and Tharin's stories to go by, but he'd learned them well. He quizzed his friend on the royal lineage, as well, lining the little kings and queens from the box up on the Palace roof.

During the day they roamed the woods and meadow wearing little more than short linen kilts. It was too hot most days for more. Even Arkoniel adopted their fashion and didn't seem to mind when they snickered at his pale hairy body.

Lhel stripped for the heat, too. Tobin was shocked the first time she stepped from the trees to greet them clad only in a short skirt. He'd seen most of Nari often enough when she changed her shift or bathed, but never any other woman. And Nari was small-breasted, soft and pale. Lhel was nothing like that. She was brown all over, and her body was almost as hard as a man's, but not flat and angular. Her breasts hung like huge ripe plums and they swayed as she walked. Her legs and flanks were firm, her hips wide and rounded, and her waist slender. Her hands and feet were as dirty as ever, but the rest of her looked as clean as if she'd just come from swimming. Tobin wanted to reach out and touch her shoulder, just to see what it would feel like, but the very thought made him blush.

He saw Ki blushing, too, that first time, though he didn't look all that embarrassed. They both soon grew used to the sight of her, but Tobin did sometimes wonder what her skirt might hide. Ki said a woman's nether parts were nothing like a man's. Now and then he'd find Lhel watching him as if she knew his thoughts and he'd have to look away, coloring more hotly than ever.

Chapter 33

Do you think Prince Korin has to fill the wash kettle at the Palace?" Ki complained as he and Tobin toiled into the kitchen yard with their buckets. The wooden horse carving he wore stuck against his sweaty brown chest as he heaved his bucket up onto the edge of the steaming wash cauldron. It wasn't even noon yet, but the Lenthin day was already sweltering.

Sweat ran off Tobin's nose as he emptied his own bucket. Leaning over the cauldron, he blew the steam out of the way and let out an exasperated groan. "Bilairy's balls! Not even half full yet. Two more trips and we're taking a swim. I don't care if Cook yells herself hoarse."

"Command me, my prince," Ki chuckled, following Tobin back out the gate.

The most recent drought had lowered the river between its banks. They had to pick their way over jumbled stones crusted with dead rockweed to reach the water's edge. They were almost there when Ki stubbed his toe badly. He let out a strangled groan as he bit back a forbidden word; Nari had already clipped his ear once today for foul language. "Damnation!" he hissed instead, gripping his bleeding toe.

Tobin dropped his buckets and helped him hobble down to the water. "Soak it until it feels better."

Ki sat down and thrust both legs into the current up to the knees. Tobin did the same and leaned back, resting on his elbows. He was even browner than Ki this summer, he noted proudly, though Nari claimed it made him look like a peasant.

From his current vantage point he could see the line of fine golden hairs that ran down the muscled trough of Ki's spine, and the way his friend's shoulder blades flared out beneath the smooth skin. Ki reminded Tobin of the catamount they'd faced together in the mountains, tawny and supple. The sight sent a warm glow through him that he couldn't quite put words to.

"That kettle won't fill itself!" Cook called from the gate behind them.

Tobin craned his head back for an upside down look at the impatient woman. "Ki hurt his foot."

"Are *your* legs broke?"

"Nothing wrong that I can see," Ki said, throwing a handful of cold water onto Tobin's belly.

He yelped and sat up. "Traitor! See if I help you . . ."

Brother stood watching him on the far bank. Tobin had called him earlier that morning, then forgotten about him.

Brother had matched Tobin in growth, but stayed gaunt and fish-belly pale. No matter where Brother appeared, the light never struck him the way it did a living person. At this distance, his unnatural eyes looked like two black holes in his face. His voice had grown fainter, too. It had been months since Tobin had heard him speak at all.

He stared at Tobin a moment longer, then turned and gazed down the road.

"Someone's coming," Tobin murmured.

Ki glanced down the meadow, then back at him. "I don't hear anything."

A moment later they both heard the first faint jingle of harness in the distance.

"Ah! Brother?"

Tobin nodded.

By now they could both hear the riders clearly enough to know there were at least a score. Tobin jumped to his feet. "Do you suppose that's Father?"

Ki grinned. "Who else could it be, coming here with that many?"

Tobin scrambled back up the rocks and ran onto the bridge for a better view.

The sun-baked planks burned his feet. He danced impatiently from foot to foot for a minute, then set off along the grassy verge to meet the riders.

"Tobin, come back! You know we're not supposed to."

"I'll just go part way!" Glancing over his shoulder, he saw Ki limping toward the bridge. The other boy pointed at his hurt foot and shrugged.

Tobin's heart beat faster as he caught the flash of sunlight off steel through the trees. Why were they coming so slowly? His father always took the last mile at a gallop, raising a cloud of dust that could be seen above the trees long before the riders appeared.

Tobin stopped and shaded his eyes. There was no dust cloud today. Uneasy, he stood poised to run if it proved to be strangers after all.

When the first riders came into sight at the bottom of the meadow, however, he recognized Tharin in the lead on his roan, with old Laris and the others close behind. There were two other lords with him, too. He recognized Nyanis by his shining hair and Solari by his bushy black beard and green-and-gold cloak.

The fighting must be over. He's brought guests for a feast! Tobin let out a whoop and waved both arms at them, still searching for his father among the press of riders. Tharin waved an answering salute but didn't spur his horse. As they came up the hill Tobin saw that the captain was leading a horse on a long rein—his father's black palfrey. It was saddled but riderless. Only then did Tobin note that all the horses' manes were shorn close to their necks. He knew what that meant. The men had told him tales in the barracks yard—

The air beside Tobin darkened as Brother shimmered into view. His voice was scarcely audible above the sound of the river but Tobin heard him clearly enough.

Our father has come home.

"No." Tobin marched on stubbornly to meet the riders. His heart was pounding in his ears. He couldn't feel the road beneath his feet.

Tharin and the others reined in as he reached them. Tobin refused to look at their faces. He looked only at his father's horse and the things strapped across the saddle: hauberk, helm, bow. And a long clay jar slung in a net.

"Where is he?" Tobin demanded, staring now at one worn, empty stirrup. His voice sounded almost as faint as Brother's in his ears.

He heard Tharin dismount, felt the man's big hands on his shoulders, but he kept his eyes on the stirrup.

Tharin turned him gently and cupped his chin, making Tobin look at him. His faded blue eyes were red-rimmed and full of sorrow.

"Where is Father?"

Tharin took something from his belt pouch, something that glinted black and gold in the sunlight. It was his father's oak tree signet on its chain. With shaking hands, Tharin placed it around Tobin's neck.

"Your father died in battle, my prince, on the fifth day of Shemin. He fell bravely, Tobin. I brought his ashes home to you."

Tobin looked back at the jar in the net and understood. *The fifth of Shemin? That was the day after Ki's name day. We went swimming. I shot two grouse. We saw Lhel.*

We didn't know.

Brother stood beside the horse now, one hand resting on the dusty jar. Their father had been dead nearly a month.

You once told me about a fox dying, he thought, staring at Brother in disbelief. *And about Iya coming. But not that our father was dead?*

"I was there, too, Tobin. What Tharin says is true." That was Lord Solari. He dismounted and came to stand by him. Tobin had always liked the young lord but he couldn't look up at him now, either. When he spoke again, it sounded as if the man was far away, even though Tobin could see Solari's boots right there next to him in the road. "He gave his war cry until the end and all his wounds were in the front. I saw him kill at least four men before he fell. No warrior could ask for a better death."

Tobin felt light, like his body was going to drift away on the breeze like a milkweed seed. *Perhaps I'll see Father's ghost*. He squinted, trying to make out his father's shade near the jar. But Brother stood alone, his black eyes dark holes in his face as he slowly faded from sight.

"Tobin?"

Tharin's hands were firm on his shoulders, holding him so he wouldn't blow away. Tobin didn't want to look at Tharin, didn't want to see the tears slowly scouring twin trails through the dust on the man's cheeks. He didn't want the other lords and soldiers to see Tharin crying.

Instead, he looked past him and saw Ki running down the road. "His foot must be better."

Tharin brought his face closer to Tobin's, looking at him with the oddest expression. Tobin could hear some of the other men weeping softly now, something he'd never heard before. Soldiers didn't weep.

"Ki," Tobin explained, as his gaze skittered back to his father's horse. "He hurt his toe, but he's coming now."

Tharin took a scabbard from his back and placed the duke's sheathed sword in Tobin's hands. "This is yours now, too."

Tobin clutched the heavy weapon, so much heavier than his own. *Too large for me. Just like the armor.* One more thing to be saved for later. Too late.

He heard Tharin talking, but it felt as if his head was stuffed with milkweed fluff; it was hard to make sense of anything. "What do we do with the ashes?"

Tharin hugged him closer. "When you're ready, we'll take them to Ero and lay them with your mother in the royal tomb. They'll be together again at last."

"In Ero?"

Father had always promised to take him to Ero.

Instead, it seemed that he must take his father.

Tobin's eyes felt hot and his chest burned as if he'd run all the way from the town, but no tears would come. He felt as dry inside as the dust beneath his feet.

Tharin mounted his horse again and someone helped Tobin up behind him, still clutching his father's sword.

Ki met them halfway, breathless and limping. He seemed to know already what had happened and burst into silent tears at the sight of the arms lashed to the empty saddle. Going to Tobin, he clasped his friend's leg with both hands and rested his forehead against his knee. Koni came and gave Ki a hand up onto his horse.

As they rode the rest of the way up the hill, Tobin could feel his father's gold signet swing heavily against his heart with every beat of the horse's hooves.

Nari and the others met them at the main gate and set up an awful wailing before Tharin could even tell them what had happened. Even Arkoniel wept.

Nari caught Tobin in a fierce embrace as he climbed down. "Oh, my poor love," she sobbed. "What will we do?"

"Go to Ero," he tried to tell her, but doubted whether she heard him.

The arms and ashes were carried into the hall and laid before the shrine. Tharin helped Tobin cut off Gosi's mane and burn it with a lock of his own hair in the barracks yard to honor his father.

Then they sang sad songs at the shrine that everyone except Tobin seemed to know, and Tharin kept both hands on Tobin's shoulders as he said prayers to Astellus and Dalna to take care of his father's spirit, then to Sakor and Illior, asking them to protect the household.

For Tobin it was all a blur of words. When Brother appeared and placed one of his dirty, twisted tree roots on the shelf of the shrine, Tobin was too tired to sweep it away. No one else noticed.

When the prayers and songs were done, Tharin took Tobin aside and knelt beside him, pulling him close again. "I was with your father as he died," Tharin said softly, and he had that odd look in his eyes again. "We spoke of you. He loved you more than anything in the world and was so sad to be leaving you—" He wiped at his eyes and cleared his throat. "He charged me to be your protector, and so I shall for the rest of my life. You can always depend on me."

He drew his sword and placed it point down before him. Taking Tobin's hand, he placed it on the worn hilt and covered it with his own. "I pledge by the Four and my honor to stand by you and serve you the rest of my days. I gave the same oath to your father. Do you understand, Tobin?"

Tobin nodded. "Thank you."

Tharin sheathed his sword and embraced him for a long moment. Pulling back, he stood and shook his head. "By the Four, I wish it was my ashes in that jar and not his. I'd give anything for it to be so."

Daylight was failing by the time it was all finished. Mealtime came and went, but no one lit a fire or cooked, and everyone spent the night in the hall. A vigil, Tharin called it. As night fell, he lit a single lamp in the shrine but the rest of the house was left dark.

Some of the servants lay down to sleep, but the warriors knelt in a half circle around the shrine, their swords unsheathed before them. Nari made a pallet for Tobin by the hearth, but he couldn't lie down. He joined the men for a while, but their silence made him feel shut out and alone. At last he crept away to the far end of the hall and slumped down in the rushes near the staircase.

Ki found him there and sat down beside him. "You've never seen anything like this, have you?" he whispered.

Tobin shook his head.

"They must have done something when your mother died?"

"I don't know." Thinking about that time still sent a shiver through him. Ki must have noticed, for he shifted closer and put an arm around him, just as Tharin had. Tobin slumped against him and rested his head on Ki's shoulder, grateful for the solid, simple comfort. "I don't remember. I saw her lying on the ice, then she was just gone."

He'd never asked what had happened to her. Nari had tried to speak of it once or twice soon after, but Tobin hadn't wanted to hear it then. He'd put his fingers in his ears and burrowed under the covers until she went away. No one in the house had spoken of it since, and he'd never asked. It had been bad enough, knowing that his mother's spirit still walked in the tower; it hadn't mattered to him where her body was.

Sitting here in the dark now, though, he considered what Tharin had said. His mother was in Ero.

Little as he recalled of that terrible day, he knew that the king had been gone by the time he'd been let out of bed. And so had his mother.

Like a tiny seeding stone dropped into one of Arkoniel's alchemical solutions, the thought crystallized years of half-realized memories into a single sharp-edged conviction: the king had taken his mother away. His grief-clouded mind worried at this like a bad tooth too painful not to touch and prod.

No, Brother whispered in the dark.

"My mam died when I was six," Ki said softly, drawing him back to the present.

"How?" For all their talking, they'd never spoken of this before.

"She cut her foot on a scythe and the wound wouldn't heal." A hint of the old upcountry accent crept back. "Her leg went all black and her mouth locked shut and she died. The ground was froze, so Father left her wrapped in the byre loft 'til spring. I used to climb up and sit by her sometimes, when I was lonesome. Sometimes I'd even pull back the blanket, just to see her face again. We buried her in the spring before the leaves came out. Father had brought Sekora home by then and her belly was already big. I remember staring at it whilst we sang the songs over my mam's grave." His voice broke high.

"You got a new mother," Tobin murmured, suddenly feeling heavy and tired beyond words. "Now I've got no mother or father at all."

Ki's arm tightened around him. "Don't suppose they'd let you come back home with me, eh? We'd hardly notice one more underfoot."

Still dry-eyed and aching inside, Tobin drifted off and dreamt of sleeping with Ki in a great pile of brown-haired children—all of them snug together like a litter of pups while dead mothers lay frozen in the byre outside.

Chapter 34

Arkoniel woke with a stiff neck just after dawn. He'd propped himself in a corner near the shrine, meaning to keep the vigil with the others, but dozed off sometime in the night.

At least I wasn't the only one who fell asleep, he thought, looking around the hall.

The lamp in the shrine still burned, and by its dim light he could see dark forms sprawled on benches and in the rushes by the hearth. He could just make out Ki and Tobin near the stairs, slumped together with their backs to the wall.

Only the warriors had stayed awake, spending the night on their knees to honor the man whom they'd followed for so long.

Arkoniel studied their worn faces. Nyanis and Solari were new to him; from what he'd heard from Nari and Cook last night, both had been loyal liegemen, and so perhaps future allies for Rhius' daughter.

He looked over at Tobin again; in this light he could have been any urchin from the slums of Ero, sleeping against a wall. Arkoniel sighed, recalling what Iya had told him of her own visions.

Too uneasy to sleep again, Arkoniel went outside and wandered onto the bridge to watch the sun come up. A few deer were grazing at the edge of the meadow, and several others had picked their way over the river's stony banks to the water's edge. A tall white heron stalked the shallows, looking for its breakfast. Even at this hour the day promised to be hot.

He sat down at the middle of the bridge and let his legs dangle over the edge. "What now, Lightbearer?" he asked softly. "What are we to do, if those who protect this child keep being taken away?"

He waited quietly, praying for some answering sign. All he could see, however, was Sakor's fiery sun staring him in the face. He sighed and began composing a letter to Iya, trying to convince her to come back from her long wandering and help him. He hadn't heard from her in months, though, and wasn't even sure where to send it to reach her.

He hadn't gotten very far with this when he heard the gate open behind him. Tharin strode out to join him on the bridge. Sitting down beside the wizard, he stared out over the meadow, hands clasped between his knees. His face was pale and deeply lined with grief. The morning light leeched the color from his eyes.

"You're exhausted," said Arkoniel.

Tharin nodded slowly.

"What do you think will happen now?"

"That's what I came out to talk to you about. The king spoke with me at Rhius' pyre. He means to send for Tobin. He wants him in Ero with Prince Korin and the Companions."

It was hardly a surprising turn of events, but Arkoniel's gut tightened all the same. "When?"

"I'm not certain. Soon. I asked him to give the boy some time, but he didn't give me an answer on that. I don't imagine he wants Tobin out of his reach for too long."

"What do you mean?"

Tharin didn't answer at once, just stared out at the deer. At last he sighed and said, "I knew you as a boy when you and Iya guested in Atyion. Since you've been here I've seen the man you've become. I've always liked you and I believe I can trust you, especially where Tobin is concerned. That's why I'm about to put my life in your hands." He turned and looked Arkoniel in the eye. "But if you prove me wrong, by the Four, you'll have to kill me to put me off your trail. Do we understand one another?"

Arkoniel knew this was no idle threat. Yet behind the man's harsh words he also heard fear, not for himself but for Tobin.

Arkoniel held up his right hand and pressed his left over his heart. "By my hands, heart, and eyes, Sir Tharin, I swear to you I will lay down my life to protect Rhius and Ariani's child. What is it you want to say to me?"

"I have your word you'll tell no one else?"

"Iya and I have no secrets, but I can vouch for her as I do myself."

"Very well. I've no one else to turn to anyway. First of all, I believe the king wanted Rhius dead. I think he may have even had a hand in getting him killed."

Arkoniel had little experience of court, but even he realized that Tharin had just placed his life in Arkoniel's hands twice over. Tharin must have known it, too, but he didn't hesitate as he went on. "Ever since the princess died Erius has pushed Rhius into the worst of any battle. Rhius saw it, too, but he had too much honor to say so. But some of the orders we followed were just foolhardy. There are hundreds of good Skalan warriors who'd still be upright and drawing breath in Atyion and Cirna if the king had shown a bit more sense in his placement of attacks.

"The day Rhius was killed, Erius ordered us into marshland on horseback. We were ambushed as we tried to get out the other side."

"What makes you think the king had anything to do with that?"

Tharin gave him a bitter smile. "You don't know much about cavalry, do you, Wizard? You don't send horsemen into such ground in the summer, with no decent footing and no cover. And not when there's a good chance of the enemy being well entrenched on the other side and all ears for your approach. An arrow took Rhius in the thigh before we got anywhere near solid ground. I was struck in the shoulder, and another shaft killed my horse under me. I fell and he charged on— It was a damn massacre. There must have been two or three hundred foot soldiers and archers, and if they weren't waiting just for us then someone was making damn poor use of their forces. Even with the arrow wound, Rhius fought like a wolf, but Laris told me a pikeman killed the duke's horse and took him down. Rhius was pinned under the beast and the enemy was on him with axes before— Before I could get to him."

A tear rolled down and clung to the stubble on Tharin's cheek. "The life was running out of him by the time I found him. We got him away, but there was nothing we could do."

More tears fell, but Tharin didn't seem to notice. Something told Arkoniel that he'd grown accustomed to weeping. "Rhius felt Bilairy coming for him. He pulled me down close and spoke so only I could hear. His last words in this life were, 'Protect my child with your life, by any means. Tobin must rule Skala.'"

Arkoniel's breath caught in his chest. "He said that to you?"

Tharin looked him in the eye, holding his gaze. "I thought then that it must be death addling his thoughts. But looking at your face right now, I think I'm about to change my mind. Do you know what he meant?"

Trust your instincts, Iya had counseled before she left. Those instincts had always told him to trust Tharin. All the same, Arkoniel felt like a man about to leap off a high cliff with only mist below. The secret was a danger to whoever carried it.

"I do. It's all Iya and I have worked for since before Tobin was born. But you must tell me truthfully, can you still serve Tobin knowing no more than you do right now?"

"Yes. Only—"

Arkoniel studied Tharin's stricken face as the man

groped for words. "You're wondering why Rhius didn't tell you more . . . before?"

Tharin nodded, mouth pressed in a tight line.

"Because he couldn't," Arkoniel said gently. "Rhius never doubted your loyalty; you must believe that. One day I'll be able to explain everything to you and you'll understand. But don't ever doubt the duke's faith in you. He proved it with his last breath, Tharin. What he passed to you was the most sacred trust of his life.

"What Tobin needs now is protection, and allies later on. How many troops could we summon today if we needed them?"

Tharin rubbed a hand over his beard. "Tobin's not quite twelve, Arkoniel. That's too young to command, too young even to inspire much of a following without a powerful lord to back him." He pointed back at the keep. "Nyanis and Solari are good men, but Rhius was the warlord who led. If Tobin were sixteen or seventeen, say—perhaps even fifteen—it might be a different story, but as things stand, the only close kin he has with any power is the king. Still—"

"Yes?"

"Between you and me, there are those among the nobles who won't stand by and watch any child of the female line of Skala come to harm, and others with good cause to remember who Tobin's father was."

"You know who these nobles are? Whom Tobin can trust?"

"There are few people I'd stake my life on, the court being what it is these days, but I've spent my life at the duke's side and in his confidence. I have a fair sense of how the wind blows."

"Tobin will need your guidance there. What about the soldiers who owed their loyalty to Rhius?"

"The common men are tied to the lands they work. By right, they serve whoever holds those. Until Tobin is of age to lead, I imagine that will be whoever the king wants it to be." He shook his head. "A lot can change between now and then, I'm afraid. Erius is sure to appoint his own regents and stewards for the estates."

"Too much has changed already for the child," murmured Arkoniel. "All the same, he's fortunate to have a man as loyal as you to stand by him."

Tharin clapped Arkoniel on the shoulder and stood up. "Some serve for loyalty or glory, some for pay," he said gruffly. "I served Rhius for love, and Tobin, too."

"Love." Arkoniel looked up, struck by something in the man's tone. "I've never thought to ask before. You have an estate somewhere. Do you have a family of your own there?"

"No." Before the wizard could read his face, Tharin turned and strode back to the keep.

"That a good man," Lhel whispered unseen, her voice mingling with the rushing of the water below his dangling feet.

"I know," Arkoniel replied, comforted by her disembodied presence. "You know about Lord Rhius?"

"Brother tell me."

"What am I going to do, Lhel? The king wants him to go to Ero."

"Keep Ki by him."

Arkoniel let out a bitter chuckle. "Is that all? I'm glad to hear it. Lhel?"

But she was already gone.

Chapter 35

The morning after the vigil Tobin woke filled with a strange stillness. Ki was still asleep against his shoulder, head pressed against Tobin's cheek. Tobin sat very still, trying to fathom the strange emptiness under his ribs. It wasn't the same as what he'd felt when his mother died; his father had died a warrior's death, falling with honor in battle.

Ki was heavy. Tobin shifted to ease his weight and Ki jerked awake. "Tob, are you well?"

"Yes." He could still speak, at least. But the sense of stillness inside him felt like a lightless hole, or the cold deep spring by Lhel's house oak. It was as if he was staring down into that dark water, waiting for something. He just didn't know what it was.

He got up and went to the shrine to pray for his father. Tharin and the nobles were gone, but Koni and some of the others were still there on their knees.

"I should have kept the vigil with you," he mumbled, ashamed at having slept.

"No one expected that, Tobin," Koni said kindly. "We shed blood with him. You could make the offerings for the shrine, though. Fifty-one wax horses, one for each year he lived."

Koni saw the root that Brother had left and moved to sweep it away. Tobin stopped him. "Leave it." There was an acorn next to the root now, too.

He and Ki spent the morning sitting on the toy room floor with his chunks of beeswax. He'd never made so many figures at once and his hands were soon sore, but he wouldn't stop. He let Ki knead the wax to soften it for him, but insisted on shaping all the horses himself. He made them as he always had, with arched necks and small pointed heads, like the Aurënfaie horses he and his father rode, but this time his thumbnail pinched out short strokes for the manes, making them cropped for mourning.

They were still at work when Solari and Nyanis came to the door in their riding cloaks.

"I've come to take my leave, Prince Tobin," Nyanis said, coming to kneel beside him. "When you come to Ero you must count me among your friends."

Tobin looked up from his wax and nodded, wondering at how faded and dull Nyanis' hair had become since he'd last seen the man. When he was little he'd always liked to watch the firelight shining on it as they played goose stones by the fire.

"You can always depend on me, too, my prince," said Solari, touching his fist to his breast. "For your father's sake, I shall always consider myself the ally of Atyion."

Liar, Brother hissed, hovering just behind the man. *He told his captain he would be lord of Atyion himself in a year.*

Stunned, Tobin gasped out, "In a year?"

"In a year, and always I hope, my prince," Solari replied, but as Tobin looked into the man's eyes, he knew Brother had spoken the truth.

Tobin rose and gave both men a bow, just as his father would have.

As they went off down the corridor Solari's loud whisper echoed back to him. "I don't care what Tharin says. The boy's not—"

Tobin stared at Brother. Perhaps it was only a trick of the light, but the ghost seemed to be smiling.

Nari wanted to fuss over Tobin, even offering to sleep in the bed with him again as she had when he was little, but he couldn't bear it and pushed her away. Arkoniel and Tharin kept their distance, but always seemed to be close by, quietly watching.

The only company Tobin could bear was Ki's, and over the next few days they spent hours together outside the keep. Riding was forbidden during the four days of official mourning, as were hot meals or fires after sundown, so they walked the trails and the riverbanks instead.

The feeling of inner stillness persisted; Ki seemed to sense it and he stayed uncommonly quiet. He never questioned Tobin's lack of tears for his father, either, though he shed enough of his own.

And he wasn't the only one. During those first few days Tobin often caught Nari and Tharin dabbing at their eyes, and a good many of the men around the barracks, too. Clearly something was wrong with him. He went to the shrine alone at night and stood with his hands on the jar of ashes, trying to find tears, but they wouldn't come.

The third night after the vigil it was too hot to sleep. He lay awake for hours, watching the moths flittering around the night lamp and listening to the chorus of frogs and crickets in the meadow below. Ki was fast asleep beside him, sprawled on his back with his mouth open, bare skin dewed with sweat. His right hand lay a few inches from Tobin's thigh and every so often the fingers would twitch in some dream. Tobin watched him, envious of the ease with which his friend slept.

The more Tobin longed for sleep, the more it eluded him. His eyes felt dry as cold embers and the beating of his heart seemed to shake the bed. A ray of moonlight fell on the suit of mail on its stand in the corner, complete now with the sword that they said was his. Too soon for the sword, he thought bitterly, and too late for the armor.

His heart was beating harder than ever now. Abandoning the bed, he pulled on a wrinkled shirt and crept out into the corridor. There would be servants sleeping in the hall, he knew, and if he went upstairs, chances were

Arkoniel would still be awake. Tobin didn't feel like talking to him. Instead, he went into the toy room.

The shutters were open to the moon. In its glow the city looked almost real. For a moment he imagined himself an owl, flying over Ero in the night. He stepped closer and it was just a toy again, the wonderful creation his father had made for him and spent so many happy hours with, teaching him the streets and byways.

And the queens.

Tobin didn't need to stand on a chair anymore to reach the shelf that held the box of figures. Taking it down, he sat beside the city and lined the kings and queens up on the roof of the Old Palace: King Thelátimos and his daughter, Ghërilain the Founder stood together, as always, then poor poisoned Tamír, victim of a brother's pride. Then came the first Agnalain, Klia and all the others up to Grandmama Agnalain, who'd been as mad as her own daughter. Arkoniel's history lessons had been far more detailed than any he'd had from his father or Nari. He knew about Grandmama's crow cages and her gibbets, and all her poisoned and beheaded consorts. No wonder the people had let Uncle Erius put aside the Prophecy and take the throne after she died.

He took the last battered, much-repaired wooden figure from the box: The King Your Uncle. He was still hardly more than a name in a story, a face glimpsed once out a window.

He took Mama away.

Tobin turned the little figure over in his hands, thinking of all the times his father had brought out the glue pot and pieced it back together after one of Brother's attacks. Brother hadn't bothered to break the carving in years.

A tiny sound made him blink; looking down, Tobin found he'd snapped the king's head off. He dropped the pieces into the shadows of the citadel and listened to the brief clatter of their descent.

His father wouldn't come with the glue pot to mend it.

This memory brought others with it, image after image of his father laughing, teaching, playing, riding. Yet he could not weep.

Just then Tobin heard a soft step behind him and smelled wood smoke and crushed green shoots. Lhel's black hair tickled his cheek as she pulled his head down on her breast.

"I tell you a true thing now, keesa," she whispered. "Your father, he make this city for you and you for this city."

"What do you mean?" He pulled away and found himself alone in the moonlight.

"What're you doing in here?" Ki mumbled, leaning sleepily in the doorway. When Tobin didn't reply, Ki shuffled over and led him back to bed. Sprawling down beside him with a hand pressed over Tobin's heart, he was asleep again as soon as his eyes closed.

Tobin wanted to puzzle out what Lhel could have meant, but the sure pressure of Ki's hand and the witch's lingering scent lulled him to sleep, free of dreams for now.

Chapter 36

Erius didn't wait long. Less than two weeks after Tharin's return Arkoniel glanced out his workroom window to see a cloud of dust rising on the Alestun road.

It would take at least a squadron of riders to raise such a cloud, and Arkoniel had no doubt who'd sent them.

Cursing himself for not being more vigilant, he was about to cast a sighting for the boys when he spied them at the far end of the meadow. Half naked as always in the heat, they crouched under a thick clump of willow bay by the riverbank.

"Run!" Arkoniel called out, knowing they couldn't see the dust rising from there, or hear the horses over the river noise. They couldn't hear him, either, of course, but something spooked them. They took off through the long grass, making for the woods on the far side of the meadow.

"Good boys," he whispered.

"Riders!" Tharin shouted in the yard below.

He and the others had been making repairs to the barracks roof. Tharin stood there now, shading his eyes with one hand as he looked up at the wizard. "Who is it?" he called.

Arkoniel covered his eyes and quickly cast the sighting. "Two score or so armed men coming on at a gallop. They're led by a King's Herald, and a nobleman—I don't know him."

"What colors?"

"I'm not sure, with the dust," Arkoniel replied. The tunics he could see could easily be grey. When he opened

his eyes again, Tharin had already disappeared down the
ladder.

The wizard's legs felt shaky as he locked up his rooms
and dashed downstairs. What if there was a Harrier wizard
among those riders? He had no idea what powers he was
facing, or if he had the skill to best them.

He met Nari coming out of Tobin's room. "I saw riders!" she exclaimed, wringing her hands. "Oh Arkoniel,
what if something's happened at last? What if they know?"

"Calm yourself. I think it's only a herald," he told her,
convincing neither of them. Together, they ran down the
stairs and found Tharin and the others armed and ready in
the hall.

"Quite an escort for a messenger, wouldn't you say?"
Tharin observed grimly.

"It won't do for them to see me here," Arkoniel told
him. "You greet them. I'll find the boys and keep them out
of sight until we see which way the wind is blowing. Send
Koni down the meadow for us if you think it's safe."

"Let me come, too!" begged Nari.

"No. Stay here and welcome them."

He slipped out the front gate and ran for the woods.
He could hear the riders clearly now. They'd be in sight
any moment.

He was halfway down to the river when Lhel's face
and shoulders shimmered into view in front of him.
"Here!" she urged, pointing him back to a spot he'd just
passed.

Arkoniel dashed into the trees, then let out a startled
cry as the ground went out from under him. He tumbled
down a small slope and found himself at the bottom of a
leaf-choked gully just inside the trees. He landed with his
feet uphill and one arm in a muddy runnel. Righting himself, he climbed back up to join Lhel and the boys, keeping watch over the edge of the gully. In their stained kilts,
with dead leaves stuck to their arms and legs, and knives

at the ready, Tobin and Ki looked like a pair of young forest bandits.

"Who's coming?" Tobin asked, watching the mouth of the road.

"Just a messenger from the king, I hope."

"Then why did Brother tell Tobin to hide?" Ki demanded.

"Well, he does have rather a lot— You say Brother told you?" He glanced at the witch. "But I assumed—"

"I be watching, too." Lhel waved toward the road. "Brother say there's a wizard with them."

"Is it those Harriers?" Ki asked.

"I don't know." Arkoniel felt for the crystal wand in his belt pouch, praying he and Lhel together could hold them off long enough for Tharin to get Tobin away. "We must be very careful until we find out."

Tobin nodded, showing no hint of fear. Ki left his side just long enough to find a stout stick, then settled back beside the prince, ready to face down a legion of wizards.

The riders emerged from the forest and thundered up the hill to the bridge. Creeping to the edge of the trees for a better look, Arkoniel could make out their leader speaking with someone at the gate. A dozen or so of the newcomers went in, leaving the rest to water the horses at the river.

There was nothing to do now but wait. The dust cloud hung over the road. Cicadas sawed out a hot-weather warning. A murder of crows argued loudly among themselves nearby, underscored by the mournful bell-like calls of doves. A moment later they heard the single, unexpected hoot of an owl. Arkoniel made a luck sign for reverence and mouthed *Lightbearer, keep your hand over this child!*

Time dragged on. Tobin caught a shiny green beetle and let it crawl over his fingers, but Ki remained watchful, eyes darting to follow every sound.

Tobin looked up from his beetle suddenly and whispered, "The wizard is a man with yellow hair."

"Are you certain?" Arkoniel asked. This was the first time in months that Tobin had shown any signs of fore-knowing.

"That's what Brother says," the boy replied, looking to the empty air next to him for confirmation.

So it wasn't foreknowing after all, but forewarned. For once the wizard had cause to be grateful to the ghost.

At last Koni came running along the verge of trees. Arkoniel turned to warn Lhel, but she'd already disappeared.

"Here!" Ki called, hailing the young soldier.

Koni skidded to a halt and bounded in to join them.

"The king—" he panted. "The king's sent a lord with a message. Lord Orun."

"Orun?" Arkoniel had heard the name but couldn't place it.

Koni rolled his eyes. "Old Lord High and Mighty. Knows Tobin's family from way back. He's Chancellor of the Treasury now. A great pompous— Well, never mind that. Tharin says you should come up now. We're to go around the back if you can manage it. Nari will have clothes for you in the kitchen, Tobin." He turned to Arkoniel. "There's no sign of them white wizards with 'em, nor any others, but Tharin says maybe you ought to lie low all the same."

"No wizard?" Tobin had sounded very certain on the matter. Best not to take chances. "Don't worry, Tobin. I won't be far away."

Tobin barely acknowledged the assurance. Squaring his bare shoulders, he set off for the keep without a backward glance.

Tobin wasn't afraid. Brother was still with him and would have said if it were dangerous to go back. And Ki was there, too, faithful as any squire in a ballad. Tobin glanced sidelong at his friend and smiled; armed with a knife and a twisted branch, Ki looked as fearless as he had charging that catamount.

They reached the kitchen without meeting any of the strangers. Nari and Cook were waiting for them there.

"Hurry along now, pet. Lord Orun won't speak to anyone but you, and he's in an almighty hurry," Nari fussed as she hustled them into their best tunics and combed the leaves from their hair. She didn't say so, but Tobin could tell that she didn't like this Orun fellow any better than Koni had. He could see that she was worried and trying not to show it. Tobin leaned forward and kissed her soft cheek. "Don't worry, Nari."

She threw her arms around him, hugging him tight. "What would I worry about, pet?"

Tobin freed himself and turned for the hall, with Ki and Koni flanking him as if he was the lord of the house.

He faltered a little at the sight of ranks of strange soldiers standing at attention in the hall. Tharin and his men were there, too, but they looked like a rabble by comparison. Most of them had on their dirty work clothes instead of uniforms, and didn't look nearly as grand as the others, who wore badges of red and gold on the breasts of their black tunics. He quickly looked them over; there were plenty with blond hair, but he saw no one in wizard's robes.

No sooner had the thought crossed his mind, however, then he spied Brother peeping at him from behind one of the soldiers, a fair-haired man with cheeks reddened with the sun. Brother didn't touch him, just stared until the man shifted his feet and cast a nervous look around.

Two men in richer dress stood in front of the soldiers, flanked by several servants and squires. The man in boots and dusty blue carried the silver horn and white baton of a King's Herald. He stepped forward and bowed very low to Tobin. "Prince Tobin, may I present an emissary from your uncle, the king. Lord Orun, son of Makiar, Chancellor of the Treasury and Protector of Atyion and Cirna."

Tobin went cold. Atyion and Cirna were his father's lands.

Lord Orun stepped forward and bowed. He wore a short robe of vermilion silk with extravagantly cut sleeves edged with dangling gold beads. The skirts were embroidered with scenes of battle, but Tobin doubted this man had ever been a warrior. He was old and very tall, but soft and pale as a woman, with deep lines bracketing a thick, moist-looking mouth. He had no hair on his head at all; his wide hat of puffed silk looked like a cushion balanced on a boiled egg. He smiled at Tobin with his thick lips, but not his eyes. "How I have longed to meet the son of Ariani and Rhius!" he exclaimed, coming forward to clasp Tobin's hand. His huge hands were unpleasantly cool and moist, like mushrooms.

"Welcome," Tobin managed, wanting to pull away and run back up the stairs.

Orun's eyes slid to Ki and he leaned toward him. "And who is this fellow, my prince? Your huntsman's boy?"

"This is Prince Tobin's squire, Kirothius, son of Sir Larenth, a knight in the service of Lord Jorvai," Tharin put in gruffly.

Orun's smile slipped. "But I had thought— That is, the king was not aware that a squire had been chosen for the prince."

"Duke Rhius blessed the bond some time ago."

Tharin spoke respectfully, but Tobin sensed an unspoken tension behind the exchange.

Lord Orun stared at Ki a moment longer, then motioned to the herald.

The herald laid his baton at Tobin's feet, bowed again, and produced a rolled parchment heavy with seals and ribbons. "Prince Tobin, I bring word from your uncle, King Erius."

He broke the seals and unrolled the parchment with a flourish. "From Erius of Ero, King of Skala, Kouros, and the Northern Territories, to Prince Tobin of Ero at Alestun Keep, written this the ninth day of Shemin month.

"Nephew, it is with a heavy heart that I write to you of the death of your father, our beloved brother Rhius. Your father was my most valued commander and while his death was a noble one, befitting a warrior, words cannot convey my despair at his loss.

"In honor of your mother's dear memory—may Astellus guide her spirit to peace—and for the love I bear you, my nearest kin, I acknowledge you as my ward until you attain the age to govern the holdings left you by your esteemed parents and take your father's place among my councilors. I appoint my trusted servant, Lord Orun, to oversee the stewardship of your lands until you reach the age of twenty-one years and I send him to act as your guardian until I return to Skala.

"I have instructed Lord Orun to escort you to Ero, where you shall take your rightful place among my son's Royal Companions. It is my fondest wish that you will be a beloved brother to Prince Korin and he to you. In the Companions you will be trained to take your place at his side when he comes to rule, just as your father served me.

"How I long to embrace you again, as I did the night of your birth! Pray for our victory in Mycena."

The herald looked up. "It is signed and sealed, 'Your most loving and affectionate Uncle, Erius of Ero, King of Skala.' My prince, here ends the message."

Everyone was looking at Tobin, expecting some response, but his tongue had fixed itself to the roof of his mouth. When Tharin had said they'd go to Ero, he'd pictured himself riding with his friends to the house of his birth, or perhaps to grand Atyion.

He looked at his so-called guardian again, already hating the man. Anyone could see that this was no warrior, just a fat, sweating pig with eyes like two dried currants pressed into dough. The arrival of the soldiers hadn't frightened him at all; the thought of this man taking him away left him sick and cold all over. *No!* he wanted to cry out, but he was struck dumb as a stone.

Brother answered for him. Moving more quickly than even Tobin could follow, he snatched the scroll from the startled herald's hand and ripped it in two, then knocked off Lord Orun's silly hat. His servants scattered, some chasing the hat, others running for cover.

A strong wind swirled out of nowhere, whipping the soldiers' hair into their eyes and snatching away badges and daggers. Some of the guardsmen flinched and broke formation. Lord Orun let out an unmanly squeal and dove for cover under a nearby table. Tharin's men laughed aloud and Tobin nearly joined in, grateful for once for Brother's tricks. Instead, he found his voice and shouted, "Enough!"

Brother ceased instantly and came to rest by the shrine, watching Tobin. The spirit's face showed no emotion, but in that shared moment Tobin sensed that Brother was ready to do murder for him.

What would he do to Orun if I asked? Tobin wondered, then hastily pushed the unworthy thought away.

Tharin's men were still laughing. The chagrined guardsmen muttered among themselves and made warding signs as they moved back into formation. Among the few who'd stood fast was the blond man Brother had pointed out to him. He was watching Tobin with a smile that showed only in his eyes. Tobin didn't know what to make of that, except that he already liked him better than Lord Orun, who was currently being helped out from under the table by his servants.

"I welcome you as guests in my house," Tobin began, trying to make himself heard.

"Silence for the prince!" Tharin roared in a battlefield voice, making even Tobin jump. Silence fell and everyone turned their way.

"I welcome you as guests in my house," Tobin said again. "Lord Orun, I extend to you the courtesy of my hearth. My servants will bring you water and wine. Your men can rest themselves in the meadow until a meal is prepared."

Orun bristled visibly. "Young sir, the king's orders—"

"Have taken Prince Tobin by surprise, my lord. He is still mourning the loss of his father," Tharin interrupted. "I'm certain the king would not wish his only nephew discomforted further." He leaned his head close to Tobin, as if listening to some whispered order, then turned back to Orun. "You must allow his highness to withdraw for a time and meditate on his uncle's words. He will attend you when he has rested."

Orun recovered enough to make a passable bow, though there was no mistaking the suppressed outrage in his face. Tobin stifled another laugh. Turning his back on the courtier and his men, he strolled up the stairs as nonchalantly as he could manage. Ki and Tharin followed. Behind him, he could hear Tharin's second in command, old Laris, barking out orders for the visitors' accommodations.

Arkoniel was waiting for them in Tobin's bedchamber.

"I heard most of it from the top of the stairs," he said, looking uncommonly grim. "Tharin, it seems the time has come to call upon your knowledge of court. Do you know Lord Orun?"

Tharin pulled a face like he'd eaten something bitter. "He's Royal Kin, a distaff cousin of some degree. He's no use in the field, but I've heard it said that he's an able enough chancellor, and the funnel through which a great deal of information flows to the king's ear."

"I don't like the looks of him," Ki growled. "He can say what he likes about me, but he spoke to Tobin like he was a scullion. *'My young sir'!*"

Tharin gave him a wink. "Don't fret yourself. Orun's a painted bladder, more wind than substance."

"Do I have to go with him?" Tobin asked.

"I'm afraid so," Tharin told him. "A king's summons can't be ignored, not even by you. I'll be with you, though, and so will Ki."

"I—I don't want to go," Tobin said, and was ashamed to hear the quaver in his voice. Clearing his throat, he added, "But I will."

"It won't be so bad," Tharin said. "Your father and I served among Erius' Companions when we were boys, you know. The Old Palace is a fine place and you'll train with the best in the land. Not that they'll have much to teach you, with all the training you've done here. The pair of you may even show those city-bred dandies a thing or two." He grinned at them, warm and sure as ever. "Prince Korin is a good lad, too. You'll like him. So don't lose heart. You show everyone who Princess Ariani's son is, and I'll keep an eye on old Orun for you."

Leaving the boys to calm down, Arkoniel brought Tharin upstairs to his workroom and locked the door. From here they had a clear view of the soldiers waiting in the meadow.

"You and Tobin snubbed the reins nicely down there."

"He did well, didn't he, once he got started? A proper little princeling with his back up. And I believe that's the first time I've ever been pleased to have that demon of his show up."

"Indeed. Tell me, when you were talking to the boys just now I had the impression you knew more about Orun than you let on."

Tharin nodded. "The first time I met Lord Orun he was guesting with Rhius' father at Atyion. I was about Ki's age at the time. Orun stumbled out of the feast blind drunk and ran into me in a deserted passageway. He backed me into a corner and offered me a cheap gilt ring if I'd let him bugger me."

Arkoniel sat down heavily on his stool. "By the Four! What did you do?"

Tharin gave him a humorless smirk. "I told him if he had to pay he couldn't be much good at it and legged it out of there. A day or two later I saw that same ring on the hand of one of the kitchen girls. Guess she was less particular."

Arkoniel gaped at him. "And *this* is who the king sends for his nephew?"

Tharin shrugged. "Creatures like Orun don't prey on their own kind. They stick to servants and peasants, those who won't complain or be listened to if they do."

"I met with a few of that kind in my day, too. Iya taught me some choice spells to deal with them. But you were no peasant boy."

"No. As I said, he was drunk. Luckily for him, I was too angry and shamed to say anything when I should have, and he was too far gone at the time to remember me later, so I let it pass. He'd never dare lay hands on Tobin, I'm certain of it."

"But what about Ki?"

"That would be almost as foolish, given his station, but I'll have a word with the boy. Don't worry, Arkoniel. I'll be with them every step of the way until they're safely delivered to the companion's quarters. Arms Master Porion is a good man and keeps a close eye on his boys. They'll be safe with him. If Orun tries to get up to anything before then, I'll be more than happy to reintroduce myself." He paused. "Am I right in thinking you can't come with us?"

"Iya wants me here, unnumbered by the Harriers. But it's only a day's ride if you need me."

"That it should come to this." Tharin ran a hand wearily back though his hair. "You know, I was right beside Rhius until that last bad moment. If my horse hadn't been hit— If I'd been where I was supposed to be, where I've *always* been—" He pressed his hand over his eyes.

"You couldn't control where the arrows went."

"I know that! But by the Four, it should be Rhius here alive and talking to you, and not me! Or both of us dead together."

Arkoniel studied the man's grief-stricken face, thinking again of their conversation on the bridge after the vigil. "You loved him a great deal."

Tharin looked up at Arkoniel and his expression softened a little. "No more than he deserved. He was my friend, just like Tobin is with Ki—"

A soft knock came at the door. "Tharin, are you there?" Nari called, sounding frantic.

Arkoniel let her in. The woman was in a terrible state, teary-eyed and wringing her hands. "Lord Orun is raising a fuss downstairs! He's frightened to death of the demon and says Tobin is to leave with him within the hour. He says that the king's order gives him the right to force the child. You mustn't allow it! Tobin doesn't even have anything proper to wear to court. Ki has his sword drawn and says he'll kill anyone who comes in the bedchamber!"

Tharin was halfway out the door before she'd finished. "Has anyone tried?"

"Not yet."

He turned to Arkoniel, eyes blazing. "What shall we do, Wizard? The bastard sees an orphaned boy surrounded by servants and thinks he can play the master in a dead man's house."

"Well, bloodshed won't do." Arkoniel pondered the situation a moment, then smiled. "I think it's time Prince Tobin set a few terms of his own. Send Tobin up to me. Tharin, you go with Nari and calm Ki down. I need to speak with the prince privately."

Tobin entered his chamber a few minutes later, looking pale but resigned.

"Ki hasn't killed anyone yet, has he?" Arkoniel asked.

Tobin didn't smile. "Lord Orun says we must go at once."

"What do you think of Lord Orun?"

"He's a fat, pompous bastard the king left behind because he's not fit for battle!"

"You're a fine judge of character. And who are you?"

"Me? What do you mean?"

Arkoniel folded his arms. "You're Prince Tobin, son of Princess Ariani, who by right of Oracle should have been Queen of Skala. You are the first-born son of Duke Rhius, Lord of Atyion and Cirna, the richest lord and the greatest warrior in the land. You are the nephew of the king and the cousin of his son, the future king. No matter how many guardians and stewards they put between you and what is rightfully yours, you mustn't forget one jot of that, or let anyone else forget it, either. You're a true noble of the purest blood, Tobin, modest and brave and forthright. I've seen it proven a hundred times over in my time here.

"But now you're going to court and must learn to wear a few masks besides. People like Orun must be fought with their own weapons: pride, arrogance, disdain, or whatever approximation you can summon from that honest heart of yours. You mustn't imagine that your father would treat a cur like that with respect when none is offered in return. If someone slaps you in the face, you must slap him right back, and harder. Do you understand?"

"But—but he's a lord and my uncle's—"

"And you are a *prince* and a warrior. Your uncle will see that when he returns. In the meantime, you're going to have to make your own reputation. Be gracious to those who respect you, but have no mercy on those who don't."

He could see Tobin taking all this in and weighing it. At last he set his jaw and nodded. "Then I don't have to be polite to Lord Orun, even though he's a guest?"

"He's behaved offensively. You owe him nothing more than the assurance of safety beneath your roof. You've given him that already, calling off Brother." Arkoniel smiled again. "That was nicely done, by the way. Tell me, if you asked Brother to cause a stir, would he do it?"

"I don't know. I've never asked him to do anything, only to stop."

"Would you like to find out?"

Tobin frowned. "I won't have him hurt anyone. Not even Orun."

"Of course not. But Lord Orun doesn't need to know that, does he? You must go downstairs now and inform our guest that you will need until tomorrow to put your household in good order."

"What if he says no?"

"Then I hope that Brother will be good enough to convey your displeasure. Is he here now? No? Why not call him?"

Tobin still looked faintly embarrassed as he spoke the summoning, although it wasn't the first time the wizard had seen him do it. Arkoniel felt a change in the air, and knew by the way Tobin turned his head slightly that Brother had appeared behind him. The wizard shifted uneasily on his stool, not liking the thought of an unseen guest at his back.

"Will you help me?" Tobin asked.

"What does he say?"

"Nothing. But I think he will." Tobin thought of something and frowned. "Where is Lord Orun to sleep, if he stays the night? The only guest chamber we have is next to your room up here."

Arkoniel knew that Rhius and Ariani's bedchambers could be offered, but hated the thought of that creature so close to the boys. "I suppose we could put him in the tower." He'd meant it as a joke, but Tobin's stricken look killed the smile on his lips. "It was only a jest, Tobin, and a bad one. He can make do with the hall. Have the servants set up a good bedstead with hangings for him, and a decent one for the herald, as well. They can hardly complain about that in a country house."

Tobin turned to go, but a sudden pang of fear and affection made Arkoniel call him back. When Tobin stood before him, however, he hardly knew where to begin. Laying a hand awkwardly on Tobin's shoulder, he said, "You will have to go with him, you know. And life will be different in the city. You've led such a quiet life here, with people you could trust. It isn't that way at court." He groped for the right words. "If anyone should—"

Tobin's face betrayed little, but his rigid stance and the darting glance he stole at the hand on his shoulder made the wizard draw back in confusion. "Well, you must have a care for strangers," he finished lamely. "If anything confuses you, you should speak of it to Tharin or Ki. They both have a wider experience of the world than you." With a final burst of false heartiness, he waved Tobin off to the door. "You'll soon find your feet."

As soon as the door closed behind the boy, Arkoniel sank his face into his hands. "That was a fine send-off!" he berated himself, wondering why the god's will and two years of good intentions had gotten him no further into Tobin's good graces than this. He'd fought Iya to be here, to help Tobin see what a normal life might be. He wanted nothing more than to protect him from treacherous men like Orun, or at least to warn him. A fine attempt he'd made, too, just now. He might just as well have summoned snakes from the walls and grown himself a second head.

Chapter 37

Tobin forgot all about Arkoniel's last cryptic advice, pondering instead the revelation that he was within his rights to defy the unpleasant man downstairs. By the time he reached his room, he was looking forward to putting this newfound bit of knowledge to the test.

Brother still shadowed him silently. For years Tobin had been too scared of the spirit to do anything but avoid him. Once they'd established their uneasy truce Brother had sometimes offered information, like the unexpected tattling on Lord Solari, but Tobin had never thought to seek any from him.

He paused at the far end of the corridor and whispered, "Will you help me? Will you scare Lord Orun if he insults me again?"

Brother gave him what might have been meant as the mocking semblance of a smile. *Your enemies are my enemies.*

At his own door he could hear Nari weeping. Inside, he found her and Ki packing their small collection of belongings into chests. His father's arms and sword were lashed into a bundle in a corner. Tharin stood by the foot of the bed, looking uncommonly dour.

Everyone looked to him as he came in.

"I've laid out your best tunic," Nari told him, wiping her eyes on her apron. "You'll be wanting your carving things, and your books. I suppose we can always send along anything we miss."

Tobin drew himself up and announced, "I'm not going

tonight. Our guests should be made comfortable in the hall."

"But Lord Orun ordered . . ."

"This is my house and I give the orders in it." Seeing the way they stared at him, he added sheepishly. "At least that's what Arkoniel says. I have to go tell Lord Orun now. Will you come with me, Tharin?"

"We're yours to command, my prince," Tharin replied; then, aside to Ki, "We wouldn't want to miss this."

Grinning, Ki followed them as far as the top of the grand staircase, where he gave Tobin a wink of encouragement before hiding himself to watch.

With Tharin on his left and Brother before him, Tobin felt a bit bolder as he descended into the great hall again. Orun was pacing around the hearth, looking very put out. The herald and several soldiers were sitting nearby at a wine table, the blond wizard among them.

"Well, then, are you prepared to leave?" Orun demanded.

"No, my lord," said Tobin, trying to sound like his father. "I must put my household in order and see that my things are properly packed for the journey. I'll go with you tomorrow as early as can be arranged. Until then, you shall be my guest. A feast will be prepared for the evening and a bed set up for you here by the hearth."

Orun halted and stared up at him, grey brows rising toward his hat. "You'll *what?*"

Brother began to stalk the man, flowing down toward him smooth and low as fog on the river.

"I did not come all the way to this benighted backwater to be answered back to by—"

Lord Orun's ill-fated hat flew off again. This time it landed in the middle of the smoldering hearth behind him, where it blossomed into a malodorous crimson burst of burnt silk and feathers. Orun's hands flew to his bald pate, then curled into angry fists as he rounded on Tobin.

Brother yanked at his sleeve, scattering golden beads, then crouched to spring at him, teeth bared.

"Stop," Tobin whispered in alarm, hoping he didn't have to speak the command spell in front of all these people. Brother subsided and faded from view.

"Have a care, my lord!" The blond wizard took Orun's arm, steadying him.

Lord Orun pulled away from him, then turned to give Tobin a false smile. "As you wish, Your Highness. But I fear the spirit that haunts this hall! Haven't you a more hospitable chamber to offer a guest?"

"No, my lord, I do not. But I assure you by my honor that none who wish me well will come to harm under my roof. Will you ride with me until the feast is prepared?"

It was frustrating to hide himself away at the top of the house, but Arkoniel contented himself with keeping watch. Since he'd seen no evidence of the wizard Brother had spoken of, he allowed himself the occasional sighting, following Tobin as he and his companions led Orun and a few of his escort a merry chase over a torturous mountain trail.

He was drafting a letter to Iya when Nari knocked on his door and stuck her head in. "There's someone here I think you'd best speak to, Arkoniel."

To his alarm, she ushered in one of Orun's armed escort. He was a pleasant-looking young fellow, but all Arkoniel noticed at first glance was the red-and-gold badge the man wore, and his sword. Readying a killing spell, he slowly stood up and bowed.

"What is it you want with me?"

The guardsman shut the door and bowed. "Iya sends her greetings and told me to give you this as a token of good faith." He held out his hand.

Arkoniel approached cautiously, still expecting violence, and saw that his visitor held a small pebble in the hollow of his palm.

Arkoniel took it and closed his fist around it, feeling Iya's essence infused into the stone. It was one of her tokens, the sort she left only with those she felt would be of use to Tobin's cause later. How this man had come by it remained to be learned.

When he looked back at him, however, he let out a startled gasp. Instead of a soldier, he found himself facing a man who only slightly resembled the one he'd just been looking at. He was fair-skinned and blond, and his features showed a strong strain of Aurënfaie blood. "You're a shape-shifter?"

"No, just a mind clouder. My name is Eyoli of Kes. I met your mistress last year while passing myself off as a beggar and picking pockets. She caught me at it and told me she had better work for me to do. I didn't know, you see."

"You didn't know you were wizard born?"

Eyoli shrugged. "I knew I could cloud minds and make ignorant people do as I wished. She sent me to study with a woman named Virishan at Ilear. You remember her?"

"Yes, we spent most of a winter with her, a few years back. I've met mind clouders before, but this—" Arkoniel shook his head in admiration as Eyoli resumed the form of the soldier. "And to carry it off without detection. It's a rare gift."

The young man smiled shyly. "It's my only talent, I'm afraid, but Viri does say I'm the best she's seen. I've had the dreams, Arkoniel. That's what Iya saw in me and she says that Ariani's son is part of that vision somehow, and that he must be protected. She sent word to me when she learned of the duke's death. I arrived in Ero just in time to get myself in with Orun's lot—"

"Wait." Arkoniel held up a hand. "How do I know that this is the truth? How do I know that you aren't clouding my mind now, pulling thoughts from my own mind and telling them back to me?"

Eyoli took Arkoniel's hand and placed it against his

own brow. "Touch my mind. Read my heart. Iya says you have the gift."

"It's not a gentle magic."

"I know that," he replied, and Arkoniel could tell that he'd been subjected to such tests before. "Go on. I knew you'd need to."

Arkoniel did, not a gentle brush of the mind but a deep, direct delving into the core of the man who stood so trustingly under his hand. It was not a pleasant spell, and never suffered between wizards without permission, but Eyoli allowed it, even as he groaned aloud and clutched at Arkoniel's shoulder to keep his balance.

Arkoniel pulled the substance of the other man's life from his mind like juice from a ripe grape. It was a brief life, and a sordid one in its earliest details. Eyoli had been a harbor brat, orphaned early and raised in filth, using his innate skills from an early age to keep himself fed and cared for as best he could. His talent was a meager one, and unpolished until Iya found him, but once tapped, his potential was amazing. He was right in thinking he'd never make a true wizard, but as a spy, he was quite unique.

Arkoniel released him. "You say this is all you can do?"

"Yes. I can't even make fire or light."

"Well, what you can do is extremely useful. Are you sworn to watch over Tobin?"

"By my hands, heart, and eyes, Master Arkoniel. The Harriers haven't numbered me, so I can come and go in the city. Orun and the others think I've been with them for years. They won't miss me when I'm gone."

"Amazing. Where is Iya now?"

"I don't know, Master."

"Well, I'm glad to have your help. Keep a close eye on him, and Ki, too." He held out his hand and Eyoli clasped it respectfully, wincing a little at the older wizard's firm grip.

When he was gone Arkoniel inspected the corner of

his little fingernail. Lhel had taught him how to sharpen it, how to clasp a man's hand so that it would nick without hurting, and just deep enough to draw a tiny "bitty of the red."

He squeezed the blood out and rubbed the tiny smear into the whorls of his thumb. Then, fixing the patterns in his mind's eye, he spoke the witching words Lhel had taught him. "Into this skin I go, through these eyes I see, into this heart I listen."

In Eyoli's heart he found a burning hatred of the Harriers, and a vision of Virishan's school and a shining white city in the west filled with wizards who welcomed her orphans. For that vision Eyoli would do whatever was asked of him. Arkoniel also caught a glimpse of Iya as the young man remembered her. She looked older and more tired than Arkoniel recalled.

All the same, he breathed a sigh of relief, feeling less alone than he had in years. The Third Orëska had already truly begun.

Tharin's story about Orun continued to worry Arkoniel, but the troublesome noble went to bed early in a surly humor, settled his nerves with a large pot of Cook's hippocras, and was soon snoring loudly. The herald did the same on the other side of the hearth. Meanwhile, Tharin saw to it that the men of the King's Guard were under close watch in their makeshift encampment in the meadow below.

As silence settled over the house, Arkoniel sat quietly in his darkened workroom, alert for any disturbance in the hall below.

Intent as he was on this task, he was taken quite by surprise by stealthy footsteps just outside his own door. Sending out another sighting, he saw Tobin stealing past in his rumpled nightshirt. The boy hesitated briefly outside the wizard's door as if to knock, then turned away and continued on.

Arkoniel went to the door and opened it a crack, knowing there was only one place Tobin could be going in this part of the keep.

Arkoniel had almost let himself into the tower several times, wanting to see the place Ariani had called her own, the place she'd chosen to die. But something—honor, fear, respect for the duke's wishes, perhaps—still held him back.

Tobin stood near the tower door now, arms wrapped tight around himself in spite of the humid night. As Arkoniel watched, he took another hesitant step, then stopped. Then another. It was painful to watch, and worse to feel like a spy doing it.

After a moment he leaned out and whispered, "Tobin? What are you doing up here?"

The boy whirled around, eyes huge. If not for what Arkoniel had already witnessed, he might have thought he'd been sleepwalking.

Tobin hugged himself tighter as Arkoniel approached. "Do you need my help?"

Another agonized hesitation, a sidelong glance—at Brother, perhaps? Then he sighed and fixed Arkoniel with those earnest blue eyes. "You're Lhel's friend, aren't you?"

"Of course I am. Does this have something to do with her?"

Again that sidelong glance. "There's something I have to fetch."

"From the tower?"

"Yes."

"Whatever it is, Tobin, I know Lhel would want me to help you. What can I do?"

"Come with me."

"That sounds easy enough. Do you have the key, or shall I use my magic to open it?"

As if in answer, the tower door swung open for them. Tobin flinched and stared at the open doorway as if expecting to see something there. Perhaps he did. All the wizard could make out were a few worn stone steps leading up into darkness.

"Did you tell Brother to do that?"

"No." Tobin edged forward and Arkoniel followed.

The summer night was heavy, but the moment they stepped into the tower a dank chill wrapped itself around them like the air of a tomb. High overhead the moon peered in through narrow slit windows.

Tobin was clearly frightened to be here, but he took the lead. Halfway up Arkoniel heard a stifled sob, but when Tobin glanced back at him, his face was dry. Another sob raised the hair on the back of the wizard's neck. It was a woman's voice.

A small, square chamber lay at the top of the tower. The windows on each side were tightly shuttered, so Arkoniel summoned a tiny point of light, then let out a gasp of dismay.

The place was a shambles. The furniture had been smashed to bits and scattered about the room. Mouldering bolts of cloth and tapestries covered the floor.

"Mother made her dolls here," Tobin whispered.

Arkoniel had heard of those later dolls; boys with no mouths.

The sound of weeping was more distinct here, but it was still faint, as if heard from another room. If Tobin heard it, he said nothing. As he crossed to a far corner, however, Arkoniel noted how he kept his face turned away from the fatal western window.

What had the child witnessed that final day, when he'd received that crescent scar on his chin? Closing his eyes, Arkoniel whispered a blood-seeking spell. The magic made a few scattered spots of old blood on the floor near the west window shine bright as moonlight on silver. And there was one more trace, a tiny, much-weathered half-moon smudge on the edge of the stone sill.

The outer edge, beyond the shutters.

Tobin made his way over the debris to a far corner and was shifting a small pile of refuse there.

The sobbing grew suddenly louder and Arkoniel could hear the whisper of heavy skirts, as if the weeper was pacing the room.

Caught between fear and grief, Arkoniel searched his mind for spirit spells, but all that would come was her name.

"Ariani."

It was enough. The shutters of the west window flew open and there she stood, a dark outline against the moonlight. Brother stood with her, grown as tall as his sibling even in death.

Arkoniel took a step toward her and held out his hand, face to face with the woman he'd helped wrong.

She turned to him and the light fell across her face. Black blood covered the left side, but her eyes were bright and alive and fixed on him with a terrible confusion that disturbed him more deeply than any show of anger.

"Forgive me, Lady." An echo a decade gone.

He felt Tobin beside him, clutching at his arm with trembling fingers. "Do you see her?" he whispered.

"Yes. Oh, yes." He stretched out his left hand to the pitiful apparition. She tilted her head as if bemused by his gesture, then reached as if they were partnered in a dance. As their hands met he felt a fleeting sensation like the kiss of snow shaken from a branch. Then she was gone, and Brother with her.

Arkoniel brought his hand to his nose and caught the faint scent of her perfume mingled with blood. Then a deathly chill closed in around him. It felt as if someone was reaching into his chest and squeezing his heart to stop it. Another hand, this one hard and warm, found his and dragged him from the room. Doors slammed shut behind them as he and Tobin fled the tower.

In his workroom Arkoniel locked the door, latched

the shutters, and lit a small lamp, then collapsed trembling on the floor with his face in his hands. "By the Light!"

"You saw her, didn't you."

"Oh yes. Maker forgive me, I did."

"Was she angry?"

Arkoniel thought of the crushing sensation he'd felt in his chest. Had that been her doing, or Brother's? "She looked sad, Tobin. And lost." He looked up and only then noticed what Tobin had brought back with him from the tower. "Is that what you went up for?"

"Yes." Tobin clutched an old cloth sack to his chest. "I—I'm glad you caught me tonight. I don't think I could've done it alone again and I'd never have been able to ask anyone to go—"

"*Again?* You mean you did that before? All by yourself?"

"When I put it up there. That night Ki arrived."

"You saw your mother then, didn't you?"

Tobin knelt beside him and began plucking at the knotted string that held the sack closed. He was shivering. "Yes. She reached out for me, like she was going to throw me out the window again."

Arkoniel searched for something to say, but words failed him.

Tobin was still busy with the sack. "You might as well see. This was my mother's. She made it." The string came loose and he pulled out a crude muslin rag doll with a badly drawn face. "She always carried it."

"Your father mentioned it in his letters."

He thought of the fine dolls she'd made in Ero. All the great ladies of Ero had wanted one, and many of the lords, too. This thing that Tobin cradled so carefully was a grotesque parody, the embodiment of her ruined soul.

This thought was quickly replaced by another, however, and the hair rose on his neck and arms for the second time that night. The doll wore a necklace of hair wound tightly around its neck. Hair as black as Tobin's own. Or his mother's.

This must be it, he thought with a thrill of triumph. *This is the secret.*

He'd known from that first day in the kitchen that the words Tobin spoke were not enough to control Brother. There had to be something more; a talisman of some sort that joined the two. Something that had perhaps been passed from mother to child.

"Did your mother give this to you?"

Tobin stared down at the doll. "Lhel helped my mother make this. Then she made it mine."

"With your hair?"

Tobin nodded. "And some blood."

Of course. "And this helps you call Brother?"

"Yes. I wasn't supposed to show it to anyone, so I hid it in the tower. I think maybe that's why Brother doesn't always stay away when I tell him to. When Lord Orun said I must go to Ero I knew I had to get it. . . ."

"But why not leave it here? Leave him here?"

"No, I have to take care of him. Lhel said so."

"If a wizard put his mind to it, he might be able to smell it out."

"You didn't."

Arkoniel let out a rueful chuckle. "I suppose not, but I wasn't looking. All the same, there are plenty of wizards in Ero. You must be careful of all of them, especially those who wear the white robes of the King's Harriers."

Tobin looked up in alarm. "What about the one with Orun's men?"

"A blond young man dressed as a soldier?"

"Yes, that's the one."

"He's a friend, Tobin. But you mustn't let on that you know about him. Iya sent him to keep watch over you, that's all. It's a secret."

"I'm glad he's not a bad wizard. He has a kind face."

"You mustn't only judge people on their faces—" Arkoniel caught himself, not wanting to scare the boy, or give too much away for a Harrier to find in Tobin's mind later, should one have cause to look. "There are many kinds of people in the world, Tobin, and as many kinds of wizards. Not all of them mean you well. By the Four, you didn't trust me and I mean you nothing but good! Don't go lowering your guard to someone just because they tip you a winning smile." He looked down at the doll again. "Now, are you certain you must take this with you? Couldn't you leave it here with me?"

"No, Lhel says I have to keep it and care for Brother. No one else can do that. He needs me and I need him."

Him.

Oh dear, thought Arkoniel. Here was another plan that had worked too well until now. Thanks to Lhel's magic, the king had been shown the body of a dead girl child, and so the world had heard the story; Tobin knew the truth. If someone saw Brother or heard Tobin speak of "him," uncomfortable questions would be raised.

Tobin was watching him with those eyes that saw too much and Arkoniel felt the terrible fragility of the new bond they'd created in the tower just now.

He thought of Iya's bag lying under his worktable; no wizard could see through its magics to the bowl swathed in silk and spells inside. For an instant he seized on the notion of making such a bag for the doll. This, at least, he had the magic for, and the makings: dark silk and silver thread, a crystal wand, needles and razors of iron, censers for burning resins and gums. Everything lay in easy reach. With these he could make a bag that would hold Brother in and keep out the prying eyes of any Harrier.

But the bag itself would be seen. He or Iya might carry such a thing with impunity, but an ordinary eleven-year-old child of warrior birth could not.

He sighed and picked up the discarded flour sack.

Ordinary. As ordinary as an old doll left as a keepsake for an orphaned child.

"This changes everything, you know," he mused, an idea already taking form. "That little display we had Brother put on in the hall was all well and good as the antics of a house spirit. At court no one, especially you, can afford any taint of necromancy and there are plenty who might assume just that if they think you can control Brother. You mustn't speak of him except as the demon twin they know of. It's an old story there."

"I know. Ki told me some people even claim it was a girl child."

Arkoniel covered his surprise quickly; he supposed if rumors would come from anyone, it would be Ki. It seemed his work was done for him after all. "Let them go on thinking that. There's no use arguing. Say nothing at all about it, and never let anyone see him. And you must *never* let on that you know anyone like Lhel. Her sort of magic isn't necromancy, but most think it is, and because of that her kind are outlawed from Skala." He gave Tobin a conspiratorial wink. "That makes us outlaws, you and I."

"But why would Father have dealings with her if—"

"That's a question best left 'til you're older, my prince. For now, trust in your father's honor as you always have and promise me that you'll keep Lhel and Brother your own secret."

Tobin fidgeted with one of the doll's mismatched legs. "I will, but sometimes he just does what he wants to."

"Well, you must try very, very hard for your sake. And Ki's, too."

"Ki?"

Arkoniel rested his elbows on his knees. "Here at the keep you and Ki have lived as brothers and friends. Equals, if you like. But once you're at court, you'll soon learn that you're not. Until you're of age, Ki has no protection but your friendship and your uncle's whim. If you were accused of necromancy the king might save you, but Ki would be executed very horribly and there'd be no saving him."

Tobin went pale. "But Brother's nothing to do with him!"

"It wouldn't matter, Tobin. That's what I'm trying to make you understand. It has nothing to do with truth. All it would take would be a Harrier wizard's accusation. It happens often these days. Great wizards who've never done harm to anyone have been burnt alive on nothing more than a secondhand tale."

"But why?"

"In their zeal to serve the king, they have taken a different road than the rest of us. I can't explain it because I don't understand it myself. For now, promise me you'll be careful and make Ki be careful, too."

Tobin sighed. "I wish I didn't have to go away. Not like this. I wanted to go with Father and see Ero and Atyion and go to war, but—" He broke off and rubbed at his eyes.

"I know. But Illior has a way of putting our feet on the right path without shining the Light very far ahead. Put your trust in that, and in the good friends the Lightbearer has sent to walk with you."

"Illior?" Tobin gave him a doubtful look.

"And Sakor, too," he added quickly. "But look whose mark you wear on your chin."

"But what about the doll? What do I do with it?"

Arkoniel picked up the flour sack. "This should do well enough."

The boy gave him an exasperated look. "You don't understand. What if the prince sees it? Or the Arms Master? Or *Ki?*"

"What if he did?" To his astonishment, Tobin blushed. "You think Ki would think less of you for it?"

"Why do you think I had it up in the tower?"

"Well, I've seen it, and I certainly don't."

Tobin rolled his eyes. "You're a *wizard*."

Arkoniel laughed. "Has my manhood just been insulted?"

"You're not a warrior!" Some strong emotion shook Tobin now, making his eyes flash and his voice break. "Warriors don't want dolls. I only have this one because Lhel says I must. For Brother."

Arkoniel watched him closely. The way Tobin still clasped the lopsided doll belied every word he spoke.

She spoke, he amended. For the first time in a very long time, Arkoniel allowed himself to make the correction, though he saw little sign of the hidden princess in the angry youth before him—except perhaps for the way the strong, callused hands neither crushed nor threw away what they professed to be ashamed of.

"I believe you misjudge your friend," he said quietly. "It's a keepsake from your dead mother. Who would begrudge you that? But you must manage that as you see best."

"But—" Confusion warred with stubbornness on the boy's drawn face.

"What is it?"

"The night Ki came, Brother *showed* me. He showed me Ki finding the doll, and how disappointed and shamed everyone was that I had it. Just like Father told me. And everything else he's shown me has come true. At least I think so. You remember the fox with the broken back? And I knew when Iya was coming. And— And he told me that Lord Solari wants to take Atyion away from me."

"Does he, now? I'll pass that along to Tharin. As for the rest of it, I don't know. It's possible that Brother could lie when he wants. Or that what he shows you can change with time, or that perhaps you don't always understand what he shows you." He reached to pat Tobin's shoulder and this time the boy allowed it. "You're not wizard born, but you've a bit of the sight in you. You should have shared your visions with Lhel or me. It's our gift and our service."

Tobin's shoulders sagged. "Forgive me, Master Arkoniel. You've always helped me and I've shown you poor courtesy."

Arkoniel waved aside the apology. For the first time since his arrival here he felt that a true link had been forged between them. "I don't expect you to understand it yet, but I've pledged my life to protecting you. Perhaps one day you'll remember what we've shared here tonight and know that I'm your friend. Even if I am only a wizard." Grinning, he held out his hand in the warrior style.

Tobin clasped it. The old guarded look had not completely left him, but in his eyes the wizard saw a respect that hadn't been there before.

"I'll remember, Wizard."

Exhausted beyond words, Tobin crept back to his bedchamber and hid the doll deep in one of the traveling chests.

He tried to slip into bed without disturbing Ki, but as he lay back he felt Ki's hand on his arm.

"Are you sick, Tob? You were gone a long time."

"No—" Arkoniel thought he should tell Ki about the doll, and suddenly he was badly tempted to. Maybe Ki wouldn't care, after all. He hated having secrets between them and the doll was so close, just a few feet away. But the memory of Brother's fury when he'd tried to show it to Nari was still too clear.

"I just wanted to say good-bye to Arkoniel," he mumbled.

"We're going to miss him. I bet he has a few spells up his sleeve that would shut Lord Orun up."

It was too hot for blankets or shirts. Sprawled on their backs, they stared up into the shadows.

"It's been a rotten few weeks, hasn't it?" Ki said after a while. "With your father—" His voice choked off for a moment. "And old Slack Guts downstairs? Not quite the way we meant to go east."

A lump hardened in Tobin's throat and he shook his head. His father's death, his mother's ghost, the summons to Ero, Arkoniel's warnings tonight, and the business with Brother, the pack of strangers waiting for them downstairs—

All the tears he hadn't been able to find over the years suddenly seemed to find him and rolled silently down his cheeks into his ears. He didn't dare sniff or wipe at them for fear Ki would know.

" 'Bout time," Ki muttered huskily, and Tobin realized his friend was weeping too. "I was starting to think you didn't know how. You've got to mourn, Tobin. All warriors do."

Is that what this pain was? Tobin wondered. But it felt so big. If he let it loose, it would sweep him away and he'd be lost. Easier to retreat again into the numbing silence that had protected him for so long. He imagined it flowing into him like liquid darkness, filling his lungs, spreading out to his limbs and head until he was nothing more than a black shape himself.

"That's not good way, keesa."

Tobin looked over to find Lhel standing in the doorway. It was dawn.

She beckoned to him, then disappeared in the direction of the stairs. He hurried after her, but caught only the sight of her ragged skirt as she slipped out the door of the great hall. Lord Orun was snoring loudly behind the curtains of his bed. Tobin hurried out through the open gate in time to see Lhel disappearing into the forest across the bridge.

"Wait!" he called, then clamped a hand over his mouth in alarm. The dew-soaked meadow below the keep was filled with Orun's escort. He'd thought there were only two score or so yesterday, but now it looked like there were at least a hundred. A few sentries were gathered around the morning cook fire, but no one noticed him as he ran barefoot into the woods.

As soon as he reached the shelter of the trees he understood. This wasn't the real forest; it was the one he'd come to so often in visions after his mother's death.

This time he didn't need Brother to guide him. He found the river path easily and followed it to the clearing where the two gentle deer grazed by the hole in the ground. When he entered the opening this time, he found himself inside Lhel's oak.

The witch and his mother sat by the fire. His mother was suckling an infant at her breast. Lhel held the rag doll on her lap instead of the rabbit.

"This is a seeing dream, keesa," Lhel told him.

"I know."

Lhel gave him the doll and shook her finger at him. "Don't you be forgetting him."

"I won't!" What else had he been worrying about all night?

His mother looked up from the baby, her blue eyes clear and sane, but full of sadness. "I want to be there, too, Tobin. Don't leave me in the tower!" She held up the baby. "He'll show you."

Lhel jumped, as if startled to find her here. "Keesa can't be worried about that. Go!"

Ariani and the baby disappeared, and Lhel drew Tobin down onto the pallet beside her. "Don't you be worried about her. That's not your burden now. You look out for you and Brother. And Ki."

She cast a handful of herbs and bones into the fire and studied the pattern of their burning. "This hairless man? I don't like him but you must go. I see your path. It takes you to the stinking city of the king. You don't know this king yet. You don't know his heart." She threw in more herbs and rocked slowly back and forth, eyes narrowed to slits. Then she sighed, and leaned close until all Tobin could see was her face. "You see blood? Don't tell nobody. Nobody."

"Like the doll." Tobin thought of his near slip with Ki.

Lhel nodded. "You love your friend, you don't tell him. You see blood, you come here to me."

"What blood, Lhel? I'm a warrior. I'm going to see blood!"

"Maybe you will, maybe not. But if you do—" She touched her finger to his heart. "You know here. And you come to Lhel."

She poked him in the chest again, harder this time, and Tobin woke in his own bed in the hot darkness with Ki snoring softly beside him.

Tobin turned on his side, pondering the dream. He could still feel Lhel's finger on his chest, and the softness of the furs he'd sat on. A seeing dream, Lhel had told him.

Wondering if he should go ask Arkoniel if it had been a vision or just a regular dream, he drifted back to sleep.

Part Three

From the memoirs of Queen Tamír II.

Ero.

When I recall the city now, the actual place, so briefly known, is overlaid in my mind by the image of the simple model my father built for me. In my dreams wooden people, clay sheep, wax geese populate the crooked streets. Flat-bottomed boats with parchment sails slide whispering across a dusty painted harbor.

Only the Palatine survives in my memory as it was, and those who lived within its walls and mazes.

Chapter 38

Tobin rode out from the keep on the twenty-third day of Lenthin and didn't look back. He'd said his farewells at dawn and let the women weep over him. With Ki and Tharin beside him, his father's ashes at his saddlebow, and a column of men at his back, he set his face for Ero, determined to uphold the honor of his family as best he could.

He'd been surprised to learn from Lord Orun that the ride would take only a day. With no heavy baggage to slow them, they rode for long stretches at a gallop and soon left Alestun behind. Beyond it the familiar road joined another that wound back into the dark forest. After several hours the forest gave way to a vast rolling countryside netted with rivers and dotted with wide-flung farmsteads and estates.

Lord Orun insisted on courtly protocol, so that Tobin was forced to ride in front beside him, with Tharin and Ki behind with the herald and servants. The men from the keep, who were now to be called Prince Tobin's Guard, rode in the column with the other soldiers. Tobin looked for the disguised wizard among them, but hadn't caught sight of him before he had to take his own position.

At midmorning they came to a broad lake that reflected the clouds overhead and the fine stone manor house on the far side. A great flock of wild geese was swimming and grazing along its shores.

"That estate once belonged to an aunt of your mother's," Tharin remarked as they rode past.

"Who does it belong to now?" asked Tobin, marveling at the grandness of the place.

"The king."

"Is Atyion as large as that?"

"Put ten of those together and you begin to match it. But Atyion has a town around it, with fields and proper walls."

Looking back, Tobin saw that his mountains were already growing smaller behind him. "How much longer until we reach Ero?"

"If we push on, I should say before sunset, my prince," Lord Orun replied.

Tobin spurred Gosi on, wondering how Alestun could have seemed so far away when the capital itself was only a day's ride. Suddenly the world seemed a great deal smaller than it had.

They passed through a market town called Korma just after noon. It was larger than Alestun and had the usual sort of traders and farmers crowding the square, as well as a few Aurënfaie in elaborately wrapped purple head cloths. Several were performing on lyres and flutes.

Lord Orun stopped at the largest inn to rest the horses and dine. The innkeeper bowed low to him, and even lower to Tobin when he was introduced. Their host made a great fuss over Tobin, bringing him all sorts of foods to try and refusing to take any payment except Tobin's kind remembrance. He wasn't used to such a commotion and was very glad to set off again.

They rode at a more leisurely pace through the heat of the day and Lord Orun took it upon himself to keep Tobin entertained. He spoke of the Prince Royal's Companions and their training and what Tobin could look forward to in the way of entertainments.

From him, Tobin learned that he might purchase anything a boy could desire simply by using his father's seal, which he still wore around his neck. Koni had shortened the chain for him.

"Oh yes," Orun assured him. "Fine clothes, a proper sword, sweets, hounds, gambling. A young man of your rank must have his pleasures. A new sport, falconry, has recently been introduced from Aurënen, who had it from the Zengati. Leave it to the 'faie to import such barbarian decadence! Oh well, they breed good horses. But it's all the rage among the young bloods."

He paused and his thick lips curved into a knowing smile. "Of course, any transaction of substance—say, to sell land or raise a levy of troops, the purchase of grain or iron, or the collection of rents from your lands—for that you must also have the seal of your uncle or myself until you are of age. But you're too young to trouble yourself about such things! All will be managed for you."

"Thank you, Lord Orun," Tobin replied, but only because good manners seemed to demand it. He'd disliked the man on sight yesterday, and familiarity had only strengthened the impression. There was something greedy behind Orun's smile; it made Tobin think of something cold and nasty stepped on in the dark.

More damning was the way he treated Ki and Tharin. Despite his fine manners to Tobin, Orun treated them as if they were his own servants, and managed to hint repeatedly that Tobin might consider finding a more suitable squire once he was at court. If it hadn't been for Arkoniel's warning, he might have summoned Brother again. Secretly, he made up his mind to find out how to make his friends into such rich lords that Orun would have to bow to them.

Ki could tell that Tobin was miserable riding with Orun, but there didn't seem to be any help for it. The long ride did give him the first opportunity he'd had to speak with Tharin since he'd returned from Mycena.

Ki had seen from the first that Tharin was suffering but hadn't known what to say to him, though in his heart he guessed the cause. Tharin believed he'd failed Rhius. A squire did not come home without his lord. Yet from what Ki had been able to glean from the other men in the days since their return, it had been no fault of Tharin's. Rhius had fallen in battle and Tharin had tried to save him. Ki clung to that, unable to believe anything less of his hero.

Now they had a new kettle of trouble to stir, and Tharin looked hollow-eyed and exhausted.

Riding a respectful distance behind the nobles, he reined Dragon in close to Tharin's horse and kept his voice low as he asked, "Are we going to have to live with *him* now?"

Tharin grimaced. "No, you'll live in the Old Palace with the other Companions. You'll only have to dine with Lord Orun now and then, so he can make reports to the king."

Ki had glimpsed the Palace over the citadel walls. "It's so big! How will we ever learn our way around?"

"The Companions have their own apartments. And the others will help you."

"How many are there?"

"Seven or eight now, I think, and their squires."

Ki fiddled with his reins. "The other squires—are they like me?"

Tharin looked at him again. "How do you mean?"

"You know."

Tharin gave him a sad little smile. "I believe all of them are the sons of highborn knights and lords."

"Oh."

"Yes." The way Tharin said it let Ki know that he understood his fears. "Don't let them bully you. Only one other of them can claim he's squired to a prince. And I promise you, Ki, there's not another boy there who surpasses you in honor." He nodded in Tobin's direction. "Keep him uppermost in your heart and you'll always do what's right."

"I don't want to fail him. I couldn't bear it."

Tharin reached out and gripped his arm hard enough to make Ki wince. "You won't," he said sternly. "You have to look after him for me now. You swear on your honor to do that."

The challenge hurt more than the hold on his arm. Ki straightened in the saddle and cast all his shameful doubts aside. "I swear it!"

Tharin released him with a satisfied nod. "We'll be his personal guard in name, but you're the one who'll be at his side. You must be my eyes and ears, Ki. If you smell any kind of trouble for him, you come to me."

"I *will*, Tharin!"

For a moment Ki feared he'd gone too far and angered the man, but Tharin only chuckled. "I know you will."

But Ki could see that he was still worried, and that made him check the lacings on his scabbard. He'd never imagined that going to the capital would feel like riding into enemy territory. He only wished he knew why.

The day wore on. The road they followed took them into flat bottomland laid out in long strips and farmed by tenants. Some of the strips lay fallow, grown over with weeds. Others were planted, but sparsely grown, or spoiled by disease. Great swaths of grain lay grey and rotted and flat.

In the villages here Tobin saw children with skinny legs, big bellies, and dark circles under their eyes. They reminded him of the way Brother used to look. What few cattle remained were raw-boned, and there were carcasses bloating in the ditches with ravens picking at their eyes. Many of the cottages in the village were empty, and several had been burnt. Most of those that remained had the crescent of Illior painted or chalked on the front door.

"That's odd," he said. "You'd think they'd be praying to Dalna for healing or good crops."

No one replied.

As the sun began its slow descent behind them, a cool breeze freshened out of the east, blowing their hair back and cooling the sweat on their brows. It carried the first hint of a sweet new smell Tobin didn't recognize.

Orun noticed him sniffing and smiled indulgently. "That's the sea, my prince. We'll be in sight of it soon."

A little further on they met a cart piled with the strangest crop he'd ever seen. A mass of some greenish brown plant quivered with every jounce and bump of the cart's wheels. A queer odor rose from it, salty and earthy.

"What is that?" he asked, wrinkling his nose.

"Seaweed, from the coast," Tharin explained. "Farmers manure their fields with it."

"From the sea!" Urging Gosi closer, Tobin leaned over and plunged his hand into the smelly stuff. It was cold and wet underneath, and had a leathery feel like the surface of Cook's calves' foot jelly after it cooled.

Dry brown hills like shoulders with no heads rose up against the sunset. The thin sliver of Illior's moon climbed over them as Tobin watched. Orun had said they'd be in Ero by sunset, yet it seemed they were in the middle of nowhere instead.

The road was steep here. Leaning forward in the stirrups, he urged Gosi up the last few yards to the top, then looked up to find a huge, unimaginable expanse of sparkling water stretching out below him. The glimpses he'd had in his vision journeys with Arkoniel hadn't prepared him for this; they'd been fuzzy and bounded by darkness, and he'd been focused on other things.

Ki rode up beside him. "What do you think of it?"

"It's—big!"

From here he could see how the water curved away to the horizon, broken in the distance by islands of all sizes sticking up through the waves. Tobin gaped, trying to take in the sheer size of it; beyond all that lay the places his father and Arkoniel had told him of: Kouros, Plenimar, Mycena, and the battlefield where his father had bravely fought and died.

"Think of it, Ki. Someday we'll be out there, you and I. We'll stand on the deck of some ship and look back at this shore and we'll remember standing here right now." He held up his hand.

Grinning, Ki grasped it. "Warriors together. Just like—"

He stopped in time, but Tobin knew what he'd meant. *Just like Lhel had foreseen, the first time she'd met Ki on that snowy forest road.*

Tobin looked around again. "But where's the city?"

"Couple miles north, Your Highness." It was the blond wizard. He saluted Tobin, then disappeared back into the milling ranks.

They followed the road over the hills, and before the last light faded in the west they crested a final rise and saw Ero shining like a gem above her wide harbor. For a moment Tobin was disappointed; at first glance it didn't look at all like the toy city his father had made for him. There was a broad river flowing past it, for one thing, and the city was spread out over several rolling hills that curved around the bay. On closer inspection, however, he could make out the undulating line of the city wall ringing the base of the largest one. The Palatine crowned this hill and he thought he could make out the roof of the Old Palace there, glowing like gold in the slanting sunset light.

For the first time he seemed to feel his father's spirit beside him, smiling as he showed Tobin all the places he'd taught him of. This was where his father had gone when he'd left the keep, riding on this road, to that market, to that hill, to those shining palaces and gardens. Tobin could almost hear his voice again, telling him tales of the kings and queens who'd ruled here, and the priest kings who'd ruled all the Three Lands before them from their island capital, back when Ero was nothing but a fishing village beset by raiders from the hills.

"What's wrong, Tobin?" Tharin was looking at him with concern.

"Nothing. I was just thinking of Father. I feel like I know the city a little already—"

Tharin smiled. "He'd be pleased."

"There's a lot more to it, though," Ki replied, ever practical. "He couldn't make all the houses and slums and all. But he got the main ways right."

"See that the pair of you stay out of alleys and side lanes," Tharin warned, giving him a sharp look. "You're still too young to be roaming the streets on your own, day or night. I'm sure Master Porion will keep you too busy to wander very much, but all the same, I want your word that you'll behave yourselves."

Tobin nodded, still taken up with the wonders spread out before him.

Setting off at a gallop, they rode along the edge of the harbor and the salt air cleared the dust from their throats. An enormous stone bridge spanned the river, broad enough for the column to ride ten abreast. On the far side they entered the outskirts of Ero, and here Tobin discovered for himself why the capital was called Stinking Ero.

Tobin had never seen so many people crowded together, or smelled such a stench. Accustomed as he was to nothing worse than cooking smoke, the mingled reek of offal and human waste made him gag and clench his teeth. The houses that lined the narrow streets here were rude hovels, worse than any byre in Alestun.

And it seemed that everyone here was maimed somehow, too, with stumps where hands or legs had been, or faces rotted with disease. Among the many carts on the road, he was shocked to see one loaded with dead bodies. They were stacked like firewood and their limbs shuddered with every bump. Some had black faces. Others were so thin their bones showed through their skin.

"They're headed there," Ki said, pointed to a column of black smoke in the distance. "Burning ground."

Tobin looked down at the jar of ashes hanging against Gosi's side. Had his father been hauled away in a dead cart? He shook his head, pushing the thought away.

Passing a wayside tavern, he saw two filthy children huddled next to the body of a woman. The bodice of her ragged gown was torn open to show her slack breasts and the skirt was pushed up over her thighs. The children held their hands up, crying for alms, but people simply walked past them, paying them no mind. Tharin noticed him staring and reined in long enough to flip a silver half sester their way. The children pounced on the coin, spitting at each other like cats. The woman settled it by rearing up and cuffing them both away. Grabbing up the coin with one hand, she cupped a breast in the other and flapped it at Tharin, then walked away with the children whining after her.

Tharin looked at Tobin and shrugged. "People aren't always what they seem, my prince. This is called Beggar's Way here. They come out to fleece country folk coming to market."

Even at this hour the road to the south gate was crowded with carts and riders, but the herald blew his silver trumpet and most of them gave way.

Tobin felt embarrassed and important all at once when Tharin greeted the captain of the guard at the city gate in his name, as if he were a grown man. Looking up, he saw Illior's crescent and Sakor's flame carved on the gate head and touched his heart and sword hilt reverently as they passed beneath.

Inside the city walls the wider streets were paved and provided with gutters. This did little to improve the smell of the place, however, as householders could be observed emptying their slop buckets out of front doors and upper windows.

The streets leading up to the Palatine sloped steadily upward, but the city's builders had cut terraces in the hillside for the larger marketplaces, parks, and gardens. Otherwise, houses and shops were stacked up the hillsides like the painted blocks of Tobin's city. They were tall rather than broad, four or five stories some of them, and built of timber over stone foundations, with roofs of baked tile.

Despite all his lessons, Tobin was seldom sure of just where they were. As Ki had said, there were a thousand side ways off the main routes and no way of knowing what street you were in without asking. Glad of his escort, he let Orun take the lead and turned his attention to the city as night fell around them.

In the lower markets the shops were already putting up their shutters for the night, but higher up many were open and lit by torches.

There were still beggars and dead dogs, pigs and dirty children, but now they also met with lords and ladies on horseback who carried hooded hawks on their fists and had a dozen servants in livery at their heels. There were Aurënfaie, too, and these must have been lords as well, for they were dressed finer than the Skalans themselves and Lord Orun bowed to many of them as they passed.

Actors and musicians in outlandish clothes performed by torchlight on little platforms in the squares. There were maskers and pie sellers, drysians and priests. He also saw a few robed figures wearing strange, beaklike devices on their faces; these must be the deathbirds Arkoniel had told him of.

Merchants sold their wares from poles and pushcarts and open-fronted shops. Passing through one wide courtyard, Tobin saw carvers of all sorts at work in booths there. He wanted to stop and watch but Orun hurried him on.

There were wizards, too, in robes and silver symbols. He saw one in the white robes Arkoniel had warned him about, but he looked no different to Tobin than any of the others.

"Hurry on," Orun urged, pressing a golden pomander to his nose.

They turned to the left and followed a broad level way until they could see the harbor below them, then turned again and climbed to the Palatine Gate.

The captain of the guard spoke a moment with Orun, then raised his torch and saluted Tobin.

Inside the walls of the Palatine it was dark and quiet. Tobin could make out little more than a few lighted windows and the dark bulk of buildings against the stars overhead, but he could tell by the way the air moved that it was less crowded here. The breeze was stronger, and carried the smells of fresh water, flowers, shrine incense, and the sea. In that moment the kings and queens weren't just names in a lesson anymore. They were his kin and they'd stood where he was standing and seen all this.

As if hearing his thoughts, Tharin bowed in the saddle and said, "Welcome home, Prince Tobin."

Ki and the others did the same.

"The Prince Royal will be most anxious to welcome you," Orun said. "Come, he should still be at table with the Companions at this hour."

"What about my father?" Tobin asked, laying his hand on the urn. His father had walked here, too. He'd probably stood on this very spot. Suddenly Tobin felt very tired and overwhelmed.

Orun raised an eyebrow. "Your father?"

"Lord Rhius asked that his ashes be laid with those of Princess Ariani in the royal tomb," Tharin told him. "Perhaps it would be best to see to the dead before we attend the living. All the rites have been observed. There's only this left to do. Prince Tobin's had the burden of it long enough, I think."

Orun made a fair job of hiding his impatience. "Of course. Now that we're safely arrived, however, I suppose we can do without our escort. Captain Tharin, you and your men should go to your rest. Your old billet has been maintained."

Tobin shot Tharin an unhappy look, dismayed at the idea of being left with Orun in this strange place.

"Prince Tobin, we accompanied your father where-ever he went," Tharin said. "Will you permit us to see our lord to his final rest?"

"Certainly, Sir Tharin," Tobin replied, relieved.

"Very well, then," Orun sighed, dismissing his own guard.

Tharin and Koni borrowed torches from the soldiers at the gate and led the way along a broad avenue lined with tall elms. The ancient trees arched to form a rustling tunnel overhead, and through their trunks to his right Tobin caught fleeting glimpses of firelight glowing be-tween pillars and high windows in the distance.

Leaving the tunnel of trees, they rode through an open park to a low-set building with a flat tile roof sup-ported by thick age-blackened wooden pillars. At Tharin's command the men-at-arms formed a double line flanking the entrance and knelt with their drawn swords point down before them.

Tobin dismounted and took the jar in his arms. With Tharin and Ki beside him, he carried his father's ashes be-tween the kneeling soldiers and entered the tomb.

An altar stood at the center of the stone platform in-side, and a flame burned on it in a large basin of oil. This flame illuminated the faces of the life-size stone effigies that stood in a semicircle around the altar. Tobin guessed that these were the queens of Skala. Those Who Came Be-fore.

A priest of Astellus appeared and led them down a stone stairway behind the altar to the catacombs below. By the light of his torch Tobin saw dusty jars like the one he carried stacked in shadowed niches, as well as bundles of bones and skulls piled on shelves.

"These are the oldest dead, my lord, your oldest ancestors who have been kept," the priest told him. "As each level fills, a new one is excavated. Your noble mother lies in the newest crypt, deep below."

They descended five narrow flights to a cold, airless chamber. The walls were carved floor to ceiling with niches and the floor was covered with wooden biers. Here lay bodies tightly wrapped with bands of thick white cloth.

"Your father chose for your mother to be wrapped," Tharin said softly, guiding Tobin to one of the niches on the far wall. An oval painting of his mother's likeness covered her face, and her long black hair hung free of the wrappings in a heavy braid coiled on her breast. She looked very thin and small.

Her hair looked just as it had when she was alive, thick and shining in the torchlight. He reached to touch it, then drew his hand back. The painting of her face was well done, but she was smiling in a happy way he'd never seen in life.

"Her eyes were just like yours," whispered Ki, and Tobin recalled with mild surprise that Ki had never known his mother. It seemed to him now that Ki had always been with him.

With Tharin's help, he lifted the jar from the netting and laid it between his mother's body and the wall. The priest stood mumbling prayers beside him, but Tobin couldn't think of a thing to say.

When they were finished Ki looked around the crowded chamber and whistled. "Are these all your kin?"

"If they're here, then I suppose they must be."

"I wonder why there are so many more women than men. You'd think with a war on and all, it'd be just the other way around."

Tobin saw that Ki was right, though he'd taken no

notice of it before. While there were a number of jars like the one he held, there were many more cloth-wrapped bodies with braids, and not all of them were grown women, either; he counted at least a dozen girls and babes.

"Come on," he sighed, too weary of death to concern himself with strangers.

"Wait," said Tharin. "It's customary to take a lock of hair as a remembrance. Would you like me to cut one for you?"

Tobin raised a hand absently to his lips as he considered this, and his fingers lingered on the small faded scar on his chin. "Another time, perhaps. Not now."

Chapter 39

After leaving the tomb, Lord Orun led them back the way they'd come and turned onto an avenue that took them past open riding grounds bounded by more trees. The moon was high now and cast a pale glow over their surroundings.

This part of the Palatine was a shadowed jumble of gardens and flat rooflines. Tobin caught the shimmer of water in the distance; there was a large artificial pond here, built by one of the queens. In front of them, past more trees, he could see a rambling, uneven mass of roofs bulking low on the eastern side of the walled citadel.

"That's the New Palace there," Tharin explained, pointing to the longest silhouette to their left, "and that directly in front of us is the Old. All around them is a rabbit's warren of other palaces and houses, but you won't have to concern yourself with those for now. When you get settled in, I'll bring you to your mother's house."

Tobin was too exhausted to register more than an impression of gardens and colonnades. "I wish I could live there."

"You will, when you're grown."

The entrance of the Old Palace loomed before them out of the darkness, flanked by huge columns, flaring torches, and a line of guards in black and white tunics.

Tobin clasped hands with Tharin, fighting back tears.

"Be brave, my prince," Tharin said softly. "Ki, make me proud."

The moment of parting couldn't be put off any longer. Tharin and the others saluted him and rode off into the darkness. Strangers in livery surged in around them, anxious to take charge of their baggage and horses.

Lord Orun swooped in as soon as Tharin was out of the way.

"Come along, Prince Tobin, Prince Korin mustn't be kept waiting any longer. You, boy." This to Ki. "Fetch the prince's baggage!"

Ki waited until the man's back was turned and made him an obscene salute. Tobin gave him a grateful grin. So did several of the palace servants.

Orun hurried them up the stairs, where more servants in long white and gold livery met them at a huge set of bronze doors covered with rampant dragons. Inside, a stiff-backed servant with a white beard led them down a long corridor inside.

Tobin looked around, round-eyed. The walls were painted with wonderful glowing patterns, and in the center of the broad stone corridor there was a shallow pool where colorful fish swam among tinkling fountains. He'd never imagined such grandeur.

They passed through a series of huge rooms with ceilings so high they were lost in shadow. The walls were covered in more faded but wonderful murals and the furnishings were wonders of carving and inlay work. There were gold and jewels everywhere he looked. Bowed under a load of bags, Ki appeared equally awed.

After several more turns, the old man opened a creaking black door and ushered Tobin into an airy bedchamber half the size of the great hall back at the keep. A tall bed with hangings of black and gold stood on a raised platform in the center of the room. Past that, a balcony overlooked the city beyond. The walls were painted with faded hunting scenes. The room smelled nicely of the sea and the tall pines visible outside the window.

"This is your room, Prince Tobin," the man informed him. "Prince Korin occupies the next chamber."

Ki stood gaping until the man showed him to a second, smaller room at the back where wardrobes and chests stood. Next to this was an alcove containing a second bed built into the wall like a shelf. It was made up with rich bedding, too, but reminded Tobin too much of the place where his mother had been laid.

Orun hustled them out again and they followed the sound of music and boisterous laughter to an even larger chamber filled with performers of all sorts. There were minstrels, half-naked tumblers, jugglers tossing balls, knives, burning torches—even hedgehogs—and a girl in a silken shift dancing with a bear she led on a silver chain. A glittering company of youths and girls sat on a raised dais on a balcony at the far end of the room. The least of them was dressed more finely than Tobin ever had been in his life. Suddenly he was aware of the thick coating of dust on his clothes.

The diners didn't seem to be paying the entertainers much mind, but sat talking and jesting among themselves over the wreckage of their feast. Servants went among them with platters and pitchers.

Tobin's approach attracted their notice, however. A black-haired youth sitting at the center of the table suddenly vaulted over and strode across to meet him. He was a stocky lad of about fifteen, with short, curling black hair and smiling dark eyes. His scarlet tunic was embroidered with gold; rubies glowed on the gold hilt of a dagger at his belt and in a small jewel dangling from one ear.

Tobin and Ki copied the low bows the others made him, guessing that this was Prince Korin.

The older boy studied them a moment, looking uncertainly from Tobin to Ki. "Cousin, is this you arrived at last?"

Tobin straightened first, realizing his mistake. "Greetings, Prince Korin. I'm your cousin, Tobin."

Korin smiled and held out his hand. "They tell me I was at your naming, but I don't remember it. I'm glad to meet you properly at last." He glanced down at the back of Ki's bowed head. "And who's this?"

Tobin touched Ki's arm and he stood up. Before he could answer, however, Lord Orun thrust himself into the conversation.

"This is Prince Tobin's squire, Your Highness, the son of one of Lord Jorvai's minor knights. It seems Duke Rhius chose him without your father's knowledge. I thought it best for you to explain—"

Ki dropped to one knee before the prince, left hand on his sword hilt. "My name is Kirothius, son of Sir Larenth of Oakmount Stead, a warrior in your father's service in Mycena, my prince."

"And my good friend," Tobin added. "Everyone calls him Ki."

Tobin saw the hint of a smile tug at the prince's mouth as he looked from Orun to Ki. "Welcome, Ki. Let's find a place for you at the squire's table. I'm sure you must be wanting your own bed after such a long ride, Lord Orun. Good night to you."

The chancellor did not look pleased, but he could not argue with the prince. With a last bow, he swept from the room.

Korin watched the man go, then motioned for Tobin and Ki to follow him to the banquet table. Throwing an arm around Tobin's shoulders, he asked softly, "What do you think of my father's choice of guardian?"

Tobin gave a cautious shrug. "He's discourteous."

Korin smelled strongly of wine and Tobin wondered if he was a little drunk. But his eyes were clear and shrewd enough as he warned, "Yes, but he's also powerful. Be careful."

Following just behind, Ki ducked his head nervously and asked, "Excuse me for speaking out of turn, my prince, but am I right in thinking that the king chose someone else to be Tob—Prince Tobin's squire?"

Korin nodded and Tobin's heart sank. "Since you've grown up so far from court, Father felt it would be best for you to have someone knowledgeable of the ways here. He left the choice to Lord Orun, who chose Sir Moriel, third son of Lady Yria. See that fellow at the lower table with the white eyebrows and a nose like a woodpecker's beak? That's him."

They'd reached the balcony and Tobin could see the squire's table to the right of the long feast table. Korin's description was an apt one. Moriel was already striding over to present himself. He was about Ki's age and height, with a plain face and white-blond hair.

Tobin started to object but Korin forestalled him with a smile. "I see the way things are." He gave Tobin a wink and whispered, "Just between us, I've always considered Moriel a bit of a toad. We'll manage something."

Moriel distinguished himself immediately by bowing deeply to Ki. "Prince Tobin, your servant and squire—"

"No, that is his squire." Korin hauled Moriel up by the arm and pointed him at Tobin. "This is Prince Tobin. And since you can't distinguish between a squire and a prince, we'd best leave the job to someone who can."

Moriel's pale face went pink. Those at the table close enough to hear the exchange burst out laughing. Moriel redirected his bow awkwardly to Tobin. "My apologies, Prince Tobin, I— That is, I couldn't tell—"

The others were staring at them now, nobles and servants alike. Tobin smiled at the mortified youth. "That's all right, Sir Moriel. My squire and I are equally dusty."

This earned him another laugh from the others, but Moriel only colored more deeply.

"My Companions and friends," said Korin. "I present to you my beloved cousin, Prince Tobin of Ero, who's come to join us at last." Everyone rose and bowed. "And his squire, Sir Ki of—"

"Now, I think you know better than that, my lord," a deep voice rumbled behind them. A heavy-set man with a long grey mane of hair stepped onto the balcony and gave

Prince Korin a wry look. His short plain robe and wide belt were not the clothes of a noble, but every boy except Korin bowed to him.

"Your father charged Lord Orun with the choice of a squire for Prince Tobin, I believe," he said.

"But as you see, Master Porion, Tobin already has a squire, and one bonded to him by his father," Korin told him.

This was the royal arms master Tharin had spoken so well of. Korin may not have bowed to him, Tobin noted, but he spoke to the man with a respect he hadn't shown to Orun.

"So I've heard. Lord Orun's just been round to my rooms with word of him." Porion sized up Ki. "Country bred, are you?"

"Yes, sir."

"I don't suppose you're familiar with court life, or the city?"

"I know Ero. A bit."

Some of the Companions snickered at this and Moriel began to puff up again.

Porion addressed both boys. "Tell me, what is the highest duty of a squire? Moriel?"

The boy hesitated. "To serve his lord in any fashion required."

Porion nodded approvingly. "Ki, your answer?"

Ki set his hand on his sword hilt. "To lay down his life for his lord, Arms Master. To be his warrior."

"Both worthy answers." Porion pulled a golden badge of office from the neck of his robe and let it fall on his chest with a thump. Grasping it, he stood a moment in thought. "As Master of the Royal Companions, I have the right to judge this in the king's absence. According to the ancient laws and customs, the bond contracted between the fathers of Prince Tobin and Squire—" He leaned over to Ki and whispered loudly, "What's your name again, boy? —and his squire Kirothius, son of Larenth of Oakmount, is a sacred one before Sakor and must be recognized. Ki's place in the Companions must stand until such time as the king says otherwise. Don't take it hard, Moriel. No one knew when they chose you."

"May I withdraw, Your Highness?" Moriel asked.

Korin nodded and the boy turned away. Tobin saw him cast a poisonous glance in Ki's direction as he stalked from the chamber.

"Have you a title, boy?" Porion asked Ki.

"No, Swordmaster."

"No title!" Korin exclaimed. "Well, that won't do for a prince of Skala, to be served so! Tanil, my sword."

One of the young men at the squire's table hurried forward with a handsome blade. "Kneel and be knighted," he ordered Ki.

The other squires cheered and pounded the table with their footed drinking cups.

Tobin was delighted but Ki hesitated, shooting him a strange, questioning look.

Tobin nodded. "You'll be a knight."

Ki bowed his head and knelt. Korin touched him on the shoulders and both cheeks with the flat of his blade. "Rise, Sir Ki—what was it? Kirothius, Knight of Ero, Companion of the Prince Royal. There. Done!" Korin tossed the sword back to his squire and the rest of the table pounded their cups.

Ki rose and looked around uncertainly. "I'm a knight now?"

"You are." Porion clapped him on the shoulders. "Welcome your little brother, squires. Give him a full mazer and a good place among you." This brought on another round of cup banging.

With a last doubtful look over his shoulder at Tobin, Ki went to join the others.

Korin brought Tobin to the long table and set him in a

fine carved chair on his right. The feast was long over, the cloth covered with rinds, bones, and nutshells, but fresh trenchers and bowls had been set ready for him.

"And now you must meet your new brothers," Korin announced. "I won't trouble you with everyone's lineage tonight. This is Caliel." Korin ruffled the hair of the handsome fair-skinned youth on his left. "This great red bear with the scruffy chin next to him is our old man, Zusthra. Then we have Alben, Orneus, Urmanis, Quirion, Nikides, and little Lutha, the baby until your arrival."

Each boy rose and clasped hands with Tobin, greeting him with varying degrees of interest and warmth. There was something odd in their handclasps. It took him a moment to realize that it was the smoothness of their palms.

Lutha's smile was the broadest. "Welcome, Prince Tobin. You make our number even again for drills." He had a sharp face that put Tobin in mind of a mouse, and his brown eyes were friendly.

The feast resumed. Korin was lord of the table and everyone deferred to him as if he were lord of the castle. With the exception of Zusthra, no one at the table looked to be any older than Korin, but all went on as if they ruled great estates of their own already, talking of horses, crops, and battles. They drank wine like men, too. Prince Korin's mazer was always in his hand and a butler always at his shoulder. Master Porion had taken a place at the far end of the table and seemed to be watching the prince without looking at him too often.

The rest in the company were the children of Skalan nobility and foreign dignitaries. The young men and boys wore elaborate tunics and jeweled daggers and rings. The dozen or so girls at the table wore gowns decorated with wide bands of embroidery, and strands of ribbon or jewels twisted into their hair under gauzy veils. Tobin couldn't keep track of all the names and titles. He did sit forward and take note, however, when a dark-haired boy was introduced as an Aurënfaie from Gedre. Tobin had overlooked him before, for he was dressed like the rest, and wore no sen'gai.

"Gedre? You're Aurënfaie?"

"Yes. I'm Arengil í Maren Ortheil Solun Gedre, son of the Gedre Khirnari. Welcome, Prince Tobin í Rhius."

One of the older girls leaned in beside Tobin, resting an arm across the back of his chair. She had thick auburn hair and a mix of freckles and pimples across her sharp chin. Tobin struggled to recall her name. Aliya something, a duke's daughter. Her green gown was embroidered with pearls and showed the first hint of a womanly form. "The 'faie love their long, fancy names," she said with a smirk. "I'll bet you a sester you can't guess Ari's age."

Everyone groaned, including Korin. "Aliya, let him be!"

She pouted at him. "Oh, let him guess. He's probably never even seen a 'faie before."

The Aurënfaie boy sighed and rested his chin on one hand. "Go on," he offered.

Tobin had seen a few 'faie, and learned a great deal more from his father and Arkoniel. This boy looked to be about Ki's age. "Twenty-nine?" he guessed.

Ari's eyebrows flew up. "Twenty-five, but that's closer than most get it."

Everyone laughed as Aliya slapped a coin down in front of Tobin's trencher and flounced away.

"Don't mind her," chuckled Korin, quite drunk now. "She's gone sour ever since her brother went to Mycena." He sighed and waved a hand around at the company. "So have we all. All the older boys are gone except for me and those unfortunate enough to be my Companions. We'd all be in the field now if there were a second heir to take my place. It would be different if my brothers and sisters had lived." He took a long swig from his mazer, then scowled unhappily at Tobin over the rim. "Why, if my sisters had lived, Skala could have her queen back as the moon priests would have it, but all they have is me. So I have to stay wrapped in silk here, safely kept by to rule." Korin slumped back in his chair, staring morosely into his cup. "An heir to spare, that's what we're lacking. A spare heir—"

"We've all heard that one, Korin," Caliel chided, nudging the prince. "Maybe we should tell him about the palace ghosts instead?"

"Ghosts?" Korin brightened at this. "By the Four, we have buckets of them! Half of 'em are Grandmama Agnalain's old consorts she poisoned or beheaded. Isn't that so, squires?"

The squires chorused their agreement and Tobin saw Ki's eyes widen a bit.

"And the old mad queen herself," Zusthra added, scratching sagely at his thin, coppery beard. "She wanders the corridors at night in her armor. You can hear the drag of her bad leg as she goes up and down, looking for traitors. She's been known to grab up grown men and carry them to the torture chambers beneath the Palace, where she locks them up in her rusty old cages to starve."

"What of that ghost of yours, cousin—" Korin began, but Porion cleared his throat.

"Your Highness, Prince Tobin has had a weary journey today. You shouldn't keep him so late, his first night here."

Korin leaned close to Tobin. His breath was sour with wine and his words were slurred. "Poor coz! Would you? Would you like to find your bed? You're in my dead brother's room, you know. There might be ghosts, there, too, but you shouldn't mind that. Elarin was a sweet lad—"

Porion was behind Korin's chair now, slipping a hand under his arm. "My prince," he murmured.

Korin glanced up at him, then turned back to Tobin with a charming smile that made him look almost sober. "Sleep well, then."

Tobin rose and took his leave, glad to escape this crowd of drunken strangers.

The stiff-backed servant appeared with Ki on his heels

and conducted them back to their room. Porion walked with them as far as their door.

"You mustn't judge the prince by what you saw tonight, Prince Tobin," he said sadly. "He's a good lad and a great warrior. That's the problem, you see. It weighs heavily on him, not being allowed to go to war now that he's of age. As he said, it's a hard thing being the sole heir to the throne when his father will declare no second. Such feasts as these—" He cast a disgusted look back toward the hall. "It's his father's absence. Well, when he's fresh tomorrow he'll make you a better welcome. You're to be presented to Lord Chancellor Hylus at the audience chamber in the morning. Come out to the training grounds after that so I can have a look at your skills and equipage. I understand you have no proper armor."

"No."

"I'll see to that. Rest well, my prince, and welcome. I'd like to say, too, that I remember your father as a fine man and a great warrior. I mourn your loss."

"Thank you, Arms Master," said Tobin. "And thank you for keeping Ki as my squire."

Porion gave him a wink. "An old friend of yours had a word with me, just after you arrived."

Tobin gave him a blank look, then laughed. "Tharin?"

Porion held a finger to his lips, but nodded. "I don't know what Orun was thinking. A father's choice of squire can't be put aside like that."

"Then it wasn't my answer?" asked Ki, a little crestfallen.

"You were both right," Porion replied. "And you might try to smooth Moriel's feathers if you get the chance. He knows the Palatine and the city. Good night, boys, and welcome."

Servants had lit a dozen lamps around the room and carried in a copper tub full of hot scented water. A young page stood by the bed and a young man stood ready with brushes and sheets, apparently waiting to bathe Tobin.

He sent both servants away, then stripped off and slid into the bath with a happy groan. Hot baths had been a rare occurrence at the keep. He was nearly asleep with his nose just above the water's surface when he heard Ki let out a cackle across the room.

"No wonder Moriel had his nose out of joint," he called, holding back the curtains of the wall bed. All the fine bedding was gone. "He must have had himself all moved in anticipation of your majesty's arrival. All he's left me is a bare straw tick. And, by the smell, he pissed on it as a parting remembrance, the little bastard!"

Tobin sat up and wrapped his arms around his knees. It hadn't occurred to him that they'd sleep apart, much less in such a cavern of a room.

"Sure is a big room," Ki muttered, looking around.

Tobin grinned, guessing his friend was having similar doubts. "Big bed, too. Plenty of room for two."

"I'd say so. I'll go unpack Your Highness' bags," Ki said, chuckling.

Tobin was about to settle back in the tub when he remembered the doll hidden in the bottom of the chest.

"No!"

Ki snorted. "It's my duty, Tob. Let me do it."

"It can wait. The water will get cold if you don't get in now. Come on, your turn."

Tobin splashed out of the tub and wrapped himself in one of the sheets.

Ki eyed him suspiciously. "You're as fussy as Nari all of a sudden. Then again—" He sniffed comically at his armpits. "I do stink."

As soon as Ki had taken his place in the tub Tobin hurried into the dressing room and flung open the chest.

"I said I'd do that!" Ki hollered.

"I need a shirt." Tobin pulled on a clean one, then dug out the flour sack and looked around for a safe hiding place. A painted wardrobe and several chests stood against one wall. On the other side was a tall cupboard that reached almost to the ceiling. By opening the doors, he could use the shelves inside as a creaking, cracking ladder. There was just enough space at the top to hide the bag. That would do for now.

Climbing back down, he had just time enough to shut the doors and brush the cobwebs off his shirt before Ki sauntered in wrapped in a sheet.

"What are you doing in here, taking the roof off?"

"Just exploring."

Ki eyed him again, then looked nervously over his shoulder. "Do you think there are really ghosts here?"

Tobin walked back into the bedchamber. "If there are, then they're my kin, like Brother. You're not afraid of him anymore, are you?"

Ki shrugged, then thrust his arms up and yawned until his jaws creaked, letting the sheet slide to the floor. "We better get some sleep. Once Master Porion gets a hold of us tomorrow, I'm betting he doesn't let us stand still long enough to cast a shadow."

"I like him."

Ki flung back the black hangings on the bed and launched himself into a somersault across the velvet counterpane. "I didn't say I didn't. I just think he's going to work us as hard as Tharin ever did. That's what the other squires say, anyway."

Tobin did a back flip of his own and landed beside his friend.

"What are they like?"

"The other squires? Hard to say yet. They were mostly drunk and they didn't say much to me, except for Korin's squire, Tanil. He's a duke's first son and seems a nice enough fellow. So does Barieus, squire to that little fellow who looks like a rat."

"Lutha."

"That's the one."

"But not the others?"

Ki shrugged. "Too soon to say, I guess. All the others are the second or third sons of high lords—"

It was too dark inside the hangings to make out his friend's expression, but there was something troubling in his tone.

"Well, you're a knight now. And I'm going to have you made a lord as soon as I can and give you an estate," Tobin told him. "I've been thinking about it all day. Arkoniel says I'll have to wait until I'm of age, but I don't want to wait that long. When the king comes back I'm going to ask him how I can do it."

Ki rose up on one elbow and stared down at him. "You'd do that, wouldn't you? Just like that."

"Well, of course!" Tobin grinned up at him. "Just try not to breed so much that your grandchildren end up sleeping in a heap on the floor again."

Ki lay back and folded his hands behind his head. "I don't know. From what I saw back home, breeding is great fun. And I saw some pretty girls at that banquet tonight! That one in the green dress? I wouldn't mind having a look under her skirts, would you?"

"Ki!"

Ki shrugged and stroked his faint moustache, smiling to himself. He was soon snoring, but Tobin lay awake for some time, listening to the ongoing revels echoing outside the window. He'd never seen anyone drunk at the keep. It made him nervous.

This wasn't what he'd looked for, all those years staring down the Alestun road. He was a warrior, not a courtier, drinking wine half the night in fancy clothes. With girls!

He frowned over at Ki's peaceful profile. The soft down covering his cheeks caught the faint light coming in through the hangings. Tobin rubbed at his own smooth cheeks and sighed. He and Ki were the same height, but his shoulders were still narrow and his skin still bare of the spots and stray hairs that Ki was developing. He tossed a while longer, then realized that he'd forgotten all about Brother.

Barely moving his lips, he whispered the words. Brother appeared crouching on the end of the bed, face as inscrutable as ever.

"You mustn't go wandering about," he told him. "Stay close and do as I ask. It isn't safe here."

To his amazement, Brother nodded. Crawling slowly up the bed, he touched Tobin's chest, then his own, and settled back at the end of the bed.

Tobin lay back and yawned. It was comforting having someone else from home here, even if it was only a ghost.

At the New Palace, in a wing adjoining the king's own now-empty rooms, the wizard Niryn stirred in his sleep, disturbed by a half-formed image that would not quite take shape.

Chapter 40

Tobin woke at sunrise and lay listening to the new morning sounds outside. He could hear crowds of people laughing and talking and whispering loudly just outside the door. From the open balcony came the sounds of riders and birds, splashing water, and the distant cacophony of the waking city. Even here, the scent of flowers and pines could not mask the rising stink of the place carried in on the warm sea breeze. Had it really only been a day ago that he'd woken in his own bed? He sighed and shook off the wave of homesickness that threatened to overwhelm him.

Ki was a softly snoring lump on the far side of the bed. Tobin tossed a pillow at him, then rolled out between the heavy curtains and went to have a look outside.

It was another clear summer day. From here he could see over the Palatine wall to the southern city and the sea. It was incredible. With the mist rising off the water and the sun slanting low as it rose, it was hard to tell where the sky stopped and the sea began. In the wash of dawn, Ero appeared to be made of fire, trees and all.

Outside his window, a colorful garden stretched away to the belt of elms he'd ridden past the night before. There were already servants at work with shears and baskets, like bees in the meadow at home.

To either side he could see other balconies, pillars, and the jut of tiled roofs with fancy cornices and bits of sculpture on top.

"I bet we could go all the way from the Old Palace to the New over the roofs," Ki said, coming up behind him.

"You can," a girl's voice agreed, seeming to come from the air over their heads.

Both boys whirled and looked up just in time to see a dark-haired blur of motion disappear beyond the eaves above their balcony. Only the rapidly fading scuffle of feet over tiles betrayed their visitor's retreat.

"Who was that?" laughed Ki, looking for a way to follow.

Before they could find an easy way up, a young manservant came in, followed by an entourage of others laden with clothes and packages. He went to the bed, then spied them on the balcony and bowed deeply.

"Good morning, my prince. I am to be your manservant at the Palace. My name is Molay. And these—" He indicated the line of laden servants behind him. "They all come bearing gifts from your noble kin and admirers."

The servants came forward in turn, presenting handsome robes and tunics, under robes, fine shirts and trousers, soft velvet hats, jewels in delicate caskets, ornate swords and knives, and colorful belts, two matched hounds who cringed and growled at Tobin when he tried to pet them, and a pretty falcon with golden ornaments on her plumed hood and jesses from Prince Korin. There were boxes of sweets, caskets of incense, even baskets of bread and flowers. Among the jewels he found an earring from the prince similar to the one Korin wore and a ring from Lord Orun. Best of all, however, were the two shirts of shining, supple mail sent by Porion from the Royal Armory.

"At last, one that fits!" Ki exclaimed, throwing one over his nightshirt.

"It is customary when a new Companion arrives in the city," Molay explained, seeing Tobin's consternation. "Perhaps I might assist you in such matters?"

"Yes, please!"

"Your Highness must of course wear first the suit of clothes sent by Lord Chancellor Hylus for your audience with him this morning. I see he has had it done in black, out of respect for your loss— But I see you have no mourning ring!"

"No. I didn't know how to get one."

"I shall call in a jeweler for you, my prince. For now, you might wear this jewel from the Prince Royal, and of course this ring from your guardian. And then each gift in turn according to the rank of the giver."

"I thought I heard voices!" Korin strode out of the dressing room with Caliel. Both wore fighting leathers with fantastically elaborate raised work and metal fittings. Tobin wondered how they could move properly in such a costume, or how they'd dare risk damaging it.

"There's a connecting door between our rooms," Korin explained, taking Tobin to the back of the dressing room and showing him where a small panel swung back on a short dusty passage. At the far end he had a glimpse of gold and red hangings and a pack of hounds watching expectantly for their master's return. "It only opens from my side, but if you knock I can let you through."

They went back to Tobin's chamber to inspect the jumble of gifts. "Not a bad haul, coz. I'm glad to see you've been shown the proper respect even though no one knows you yet. Do you like my hawk?"

"Very much!" Tobin exclaimed, though in truth he was a little afraid of her. "Will you show me how to hunt with her?"

"Will he? It's all he wants to do, besides sword fighting," Caliel exclaimed, stroking the falcon's smooth wings.

"Gladly, but Caliel's our best falconer," Korin demurred modestly. "He has some Aurënfaie blood, you know."

"Her name is Erizhal," Caliel told Tobin. "It's 'faie for 'arrow of the sun.' The royal falconer will keep her in good trim for you. We'll have to bring Ari along, too. He's got a wizard's touch with hawks."

With the help of the older boys, Tobin sorted through

the gifts. Those sent by lesser nobles were by custom passed to his squire, so Ki came out of it quite well, too. Korin drew up a list of proper return gifts and Tobin used his father's seal to authorize the deliveries.

"There, now you're a true Ero noble," laughed Korin. "To be one, you must spend exorbitant amounts of money and drink exorbitant amounts of wine. We'll get to the wine later."

The sun was well up by the time they'd finished. Korin and Caliel went back the way they'd come, promising to meet Tobin on the training field later.

Molay helped the boys dress, and by the time he'd finished they hardly recognized each other. Tobin's robe from Chancellor Hylus was of fine black wool split at the front, cut slim in the waist and embroidered in red and golden silk with the Dragon of Skala on the breast and the hems. The oversleeves were cut full to show off the sleeves of the red under robe. When he'd put on shoes of soft red leather and the first jewels he'd ever worn, he hardly felt like himself at all. As for Ki, he looked like a dapper fox in russet and green. Standing at the polished bronze mirror together, they both burst out laughing. Molay offered them each a new sword, but they kept the plain, serviceable blades Tobin's father had given them, accepting no other.

Molay was very pleased with them, and fussed over the trimming of their hair and nails as much as Nari ever had. When he was satisfied, he sent the young page scampering off for their escort. To Tobin's considerable disappointment, this proved to be not Tharin, but Lord Orun. He was more resplendent than ever, in shimmering silken robes of sunbird gold, with a black and gold hood of office over his shoulders. A jeweled triangle of heavy black velvet covered his bald head.

He paused in the doorway and raised an approving eyebrow. "Well, now you do look like a young prince,

Your Highness. Ah, and I see you received my token. I hope it pleases you?"

"Thank you, my lord. It was most generous of you," Tobin said, holding out his hand to show off the ring. After the incident with Moriel last night, and what Korin had said, he was glad to be able to please his guardian a little today.

The audience chamber was in the New Palace, far enough away that they found their horses saddled and ready for them as they came out of the palace gate. Ki made a show of checking the saddles before Tobin mounted, and rode at Tobin's left as Tharin had taught him.

The New Palace dwarfed the Old in both size and grandeur. Many of its pillared courtyards stood open to the sky and had splashing fountains to make music through the corridors beyond. Windows with panes of colored glass cast patterns on the marble floors, and shrines as tall as the keep tower filled the palace with their incense.

The audience chamber was equal in scale to all the rest. The vaulted white stone roof was held aloft by ranks of pillars carved with twisting dragons.

The huge chamber was filled with people in clothing of every sort, from rags to fine robes. There were Aurënfaie in white tunics and jewels and sen'gai of every color, and other foreigners Tobin did not recognize at all—people in blue tunics that billowed like tents around them, and men in brightly striped robes with skin the color of dark tea and curly black hair like Lhel's.

Some stood in intent knots, speaking in hushed, rapid voices. Others lounged at their leisure on couches or on the edges of the great fountains, toying with their hawks or the hounds and spotted cats they led on chains.

At the far end of the chamber a beautiful golden throne stood on a wide dais, but no one sat there. A cape bearing the king's crest was draped over it and a crown had been placed on the seat.

Two men sat in lower chairs before it. The older of the pair was listening to each petitioner in turn, just as Tobin's father had in the hall at the keep. He had a short white beard, a number of heavy gold chains and seals around his neck, and wore long black robes and a hat like a red velvet pancake on his head.

"That is Lord Chancellor Hylus, the King's Regent," Orun told him as they approached. "He is a distant kinsman of yours."

"And the other?" asked Tobin, though he'd already guessed.

The other man was much younger, with jasper-colored eyes and a forked beard that shone coppery red in the sunlight. But all Tobin saw at first were his robes. They were white as sunlit snow, with sweeping designs over the shoulders and skirts picked out in glittering silver thread. This was one of the Harriers that Arkoniel had warned him about. He'd been sure to send Brother away last night, but he looked around quickly just to be sure.

"That is the King's Wizard, Lord Niryn," said Orun, and Tobin's heart skipped a beat. This was not only a Harrier, but *the* Harrier.

He feared that they'd spend the whole morning waiting their turn, but Lord Orun led them right up to the front and bowed to Hylus.

Tobin had thought that the Lord Chancellor Hylus had a harsh face, for he'd been dealing sternly with a baker accused of selling underweight loaves when they approached. As soon as Orun introduced Tobin, however, the old man's face softened into a warm smile. He held out his hand and Tobin climbed the steps to join him.

"It's as if I see your dear mother looking at me out of your eyes!" he exclaimed, clasping Tobin's hand between ones that felt like they were made of bones and thin leather. "And her grandmother, too. Most extraordinary. You must dine with me soon, dear boy, and I will tell you stories of them. You'll have met my grandson Nikides among the Companions?"

"I'm sure, my lord." Tobin thought he remembered the name, but couldn't summon a face to go with it. There had been so many last night.

The chancellor appeared pleased. "I'm sure he'll be a good friend to you. Have they given you a squire?"

Tobin introduced Ki, still standing with Orun below. Hylus squinted down at him for a moment. "Sir Larenth? I don't know that name. This is a fine-looking young fellow, though. Welcome to you both." He looked at Tobin a moment longer, then turned to the man beside him. "And allow me to present your uncle's wizard, Lord Niryn."

Tobin's heart knocked against his ribs again as he acknowledged Niryn's bow. Yet it was Arkoniel's warning that made his heart race rather than anything in the man's appearance, for Niryn was a perfectly ordinary looking man. The wizard inquired politely about his journey and his home, spoke kindly of his parents, then asked, "Do you enjoy seeing magic, my prince?"

"No," Tobin said quickly. Arkoniel had done his best to interest him in tricks and visions—Ki loved anything of the sort—but Tobin still found most of it disconcerting. He didn't want to give this stranger any encouragement.

The wizard didn't seem insulted. "I remember the night of your birth, Prince Tobin. You did not have this mark on your chin then. But there was another, I think?"

"It's a scar. You're thinking of my wisdom mark."

"Ah yes. Curious things, such marks. May I see how it has developed? I have made a study of such things."

Tobin pushed back his sleeve and showed Niryn and Hylus the red mark. Nari called it a rosebud, but to him it looked like a grouse's heart.

Niryn covered it with the tips of two fingers. His expression did not change, but Tobin felt an unpleasant tingle pass through his skin and saw the man's jasper eyes go hard and distant for an instant, just the way Arkoniel's did when he made magic. But Arkoniel had never done any magic on him without first asking permission.

Shocked, Tobin pulled away. "Don't be rude, sir!"

Niryn bowed. "My apologies, my prince. I was merely reading the mark. It does indeed denote great wisdom. You are most fortunate."

"He did say he does not like tricks," murmured Hylus, looking displeased with the wizard. "His mother was much the same at that age."

"My apologies," Niryn said again. "I hope you will allow me to redeem myself another day, Prince Tobin."

"If you wish, my lord." For once Tobin was grateful when Orun loomed up behind him to shepherd him away. When he was sure they were out of sight of the dais he pushed his sleeve back and looked at his birthmark, wondering if Niryn had done anything to it. But it seemed just the same.

*T*hat went well enough, I suppose," Orun sniffed as he escorted them back to their room. "You would do better to be civil to Niryn, though. He's a powerful man."

Tobin wondered angrily if any of the powerful men in Ero were pleasant. Orun left them with a promise to feast with Tobin in a few days and went on his way.

Ki made a face at Orun's back, then turned to Tobin with concern. "Did the wizard hurt you?"

"No. I just don't like to be pawed at."

Molay had laid out a pair of fine leather jerkins for them, similar to those Korin and Caliel had worn, but they were far too stiff and fancy for Tobin's taste.

Instead, he sent Ki to find the worn leathers they'd brought with them from home. Molay was clearly dismayed at the thought of Tobin wearing such plain garb but Tobin happily ignored him, glad to be back in comfortable old clothes again. Gathering up their swords, helms, and bows, he and Ki followed the waiting page to the main entrance.

So happy was he to finally be doing something war-riorlike, he didn't notice the odd looks they were attract-ing until Ki tugged on his sleeve and tilted his chin at two robed noblemen staring at them disapprovingly.

"I should be carrying your gear," Ki muttered. "They must think we're a couple of peasant soldiers who wan-dered in from the street!"

The page heard him. Throwing his shoulders back, he cried out in a ringing voice, "Make way for His Highness, Prince Tobin of Ero!"

The words worked like magic. All the muttering, glit-tering nobles parted and bowed to Tobin and Ki as they strode past in their dusty shoes and scarred leathers. Tobin tried to copy Lord Orun's haughty nod, but Ki's smothered snort behind him probably spoiled the effect.

At the palace entrance the page stepped aside and bowed deeply, though not quickly enough to hide his own grin.

"What's your name?" asked Tobin.

"Baldus, my prince."

"Well done, Baldus."

The Companions trained on a broad stretch of open land near the center of the Palatine. There were riding grounds, sword fighting rings, archery lists, stables, and a high stone Temple of the Four, which the boys ran to each morning to make sacrifice to Sakor.

The Companions and their squires were shooting in the archery lists when Tobin and Ki arrived. Even at a dis-tance, Tobin could see that all of them wore fine clothes like Korin's. There were scores of other people around the field, as well. Tobin recognized some of the guests from the banquet last night, though he could recall few names. Many of the girls were there, too, in bright gowns and light capes of silk that fluttered in the morning breeze like butterfly wings. Some rode their palfreys around the pe-rimeter. Others were shooting at targets or flying their hawks. Ki's eyes followed them, and Tobin suspected he was looking for auburn-haired Aliya.

Master Porion didn't seem to mind how they were dressed.

"From the looks of your leathers, you've been practicing with bears and wildcats!" he said. "The others are at their shooting, so you may as well begin there."

Korin might be lord of the mess table, but Porion was master here. At his approach all eighteen boys turned and made him a respectful salute, fist to heart. A few also raised their hands to smother smirks at the sight of Tobin and Ki's leathers. Someone in the crowd watching the Companions laughed aloud and Tobin thought he caught a glimpse of Moriel's pale head.

The Companions' practice jerkins were as ornate as their banquet garb, worked with raised patterns and colors to show hunting or battle scenes. Fancy gold and silver work glittered on scabbards and quivers. Tobin felt dull as a cowbird by comparison. Even the squires were better turned out than he was.

Remember whose son you are, he thought, and squared his shoulders.

"Today you become a Royal Companion in earnest," Porion told him. "I know I don't have to teach you of honor; I know whose son you are. Here I charge you to add to it the Companion's Rule: Stand together. We stand for the Prince Royal, and we stand with him for the king and Skala. We don't fight among ourselves. If you have a grievance with one of your fellows, you bring it to the circle." He pointed to the stone outline of the sword fighting ground. "Words are met with words and judged by me. Blows are exchanged only here. To strike another Companion is a serious offense, punishable by flogging on the Temple steps. A Companion who breaks the rule is punished by Korin, a squire by his own lord. Isn't that so, Arius?"

One of the squires who'd smirked at Tobin's jerkin gave the arms master a sheepish nod.

"But I don't imagine that will be a problem with you two. Come on and let's see how you shoot."

As Tobin stepped up to the lists, he began to feel a little steadier. After all, these were the same sort of targets he'd trained on at home: bulls and wands and straw-filled sacks for straight shots, and clouts tossed out for arching. Tobin checked his string and the breeze as he'd been taught, then set his feet well apart and nocked one of Koni's fine new arrows to the string. The king vanes were made from striped owl feathers he'd found in the forest one day.

A puff of wind across the field carried his first shaft wild, but the next four found their marks on the bull, all striking close inside the center ring. He shot five more at the sack, and then managed to hit three of the five wands set in the ground. He'd shot better, but when he was done the others cheered him and clapped him on the shoulders.

Ki took his place and pulled just as well.

They moved on to the sword ground next, and Tobin was paired with plump, sandy-haired Nikides, the lord chancellor's kinsman. He was older than Lutha, but closer to Tobin in height. His steel helm was burnished like silver and had fancy bronze work around the rim and down the nasal, but there was something unsure in his stance. Tobin clapped on his own plain helmet and stepped into the circle to face him. As they saluted each other with their wooden practice blades, Tobin's first bout with Ki came back to him. A new opponent wouldn't catch him off guard this time.

Porion set them no slow drills or forms, just raised his own sword, then dropped it with the cry, "Have at it, boys!"

Tobin lunged forward and got past Nikides' guard with surprising ease. He expected a swift reprisal, but Nikides proved to be clumsy and slow. Within a few minutes Tobin had driven him to the edge of the circle, knocked his sword from his hand, and scored a killing thrust to the belly.

"Well fought, Prince Tobin," the boy mumbled, clasping hands with him. Tobin noted again how soft his palm was, compared to the warriors he'd grown up among.

"Let's try you with someone a bit tougher," Porion said, and called Quirion into the ring. He was fourteen, a hand taller than Nikides, and leaner built. He was left-handed, too, but Tharin had made Tobin practice with Manies and Aladar back home so this didn't throw him. He shifted his weight to accommodate the difference and met Quirion's opening attack solidly. This boy was a better fighter than Nikides and scored a bruising blow on Tobin's thigh. Tobin quickly recovered and got his blade under Quirion's, forced it up, then gutted him. Ki hooted triumphantly outside the circle.

This time Porion said nothing, just motioned Lutha into the ring. Lutha was smaller than Tobin, but he was sharp-eyed, quick, and had the advantage of having watched Tobin fight. Tobin soon found himself being pushed, and had to turn to keep from being forced past the stone perimeter. Lutha grinned as he fought, and Tobin could almost hear Tharin's voice saying *a real warrior, this little one*.

Tobin rallied and beat him back, raining blows down at his head that Lutha had no choice but to fend off. Tobin was dimly aware of the cheering around them, but all he could see was the bowed figure before him, boldly facing him down. He was sure Lutha was about to fall back when his own blade shattered. Lutha sprang at him and Tobin had to dodge sideways to avoid a killing swing. Using one of the tricks Ki's sister had shown them, he checked his own rush and took advantage of Lutha's overbalanced stance to trip him up. Much to his surprise, it worked, and Lutha went sprawling on his belly. Leaping on the boy's back before he could recover, Tobin got an arm around his neck and pretended to cut his throat with his broken sword.

"You can't do that!" Caliel protested.

"You can if you know how," said Porion.

Tobin climbed off Lutha and helped him up.

"Who taught you that move?" the boy asked, dusting himself off.

"Ki's sister."

The statement was met with resounding silence. Tobin saw a mix of disbelief and derision in many of the faces of the onlookers outside the circle.

"A girl?" Alben sneered.

"She's a warrior," Ki said, but no one seemed to hear him.

Lutha clasped hands with Tobin. "Well, it's a good one. You'll have to teach it to me."

"Who's next in the ring with our mountain wildcat?" asked Porion. "Come on, he's whipped three of you. No, not you Zusthra. You know you're too big for him. Same for you, Caliel. Alben, I haven't heard much from you yet today."

Alben was fourteen, tall, and dark, with a sulky mouth and shining blue-black hair that he wore in a long tail down his back. He made a show of knotting this up behind his neck, then ambled into the ring to face Tobin. Many of the girls in the crowd pushed forward to watch, Aliya and her friends among them.

"None of your tricks now, Prince Wildcat," he murmured, twirling his wooden blade from hand to hand like a juggler's stick.

Distrustful of such showy moves, Tobin took a step back and assumed the salute position. With a sly, knowing nod, Alben did the same.

When they fought, all the showiness disappeared. Alben fought like Lutha, hard and skillfully, with more height and strength behind it. Already tired from the previous bouts, Tobin was hard pressed to keep up his guard, much less press an attack. His arms ached and his leg hurt where Quirion had struck him. If he'd been at practice with Tharin, he might have given, or called truce. Instead, he thought of the sneering way this boy had spoken of Ki's sister and threw himself into the fight.

Alben fought rough, butting him with his shoulders and head whenever he saw an opening. But Tobin was no stranger to this sort of rough-and-tumble, thanks to Ki, and responded in kind. He began to think it might be in fun after all, that he and Alben had found a way to make friends, but the look on the older boy's face told him otherwise. He didn't like being matched by a younger boy, or at least not by Tobin. Tobin gave rein to his own anger again. When Alben caught him in the nose with his elbow, the pain only put the strength back into him and he laughed aloud as he felt the shock of his blade against the other boy's.

Sakor's luck was still with him, or maybe the gods hated a sneerer that day, for he was able to trip up Alben with the very same trick he'd used on Lutha. Alben went down on his back with the wind knocked out of him. Tobin sprang on him and put his sword to his heart.

"Do you yield?"

Alben glared up at him but saw that he had no choice. "I yield."

Tobin withdrew and walked out of the circle to where Korin and Ki stood with Porion.

"Our new Companion's been bloodied," the arms master observed.

Tobin looked at him, then at the cloth Ki was holding out to him.

"Your nose, Tobin. He scored one hit on you, anyway."

Tobin took the cloth and wiped at his bloody nose and chin. The sight of the stained cloth brought back the fleeting fragment of a dream.

You see blood, you come here.

He shook his head as Korin and some of the others thumped his back and told him what a fine swordsman he was. This was an honorable bloodying. Why would he go running home for that? It had just been a silly dream.

"Look at you! Scarce half-grown and you've already taken down half the Royal Companions," said Korin. He was clear-eyed today, and Tobin found himself basking in the older boy's praise. "Who taught you to fight so well, coz? Not Ki's sister, surely?"

"My father and Sir Tharin were my teachers," he told him. "And Ki. We practice together."

"When you've rested a bit, would you two fight for us?" asked Porion.

"Certainly, Arms Master."

Ki fetched him a mug of cider from a barrel nearby, and they watched Korin and Caliel fight a practice match while Tobin rested. Lutha and Nikides joined them with their squires, Barieus and Ruan. The others kept their distance and watched the prince. After the praise from the prince and Porion, it felt awkward to be standing apart.

"Did I do something wrong?" Tobin asked Lutha.

The other boy looked down at his feet and shrugged. "Alben doesn't like to be beaten."

"Neither did you two."

Lutha shrugged again.

"Lutha will beat you next time, now that he knows how you fight," said Nikides. "Or maybe not, but he'll have a chance and he's always good-hearted about it. I won't, though."

"You might," Tobin told him, though he guessed the boy was right.

"No, not against you," Nikides insisted, apparently unconcerned. "But that's no matter. Not all of us are here because we're great warriors, Prince Tobin."

Before Tobin could ask what Nikides meant, the older boys had finished their match and Porion was calling them into the ring.

"All right, then. Let's give 'em a proper show," Ki whispered happily.

Putting aside their wooden swords, they drew steel and fought, no holds barred, using elbows and knees and butting helmets. They yelled their war cries and fought until the dust rolled higher than their heads and sweat soaked through their mail and jerkins. Steel rang on steel as they battered at each other's guards and Ki came close to smashing Tobin's sword hand. Tobin caught him a flat-bladed smack on the helmet in return, but neither would give. For the space of the battle nothing else mattered and Tobin lost himself in the familiarity of the fight. They'd done this so often and were so well matched that they eventually fought each other to a standstill and Porion called a draw.

They stepped apart, panting and winded, and found themselves in the center of a crowd of spectators. Many of Alben's female admirers were watching them now. Ki noticed and nearly tripped over his own feet. Aliya turned and said something to a slender blond girl beside her and they both laughed. Behind them, a brunette closer to Tobin's age stood watching him with dark, serious eyes. He didn't remember seeing her before. She caught him looking and disappeared into the surrounding crowd.

"By the Flame!" Korin exclaimed. "You weren't joking when you said you did nothing else back in your mountains but fight!"

Not even proud Alben could hang back in the face of Korin's obvious approval. The pair was allowed to rest again, but both were in demand for the rest of the afternoon among the younger Companions and squires.

But not against Prince Korin, Tobin noted. Korin fought only against Caliel and Porion, and defeated both of them most of the time. Tobin was glad not to have been paired against him. Alben had been hard enough to defeat. Of all of them, however, he'd already set Lutha as his main challenger. He was as slippery as Alben, but Tobin liked him a good deal better.

Chapter 41

Ki was glad that there was no great feast on their second night in Ero. Instead, he began his regular duties at table in the Companion's mess. This meal, eaten in a smaller hall, was conducted like any noble table. A few musicians entertained them, and couriers from the king read out dispatches and descriptions of the latest battles.

Each squire had his appointed role. Tanil served as carver of the meats in each course, and Caliel's squire Mylirin as panter, with his four knives for the different breads. These were the services of highest distinction.

Garol had the alchemist's task of butler, mixing the wines and spices with water. It could be a dangerous task; the butler must always "prove by the mouth" to test the wine's quality and therefore was usually the first to be poisoned if someone meant to kill the host. According to Squire Ruan, Garol was more likely to kill the rest of them by mixing the wine too strong.

Orneus' squire, a quiet, graceful boy nicknamed Lynx, was the mazer, whose task it was to keep the footed cups filled with the appropriate wines during each course. Ruan served as almoner, in charge of collecting scraps to be sent out to the beggars at the Palatine gates. Ki and the rest were sent off as ushers to carry in food from the kitchens, with Zusthra's squire, Chylnir, as their captain. Unfortunately, this left Ki at the mercy of his least sympathetic companions in arms.

Even with friendly Squire Barieus to help him, Ki was always one step behind or forgetting something. The other ushers, Mago and Arius, were too busy looking down their long noses at him to give him any help. Chylnir had little patience with any of them.

It hurt Ki's pride to make such a poor showing for Tobin in front of the others. He managed to upset two sauce basins that first night, and nearly dumped a steaming swan's-neck pudding on Korin's head when Mago bumped his elbow. He ended the evening splattered with grease and plum sauce, then had to endure the snickers and smirks of the others during the evening's hearth entertainments. Korin passed it off graciously with a joke and Tobin was happily oblivious, clearly not feeling dishonored in the least. Ki sat outside the circle of firelight, feeling low-spirited and out of place.

*T*obin guessed that something was bothering Ki, but couldn't guess what it might be. Tobin had been proud of him at table; he'd even gotten praise from Prince Korin.

Ki's mood didn't seem to lighten any when Porion and the older boys began telling more tales of the palace ghosts around the hearth that night, elaborating on where the different apparitions were most likely to be found. There were weeping maids and headless lovers at every turn, if all the stories were to be believed, but the most fearsome ghost was that of Mad Agnalain herself.

"Our grandmother wanders these very halls," Korin said, sitting close beside Tobin as he imparted the tale. "She has a golden crown on her head, and blood runs down from it into her face and over her gown—the blood of all the innocents she sent to the torture chambers and gibbet and crow cages. She has a bloody sword in her hand, and a golden girdle hung with the pricks of all the consorts and lovers she took."

"How many are there?" asked someone, and it sounded like an old question.

"Hundreds!" everyone chorused.

Judging by the grins being exchanged among the younger boys, Tobin guessed that this was a test to see if the new Companions would show fear. Tobin had been in enough haunted places in his life to know the feel of one; so far he hadn't sensed anything at all here at the Palace, or even in the royal tombs among the dead.

He stole another glance at Ki, sprawled on the rushes at the edge of the fire-lit circle. He was maintaining a carefully bored expression, but Tobin thought he saw some uneasiness in his friend's eyes. Perhaps living around Brother for so long hadn't cured him of his fears, after all.

As the tales went on of floating heads and ghostly hands and unseen lips that blew out lamps in the night, Tobin found he wasn't feeling all that brave himself. By the time they went back to their huge, shadowy room he was more glad than usual of Ki's company and for little Baldus on his pallet by their door.

"Have you ever seen a ghost here?" he asked when the other servants had gone away for the night. Molay slept on a pallet outside their door to keep guard.

"Oh, yes! Lots," the boy said, sounding quite cheerful about it.

Tobin pulled the bed curtains tight, then exchanged a troubled look with Ki. The bed might be large enough for a whole family, but they settled down close enough to touch shoulders all the same.

They were awakened sometime later by ominous scuffling and clacking sounds that came from all directions at once.

"Baldus, what is that?" Tobin called out. Someone had put out all the lamps. He couldn't see a thing.

The noises grew louder and surrounded the bed. Both boys lurched up onto their knees, back to back.

The unnatural glow of lightstones broke in on them as dead white hands yanked back the bed curtains.

Tobin choked back a cry of alarm. The room was filled with shaggy humped figures that moaned and clacked long white bones together in their hands as they marched around the bed.

The cry quickly turned to a muffled laugh. Even in this light, he recognized Korin and Caliel beneath the black and white paint that covered their faces. They had on long black cloaks and what appeared to be wigs made out of frayed rope. The light came from several lightstones set on long poles that some of the others carried. There were too many for this to be only the Companions; looking more closely, he made out some of the young noble boys and girls who hung about the training grounds. Tobin could smell the wine on them, too. Baldus was crouched on his pallet by the door, both hands pressed over his mouth, but he looked to be shaking with laughter rather than fear.

"Are you ghosts?" Tobin asked, trying hard to keep a straight face.

"We are the ghosts of the Old Palace!" Caliel wailed. "You must prove your worth, New Companion. You and your squire must enter the forbidden chamber and sit on the throne of the mad queen."

"Very well. Come on, Ki." Tobin slid out of bed and pulled on his discarded trousers.

Their ghostly escort blindfolded them, then hoisted them up and carried them for what felt like a long way to a cold, quiet place that smelled of rot and the sea.

When Tobin was set on his feet and the blindfold pulled away, he found himself standing beside Ki in a corridor similar to most they'd seen in the Old Palace, except that this one had gone to ruin. The fish pool down its center was empty and choked with dead leaves, and stars showed through holes in the roof overhead. What murals remained on the rain-washed walls were flaking and faded. Before them was a set of doors similar to those at the front of the Palace, but these were sheathed in gold and sealed with great plugs of lead pounded in around their edges and struck with official-looking imprints.

His captors didn't look quite so silly in their robes and wigs here.

"This is the old throne room, the forbidden chamber," Korin intoned. "Here Mad Agnalain had a hundred traitors executed in a single day and sat drinking their blood. Here she took a dozen consorts, then sent them to their dooms. On this very throne she commanded that five hundred crow cages be set up on the high road, from here to Ylani, and that every cage be filled. She still walks these halls, and she still sits upon that throne." He raised a white hand and pointed at Tobin. "Here, in the sight of these witnesses, you and your squire must join her. You must enter this chamber and sit in the mad queen's lap or you are not one with us, and no warriors!"

Their escort dragged them through a side door and into a long room where a narrow window stood open. From here, they had to crawl onto a wide ledge high above the gardens and climb into the audience chamber beyond through a broken shutter.

It was a simple enough matter to get into the chamber, but once in, it was as if they'd dropped into a black void. They could see nothing at first, and the echo of every whisper and shuffling step seemed to be swallowed up in endless space around them.

Tobin could hear the others on the ledge outside and knew they were being listened to. Someone tossed in one of the glowing stones, a tiny one that cast light no more than a few feet around. Still, it was better than nothing.

"Tobin, son of Rhius!" a woman's voice whispered from the darkness.

Tobin jumped as Ki clamped a hand around his wrist.

"Did you hear that?" Ki whispered.

"Yes."

"Do you think it's her? Queen Agnalain?"

"I don't know." He tried to sense what he felt when Brother was around, but the place just felt drafty and deserted.

"Come on, they're just playing tricks on us. If there really was a ghost who'd kill us, they wouldn't send us in, would they?"

"You don't think so?" muttered Ki, but he followed when Tobin handed him the lightstone and strode off into the darkness.

At first it felt like stepping off a cliff, but with the lightstone behind him and the starlight that filtered in around the shuttered windows to his right, Tobin soon made out the rows of pillars that marched away into the darkness on either side of the long chamber.

This had been Queen Ghërilain's audience chamber, her throne room. He paused, visualizing the one at the New Palace. The throne there had been at the end farthest from the doors. The doors here should be to his right, so the throne would be to his far left.

"Prince Tobin!" the ghostly voice called. It was coming from his right instead.

He stopped again, recalling the toy palace his father had made for him. It had been a simple box with a roof that lifted off, but inside had been the queen's throne room. This room. And the throne had been in the middle, not at the end, with the golden tablet of the Oracle beside it. Squinting, he could just make out a dark shape to his right that could be a dais. Suddenly he wanted very much to see that throne, and touch that golden tablet for himself. Even if there was a ghost there, she was his kin.

He turned and bumped into Ki, who jumped and grabbed for him again. "What is it? Did you see something?"

Tobin felt for his friend's shoulder; sure enough, Ki was shivering.

Putting his mouth close to Ki's ear, he whispered, "There aren't any ghosts here. Korin and the others were just trying to scare us with their stories tonight so we'd be worked up for this. I mean, look what they had on! Who knows better than *I* do what a real ghost looks like?"

Ki grinned, and for a fleeting moment Tobin considered turning Brother loose here to show the others what a real spirit was capable of. Instead, he raised his voice for the benefit of those listening behind them and said, "Come on, Ki, the throne is just over here. Let's go visit my grandmother."

Their footsteps echoed bravely in the unseen vaulting overhead, disturbing some creatures that ruffled the night air with their soft wings. Perhaps it was the spirits of the dead, but if so, they kept their distance.

Just as he'd guessed, the throne stood on a broad platform in the middle of the chamber. It was approached by two stairs and was shrouded in some dark covering.

"We have to sit on the throne," Ki reminded him. "After you, Your Highness."

Tobin acknowledged Ki's mocking bow with a salute Nari would not have approved of and climbed the steps to the throne. As he bent to draw aside the cloth that shrouded it, the dark stuff gathered itself together into a white-faced figure that leaped at him, brandishing a sword and shrieking, "Traitor, traitor, execute him!"

More startled than frightened, Tobin would have tumbled backward down the stairs if Ki hadn't been there to catch him and push him upright again. Both of them recognized that voice, distorted as it was.

It was Aliya.

"Good—good evening, Grandmother!" he managed, as the rest of the supposed ghosts ran over with their lights to join them. He tried to grasp her hand and kiss it, but she snatched it away.

"Oh, he's no fun at all!" Aliya cried out, stamping her foot in frustration.

"I told you he'd stand fast!" Korin hugged Tobin off his feet. "You owe me ten sesters, Alben. By the Flame, no blood of mine is a coward. And you, too, Ki, though I saw you shaking when you went in. Don't worry; you should have seen Garol." Korin reached out and pulled off the other squire's wig. "He fell down the stairs and almost dashed his own brains out."

"I tripped," Garol grumbled.

"I nearly did, too," Tobin admitted. "But only because Aliya surprised me. She hides better than she haunts."

"I suppose you'd know?" she shot back.

"Yes, I do. Korin, may I see the golden tablet?"

The prince cocked his head. "The what?"

"The golden tablet with the Prophecy of Afra on it. It's here somewhere beside the throne—"

"There's nothing like that here." Korin took Tobin's arm and walked him around the dais. As he'd said, there was no sign of a tablet. "Come on, you two, we've got to celebrate your great triumph here tonight."

Pleased as he was to have passed the test, Tobin was terribly disappointed not to find the tablet. And how could Korin not know of it, growing up here his whole life? Could his father have been mistaken?

As they walked back toward the window, he twisted around for a final look, then pulled free of the prince and exclaimed, "Oh, look! Korin, look!"

There was a ghost here, after all. The carved throne was undraped now and a woman sat upon it. The jostling and noise of the other Companions seemed to fade away around Tobin as he gazed at her. He didn't recognize her but he knew who she was: one of Those Who Came Before—no longer just a figure in a box, or a name in a tale, or one of Korin's silly conjurings, either. This was a ghost as real and knowing as his own twin.

She wore a golden crown and armor of ancient design. Staring at him with eyes as dark and unblinking as Brother's, she rose and unsheathed the sword that hung at her side, then held it out to him like an offering on her open palms.

And there at the foot of the dais stood the golden tablet, as tall as Tobin was himself. It caught the light like a mirror and the lines of lettering on it shimmered and moved as though they were written in fire. He couldn't read the script but he knew by heart what they said.

He wanted to walk back and speak to the queen, learn her name and touch the sword she held, but he couldn't move. He looked around to find everyone staring at him, their faces strange and wary behind their paint. When Tobin looked back at the throne again he saw only darkness. There was no throne, no queen, and no tablet. He was too far away to see anything at all.

Then Ki grinned and said, "You fooled them well, my prince. You even had me looking!"

Korin burst out laughing. "By the Four, cousin, you're a quick one! You've turned our own joke back on us."

"The little trickster!"

Aliya grabbed Tobin and kissed him on the lips. "You terrible child! You even scared me!"

Tobin couldn't help stealing a last look back toward the throne as they continued on. He wasn't the only one to do so.

His victory celebration took place in the gardens below, with wine and cakes the Companions had stolen from the kitchens.

The old audience chamber was forbidden ground, the seals on its door real, though no one seemed to know quite why. Korin and Caliel had invented the game years ago, and carried it on in defiance of the king and Master Porion.

Korin and his marauders took Tobin and Ki to a sheltered bank under a tangled overhang of rose hedge. Lying on the soft, damp grass, they passed the wineskins and cakes.

"So you weren't scared a bit?" Alben jeered.

"Were you when you had to go?" Tobin shot back.

"He was! Don't let him tell you any differently," Aliya scoffed.

Everyone laughed except Alben, who sniffed and flipped his long, black hair over his shoulder, looking offended.

"It's because you know of ghosts already, isn't it?" Lynx asked, made bold by the wine. "I don't mean any offense, Prince Tobin, but we all know the story. They say your twin was stillborn with her eyes open, or under a caul, and turned demon so that your family had to leave the city. They say the ghost followed you all the way to the mountains. Is it true? Do you really have a demon twin?"

Tobin shrugged. "It's nothing, really. Just a haunting spirit."

Ki began to sputter, but Tobin nudged his foot and he subsided.

"My father says that's what comes of consorting with wizards," Zusthra put in. "Go messing about with magic too much and you end up with all sorts of creatures you don't care for lurking about."

"You wouldn't want Lord Niryn to hear that opinion, I'm sure," someone said, and Tobin realized that the would-be squire, Moriel, had been with them all along. He just hadn't noticed him under the wig and paint until he spoke. "Lord Niryn believes that wizards can help strengthen the throne of Skala. What do you say, Korin? You see enough of the fellow."

Korin took a long pull from the wineskin and laid his head in Aliya's lap. "My father's wizard has eyes like two brown stones polished by the sea surf. I can't ever tell what's going on behind those cold hard orbs. So long as he keeps us in lightstones and tricks, I've nothing against the man, but when I'm king I won't need any wizards to win my wars for me, or to guard my throne. Just give me you lot!" He waved the wineskin, spraying its contents liberally over those lying closest to him. "Skalan steel and a brave Skalan to wield it!"

This toast led to singing, and the singing to more drinking. Even Tobin let himself get a little drunk before Ki hauled him off to bed in disgust.

Chapter 42

Tobin and Ki came off the training field a few days later to find Tharin and half a dozen of his men waiting for them. Tobin hardly recognized them at first. Koni and the others wore new uniforms similar to those of the King's Guard, with silver badges instead of gold. Tharin was dressed like a lord in somber brown edged with black, and wore a silver chain.

"My prince," said Tharin. "The steward sends word, asking if your highness will inspect your house today. Everything has been made ready for you."

Tobin strode up to hug him, he was so glad to see a familiar face, but Tharin gently held him off and shook his head ever so slightly. Ki hung back, looking like he wanted to do the same.

They got leave from the arms master and followed Tharin into the labyrinth of noble dwellings that filled the grounds between the two great palaces.

The house that had belonged to Tobin's mother was actually a small wing attached to the outer wall of the Old Palace, surrounded by its own walls and courts. The gardens inside the main courtyard had been well tended, but once inside the house itself Tobin felt a strange emptiness close in around him, even though the hall had fine carved furnishings and brightly painted walls. Half a dozen servants in livery bowed to him as he entered. The steward was a middle-aged man Tharin introduced as Ulies, old Mynir's son.

"I grieve for your loss," Tobin told him.

Ulies bowed again. "And I for yours, my prince. I am

honored that he served you and your family, and hope
that I may do the same."

Tobin turned slowly, taking in the great hall, with its
ancient sideboards, hangings, and elegant carvings on the
beams and walls. A broad staircase led up to his left.

"Your father carried you down those stairs the day
you were named," Tharin told him. "You should have
seen this room, filled with all the great nobles of Skala.
The king himself stood just there at the bottom of the
stairs with Prince Korin on his shoulders. By the Four,
how proud we all were!"

Tobin looked up at him. "Where was my mother?
Was—was she well then?"

Tharin sighed. "No, Tobin, she wasn't. From the night
of your birth she wasn't, but that's no fault of yours. She
stayed up in her room."

"May I see it?"

"Of course. This is your house now and you can go
anywhere you like. But the upstairs rooms haven't been
lived in since your mother left. Your father and I used
chambers on this floor when we were in Ero, and the men
have a barracks in the back court. Come on."

Tobin looked around for Ki. "Well, come on!"

They were halfway up the stairs when Brother appeared above them, waiting for him at the top.

He shouldn't have been there. Tobin hadn't called
him all day.

Actually, he hadn't called him since that first night, he
realized guiltily. There'd been so much to see and do here
that he'd completely forgotten.

Yet Brother was there all the same, staring at him with
black, accusing eyes. Tobin sighed inwardly and let him
stay.

"Did you see my twin, Tharin?" he asked. "The one
who died?"

"No, I was away at Atyion that night. By the time I returned all had been dealt with."

"Why didn't Father ever talk about that, and tell me what the demon really was?"

"I don't know." Tharin paused at the top of the stairs, not realizing that his hand brushed Brother's shoulder as he spoke. "Perhaps out of respect for your mother? She couldn't bear the mention of it, especially in the early days. It made her quite—wild. And then there was all the gossip around the city of ghosts and hauntings. After a while none of us spoke of it at all." He shook his head. "I assumed he'd said something to you on his own. It wasn't my place."

He lifted the latch of a door just across from the head of the staircase. "This is it, Tobin, the room where you were born."

The corridor floor was freshly laid with rushes, and smelled of strewing herbs and lamp oil. In the room beyond, however, Tobin recognized the stale smell of disuse. The shutters were open but the room was dismal and cold. Gooseflesh prickled up his arms as he stepped inside.

It had been a lady's bedchamber. A few tapestries still hung on the walls—faded scenes of ocean creatures and forest hunts. There were fish of some sort carved on the mantel, very pretty, but the hearth was cold and full of soot, and there were no ornaments or dolls on the bare stone mantel.

Across the room Brother stood at the foot of a high, tall-posted bed with a bare mattress. He was naked now, and Tobin could see the line of blood-crusted stitching on his chest again. As Tobin watched he climbed onto the bed and lay down on his back. Then he was gone.

"Do you know how my brother died?" asked Tobin softly, still staring at the bed.

Tharin looked at him. "Stillborn, Nari said. Never drew breath. But it wasn't a boy child, Tobin, it was a little girl."

Ki gave him a questioning look; surely he'd speak the truth to Tharin? But here was Brother again, standing between them with a finger to his lips. Tobin shook his head at Ki and said nothing.

Instead, he turned away, seeking some sign of his mother in this empty room. If she had changed so terribly the night he was born, then perhaps there was some trace here of who she'd been before—something to help him understand why she'd changed.

But he found nothing and suddenly he didn't want to be here anymore.

The other chambers along the corridor were the same: long since deserted and emptied of all but the largest furnishings. The more he saw, the lonelier he felt, like a stranger wandering somewhere he did not belong.

Tharin must have sensed this. He put an arm around Tobin's shoulders and said, "Come back downstairs. There's a place I think you'll like better."

They went down through the hall and along a short corridor to a cozy, dark-paneled bedchamber that Tobin recognized at once as having been his father's. Rhius hadn't been here in months and would never return, but there was still a feeling of life in this room. The heavy dark red hangings around the bed were just like the ones at the keep. A pair of familiar shoes stood on a chest. A half-finished letter in a bold scrawl lay curling on the writing desk beside an ivory portrait of Tobin. Tobin breathed in the familiar mix of scents: sealing wax, oiled leather, rust, herbs, and his father's own warm, manly smell. On a shelf by the writing desk Tobin found a collection of his wax and wooden sculptures—gifts to his father over the years—lined up and saved just as Tobin had saved the tokens his father had sent to him.

All at once the ache of loss he'd managed to hold at bay returned full force. He clenched his teeth against it, but the hot tears came anyway, blinding him as he sank down. Strong arms caught him; not his father, but Tharin holding him tight, patting his back as he had when Tobin was very small. There was another hand on his shoulder, too, and this time he was not ashamed at showing weakness in front of Ki. He believed him now; even warriors had to grieve.

He wept until his chest hurt and his nose ran, but in the end he felt lighter, freed of some of the burden of sorrow he'd carried so deeply. He pulled away from them and wiped his nose on his sleeve. "I'll honor my father," he said, looking around the room again with gratitude. "I'll carry his name into battle and be as great a warrior as he was."

"He knew that," said Tharin. "He always spoke proudly of you."

"May I have this room as mine, when I stay here?"

"You don't have to ask, Tobin. It all belongs to you."

"Is that why Koni and the others are wearing different uniforms now?"

"Yes. As your parents' sole heir, you take the rank of your mother and all your father's holdings fall to you."

"My holdings," Tobin mused. "Can you show me?"

Tharin opened a chest and took out a map. On it Tobin recognized the outline of the Skalan peninsula and the territories to the north of it. A tiny crown on the eastern coast marked Ero. He'd seen maps like this before, but on this one there were other places marked in red ink. Atyion lay to the north, and Cirna was a dot on the thin bridge of land that connected Skala to the mainland. There were red dots up there in the territories, too, and across the mountains on the northwestern coastline where there were almost no cities at all. Which ones would Ki like best, he wondered?

"All these belong to the Crown until you're of age, of course," Tharin said, frowning down at the map.

"That worries you."

"It's nothing we have to think about for now." Tharin tried to smile as he put the map away. "Come and see my room."

They walked to the next door along the passageway and Tharin showed them in.

This chamber was austere to the point of severity by comparison, with plain hangings and few comforts. The only exceptions were a fine collection of weapons hung on one wall, collected from many battlefields, and more of Tobin's little creations on a table near the window. Tobin went over and picked up a lopsided wax man with a wood splinter sword in one round fist. He wrinkled his nose. "I remember this one. I threw it out."

Tharin chuckled fondly. "And I saved it; it's the only portrait ever done of me. These others were gifts from you, remember?" He pulled a crude little wooden Sakor horse on a knotted bit of string from the neck of his tunic. "This is the first one you ever made for me. All the other men have them, too. We wear them for luck."

"You should have him make you a new one," said Ki with a laugh. "He's improved quite a lot since then."

Tharin shook his head. "It was a gift from the heart. I wouldn't trade this little fellow for all the horses of Atyion."

"When can I go to Atyion?" Tobin asked. "I've heard tales of it all my life. Even Ki's seen it, but not me! And Cirna and all the other estates and holdings?"

There was that hint of a frown again as Tharin replied, "You'll have to speak to Lord Orun about that. He's the one who must arrange any travel outside the city."

"Oh." Tobin made no effort to hide his dislike here. "When do you think the king will come back? I'm going to ask him to give me a new guardian before he goes away next time. I don't care how rich or powerful Orun is, I can't stand the sight of him!"

"Well, I've been hoping to have a talk with you about that. That's one of the reasons I brought you here today." Tharin closed the door and leaned against it, rubbing a hand over his bearded chin.

"You're young, Tobin, and you've no experience of court life. I can't say I'm sorry about how you've turned out because of that, but now that you're here, it may hurt you, not knowing how things are done. Illior knows, there hasn't been much time to speak of all the changes— It took us all by surprise when he showed up. But now that we're all split up this way, there are some things you need to hear. I swore to your father that I would watch over you, and I don't know of anyone else who can tell you what I'm about to tell you. Ki, you listen well, too, and don't you ever breathe a word of it to anyone."

He sat the boys on the edge of his bed and pulled up a chair.

"I don't care much for Lord Orun, either, but you keep that to yourselves. He's the king's friend, and one of his highest ministers, so it wouldn't do you any good if that's the first thing your uncle hears from you when you meet. Understand?"

Tobin nodded. "Prince Korin says I should be careful of him, because he's a powerful man."

"That's right. At court you must say less than you think and only speak as much of the truth as will do you good. I'm afraid that's something we didn't teach you before, but you always were a good one at keeping quiet about things. As for you, Ki—"

Ki blushed. "I know. I'll keep my mouth closed."

"It's for Tobin's sake. Now, it costs me some pride to say it, but I want you both to keep on Lord Orun's good side while you have to."

"You sound like you're scared of him!" Ki blurted out.

"You could say that. Orun was already a powerful lord at court when Rhius and I were in the Companions. He was only the third son of a duke, but his father was rich and had the mad queen's ear. I mean no disrespect to your family, Tobin, but your grandmother Agnalain was mad as a cat in a high wind by the end and Orun still managed to come out alive and with power. Erius likes him, too, which is more than your father or I could ever fathom. So crossing Orun is only fouling your own nest. Keep peace between you. And . . ." He stopped, as if unsure what to say next.

"Well, if either of you has any trouble with him, you come to me. Promise me that."

"You know we will," Tobin replied, though it seemed to him that Tharin was looking at Ki as he said this.

A knock came at the door and Tharin went to deal with a courier who'd arrived. Tobin sat a moment, pondering all he'd been told, then rose to go back to the hall. When he came out into the passage, however, Ki tapped his shoulder and whispered, "I think our friend is here. I've been feeling him since we were upstairs."

Tobin turned in surprise, realizing that Ki meant Brother. "You can feel him?" he whispered back. He'd lost track of the spirit upstairs and hadn't seen him since.

"Sometimes. Am I right?"

Tobin looked around and, sure enough, there was Brother behind them, beckoning for Tobin to follow him down the passage in the opposite direction. "Yes. He's there. I didn't call him, though."

"Why should he act any different here?" muttered Ki.

Following Brother, the boys passed through a succession of narrower passages and out into a small disused courtyard surrounded by a high wall. There was a summer kitchen here, but the mossy roof over the outdoor oven had fallen in years ago and never been repaired. Near the center of the yard stood a huge, dead chestnut tree. Its twisted branches stretched their broken fingers over the yard like a netted roof, grey and scabrous against the blue sky. Its knobby roots humped up out of the packed earth like serpents writhing across the ground.

"Can you still see him?" Ki whispered.

Tobin nodded. Brother was sitting at the base of the tree between two big roots. His legs were drawn up tight against his chest and his forehead rested on his knees. Tangled black hair hung down, covering his face. He looked so forlorn that Tobin slowly moved closer, wondering what the matter could be. He was within a few feet of the spirit when Brother raised a pale, tear-streaked face to him and whispered in a dry, weary voice Tobin had never heard before, "This is the place," and faded from sight again.

Baffled, Tobin stared up at the tree, wondering what was remarkable about this spot. He'd understood about the bed; Brother had been stillborn upon it and seemed to remember it. But why would he remember this yard, or this tree? He looked back at where Brother had been sitting and spied a small opening beneath one of the roots. Squatting down, he examined it more closely. It was larger than it had looked at first glance; eight or ten inches wide and a few inches high on the outside. It reminded Tobin of the sort of place he used to look for in the forest as a hiding place for the doll.

The soil here was sandy and hard, well sheltered by the tree. Curious, he reached inside to see if the hole was as dry as it looked.

"There could be snakes," Ki warned, hunkering down beside him.

It was larger inside than he'd have guessed, large enough for the doll if he could get it through the opening. His fingers found no snakes, only a few spiky chestnut husks among the dead leaves. As he moved to withdraw his hand, however, his fingers brushed across a rounded edge. He felt more closely, then got enough of a grip on it to dislodge it from the soil. Drawing it out, he saw that it was a gold ring set with a carved stone like the one Lord Orun had given him. He rubbed it on his sleeve to clean it. The large flat stone was the same deep purple as the throat of a river iris, and carved with the intaglio profiles of a man and a woman, side by side with the woman's foremost.

"By the Flame, Tobin, isn't that your father?" asked Ki, peering over his shoulder.

"And my mother." Tobin turned the ring over in his hands and found an *A* and an *R* engraved on the gold band behind the stone.

"I'll be damned. Brother must have wanted you to find it. See if there's anything else."

Tobin felt again, but there was nothing more in the hole.

"Here you are!" said Tharin, coming out into the yard. "What are you doing down in the dirt?"

"Look what Tobin found under this dead tree," said Ki.

Tobin showed him the ring and Tharin's eyes widened. "It's been years— How did that get out here?"

"Was it my mother's?"

The tall man sat down and took the ring from him, gazing at the two profiles on the stone. "Oh, yes. It was her favorite among the betrothal gifts your father gave her. It's Aurënfaie work. We sailed clear to Virésse just so he could have the finest carvers make it for her. I remember the look on her face— We never did know what happened to it after she got sick, or some of her other things either." He looked down at the hole. "How do you suppose it ended up out here? Well, it's no matter. It's found now, and yours to keep. You should wear it in their memory."

It was too large for Tobin's fingers so he hung it on the golden chain with his father's seal, then looked at the carving again. His parents looked young and handsome together, not at all like the troubled people he'd known.

Tharin reached down and took the ring and seal together on his palm. "Now you can carry something of both of them close to your heart."

Chapter 43

The weeks that followed passed in a glittering blur. Life at the keep hadn't prepared either boy for such company, though neither wanted to trouble the other with his doubts at first.

Each morning the Companions ran to the temple to make their offerings, then worked hard on the training field until midafternoon under Porion's demanding direction.

Here, at least, Ki and Tobin both excelled. Porion was a strict taskmaster, but he was as quick to praise as to chastise. He taught the Companions the fine points of buckler work and how to fight and shoot on horseback, but they also learned to use the javelin and the axe, and how to wrestle and fight with knives.

"You fine nobles may start the day in the saddle, but only Sakor knows how long you'll stay there," Porion was fond of telling them, and devised a good many drills designed to unseat them in various jarring ways.

After practice the remainder of the day belonged to the boys to amuse themselves as they pleased until mess time. Sometimes they rode about the city to see players or visit their favorite artisans and tailors. Other times they went to the hills to hunt and hawk, or to the seaside to bathe, enjoying the last warm days of summer.

In these pastimes they usually were accompanied by a great crowd of young nobles, and some not so young. Lord Orun frequently came along, together with others of his ilk—men who wore ear bobs and scent and hadn't gone off to fight. There were women and girls, too.

Ki soon realized that girls like pretty Aliya and her

friends were beyond his grasp, and that a pretty face didn't necessarily mean a pretty heart. Aliya was Alben's cousin and proved to be as spiteful as her kinsman. Prince Korin liked Aliya well enough, though, and through the gossip of the squires Ki learned that she was one of several mistresses who regularly visited the prince's bed, hoping to get him an heir so he could go off to war. What the king would say to that no one cared to speculate.

Still, there were plenty of other girls who found Ki good enough to flirt with. One in particular, Mekhari, had given him several encouraging looks while endeavoring to teach him to dance. Skilled as he and Tobin might be at the arts of war, neither had a proper dance step between them, nor played an instrument; and despite Arkoniel's best efforts, they had the singing abilities of a pair of crows. Their ill wishers took no end of delight in this lack of graces and made certain to include them in any situation that would call attention to these shortcomings.

Tobin managed to redeem himself quite by accident one night at dinner when, in a fit of boredom, he whittled one of his little sculptures from a block of cheese. Soon the girls were pestering him to carve charms and toys for them, offering kisses and favors in return. Tobin modestly refused payment as he hemmed and blushed and carved away furiously for them, clearly not knowing what to do in the face of such attentions.

This puzzled Ki. Tobin was nearly twelve and had heard enough of his tales to know what girls were about. While he might not be old enough to want one yet, it seemed odd that he'd be so standoffish about it. Two in particular seemed to plague him. Pale Lilyan, Urmanis' sister, had taken to flirting outrageously with him, though Ki was certain she only did it because she knew it made Tobin squirm.

But the other one, a slim brunette named Una, was another matter. She was skilled at hunting and riding, and had a quiet way about her that Ki found both pleasant and unsettling; she looked at you like she could read your thoughts and liked them fine. Yet Tobin was more stumble-tongued around her than anyone else. He'd nearly sliced off one of his fingers whittling her a cat.

"What in Bilairy's name is the matter with you!" Ki had chided, bathing the gash in a basin that night as they got ready for bed. "I bet Una would let you kiss her if you tried, but you act like she's got the plague!"

"I don't *want* to kiss her!" Tobin snapped, pulling his hand away before Ki could wrap the finger. Scrambling across the bed, he burrowed under the blankets as far from Ki as he could get and remained there, refusing to talk to him for the rest of the night.

That was the first time Tobin had ever been truly angry with him. Ki laid awake heartsick half the night and vowed never to tease Tobin about girls again.

He had enough to trouble him as it was.

Prince Korin had thrown several more of his lavish banquets since their arrival, ordering them up whenever the whim took him and he thought he could brook Porion's disapproval. Although this meant a respite from table service for the squires, Ki could have done without them. Everyone drank more, especially Korin, and Ki liked the Prince Royal a good deal better when he was sober.

Tobin had taken to his cousin in his usual good-hearted way, but Ki wasn't so sure of his friend's judgment this time. Korin struck him as a weak reed when drunk, too likely to take on the colors of those around him instead of shining with his own. He was more likely to tease then, and overlook the rudeness of others.

And rudeness abounded, though it was often thinly veiled in jest. Their skill on the training field had sparked jealousy among the older Companions, and Tobin's odd behavior that night in the old audience chamber had set a few tongues wagging. But they'd probably wagged before they ever arrived.

Still, seeing Tobin here brought back to Ki how strange the boy had seemed to him when they'd first met: the way Tobin talked to ghosts and witches and wizards as if it were the most natural thing in the world, and how he could read people's faces like others read tracks or weather, without even knowing he was doing it. He'd changed some since Ki had known him, but Tobin still had the eyes of a man, and still made little distinction in his manner toward noble or servant, highborn or low. He treated them all well. Ki had grown accustomed to that, too, during the slow, easy years at the keep. Here among these young lords, it was quickly brought home to him how unusual that was, and in ways that Tobin just didn't seem to understand.

But Ki understood, and so did the Companions—even the ones who were kind. Tobin hadn't understood the shame Ki felt when a drunken prince had slapped him so carelessly with a sword and dubbed him "Sir," bestowing on him a grass knight's hollow title—with its boon of a warhorse and a yearly purse of money. For all the lessons and proper speech he'd learned from Arkoniel, everyone here knew who his father was and had seen how his "knighthood" had been earned.

No, Tobin couldn't understand any of that, and Ki kept his promise to Tharin and didn't tell him. Pride kept him from confiding even in Tharin, though they visited him as often as they could.

Still, it wasn't all bad, he often reminded himself. Tobin was like a drink of sweet water in a swamp, and there were those who knew how to appreciate him. Korin did, when he was sober, and so did the better ones among the Companions: Caliel, Orneus, Nikides, and little Lutha. Their squires were courteous to Ki out of respect for that, and some of them accepted him as a friend.

On the other side of the fence were Squire Mago and his faction; it hadn't taken Ki long to peg them as trouble. They spared no effort to remind him that he was a grass knight, and a poor man's son. Whenever they could corner him out of earshot of the prince—at the stables, in the baths, or even when they were sparring in the sword circle—they hissed it at him like rock vipers: "Grass knight!"

To make matters worse, Moriel, the boy whose place Ki had taken, was fast friends with Mago and cousin to Quirion's squire, Arius. Evidently Moriel's appointment was to have been his way into the Companions.

There was something wrong there, Ki thought. Korin didn't seem overly fond of some of his own Companions, even though they were touted by all as a closely bound elite, the future generals and councilors of a future king. It seemed to Ki that Korin would do well to rid himself of a good many of them when he was old enough to choose for himself.

None of that is my concern, he reminded himself. He was Tobin's squire and in that he was content. Nothing the other squires could say to him would interfere with that.

Or so he thought.

By the end of Rhythin Ki was beginning to get his bearings at table. He could serve any type of dish through a twelve-course banquet without spilling a drop, knew all the right serving dishes, and was feeling rather proud of himself.

That night at mess it was only the Companions and Porion at table. Tobin was seated between the arms master and Zusthra. The older boy was still hard to read; he seemed sullen, but Porion treated him with high regard and Ki took that for a favorable sign.

Tobin seemed happy enough, if quiet. Korin was drinking and going on again about the latest report from Mycena. Apparently the king had routed a Plenimaran attack along some river and everyone was drinking to celebrate the victory, and growing more morose as they grew drunker, convinced the fighting would be over before they were allowed to go.

Ki went out for more platters, and by the time he came back Caliel and Korin were arguing about why hounds didn't like Tobin and hawks did. Ki wished them luck with that one; even Arkoniel had had no answer for the dog question. They'd had to give Tobin's gift hounds away, but he'd turned to out be a fine hand with falcons. Caliel spent a great deal of time with him, teaching Tobin how to use the hoods, jesses, and whistles. In return, Tobin had fashioned a beautiful ring for him from wax, in the shape of a hawk with outstretched wings, and had a goldsmith cast it. Caliel wore it proudly and was the envy of the Companions. Thanks to that, Tobin had switched from wood carvings to jewelry making and their room was littered with gobs of wax and sketches. Tobin already knew half the goldsmiths near the Palatine, and was making inroads among the gem carvers as that took his fancy. Korin dubbed him the Artist Prince.

Ki was pleasantly lost in these happy thoughts as he balanced two half-empty sauce basins back to the kitchen. He was nearly to the sideboard when Mago and Arius cornered him. He glanced around quickly but Barieus was nowhere in sight. The cooks and scullions were busy with their own work.

"No, it's just we three," said Arius, guessing his thought. He jostled Ki on one side and Mago did the same on the other until they had him backed into a corner. Ki barely managed to get the sauce basins down onto a table before they spilled.

"Well done, grass knight," snickered Arius.

Ki sighed and waited for them to back off now that they'd had their fun. But they didn't.

"Well done, for a horse thief's son," sneered Mago, not even bothering to lower his voice.

Ki felt his face go hot. "My father's no thief."

"He's not?" Mago made round eyes of surprise at him. "Well, then you're the cuckold's bastard I took you for all along. Old Larenth has been stealing my uncle's horses for years and everyone knows it. He'd have hanged your brother Alon if he hadn't run away to the war before the bailiff caught him."

Ki faced him down, holding his clenched fists against his thighs. "He's no thief! And neither is my father."

"Then he's not your father," said Arius, pretending to reason with him. "Come on now, which side of the blanket were you born on, Sir Kirothius? Or do you even know?"

It doesn't matter. Ki clenched his fists so tightly he felt the nails bite into his palms. *Only honor matters. Don't dishonor Tobin by losing your temper.*

"What's a prince doing with a grass knight like you for a squire, I wonder?" said Mago.

Arius leaned in closer. "Well, you know what they say about *him*—"

Ki could hardly believe his ears. Were they daring to insult Tobin now? Both boys turned and were gone before he could gather his wits to respond.

"Ki, don't stand there dreaming. Fetch in the damson tart!" snapped Chylnir, who'd just come in.

Honor. Ki summoned Tharin's voice in his mind as he hoisted the heavy pastry dish. *Whatever a squire does reflects on the lord he serves. Keep that thought first in your heart, no matter what, and you'll always do what's proper.*

Thinking of Tharin calmed him. By the time he reached the dining room, he could wish Mago and Arius dead without so much as frowning in their direction.

Instead, he brought all his anger and resentment to the training fields the next morning and every day after. Whenever he could, he paired off with his enemies for swordplay or wrestling, and let his body speak for him. The other boys were good fighters, too, and he didn't always best them, but they soon learned to avoid him when they could.

He and Tobin were hailed as equals of all but the

oldest boys, and Ki wasn't sure they couldn't have taken some of them on, but Porion wouldn't allow it. Crowds gathered to watch the new prince fight. Some of the squires and other blades, including Lutha, began to adopt plainer garb on the training field, though nothing so worn as Tobin's old jerkin. Ki had even sided with Molay and Lord Orun on this issue, trying to talk Tobin into adopting better garb to suit his station, but he wouldn't be moved. He'd wear any finery they wanted to feasts and around the city, but remained stubborn on that point, even when he overheard some of the onlookers joking that they couldn't tell him from Ki in a match. In fact, it seemed to please him.

It was only much later that Ki realized that Tobin understood and resented the petty meanness directed at them as well as Ki did, and chose his own ways of fighting back.

Chapter 44

Autumn came on in a series of terrible thunderstorms that swept in off the sea. Lightning flashed down, striking buildings and sometimes even people. Rain ran in torrents from rooftops and through the streets, washing the year's refuse down to the sea.

The foul weather kept the Companions indoors for days. They practiced at swords in the feasting hall and played wild games of chase through the corridors, much to the despair of those nobles unfortunate enough to encounter them. Several ended up in the fish pools.

Korin held court in his great hall, surrounded by jugglers and minstrels. He brought in troupes of actors and badgered the heralds for news every few hours. And he drank.

Ki and Tobin were sweating through another round of dancing lessons when a page wearing the yellow livery of Lord Orun beneath his dripping cloak appeared and approached Prince Korin.

"Cousin!" Korin called to Tobin. "Your guardian requests our company this afternoon. I suppose we must go. You too, Caliel. I'm sure Orun can make room for you."

"Damn," sighed Ki.

"You'll have a better time here than I will there," groused Tobin. "What does he want with me now? I was just there three nights ago."

Other messengers appeared through the dreary afternoon, calling more of the boys away. Chancellor Hylus called for his grandson, Nikides, who took Ruan with him. Lutha was ill with a fever and Barieus was tending him.

Faced with Mago and few allies, Ki decided to make himself scarce until Tobin came back.

He went back to their room and cast about for something to do, but Molay had put everything in order. Even
Tobin's carving bench was tidy for a change. Deciding to
chance a ride in spite of the weather, Ki threw on old
shoes and a thick cloak and set off for the stables.

"Shall I send for your horse, Sir Ki?" Baldus called after him.

"No," Ki replied, glad of the excuse for a walk after
being shut up inside for so long.

The rain had slackened but a strong wind whipped
his cloak around his legs as he left the shelter of the
palace gardens. His shoes were soon soaked through, but
he didn't care. The pummeling of the wind and the cold,
sharp smell of the sea made his blood race and his heart
feel lighter. He turned his face up and let the wind scour
it. There was plenty of daylight left; perhaps he could get
Tharin to go for a ride by the shore.

The stables were deserted except for a few grooms
and ostlers. They knew him and bowed as he walked
through the sour darkness of the mews. A hundred glossy
rumps faced him on either side; Dragon and Gosi's stalls
were about halfway down on the left side.

He hadn't gone very far when he realized that he
wasn't alone after all.

Turning, he found Mago and Arius almost on his
heels. The sound of the storm must have covered them as
they followed him from the palace. That, and his own
inattention, he thought with sinking heart. There wasn't a
groom in sight now. These two probably had the sense to
bribe them to stay away.

"Why, fancy meeting you here, grass knight," Mago
exclaimed brightly. "And how might you be this fine afternoon?"

"Well enough, but for the company," Ki retorted. They
wouldn't let him pass; that much was clear. There was a

door at the far end of the stable, but it meant turning tail and running, and he'd be damned if he'd do that. He'd rather take a beating. Then again, surely even they wouldn't be that foolish.

"I wouldn't think you'd be so particular about what company you keep," Arius said, toying with a heavy ring on his hand. "Stuck in that rat trap old keep of the duke's with a demon and Tharin's draggle-tailed peasant soldiers? And I'm curious . . ." Arius went on twisting the ring around and around. "Perhaps you can tell me, since you lived there. Is it true what they say about Tharin and Lord Rhius? With you being his son's squire and all, I thought maybe you'd know."

The blood began to pound in Ki's ears. He had no idea what Arius was talking about, but the way he said it was insult enough.

"Maybe it runs in the family, like the madness," Mago put in with a poisonous smile. "Do you and Tobin do it, too?"

Ki began to suspect what Mago was hinting at and went cold with anger. Not at the implied act itself, but at the thought of these spotty-faced bastards dragging two such men down with their filthy leering tones, and Tobin with them.

"You take that back," he growled, advancing on Mago.

"Why should I? You share a bed, don't you? We all saw it the night we went to the old throne room."

"Everyone does where I'm from," Ki said.

"Well, we all know where you're from, don't we, grass knight?" said Arius.

"Two in a bed," Mago taunted. "Lord Orun told me that Tharin used to take it up the ass. Do you? Or is it Tob—"

Ki punched Mago without even deciding to do it. He just didn't want to hear those words, and, in the instant that his fist connected with the older squire's nose, it felt good. Mago went down cursing and landed on his back in the wet muck of a stall, blood spurting from his nose. Arius got Ki by the arm and yelled for help, but Ki threw him off and walked away.

His elation was short-lived. By the time he was out the door at the far end of the stable he knew he'd made a serious error and started running, knowing there was only one place to go. No one followed.

I failed him! he raged at himself as the enormity of the situation crashed in on him. He'd failed Tobin and Tharin. And himself. In the next instant he lashed out at his tormenters. Korin was right; they were all rotting here. Foul mouthed, soft-handed, backbiting little sneak bitches like Mago wouldn't last a day among real warriors. But that didn't change the fact that he'd dishonored Tobin. And now there'd be worse to come.

The clouds opened, the rain lashed down, and Ki ran.

Tobin hated the visits to Lord Orun's house. The rooms were too warm, the food too sweet, and the attendants—a pack of droopy, bare-chested youths—overly attentive. Orun always insisted that Tobin sit next to him and share his dish. The sight of those greasy, wrinkled fingers did little for his appetite.

It was even worse today. Tobin's head had been hurting since he woke up that morning, and he'd had a dull pain in his side that was making him tired and out of sorts. He'd hoped to sleep that afternoon, until the summons came and spoiled his plans.

Orun always insisted on inviting Moriel, as well. Though Tobin still resented this, he had to admit that the pale boy did do his best to be pleasant when they were thrown together here. Then again, almost anyone would seem pleasant company at Orun's table.

There were thirty nobles at the table today, and the king's wizard, Niryn, occupied the place of honor on Tobin's left. Between courses he entertained the company with silly tricks and illusions, like making a stuffed capon dance, or floating sauceboats around like ships in the harbor. Looking down the table, Tobin caught Korin and Caliel rolling their eyes.

He sat back with a sigh. Niryn's magic was even more pointless than Arkoniel's.

Ki managed to keep himself under control as Ulies let him in and led him to the hall. Tharin sat by the fire in his shirtsleeves. Koni and some of the other men were with him, gambling and repairing bits of tack by the hearth. They called out their usual greetings to Ki, but Tharin frowned as soon as he saw him.

"What's wrong?" he asked.

"Can we speak alone?"

Tharin nodded and took him to his room. Shutting the door, he turned and asked, "What happened?"

Ki had rehearsed half a dozen explanations on the way here but now his tongue seemed to have glued itself to the roof of his mouth. There was no fire and the room was cold. Shivering miserably, he listened to the sound of his sodden cloak dripping on the floor as he searched for the words.

Tharin sat down in the chair next to his bed and motioned for Ki to come to him. "Come on, now. Tell me about it."

Ki let his cloak fall and knelt at Tharin's feet. "I've dishonored Tobin and myself," he managed at last, fighting back tears of shame. "I struck another squire. At the stables. Just now."

Tharin's pale eyes fixed on him in a most unnerving way. "Which one?"

"Mago."

"Why?"

"He's been saying things to me."

"Insults?"

"Yes."

"Were there witnesses?"

"Just Arius."

Tharin let out a snort of disgust. "The arrogant little fool. Well, out with it. What did he say that you couldn't walk away from?"

Ki bristled. "I did walk away from a lot! Ever since we came here they've called me grass knight and bastard and a horse thief's son. And I walked away every time. But this time they got me alone in the stables and they— They—" He cringed inwardly at the thought of repeating what they'd said about Tharin. "They insulted Tobin. And Duke Rhius. And you. They said filthy lies and I lost my temper and punched Mago. Then I ran here." He hung his head, wishing he could die and be done with it. "What am I going to do, Tharin?"

"You're going to take your punishment tomorrow like any other squire. But right now I want to hear what they said that made you angry enough to do such a thing. And why being called those other things didn't. Let's start with that, shall we?"

Tharin pulled Ki up by the shoulders and sat him on the bed, then poured him a small cup of wine. Ki downed it and shivered as it burned his belly. "I don't know. Maybe because I knew most of what he said about my kin and me is true. I am a grass knight, but Tobin doesn't care and neither do you or Porion, so I don't mind it so much. And I know I'm no bastard. And that about my father? I don't know. Maybe he is a horse thief, but Tobin doesn't care about that, either, so long as I'm not one. . . . And I'm not! So I can stand any of that."

"Then what was it you couldn't stand?"

Ki clutched the cup in both hands. "Mago said that Lord Orun told him you and Duke Rhius— That you—" He couldn't say it.

"That we were bedmates when we were young? Lovers?"

Ki stared miserably down into the red depths of his

cup. "He said he thought Tobin and I did it, too. But that's not the way he put it—what you said."

Tharin sighed, but Ki could tell he was angry. "I don't suppose it was."

"Tobin and I don't!"

"I didn't imagine you did. But it is common enough among young warriors, and lots of other folk besides. I could tell Mago a thing or two about his own father that would shut him up for you. With some it's something that passes. Others stay with men all their lives. For Rhius, it passed."

He reached out and chucked Ki under the chin, making him look him in the eye. "I'd have told you myself if you'd asked me. There's no dishonor in it between friends, Ki, or half of Ero would be shamed, and some of the other Companions too, from what I've seen."

This revelation left Ki speechless.

"So they teased you all this time, and this is what broke you?"

Ki nodded.

"They poked around until they found the sore spot to goad you with. Well, here you are. What interests me the most is that Mago said he had this from Lord Orun, Tobin's own guardian. I think perhaps that was more than Orun wanted said."

"But why would he say it at all?"

"Use your brains, boy. Who wanted Moriel as Tobin's squire? Who hasn't had use for you since the day he laid eyes on you? Who got his nose put out of joint when Porion put Moriel out of the Companions in favor of you?"

"Orun."

"Whom Tobin just happens to be dining with right now, I believe?"

Ki dropped the cup and jumped to his feet. "Oh gods! He can dismiss me? I've done it, haven't I? Old Slack Guts is going to send me away!"

"He can't dismiss you, not directly. But perhaps he

thinks that Tobin won't be able to discipline you as he must, and that will reflect badly on both of you. Perhaps that's what he's hoping to put in his next report to the king."

"But why? Why does Orun give a damn who Tobin's squire is?"

"Who's closer to Tobin than you? Who would be of more use to Orun if he wanted Tobin spied on than the prince's own squire?"

"You think Orun means to harm him?"

"No, I think he means to control him. And who do you think controls Orun?"

"The king?" Ki whispered.

"Yes. You're too young for this, Ki, but since they've gone after you, you need to know. It's all a great gaming board we're on, and the stake over on the side is Atyion and all the other lands and riches that Tobin holds. You and me? We're guard stones around Tobin, and we're in their way."

"But Tobin's loyal to the king. All he wants is to go and fight for him. Why can't Erius just leave him alone?"

"That's what I don't quite understand myself. But it's not for us to solve that, only to stand by him. And to do that, you're going to have to convince Tobin to flog you properly tomorrow. And you're going to have to tell him what Mago said."

"No." Ki set his jaw. "I know what you've told me is the true way of it, but I don't ever want Tobin knowing that a squire was talking about him and his kin that way."

"But you're going to have to, Ki. You'll have to go before Porion to be judged, and he's going to ask."

"But that means saying it out in front of everyone. Then they'll all know what he said, right?"

"Probably."

"I won't do that, Tharin. I just won't! Some of the others already make fun of him behind his back on account of me, and for seeing ghosts. I don't know what Tobin would do if this all came out, too. He isn't like the rest of us. You know that." Ki was trembling again. "And I don't want him to be, either. I like him just the way he is. So let me do this my way now and I promise you I won't give Lord Orun anything more to write to the king. I'll say it was for the insults to my father and take my flogging and that'll be the end of it. To make me out a liar, Mago would have to tell what he really said, and I don't think he's going to do that. Not in front of Porion."

He stood tensely as Tharin considered this, ready to argue all night if he had to.

But Tharin nodded. "All right then. But be careful, my boy. Some mistakes you can back out of; I think you can with this one. But others you can't. Honor, Ki, always honor. I want you safe. Both of you."

Ki clasped his hand gratefully. "I won't forget again. I swear it."

Actors came in after the feast was finished, but the play was a romance of some sort, incomprehensible to Tobin. He was dozing with his chin on his hand, trying to ignore the ache in his side, when a messenger entered and whispered in Orun's ear.

Orun clucked his tongue, then leaned over to Tobin. "Dear me, there seems to have been some unpleasantness involving that squire of yours!"

Those closest to them turned to stare. Korin had heard, and Caliel, too.

Tobin stood and made a hasty bow. "With your permission, Lord Orun, may I be excused?"

"If you must. I shouldn't bother myself if I were you."

"I'd like to, all the same."

Tobin felt every eye in the room on his back as he hurried out. His side hurt worse than ever.

Baldus was waiting for him at the Palace gate and burst into tears as soon as he saw him. "Hurry, Prince Tobin!

Master Porion and the others are already in the Companion's hall. Ki hit Mago!"

"O gods! Why?" Tobin asked in alarm as they strode down the corridor.

"I don't know, but I hope he knocked his teeth out!" the boy exclaimed tearfully. "He's always been mean to the pages."

A few lamps at one end lit the hall. Ki sat on a bench, looking defiant. Porion stood grimly beside him.

On a second bench Alben sat with Mago, looking no happier. The squire's nose was swollen and his lip was split. Quirion and Arius stood with them. The rest of the Companions stood at attention across the room.

"He did this!" Alben shouted at Tobin, pointing an accusing finger at Ki.

"That's enough!" snapped Porion.

"What happened?" Tobin asked, unable to believe what he was seeing.

Ki shrugged. "Mago insulted me."

"But why didn't you say? Why didn't you tell me and bring it to the circle as we're supposed to?"

"He surprised me, my lord, and I lost my temper. I'm very sorry to have dishonored you and I'm ready to take my punishment at your hand."

Porion sighed. "That's all he'll say, Prince Tobin. He won't even repeat what Mago said."

"It doesn't matter," Ki muttered.

"It does," snapped Porion. "If it's only you he insulted that's one thing. If he said anything about your lord or some other—" He cast a baleful look at Mago. "—then it's another matter altogether. Prince Tobin, command him to speak."

"Ki, please."

Ki shot Mago a disdainful glance. "He called me a bastard and a grass knight. And he called my father a horse thief."

Porion stared at him in disbelief. "And for that you hit him?"

"I didn't like the way he said it."

Tobin looked around at the others again, wondering why Ki seemed the calmest of the lot.

The arms master gave Mago and Arius a hard look. "Is this so?"

The two boys quailed under that scrutiny. "Yes, Arms Master. It's as he said."

They're lying, thought Tobin. But why would Ki protect them?

Porion threw up his hands. "Very well. Prince Tobin, I give Ki into your charge. Alben, I give Mago over to you. Before the offering tomorrow Prince Tobin will mete out Ki's punishment on the Sakor steps. First offense is ten strokes of the lash, and a day and night of fasting vigil. Mago, a fasting vigil might curb that unruly tongue of yours, too, so the same for you. Now get out of my sight!"

Retreating to their chamber, Tobin sent the servants out and rounded on Ki. "What happened? How could you do such a thing?"

"Just being a stupid grass knight, I guess."

Tobin grabbed him by the front of his damp tunic and shook him angrily. "Don't you ever call yourself that! That's not what you are!"

Ki covered Tobin's hands with his own and eased them away. "I did what they said, Tob. I lost my temper like a fool. But they wanted me to. I think they did it on purpose to embarrass you. Don't give them the satisfaction."

"What do you mean?" Tobin demanded. "And how can I do that to you? If I'd been there I'd have hit him myself, and then they could beat the both of us together!"

"Yes, I'm sure you would have. But that's no good. They forced my hand, made me do something against my will, and now they think they've got the laugh on me."

He went to the bed and sat down. "I didn't tell Porion everything. This wasn't the first time, and Mago isn't the only one who's said things. I don't even have to say who, do I? To them, I'm just a grass knight who grew up sleeping in the dirt." He looked up and forced a tired grin. "That's true enough I guess, but the lucky thing is, it makes you strong. Stronger than they are. Ruan told me Arius cried when he got his beating a while back. You don't have enough strength in that arm of yours to make me bawl."

Tobin stared at him, aghast. "I won't hurt you!"

Ki shook his head. "You're going to have to try, though. We have to give 'em a good show, like we always do. If they think that you're too soft to keep me in line, then the king may think again about letting me stay on as your squire. That's what Tharin said. I asked him already. So put your back into it tomorrow and show them that we're tough as mountain oak."

Tobin was trembling now. Ki rose and gripped him by the shoulders. "This is for us, Tob, so we can stay together. You don't want Moriel in here, instead of me, do you?"

"No." Tobin, trying hard not to cry. If Tharin said they could still send Ki away, then it must be so. "But Ki, I don't want—"

"I know that. This is all my fault." He knelt before Tobin as he had with Tharin. "Can you forgive me?"

Tobin couldn't bear it. Weeping, he grabbed Ki and hugged him close.

Ki hugged him back, but his voice was hard as he said, "Listen to me, Tobin, you can't act like this tomorrow, you hear? It's just what they want, the bastards. Don't you give them the satisfaction!"

Tobin pulled back and looked down at Ki; the same warm brown eyes, golden skin, and prominent teeth under the dark lip scruff, but Ki looked almost man grown suddenly. "You're not scared?"

Ki stood up and grinned at him again. "I told you, you're not going to hurt me. You should have seen the hidings my father used to give us. Bilairy's balls, I'll probably doze off before you're finished. Besides, it was worth it to finally shut Mago's foul mouth!"

Tobin tried to match that grin, but it wouldn't come.

Chapter 45

It was still raining the next morning. They jogged to the temple under a cold grey canopy of clouds. Tobin gripped the heavy whip in his hands as he ran and tried to think of nothing but the solid feel of the wet earth beneath his feet; not the hot stitch throbbing in his side, or Ki running like a silent shadow beside him.

Neither of them had slept well and, when morning came, Tobin was dismayed to find his friend curled up in a blanket on the alcove bed across the room. Tobin had almost forgotten that it was there. Ki mumbled something about being restless, and they'd dressed in silence.

They were among the first to appear that morning, and Porion took Tobin aside as they waited in the portico for the rest of the Companions to arrive.

The arms master placed a stiff leather lash in Tobin's hands. It was about three feet long and as thick as his thumb, with a stiff core and a hilt like that of a sword.

"This is no toy," he warned. "Ki doesn't have a man's muscle on him yet. Strike too hard or too often in the same place and you'll open him to the bone and lay him up for days. No one wants that. Stand to his left for five strokes and to his right for the other five, and space them wide. Strike this hard—" Porion slapped the base of the whip against Tobin's palm, "and the tip strikes ten times as hard. When you're done he must kiss your hand, still kneeling, and ask your pardon."

Tobin's stomach turned over at the thought.

*   *   *

*T*he Temple of the Four resolved from the curtain of rain ahead of them, square and forbidding above its steep stairs. It stood at the center of the Palatine and was a nexus for business as well as worship. At this early hour, however, it was frequented mostly by the devout making their offerings at the altars inside.

Broad stairs led up each of the Temple's four sides. The Altar of Sakor stood on the west, and it was on these stairs that the Companions gathered for Ki's ordeal after making their offerings. The priest of Sakor stood in the open doorway at the top of the stairs. "Who has broken the Companions' peace and brought disgrace on his lord's name?" he asked, attracting a small crowd of onlookers.

Tobin looked around. There were soldiers mostly, but Aliya and her friends were there, too, muffled in veils and cloaks against the rain. So were Lord Orun and Moriel. Any goodwill Tobin had had for the boy evaporated as he recognized the gloating look in Moriel's eyes. Tharin was not there, or anyone else from Tobin's household.

"I broke the peace," Ki replied in a loud, steady voice. "I, Kirothius, son of Larenth, unworthy squire of Prince Tobin, am guilty of striking a fellow Companion. I stand ready to take my punishment."

The other Companions formed a box on the stairs around them as Ki stripped off his jerkin and shirt. Kneeling, he leaned forward and braced his hands on a step above him. Tobin took his place on Ki's right and gripped the whip.

"I beg your pardon, my prince," Ki said, his voice carrying clear and strong on the morning air.

Tobin rested the whip across Ki's back, then froze, unable for a moment to get any air into his lungs. He knew what was expected, that Ki would hold no grudge, that there was no turning back. But looking down at that familiar back, with its downy golden line down the spine and the catamount shoulder blades motionless under the sun-browned skin, he thought he wasn't going to be able to move at all. Then Ki whispered, "Come on, Tob, let's give 'em a show."

Trying to gauge as Porion had shown him, Tobin raised the whip and brought it down across Ki's shoulders. Ki didn't flinch, but an angry red welt burned where the whip had bitten.

"One," said Ki, quite clearly.

"No one expects you to count the strokes," Porion said quietly.

Tobin brought the whip down again, a few inches lower. It was too hard; Ki shuddered this time, and droplets of blood beaded the new welt.

"Two," Ki announced, just as clearly.

Someone murmured in the crowd. Tobin thought he recognized Orun's voice and hated the man all the more.

He brought the whip down three more times on that side, ending just above Ki's waist. They were both sweating, but Ki's voice stayed steady as he counted off each stroke.

Tobin changed sides and began again at Ki's shoulders, crosshatching the welts he'd already made.

"Six," said Ki, but this time it came out a hiss. Tobin had drawn blood again. The whip cut into the swollen flesh where the two stripes met and a trickle of blood inched away toward Ki's armpit.

You see blood

Tobin's empty stomach lurched again. He made seven too light, then eight and nine too fast so that Ki had to gasp out the count. By "Ten" his voice was ragged but it was over.

Ki sat back on his heels and reached for Tobin's hand. "Forgive me, my prince, for disgracing you."

Before he could kiss it, Tobin pulled him up onto his feet and clasped his hand like a warrior. "I forgive you, Ki."

Confused by this break with ritual, Ki bent uncertainly to complete the ceremony, pressing his lips to the back of Tobin's hand as they stood facing each other. Another murmur went through the crowd. Tobin saw Prince Korin and Porion both giving them curious but approving looks.

The priest was less happy about the breach. His voice was harsh as he called out, "Come and be cleansed, Squire Kirothius."

The Companions parted silently and Ki climbed the remaining stairs with his head held high, the ten uneven welts showing like fire on his bloodied back. Mago followed to begin his punishment vigil, looking a good deal less heroic.

When they'd disappeared inside Tobin looked down at the whip he still held, then over at Alben, who stood with Quirion and Urmanis. Were they smirking at him? At what he'd just done? He tossed the whip down. "I challenge you, Alben. Meet me in the practice ring. Unless you're afraid of getting your pretty clothes dirty."

Gathering up Ki's discarded jerkin and shirt, he turned on his heel and walked away.

Alben had little choice but to accept Tobin's challenge, though he didn't look too happy about it.

The rain had slackened to a sullen drizzle by the time they squared off in the stone circle. A crowd had followed them from the temple to watch what was all too clearly a grudge match.

Tobin had practiced against Alben often since his arrival in Ero and hadn't often bested the older boy, once Alben had learned to watch for tricks. But today he was driven by pent-up fury, and his years of rough practice with Ki served him well. He battered Alben down into the cold mud again and again. As he swung the wooden sword, it felt almost like the heavy whip in his hand and he wished he could bring it down on Alben's back just once. Instead, he broke through the older boy's guard and hit him across the nasal of his helmet hard enough to bloody his nose. Alben went to his knees and yielded.

Tobin bent to help him up. As he leaned close, he whispered just loud enough for Alben to hear. "I'm a prince, Alben, and I'll remember you when I'm grown. Teach your squire to keep a civil tongue in his head. And you can tell Lord Orun the same."

Alben pulled away angrily, then bowed and left the circle.

"You." Tobin pointed his sword at Quirion. "Will you fight me?"

"I have no quarrel with you. And no desire to catch the plague out here in the rain." He helped Alben back toward the Palace and their friends drifted off with them.

"I'll fight you," said Korin, stepping into the ring.

"Korin, no—" Porion warned, but Korin waved him off.

"It's all right, Arms Master. Come on, Tobin. Give me your best."

Tobin hesitated. He wanted to fight someone he was angry with, not his cousin. But Korin was already in the circle and saluting. He faced Korin and raised his blade.

Fighting Korin was like fighting against a wall. Tobin threw himself into it, wanting to give the prince his best, but Korin met every attack with a block like an iron bar. But he didn't return the attacks, just let Tobin wear himself out until he fell back panting and called a yield.

"There now, do you feel any better?"

"Maybe a little."

Korin leaned on his sword and grinned at him. "You two always have to have things your own way, don't you?"

"What do you mean?"

"Well, the kiss, for one thing. You wouldn't let Ki kneel."

Tobin shrugged. He hadn't planned that. It had just seemed the thing to do at the moment.

"Only equals do that."

"Ki is my equal."

"He's not, you know. You're a prince."

"He's my friend."

Korin shook his head. "What a funny little fellow you are. I think I'll have you for my Lord Chancellor when I'm king. Come on. Let's go eat. Ki and Mago must starve for their sins, but we don't have to."

"I'd rather stay out for a while, if you don't mind, cousin."

Korin looked to Porion and laughed. "Stubborn as his father! Or mine. Suit yourself, then, coz, but don't catch your death. I'll be needing you, as I said before." Korin and the older Companions strode away, followed by their squires.

Lutha and Nikides hung back. "Would you like company?" Lutha asked.

Tobin shook his head. All he wanted right now was to be left alone to miss Ki. He'd have ridden down to the sea if he could, but it was forbidden for Companions to leave the Palatine alone and he didn't have the heart to face Tharin yet. Instead he spent the rest of the day walking the citadel in the rain. It was a gloomy pastime and suited his mood.

He avoided the Temple, telling himself he didn't want to embarrass Ki by intruding on his vigil, but the truth was he wasn't ready to face his friend, either. The memory of the red welts rising on that smooth brown back was enough to make the bile rise in his throat.

Instead, he circled the banks of Queen Klia's great pool and watched the silvery fish jump at raindrops, then made the long walk to the grove of Dalna above the northern escarpment. It was only a few acres of trees, but they were as ancient as the city itself, and for a little while he could imagine himself back home again, on his way to Lhel's oak. He missed the strange little witch terribly. He missed Nari and the servants at the keep. He even missed Arkoniel.

A hearth shrine stood at the center of the grove; Tobin found a wooden carving in his belt pouch and cast it and a few homesick tears into the flames with a prayer to be at his home hearth soon.

Lamps were being lit around the citadel when Tobin happened past the royal tomb. He hadn't come here since the night of his arrival. Chilled and footsore, he went inside to warm himself at the altar flame.

"Father, I miss you!" he whispered, staring into the flame. Had it really only been a few months since he'd died? It didn't seem possible. Tobin felt like he'd been here for years already.

He pulled the chain from his neck and held the seal and his mother's ring in his hand. Tears blurred his eyes as he looked down at the dual profiles on the ring. He missed both of them. Right now he knew he'd even be glad to see his mama in one of her bad spells, if only he could be home again and everything as it had been.

He had no desire to visit the dead below. Instead, he said a long prayer for their spirits. When he was finished he felt a little better.

It was raining harder now. He turned and studied the effigies of the Skalan queens as he waited for it to pass, wondering if he could recognize the ghost that he'd seen in the throne room.

As an artist, he noted with interest the differing styles of the statues. The earliest, Ghërilain the Founder, was a stiff, lifeless figure with a flat face and all her clothes and accounterments molded close to her body, as if the sculptor hadn't had the skill to quite free her from the stone. All the same, he recognized the Sword of Ghërilain clutched in her gauntleted hands—the same sword that all the other statues held. His uncle carried that sword now.

Was it the same sword, perhaps, that the ghost had held out to him? He turned slowly where he stood, studying the stone faces. Which one had she been? For she had certainly been a queen. And if it had been *this* sword she'd held, why would she offer it to him?

He checked quickly to make certain that the altar priest was nowhere around, then whispered, "Blood my blood, flesh my flesh, bone my bone."

Brother appeared, looking transparent in the firelight. How long had it been since he'd last called him, Tobin wondered guiltily. Three days? A week? Perhaps longer. There had been feasts and dances and practices, then all the fuss with Ki. What would Lhel say? He didn't like to think of that.

"I'm sorry I forgot," he whispered. "Look, here are the great queens. You remember the ones in the box at home? This is their tomb. I saw one of them—her ghost. Do you know who it was?"

Brother began circling the effigies, looking up at each one in turn. He came to rest at last in front of one and seemed content to remain there.

"Is that her? Is she the one I saw at the Old Palace?"

"I beg your pardon, Prince Tobin?"

Tobin turned to find the king's wizard standing beside the altar. "Lord Niryn! You startled me."

Niryn bowed. "I might say the same, my prince. I heard you speak, yet I see no one here to listen."

"I—I thought I saw a ghost in the Old Palace once, and I was wondering if it could have been one of the queens."

"But you spoke aloud."

If Niryn could see Brother, he gave no sign. Tobin was careful not to look at the ghost as he answered. "Don't you ever talk to yourself, my lord?"

Niryn stepped closer. "Perhaps. So, do you recognize your ghost here?"

"I'm not sure. They aren't very good for faces, are they? Perhaps that one." He pointed to the one where Brother stood. "Do you know who she is?"

"Queen Tamír, daughter of Queen Ghërilain the First, I believe."

"Then I guess she'd have reason to haunt," Tobin said, trying to make light of it all. "She was murdered by her brother," he went on, nervously rattling off the lesson out of habit. "Pelis contested the Oracle and seized the throne, but Illior Lightbearer punished the land and killed him."

"Hush, child!" Niryn exclaimed, making some sign on the air. "King Pelis did not murder his sister. She died and he was the only heir. No queen has ever been murdered in Skala, my prince. It's most unlucky to even suggest such a thing. And assassins killed him, not the gods. Your teachers were most misinformed. Perhaps a new tutor is in order."

"My apologies, Wizard," Tobin said quickly, taken aback by this unexpected outburst. "I meant no offense in this holy place."

The wizard's stern expression softened. "I'm certain the shades of your ancestors would make allowances for their youngest descendent. You are, after all, the next in line for their throne after Prince Korin."

"Me?" This was even more surprising.

"But of course. The king's brothers and sisters are dead, and their issue with them. There is no one else of such close blood tie."

"But Korin will have heirs of his own." Tobin had never once imagined sitting on the throne of Skala, only that he would serve it.

"No doubt. But he is a young spark yet, and none of his paramours have kindled. Until then, you are next in the line of succession. Your parents never spoke to you of such things?"

Niryn smiled in a way that did not reach his eyes, and Tobin felt a strange, crawling feeling deep inside, like someone was stirring around in his guts with a bony finger.

"No, my lord. Father only said that I would be a great warrior and serve my cousin as he served the king."

"An admirable aspiration. You should always beware of anyone who tries to draw you from the path ordained for you by Sakor."

"My lord?"

"We live in uncertain times, my dear prince. There are forces at work disloyal to the royal house, factions who would have someone other than Agnalain's son rule. If anyone of that ilk should approach you, I hope you will do your duty and speak to me at once. Such disloyalty cannot be tolerated."

"Is that what you and the Harriers do, my lord?" Tobin asked. "Hunt down traitors?"

"Yes, Prince Tobin." The wizard's voice seemed to take on a darker timbre and fill the open space of the tomb. "As a servant of the Lightbearer, I have sworn to see the children of Thelátimos safe on the throne of Skala. Every true Skalan must serve. All falsehood must be purged with the Flame of Sakor."

Niryn reached into the altar fire and drew out a handful of flame. It rested in his palm like water.

Tobin fell back a step, disliking the reflection of this unnatural fire in the man's jasper-colored eyes.

Niryn let the flame run away to nothingness through his fingers. "Forgive me, Your Highness. I had forgotten that you do not enjoy displays of magic. But I hope that you will remember my words. As I said, we live in uncertain times and too often foul appears fair. It is difficult for one so young as you to discern the difference. I pray that the mark you bear on your arm proves a true sign, and that you will always count me among your good councilors. Good night to you, my prince."

The crawling, stirring feeling rippled through Tobin again, less strong this time, then disappeared as Niryn left the tomb.

Tobin waited until the man was out of sight, then sat down at the foot of the altar and wrapped his arms around his knees to fight the fresh chill that had overtaken him.

The wizard's veiled allusions to traitors frightened him. It was as if he was being accused of doing something, yet he knew that he'd done nothing that the wizard could disapprove of. He was loyal to Korin and the king with all his heart.

Brother squatted beside him. *There is no Pelis here*.

Tobin looked around at the effigies. After taking count and looking carefully into their faces he saw that Brother was right. No effigy of King Pelis stood among the royal dead. Niryn was wrong; the lessons his father and Arkoniel had taught him were the truth. But why would the wizard be so insistent?

All the same, Niryn had given him the name of the queen Brother had chosen—the very one King Pelis had murdered.

Tobin went to stand in front of the second queen of Skala and placed his right hand on the stone sword she held. "Hello, Grandmother Tamír."

Chapter 46

The sun came out the next day and Porion ordered them back to outdoor practice.

Tobin hardly noticed the renewed ache in his side as they ran to the Temple, wondering instead how Ki had fared. His heart swelled with relief when Ki emerged, hungry but unbowed. Mago looked the worse for wear of the two, and Ki confided later that he'd stared at the other squire for hours in the dead of night without speaking, just to put the wind up Mago's ass. Apparently it had worked.

The priests had put a salve on Ki's stripes and he joined in at practice without complaint. He joked with his friends among the squires, ignored his enemies, and served at table that night. Tobin decided that everything was settled for the best until bedtime came and Ki pulled back the curtains on the alcove bed.

"You're sleeping there again?"

Ki eased himself down on the edge of the narrow bed and laced his fingers together in his lap. Tobin could tell by the way Ki held himself that he was in more pain than he'd let on. "Baldus?"

The page rose up on his pallet. "Yes, Prince Tobin?"

"Go to the kitchens and see if the cook can make a sleeping draught for Sir Ki."

Baldus scampered out. Tobin barred the door after him and went back to Ki. "What's all this about?"

He shrugged. "I hear that most of the other squires do and—well— You know, people look at us strange enough as it is. I just thought that maybe we ought to do a few things the Ero way."

"Korin likes how we do things our own way. He told me so. He was proud of you yesterday."

"Was he? Well, Korin isn't everybody. And I'm not a prince."

"You're angry with me."

"With you? Never. But—"

For the first time since the trouble began, Ki's brave front crumbled. Tobin saw past it to the tired, beaten-down country boy slumped before him, shoulders held awkwardly to ease the pain.

Tobin sat down beside him and inspected the back of Ki's shirt. It was stained with spots of blood.

"You're bleeding. That'll stick by morning if you leave it. Here, you better let me help."

He coaxed Ki out of the shirt and threw it aside on the bed. The ache in his side was worse tonight, but he ignored it. It was Ki who needed tending now, not him.

The welts had changed from red to purple and black, and the scabs pulled and bled when Ki moved. Tobin swallowed hard, thinking of all the times he'd kept Nari from taking a switch to Ki. Now he'd done this.

"I don't like it here," he said at last.

Ki nodded and a tear dripped off the end of his nose to land on the back of Tobin's hand.

"I wish we could have just gone with Father. Or that the Companions could ride out tomorrow and go find the king. Mostly, I wish I was grown and had my lands, so I could make you a lord. I promise I will, Ki. No one is going to call you a grass knight again after that."

Ki let out a hiccuping laugh and painfully lifted an arm around Tobin's shoulders. "I don't—"

A loud crash came from the direction of the dressing room, startling them both. Tobin jumped to his feet and Ki flinched back, grabbing for his discarded shirt.

Korin and half a dozen of the older Companions and squires came staggering in by way of the hidden panel.

"Cousin, we've come to issue an invitation!" Korin

cried, and Tobin guessed that he'd been drinking steadily since they'd parted after supper. Urmanis and Zusthra were flushed and grinning, too. Orneus had his arms around Lynx and was nuzzling his ear. Caliel looked a bit clearer but Korin's squire, Tanil, was the only sober one. He gave Tobin a bow, looking embarrassed.

"We're off to the city to play and we've come to invite you," Korin went on, staggering into the middle of the room. "And more especially, the inestimable Ki. Get your clothes on, boy, and I'll buy you a whore to take your mind off your back."

Garol staggered sideways from the group and vomited loudly as the others berated him.

"Ah, Urmanis, looks like you two are next for the temple steps," Korin said, shaking his head. "Your squire's dishonored you all over my poor cousin's floor. Now, what was I saying—? Oh, yes. Whores. You're old enough, aren't you, Ki? I've seen you eyeing the girls! By the Flame, you're the best of this rotten lot. We'll get drunk and kick that pimple Mago out of bed. Alben, too, the bugger!"

"No, Cousin. Ki's tired." Tobin stood between the prince and his friend, wondering what he was going to do if Korin decided to force them to go. This was the drunkest he'd seen Korin since the night they'd arrived.

Fortunately Tanil was his ally tonight. "They're too young for your revels, your highness. Besides, Ki's so sore a whore would be wasted on him. Let's get ourselves out before Master Porion catches you and sends you back to bed."

"Damnation, we don't want that! Everyone be *quiet*, for hell's sake!" Korin roared. "Come, coz. Give us a kiss for luck. You, too, imeshamable Kirothius. Good night! Good night!"

Korin wouldn't be satisfied until everyone had kissed Tobin and Ki on both cheeks and been kissed for luck in return, but at last they stumbled out the way they'd come.

As soon as Tobin was sure they were gone he dragged the heaviest chair in the room into the dressing room and braced it against the panel, then called Brother and set him to watch.

He returned to the bedchamber to find Ki washing his face at the basin. He'd let Baldus and Molay in, and they were grumbling to each other as they cleared away Garol's sour vomit.

"It's never like this when the king's at home," Molay muttered. "When Korin was younger Porion could keep him in line, but now—! I'll burn some incense to cut the stink. Baldus, go and fetch some spiced wine for the prince."

"No, no wine," Tobin said wearily.

When the servants had finished, Tobin sent them away for the night, then pulled Ki back to the large bed. "You saw what comes of doing things the Ero way. Go to sleep."

With a sigh, Ki gave in and sprawled on his belly at the far edge of the bed.

Tobin lay back against the bolsters and tried to ignore the smell still noticeable through the roiling clouds of incense. "What was Ornews doing to poor Lynx?"

Ki snorted into his pillow. "What did you do yesterday while I was flattening my knees with Mago?"

Tobin thought back over the long grey day. "Nothing, really. But I met Niryn at the tombs last night."

"Fox Beard? What did he want?"

"He said I'm the next heir after Korin until he gets an heir of his own."

Ki turned to regard him thoughtfully. "I guess you are, at that. The way Korin was staggering tonight, you might just get your chance, too."

"Don't joke!" Tobin warned. "If the Harriers heard you even joking, I think maybe they'd come for you. Niryn scares me. Every time he's near me I feel like he's looking for something, like he thinks I'm hiding something."

"He looks at everyone that way," Ki mumbled, slipping fast toward sleep. "All those white wizards do. I wouldn't dare get around any of them. But what have we got to worry about? No one is more loyal than we. . . ." He trailed off into a soft snore.

Tobin lay awake for a long time, remembering the strange feeling he'd had around the wizard, and the secret enemies the man had spoken of. No traitor had better approach him; as little as he might care for the red-bearded wizard, he'd keep his promise to him if any man asked him to betray the rightful ruler of Skala.

Chapter 47

Think it was worth it to them?" Ki whispered to Tobin as Korin and his revelers straggled up for the morning run the next day. Porion was watching them, too, looking like a thundercloud about to burst.

Garol's purging hadn't done him any good; he was as green as a leek and swaying on his feet. The others were less wobbly but very quiet. Only Korin, who'd seemed the drunkest, was his usual self. His morning greeting to Tobin was contrite, however.

"I don't suppose you spared any kind thoughts for us after we left you?" he asked, giving Tobin a sheepish look.

"Did you have fun in the city, Your Highness?" asked Ki.

"We got as far as the gate this time before Porion caught us. We're all to do a penance vigil after training, to cleanse the poisons from us, as he put it. There's to be no wine at table for a month." He sighed. "I don't know why I do it. You will forgive me, won't you, Tob?"

Tobin hadn't been angry in the first place, and Korin's pleading smile would have melted river ice on Sakor's Day. "I'd rather you come in my front door, that's all."

Korin clapped him on the shoulder. "Then it's peace between us? Good. Come on, let's race these laggards to the temple!"

Tobin and Ki led the pack easily today, but Korin kept up with them, laughing all the way. Tobin knew Ki had his doubts about the prince, but he found himself liking the older boy almost as much for his faults as in spite of them. Even drunk he was never gross or cruel the way some of the others were, and it never seemed to affect him afterward. Today he looked as fresh as if he'd spent the whole night sound asleep.

When they'd finished with the temple devotions Porion ran them straight to the archery lists. It was a clear, windless morning and Tobin was looking forward to besting Urmanis, with whom he had a running rivalry.

As he took his place at the mark and drew the first shaft to his ear, however, the belly pain that had plagued him over the past several days took him again, this time with a sharp, sudden stitch that made him catch his breath and release without aiming. The arrow flew wild over a knot of girls watching nearby. They scattered like startled birds.

"Tobin, have you got your eyes open?" shouted Porion, still in a foul humor.

Tobin mumbled an apology. The pain passed, but left him tense and awkward.

"What's the matter, Prince Wildcat?" Urmanis chuckled, stepping up for his shot. "Snake crawl over your shadow?" His arrow sped true to the center of the bull.

Tobin ignored the jibe and nocked another shaft. Before he could draw the pain came again, gripping his bowels like hot claws. Tobin swallowed hard and made himself go on as if nothing was wrong, not wanting to show weakness before the other Companion. He took aim and released in one smooth motion, only to find Brother standing there in front of the bull as the shaft took flight.

The spirit hadn't come without being summoned since that day at his mother's house. The day he'd found her ring.

Brother was mouthing something but Tobin couldn't make it out. Another cramp took him, worse than the last. It was all Tobin could do to stay on his feet until it passed.

"Tobin?" Urmanis wasn't making fun anymore as he bent to look into Tobin's face. "Master Porion, I think the prince is ill!"

Ki and Porion were at his side at once.

"It's just a cramp," he gasped. "I ran hard—"

Porion felt his brow. "No sign of fever, but you're pale as milk. Were you sick in the night?"

Brother stood close enough to touch now. "No. It just took me now, since the run."

"Well then, you'd better go back to your bed for a while. Ki, see that the prince gets to his bed, then report to me."

Brother stayed with Tobin all the way back to their chamber, watching him with unreadable black eyes.

Molay insisted on helping him into bed while little Baldus hovered just behind. Tobin let them pull off his jerkin and shoes, then curled into a tight ball as a new wave of pain struck.

Ki shooed the others back and climbed up beside him. Pressing the back of his hand to Tobin's brow, he shook his head. "You're not feverish, but you're in a sweat. Baldus, go fetch Sir Tharin."

Tobin could see Brother standing behind Ki now, shaking his head slowly. "No, just let me rest," he gasped. "It's probably that pudding we ate last night. I shouldn't eat figs." He gave Ki a rueful grin. "Just leave me with the pot, all right? Go back and tell them I'm all right. I don't want that pack of drunkards gloating over me."

"Is that all?" Ki let out a relieved laugh. "No wonder you ran out of there so fast. All right, then. I'll carry your message and come right back."

"No, stay and practice. I'll be right soon. Porion has enough people to be angry at today."

Ki squeezed his shoulder and then pulled the curtains around the bed.

Tobin listened to him go out. He lay very still, wondering at the strange sensations in his belly. The pain was not so sharp now, and seemed to come and go like waves that made him think of the tide on the beach. As the pain receded, he was aware of another, more unsettling sensation in its wake. He got up and made certain there was no one in the chamber or dressing room. Then, with the curtain pulled tight all around, he undid his trousers and pulled them down to find a small wet stain where the two legs joined. He stared at it, puzzled. He was certain he hadn't soiled himself.

Brother was with him again, staring.

"Go away," Tobin whispered, his voice faint and shaky, but Brother stayed. "Blood my blood—"

He stopped, throat tight with fear as he gauged the position of that stain. Reaching down with shaking fingers, he felt under his privates, still so small and hairless compared to those of the other Companions. On the wrinkled underside of the sac, he felt a patch of sticky wetness on the skin. He stared at his fingertips in alarm; even in this light he could see that it was blood. He could hardly breathe for fear as he reached down again and felt desperately for some sore or wound.

The skin was unbroken. The blood was seeping through like dew.

"Oh, gods!" He knew what this was.

Plague. The Red and Black Death.

All the street-corner mummeries he'd watched came back to him, and the tales the boys shared around the hearth. First you bled through your skin, then huge black sores swelled under your arms and in your groin. In the end you thirsted so badly you'd crawl into a gutter to drink filth before you died vomiting out what blood you had left.

On the heels of this came Lhel's words again. *You see blood? You come to me.* It had been a vision after all.

"What do I do?" he whispered to Brother. But he already knew.

Don't be tell nobody. You love your friend, you don't tell him, Lhel had warned.

He mustn't tell Ki. Or Tharin. Or anyone else he loved. They'd want to help and they'd catch it, too.

He looked around at the bed he and Ki had shared. Had he made his friend sick already?

You love your friend, you don't tell him.

Tobin tied up his trousers and climbed out of the bed. Ki would never let him go off alone. Neither would Lord Orun or Porion or Tharin or anyone else. He found his tunic and got it on before pain pushed hot red fingers through his belly again, making him grit his teeth and curl forward. The seal and ring clinked against his chest inside his shirt. He pulled them out and clutched them like talismans, feeling very alone. He had to get to Lhel.

When the pain receded he went into the dressing room and buckled on his father's blade. *I'm nearly tall enough to carry it, now that I'm dying,* he thought bitterly. *Let me at least be burned with it. There's no one left to pass it to.*

He heard servants talking out in the corridor; there was no escape that way without being seen. Throwing on an old cloak, he knelt and felt at the panel that led to his cousin's room. As Korin had warned, he couldn't open it from his side, but Brother could and did.

Korin's room was similar to his own, but the hangings were richer and done in red and gold. He also had a stairway from his balcony down to the gardens, and Tobin made use of it to escape unseen.

As Ki had feared, Porion kept him at practice half the afternoon. The shadows of the thin pines were stretching into their chamber by the time he finally returned to their room.

"Tobin, how are you?"

There was no answer. He went to the bed and pulled back one of the heavy hangings, thinking his friend must still be asleep, but found the bed empty.

Puzzled, Ki looked around the room. There was the discarded jerkin; Tobin's sword and bow still hung on the carved rack where he'd left them. There were a dozen places his friend could be, and normally Ki would have been content to wait for him to show up or to meet him at the nightly feast, but Tobin's sudden illness had left him uneasy in his mind.

Just then he caught the scuffing of feet on the balcony and turned to see Tobin framed in the brightness of the doorway. "There you are!" he exclaimed, relieved. "You must be feeling better."

Tobin nodded and walked quickly into the dressing room, waving at him to follow.

"How are you feeling? You still look pale."

Tobin said nothing as he climbed to the top of the old cupboard that stood in the dressing room.

"What are you doing?" Tobin wasn't acting himself, Ki thought. Perhaps he was really ill after all. Even the way he moved seemed odd, though Ki couldn't quite say how.

"Tob, what's wrong? What're you after up there?"

Tobin twisted around and dropped a dirty cloth bag into Ki's hands. The move brought them face to face for the first time since Ki had come back to the room.

Ki looked up into those black, staring eyes and began to tremble. This wasn't Tobin.

"Brother?"

In the blink of an eye, the other stood just inches in front of him. The spirit's face reminded him of a mask—it was as if some ham-fisted carver had tried to model Tobin's face, but forgotten to put in any kindness or warmth. Ki thought suddenly of his own dead mother lying frozen in the loft all those years ago; he'd pulled back the blanket and looked into her face, seeking in vain for the loving presence he'd known. It was the same now, looking for Tobin in the face of the demon.

In spite of his fear, he found his voice again. "You're Brother?"

The spirit nodded, and something like a smile twitched its thin lips. The effect was not a pleasant one.

"Where's Tobin?"

Brother pointed to the bag. His mouth didn't move, but Ki heard a faint whisper like wind blowing over a frozen lake. *He goes to Lhel. Take this to him quickly!*

Brother vanished, leaving Ki alone in the lengthening shadows holding a dirty cloth sack that wasn't empty.

Lhel? Tobin had gone home? But why? And why would he leave without him? Ki's hand found the carved horse hanging at his throat as he fought off the hurt feelings that came with such questions. If Tobin had gone without him, then something was terribly wrong and, if that was so, then Ki's place was at his side.

But he left without me—

"Tharin. I should go tell Tharin, perhaps even Porion—"

No!

Ki jumped as Brother hissed at him from the shadows beside the doorway. It was a sign, seeing Brother at last. Tobin must be in very great danger indeed if the ghost was appearing to him. He'd better do as the thing said.

In this, at least, he had luck on his side. In the hours between duty and mess, the boys were free to do as they wished. No one would give a squire a second glance as he went between Palace and stables carrying his master's arms for repair.

Taking only their swords and the mysterious bag, he went out to the stables. Here his fears were confirmed. Gosi was gone. If Tobin had left mounted, there was no hope of catching up with him now. All he could do was follow.

"You might have shown yourself a bit earlier," he muttered as he saddled Dragon, hoping Brother was lurking close enough to hear.

A tale of a squire's errand in the city suited the Palatine guards, and another got him past those at the harbor gate. Night was falling fast and there was no sign of Brother to guide him now, but there was moon enough to light his road. Turning Dragon's head to the west, he kicked the roan into a gallop along the high road and prayed to Astellus to guide his hooves safely in the dark.

There were few riders on the roads at night, and fewer yet slight enough to be Tobin, but Ki couldn't help staring hard at every stranger he overtook.

Near midnight he stopped to rest his horse at a stream. Only then did it occur to him to look inside the bag.

It was near that same hour that Tharin found a very distraught Molay at his door.

Chapter 48

The crescent moon guided Tobin home. By its light he put the sea at his back and retraced the rivers and roads that led west to the mountains. Perhaps Gosi remembered the way, too, for they took no wrong turning through the night.

Tobin had fear to keep him awake, and the strange pain that swelled and changed as the moon pulled him onward. Sometimes it wasn't there at all and he pushed the horse into a gallop for miles at a time. Then it would close in on him again and Gosi would wander along the grassy verge while Tobin carried a basin of dull red fire sloshing between his hipbones. Eyes half closed against it, he thought of Niryn and his handful of flame at the royal tomb.

As the night dragged on, the pain often rose through him, digging in under his breastbone and spreading out beneath his skin, making his flesh hot and cold by turns on his bones. The blood in his trousers had dried, but near midnight his chest began to itch down low, between his nipples. When he reached in to scratch, his fingers came away dark and wet.

Plague plague plague. It thrummed with the beating of his heart.

Plague bringer.

Lhel must have some cure. That must be why he'd been given the vision telling him to go to her. Perhaps hill witches knew of some healing that the drysians and the royal healers of Skala did not.

They'd all heard the tales. In the port cities the death-bird plague chasers nailed plague bringers in their houses, along with anyone else unlucky enough to be there when the first victim was discovered. If anyone survived the illness, they could prove their health by breaking free.

He was a plague bringer.

Lhel had foreseen it.

Would they nail the Old Palace shut?

In the darkness his imagination conjured an army of deathbirds settling like carrion crows on the Palace with hammers and pouches of nails over their shoulders, like the workmen who'd come to the keep.

Would they follow him and nail up the keep, too?

They could put him in the tower. He'd wear their mask and be a bird like the ones who'd been his mother's only companions—

All through the long night his thoughts chased themselves round in an endless circle. He was almost surprised when he saw the jagged teeth of the mountains rising against the star-crusted sky so close ahead of him.

The first glow of dawn was warming the sky at his back when he rode through sleeping Alestun. Gosi was stumbling and blowing under him. Tobin had passed from weariness into a numbed, dreaming state and began to wonder if he would suddenly open his eyes and find himself back in Ero after all, nailed in his room by the deathbirds. Or perhaps he was really following the trail of his visions to that underground room guarded by the deer.

He left the town behind and rode on along the familiar road between autumn-colored trees. It had looked much the same the first time his father took him to Alestun nearly half his life ago. He was glad to be here again, even if it did prove to be for the last time. Better to die here than in the city. He hoped they'd leave his body somewhere in the forest. He didn't want to be on one of those stone shelves under the stone queens. He belonged here.

He'd just caught a glimpse of the tower roof over the

treetops when Lhel stepped out of the trees ahead of him. Tears of relief burned his eyes.

"Keesa, you come," she said, walking out into the road to meet him.

"I saw the blood, Lhel." His voice was as faint as Brother's. "I'm sick. I've brought plague."

She grasped his ankle and squinted up into his face, then gave his foot a reassuring pat. "No, keesa. No plague."

Pulling his foot out of the stirrup, she climbed up behind him and took the reins.

He remembered little of the ride that followed except for the warmth of her body against his back. It felt good.

The next thing he knew she was helping him down out of the saddle with hands as cool as river water. There was the house oak, with its baskets and racks, and the round shining pool of the spring glimmering like a green and gold mirror just beyond.

A cheerful fire crackled in front of the door. She guided him to a log seat beside it, pulled a fur robe around him, and placed a wooden cup of boiled herb tea in his hands. Tobin sipped it, grateful for the warmth. The soft fur of the robe was tawny cream and brown—catamount fur. Ki's catamount, he thought, wishing his friend was here.

"What's wrong with me?" he rasped.

"Show blood."

Tobin pulled down the neck of his tunic to show her the seeping patch on his chest. "You say I'm not sick, but look! What else would do this?"

Lhel touched the damp flesh and sighed. "We asked much of the Mother. Too much, I think."

"My mother?"

"Her, yes, but Goddess mother is the one I speak. You have pains there?"

"Some, but mostly in my belly."

Lhel nodded. "Blood other place?"

Embarrassed, Tobin pulled up his jerkin and showed her where the first stain had soaked through his trousers.

Lhel placed her hands on his head and spoke softly in words he didn't understand.

"Ah, too soon, keesa. Too soon," she said, sounding sad. "Perhaps I did wrong, making Brother's hekkamari keeping you so close. I must bring Arkoniel. You eat while I go."

"Can't I go with you? I want to see Nari!" Tobin begged.

"Later, keesa."

She brought him warm porridge, berries, and bread, then strode away through the trees.

Tobin huddled deeper into the robe and took a bite of the bread. Stolen from Cook's kitchen, no doubt. The taste of it made him even more homesick. He longed to run after Lhel and sit by the kitchen fire with Cook and Nari. Being so close, dressed in his old clothes, it was easy to pretend that he'd never left home at all.

Except that Ki wasn't here. Tobin ran his fingers along the edge of the catamount skin, wondering what he was going to say to him when he went back. What must Ki and Tharin and the others be thinking by now?

He pushed that worry away for later and touched the blood on his chest again. He wasn't a plague carrier after all, but something was wrong. Maybe something even worse.

It was almost daylight when Ki reached the turning of the road for Alestun, but he missed it all the same, only having been this way once before. He was clear past it when Brother suddenly appeared in the road in front of him, startling his horse.

"So there you are!" Ki muttered, snubbing the reins to calm Dragon as he shied.

The ghost pointed back the way he'd come. Ki turned and saw the marker he'd missed at the crossroads behind him. "Many thanks, Brother."

He was almost used to the ghost by now. Or maybe

he was just too tired and hungry and worried about what he was going to find at the end of this night's long ride to have any fear to spare. Whatever the case, he was glad enough when Brother stayed with him and led the way to Alestun.

It was a warm morning for mid-Erasin. A mist rose off the dripping trees, ghostly in the thin light of the false dawn.

"Is Tobin well?" he asked, assuming Brother would know something of his twin's condition. But Brother neither turned nor spoke, just moved on ahead of him in that odd, not-walking way of his. Watching him for a while, Ki began to think he'd been more comfortable alone after all.

Arkoniel looked up from his washbasin to find Lhel's face floating before him.

"You come now," she said, and there was no mistaking the urgency in her voice. "Tobin is with me. Magic has broken."

Arkoniel hastily dried his face and ran out to the stable. He didn't bother with a saddle, just grasped the bridle and clung on to his gelding's back as he rode up the mountain road to meet the witch.

She was waiting for him at the forest's edge, as always. He left the horse and followed her on foot through the trees by what felt like a shorter route than usual. For over two years he'd been her pupil, her lover, yet she had still not entrusted him with the way to her home.

At the clearing he found Tobin sitting by the fire wrapped in a catamount skin. The child's face was drawn and sallow, and there were dark circles under his eyes. He'd been dozing, but looked up sharply at their approach.

"Tobin, how are you feeling?" Arkoniel asked, kneeling in front of him. Was it his imagination, or had the familiar planes of that face shifted already, ever so slightly?

"A little better," Tobin replied, looking scared. "Lhel says I don't have plague."

"No, of course you don't!"

"But tell me what is happening to me!" Tobin showed him a bloody smear on his flat, smooth chest. "It just keeps leaking out and it's starting to hurt again. It must be the Red and Black Death. What else would do this?"

"Magic," said Arkoniel. "A magic worked on you long ago that's coming undone before its time. I'm so sorry. You were never meant to find out this way."

As he'd feared, Tobin only looked more frightened at this. "Magic? On me?"

"Yes. Lhel's magic."

Tobin cast a betrayed look at the witch. "But why? When did you do it? When you put my blood on the doll?"

"No, keesa. Much older time ago. When you is born. Iya and Arkoniel came to me, ask for it. Say your moon god want it. Your father want it. Part of your warrior path. Come, it's better to show than to tell you."

Ki had planned to go straight to the keep and fetch Arkoniel, but Brother would have none of it.

Follow, the spirit demanded in his hoarse whispery voice. Ki didn't dare disobey.

Brother guided him to a game track that skirted the meadow and crossed the river at a ford further upstream.

Ki peeked into the bag at the worn old doll as he rode, wondering how such a thing could matter to a ghost. But clearly it did, for Brother was suddenly at his stirrup and Ki felt cold all over.

Not for you! hissed Brother, gripping his leg with icy fingers.

"I don't want it!" Ki snugged the bag shut and stuffed it between his leg and the saddle.

The way quickly became steep on the other side of the ford and began to look familiar. Ki recognized a large stone that they'd used for a table one summer day, picnicking with Arkoniel and Lhel. It couldn't be much farther now.

Tired as he was, and uneasy with Brother, Ki couldn't help smiling as he thought how surprised everyone would be to see him.

*T*obin shivered as he bent over the spring's smooth surface. Lhel had made him take off his tunic and shirt. Looking down, he could see his face and the red smear on his chest. He wondered if he should wash it away, but didn't dare. Lhel and Arkoniel were still looking at him so strangely.

"Watch the pool," Lhel told him again, rustling around with something behind him. "Arkoniel, you tell."

The wizard knelt beside him. "It should have been your father who told you this, or Iya. And you should be older and ready to take your place. But it seems the gods have other plans.

"You've heard people say that your dead twin was a girl. Well, that's true, in a way."

Tobin looked up at him and saw a deep sadness in the wizard's face.

"Your mother bore two children that night: a boy and a girl. One died, as you know. But you see, the child who lived was a girl. You, Tobin. Lhel used a special kind of magic—"

"Skin binding," said Lhel.

"Skin binding, to make you appear to be a boy, and the dead boy—Brother—appear to be a girl."

For a moment Tobin thought he'd lost his voice again, as he had when his mother died. But he managed a rasping, "No!"

"It's true, Tobin. You are a girl in boy's form. And there will come a time when you must put aside that false form and take your place in the world as a woman."

Tobin was shivering now, and not because of the cold. "But— But *why*?"

"To protect you until you can be queen."

"Protect me? From who?"

"From your uncle and his Harriers. They'd kill you if they knew. The king would have killed you the night you were born if we hadn't done as we did. He'd killed others already, many others, whom he feared would challenge his right, and Korin's."

"Niryn said— But he talked of traitors!"

"No, they were innocents. And they had far less claim than you, his own sister's child. You know the Prophecy of Afra. You're a true daughter of Thelátimos, the last of the pure line. This skin binding—it was the only way we could think of to protect you. And until now it worked."

Tobin stared down at the face in the water—his eyes, his hair, the scar on his pointed chin. "No! You're lying! I want to be who I am! I'm a warrior!"

"You've never been anything else," Arkoniel told him. "But you're destined by Illior to be something more. Illior showed this to Iya while you were still in your mother's womb. Countless wizards and priests have dreamed of you. You'll be a great warrior and a great queen, like Ghërilain herself."

Tobin pressed his hands to his ears and shook his head in fury. "No! Women aren't warriors! I'm a warrior! I'm Tobin. *I know who I am!*"

The scent of musk and green herbs enveloped him as Lhel knelt on his other side and wrapped strong arms around him. "You are who you are. Let me show."

She covered the bloody place on his chest with her hand and the pain came back for a moment on crawling centipede feet. When she took her hand away, he saw a vertical line of stitching on his chest identical to the one that Brother had once shown him, tiny and fine as spider silk. But his wound had healed and the scar had faded pale. Only the lower end of it was bloody, like Brother's wound.

"The magic grow thin, the binding not hold. Must be new magic made," Lhel said. "It's not your time to show the true face, keesa."

Tobin pressed against her gratefully. He didn't want to change.

"But how—" Arkoniel began.

Lhel forestalled him with one upraised finger. "For later. Tobin, you should know your true face."

"I don't want to!"

"Yes. Is good to know. Come, keesa, look."

Lhel pressed a finger to the stitching on his chest and when she spoke again, he heard her voice inside his head; for the first time her words were clear and unbroken. "Goddess Mother, I loosen these stitches made in your name, sewn on the night of your waxing harvest moon, that they may be made sound again in this moon to protect this child with the binding of one form to another. Let this daughter called Tobin see her true face in your mirror. Ease, red moon woven strand, here." Saying this, she passed her hand across Tobin's eyes and guided him to lean over the pool's glassy surface again.

Fearfully, unwillingly, he looked down to see what stranger would peer up at him.

She was not so different.

It was a girl—there was no mistaking that—but she had his dark blue eyes, his straight nose and pointed chin, even the same scar. He'd feared to see someone soft and silly, like the girls at court, but this one had nothing soft about her. Her cheekbones might be a little higher set than his own, the lips a hint fuller, but she met his gaze with the same wariness he'd so often seen in his mirror at home—and the same determination.

"Not 'she,' Tobin," Arkoniel whispered. "You. You *are* she. You've been looking at Brother in your mirror all these years. But not all of him. Your eyes are your own."

"No binding change that. And this." Tobin felt Lhel touch the wisdom mark and heard the witch's voice inside his head again. "That did not change from your birth. That has always been a part of you. And this—" She touched the scar. "This was given to you, and this you keep. All your life you have thought to follow Sakor, but Illior marked you from birth. So it is with your memories, your training, your art, your soul. All the things that are you keep. But you shall be more than that."

Tobin shivered, remembering the ghostly queen who'd offered him the sword. Had she known, and given it as a blessing?

"You can see me, Arkoniel?"

"Yes. Oh, yes!" The wizard's voice was thick with joy. "I'm so glad to see you at last, after all these years, my lady!"

My lady.

Tobin covered her ears against the word but could not take her gaze from the reflection.

"I know what you fear, Tobin," Arkoniel told her, speaking gently. "But you know the histories. Before your uncle's time, the queens of Skala were the greatest warriors of all, and there were women generals, women captains and squires and arms masters."

"Like Ki's sister."

"Yes, like Ki's sister. And Cook, too, in her day. They're still out there in the armies, as she is. You can bring them back to court, back to honor. But only if you stay safe and hidden until the time is right. To do that, you must go back to Ero and remain Tobin to the world. Nari and Iya are the only others who know the truth, besides we two. No one else can know. Not even Ki or Tharin."

"But why?" Tobin demanded. She'd had enough of secrets already. How was she to bear this one alone?

"I gave my word to your father and to Iya that no one would learn of your true identity until the sign is given."

"What sign?"

"I don't know that yet. Illior will reveal it. For now, we must be patient."

The incident with the doll had ended any chance of Ki being at ease with the spirit or demon or whatever the hell Brother was.

Even so, he wasn't prepared when it suddenly flew at him as they climbed a steep, crumbling bank. It didn't touch him, but spooked Dragon, who reared and threw him. He went tumbling ass over tippet down the bank. Luckily the ground was soft with moss and ferns, but he still found a few rocks and logs before he fetched up against a tree halfway back down the slope.

"Damnation, what did you do that for?" he gasped, trying to get his wind back. He could see Brother at the top of the hill. The ghost had the flour sack now, and he was smiling that unsettling smile of his as he looked back at Ki. The horse was long gone.

"What do you want?" Ki shouted at him.

Brother said nothing.

Ki started to scramble up after him. When he looked up again, Brother was gone.

He climbed to the top of the rise and found Brother watching him from the mouth of a game track a few yards away. Ki took a step in his direction and Brother faded back, leading him.

Not knowing what else to do, Ki set after him, letting the ghost lead him as it would. After all, it had the doll now.

Lhel had taken Arkoniel back behind the oak some time ago, leaving Tobin alone at the spring. She knelt where they'd left her, staring down at the face in the pool and feeling the world turning upside down around her.

My face, she told herself.

Girl. Lady. Princess.

The world spun again.

Queen.

Me.

She touched her cheek to discover if it felt as different as it looked in the water. Before she could decide, the image burst in a splash that wet her from face to knees.

A cloth sack floated in the spring in front of her.

A flour sack.

"The doll!" she cried, pulling it out before it could sink. She'd forgotten it in Ero. Brother crouched on the far side of the pool, staring at her with his head cocked to one side, almost as if he were surprised to see her like this.

"Look Lhel," she called. "Brother brought it all the way from the city."

Lhel and Arkoniel ran to her and pulled her from the spring. The witch wrapped the catamount robe around her like a cloak, pulling it forward over her face.

"No, Brother couldn't have done that. Not by himself," said Arkoniel, scanning the edge of the clearing with frightened eyes.

"Then Brother must have brought Ki," said Tobin, trying to pull away. "I was so scared when I saw the blood that I just ran away and forgot the doll. Brother must have shown it to Ki and told him to bring it."

"Yes, the spirit knows his way," Lhel said, but she was looking at Arkoniel, not at the ghost. "And Ki knew the way to the keep—"

The wizard had disappeared into the trees before she could finish. She sent her voice after him, finding his mind with ease.

"No, you must not harm him."

"You know what I have sworn, Lhel."

Lhel almost followed, but knew she couldn't leave Tobin alone like this.

"What's wrong?" Tobin asked, gripping her arm.

"Nothing, keesa. Arkoniel gone to find your friend. We start the healing while he go."

"No, I want to wait for Ki."

Lhel smiled and placed her hand on Tobin's head, then spoke the spell she'd shaped in her mind. Tobin fell limp in her arms.

Lhel caught her and held her close as she stared into the trees. "Mother, protect him."

Brother kept just ahead of Ki all the way to Lhel's clearing, never close enough to question but never quite out of sight. Then he disappeared, and where he'd stood Ki could see what looked like Tobin through a break in the trees.

He opened his mouth to hail him when Arkoniel suddenly stepped in front of him. Sunlight flashed on something in the wizard's hand and everything went black.

Tobin woke on a pallet inside the oak. It was hot and his bare skin streamed with sweat. His head felt like it was filled with warm mud, too heavy to lift.

Lhel sat cross-legged beside him, holding the rag doll on her lap.

"You 'wake, keesa?"

A twinge of pain brought Tobin fully awake and he sat up with a cry of dismay. "Ki? Where's Ki?"

There was something wrong with his voice. It was too high. It sounded like—

"No!"

"Yes, daughter."

"Where's Ki?" Tobin asked again.

"He be outside. It's time for the teaching I tell you of all that time ago, when you bring me this hekkamari." She held up the doll. "The Skala moon god got path set for you. You a girl, but you got to be a boy looking for a time again. We do another binding now."

Tobin looked down and saw that her naked body was still a boy's—lean and angular with a little penis nestled like a mouse between her thighs. But there were a few smears of fresh blood there, too.

"Why am I bleeding there?"

"Binding got weak when your moon time come on you. Fight with the magic."

"Moon time?" Tobin realized uncomfortably that Lhel must mean the monthly female bleeding Ki had told her about.

"Woman got a tide in her womb like the sea, called by the moon," Lhel told her. "Give you blood and pain. Give you magic to grow baby in your belly. Some get other magic from it too, like me. And you, too. It give you dreams, sometimes, and the eye. Strong magic. Break some of my stitching."

Lhel clucked her tongue against her teeth as she took out a slender silver blade and picked out a few of the stitches on the doll's side. "Never do a binding for so long time. Maybe not meant to hold so long. Skin strong, but bone stronger. We use bone this time."

"What bone?"

Lhel pulled a handful of yellowed wool and crumbling dried herbs from the body of the doll and felt through it until she found what she wanted. Holding out her hand, she showed Tobin three ivory-colored fragments: a tiny curved splinter of rib, a fragment of skull cupped and thin as eggshell, and one whole bone small and fine as the wing bone of a swallow. "Brother's bone," she said.

Tobin's eyes widened. "His bones are in the doll?"

"Most. Some little bits still be in ground by your mama's house in the city. Under a big tree there, near cooking place."

Tobin reached up for the chain around her neck and showed Lhel the ring. "I found this in a hole under a dead tree by the old summer kitchen. Tharin says it was my mother's. Is that where he was buried?"

Lhel nodded. "I call to bring up bones from earth and flesh. Your mama—" She mimed digging into the earth, fingers bent like claws. "She make them clean and sew into the doll so she can care for the spirit."

Tobin looked at the doll with revulsion. "But why?"

"Brother angry to be dead and still skin bind to you.

His spirit be demon worse than what you know if I didn't teach your mama to make the hekkamari. We take up his little bones and put them in the doll. I bind her to it, just as I bind you. You remember?"

"With the hair and the blood."

Lhel nodded. "She his blood, too. His mama. When she die it pass to you. You know the words. 'Blood my blood. Flesh my flesh. Bone my bone.' That's a true thing."

Lhel snapped off a tiny sliver from the broken rib bone and held it up. "I put this in you, you be bind again, have Brother's face until you cut it out and be girl outside. But you know you girl inside now, keesa."

Tobin nodded miserably. "Yes, I know. Just make me look like my old self again, please?"

Lhel pressed Tobin back down on the pallet and placed the doll beside her. Then she began to sing softly under her breath. Tobin felt very sleepy all at once, though her eyes stayed open. Brother came into the oak and lay down where the doll was. His body felt as solid and warm beside her as Ki's ever had. She looked over at him and smiled, but he was staring straight up, his face as rigid as a mask.

Lhel dropped the rough dress from her shoulders. The firelight made the tattoos on her hands, breasts, and belly seem to crawl across her skin as she wove moon white patterns in the air with the silver blade and a needle. A net of light hung over Tobin and Brother when she was done.

Tobin felt the cold touch of metal between her thighs, and a sharp needle prick under her boy sac. Then Lhel was painting red on the air, so that the patterns looked like—

—*blood on river ice*

Tobin wanted to look away but she couldn't move.

Chanting softly, Lhel balanced the tiny shard of infant bone on the tip of her knife and waved it through the flames beside her until it glowed blue-white. Brother floated up into the air and turned over, so that he hung nose to nose above Tobin. Lhel reached through his luminous body and plunged the hot bone shard into the seeping wound on Tobin's breast.

The flame of the burning bone shot out under her skin, encasing her in heat. She tried to cry out in pain and fear, certain the flesh would boil off her bones, but she was still held tight by Lhel's voice. White light blinded her for a moment, then the pain lifted her off the ground and she and Brother floated together up the smoke hole of the oak, and still higher above the trees. Like a hawk, she could see everything for miles around. She saw Tharin and his men coming on at a gallop from Alestun. She saw Nari and Cook doing the wash in the kitchen yard at the keep. And she saw Arkoniel kneeling over Ki, who lay on his back just outside Lhel's clearing, looking up at the sky with unseeing eyes. The wizard had one hand pressed to Ki's brow, the other over his own eyes as if he were weeping.

Tobin wanted to go closer, see what the matter was, but something lifted her higher, until she was flying west over the mountains to a deep harbor below a cliff. Long arms of rock embraced the mouth of the harbor, and islands guarded it. She could hear the waves breaking against their steep sides now, and the lonely cries of the grey-winged gulls—

Here, a voice whispered to her. The white light swelled again, filling her eyes. Then, *You must go back,* and she was falling, falling back into the oak, into herself.

She opened her eyes. Brother was still hovering over her, but Lhel's chanting had changed. She'd exchanged knife for needle and was stitching up the bloody edges of the wound in Tobin's chest as deftly as Nari used to mend the rents in her tunics.

Nari knew all along—

But now Tobin was the tunic and had to watch as the silver needle rose and fell in the firelight, drawing a barely visible thread silvery as a snail's trail through the air, through her skin. It didn't hurt, though. With each successive flash and tug of the needle Tobin felt herself being drawn together, made whole again.

Patched, she thought dizzily.

With every stitch Brother shook above her and his face twisted into a mask of true pain. She could see the unhealed wound on his chest again, how the blood fell from it drop by drop with every pass of the witch's needle through Tobin's living flesh. His lips drew back from his white teeth and bloody tears fell from his eyes. Tobin expected to feel them on her face but they disappeared somewhere in the air between them.

Stop it! she tried to cry out to Lhel. *You're hurting him. Can't you see you're hurting him?*

Brother's eyes flew wide and he stared down at her. *Let me go!* It was a scream inside her head.

"Be still, keesa. Dead don't know pain," Lhel murmured.

You're wrong! Tobin cried out silently. *Brother, I'm sorry!*

Lhel pulled the final stitch tight and Brother slowly sank down onto Tobin, then through her, and for an instant she felt the coldness of his presence in every inch of her frame.

You must go back—

Then Brother was gone and Tobin was free, curling away from Lhel's stained hands, curling into the sweet-smelling softness of the catamount skin, and sobbing aloud with the hoarse, ugly voice of a boy.

About the Author

LYNN FLEWELLING's first novel, *Luck in the Shadows,* was chosen by Locus as a Recommended First Novel and was a finalist for the Compton Crook Award. *Traitor's Moon,* the third book in what has become the Nightrunner Series, was a finalist for the 2000 Spectrum Award. The Nightrunner books have achieved worldwide popularity and are currently published in eight countries, including Russia and the Czech Republic.

Flewelling currently resides with her family in East Aurora, New York. Her website address is www.sff.net/people/Lynn.Flewelling.

**Be sure not to miss
the next riveting book
in the Tamír Triad:**

HIDDEN WARRIOR

**Now available from
Bantam Spectra**

REALMS OF FANTASY

The biggest, brightest stars from Bantam Spectra

Maggie Furey

A fiery-haired Mage with an equally incendiary temper must save her world and her friends from a pernicious evil, with the aid of four forgotten magical Artefacts.

AURIAN ___56525-7 $6.99

HARP OF WINDS ___56526-5 $6.99

SWORD OF FLAME ___56527-3 $6.99

DHIAMMARA ___57557-0 $6.99

THE HEART OF MYRIAL ___57938-X $6.99

Katharine Kerr

The mistress of Celtic fantasy presents her ever-popular Deverry series. Most recent titles:

DAYS OF BLOOD AND FIRE ___29012-6 $6.99/$9.99

DAYS OF AIR AND DARKNESS ___57262-8 $6.99/$9.99

THE RED WYVERN ___57264-4 $6.99/$9.99

THE BLACK RAVEN ___57919-3 $6.99/$9.99

DAGGERSPELL ___56521-4 $6.99/$9.99

DARKSPELL ___56888-4 $6.99/$9.99